She sighed ... **"This isn't** ... **keep flirtin** ...

"I'm not flirting with you, Marnie. If I was flirting with you, you'd know it."

"That," she waved a finger between them, "was definitely flirting."

"No. *This* is flirting." He got up again and approached her desk, then placed his hands on the oak surface and leaned over until their faces were inches apart.

"You are a beautiful, intoxicating, infuriating woman," he whispered, his voice a low, sensual growl, "and I can't stop thinking about you. And I love the way you look today. All…unfettered. Untamed."

Heat washed over her body. "Okay." Her words shook and she drew in a breath to steady herself. "Yes, that…that was flirting."

He smiled, held her gaze a moment longer, then retreated to the chair. "Glad we got that settled."

Settled? If anything, things between them had become more unsettled. Jack Knight. The enemy. In more ways than one.

she sighed, then put down the pen.
"This isn't going to work if you
keep fighting with me."

THE MATCHMAKER'S HAPPY ENDING

BY
SHIRLEY JUMP

First published in Great Britain 2013
by Mills & Boon, an imprint of Harlequin (UK) Limited,
Eton House, 18-24 Paradise Road, Richmond, Surrey TW9 1SR

© Shirley Kawa-Jump, LLC 2013

ISBN: 978 0 263 90115 3
ebook ISBN: 978 1 472 00487 1

23-0613

Harlequin (UK) policy is to use papers that are natural, renewable and recyclable products and made from wood grown in sustainable forests. The logging and manufacturing processes conform to the legal environmental regulations of the country of origin.

Printed and bound in Spain
by Blackprint CPI, Barcelona

New York Times bestselling author **Shirley Jump** didn't have the will-power to diet, nor the talent to master under-eye concealer, so she bowed out of a career in television and opted instead for a career where she could be paid to eat at her desk—writing. At first, seeking revenge on her children for their grocery store tantrums, she sold embarrassing essays about them to anthologies. However, it wasn't enough to feed her growing addiction to writing funny. So she turned to the world of romance novels, where messes are (usually) cleaned up before The End. In the worlds Shirley gets to create and control, the children listen to their parents, the husbands always remember holidays, and the housework is magically done by elves. Though she's thrilled to see her books in stores around the world, Shirley mostly writes because it gives her an excuse to avoid cleaning the toilets and helps feed her shoe habit.

To learn more, visit her website at www.shirleyjump.com

To Mom. I miss you every day.

CHAPTER ONE ✓

MARNIE FRANKLIN LEFT her thirtieth wedding of the year, with aching feet, flower petals in her hair and a satisfied smile on her face. She'd done it. Again.

From behind the wide glass and brass doors of Boston's Park Plaza hotel, the newly married Mr. and Mrs. Andrew Corliss waved and shouted their thanks. "We owe it all to you, Marnie!" Andrew called. A geeky but lovable guy who tended toward neon colored ties that were knotted too tight around his skinny neck, Andrew had been one of her best success stories. Internet millionaire, now married to an energetic, friendly woman who loved him for his mind—and their mutual affection for difficult Sudoku puzzles.

"You're welcome! May you have a long and happy life together." Marnie gave them a smile, then turned to the street and waited while a valet waved up one of the half dozen waiting cabs outside the hotel. Exhaustion weighed on Marnie's shoulders, despite the two cups of coffee she'd downed at the reception. A light rain had started, adding a chill to the late spring air. The always busy Boston traffic passed the hotel in a *swoosh-swoosh* of tires on damp pavement, a melody highlighted by the honking of horns, the constant music of a city. She loved this city, she really did, but there were days—like today—when she wished she lived somewhere quiet. Like the other side of the moon.

Her phone rang as she opened the taxi's door and told the driver her address. She pressed mute, sending the call straight to voice mail. That was the trouble with being on the top of her field—there was no room for a holiday or vacation. She'd become one of Boston's most successful matchmakers, and that meant everyone who wanted a happy ending called her, looking for true love.

Something she didn't believe in herself.

An irony she couldn't tell her clients. Couldn't admit she'd never fallen in love, and had given up on the emotion after one too many failed relationships. She couldn't tell people that the matchmaker had no faith in a match for herself. So she poured herself into her job and kept a bright smile on her face whenever she told her clients that they could have that happy ending, too.

She'd seen the fairy tale ending happen for other people, but a part of Marnie wondered if she'd missed her one big chance to have a happily-ever-after. She was almost thirty, and had yet to meet Mr. Right. Only a few heartbreaker Mr. Wrongs. At least with her job, she had some control over the outcome, which was the way Marnie preferred the things in her life. Controlled, predictable. The phone rang again, like a punctuation mark to the end of her thoughts.

In front of her, the cabbie pulled away from the curb, at the same time fiddling with the GPS on the dash. Must be a new driver, Marnie decided, and grabbed her phone to answer the call. "This is Marnie. How can I help you make a match?"

"You need to stop working, dear, and find your own Mr. Right."

Her mother. Who meant well, but who thought Marnie's personal life should take precedence over everything else in the universe. "Hi, Ma. What are you doing up so late on a Friday night?"

"Worrying about my single daughter. And why she's working on a Friday night. Again."

The GPS announced a left turn, a little late for the distracted cab driver, who jerked the wheel to the left and jerked Marnie to one side, too. She gave him a glare in the rearview mirror, but he ignored it. The noxious fumes of Boston exhaust filled the interior, or maybe that was the bad ventilation system in the cab. The car had seen better days, heck, better decades, if the duct tape on the scarred vinyl seats was any indication.

"You should be out on a date of your own," Marnie countered to her mother.

"Oh, I'm too old for that foolishness," Helen said. "Besides, your father hasn't been gone that long."

"Three years, Ma." Marnie lowered her voice to a sympathetic tone. Dad's heart attack had taken them all by surprise. One day he'd been there, grinning and heading out the door, the next he'd been a shell of himself, and then…gone. "It's okay to move on."

"So, what are you doing on Sunday?" her mother said, instead of responding to Marnie's advice, a sure-fire Helen tactic. Change the topic from anything difficult. Marnie's parents had been the type who avoided the hard stuff, swept it under the rug. To them, the world had been a perpetually sunny place, even when evidence to the contrary dropped a big gray shadow in their way.

A part of Marnie wanted to keep things that way for her mother, to protect Helen, who had been through so much.

"I wanted to have you and your sisters over for

brunch after church," Ma said. "I could serve that coffee cake you love and…"

As her mother talked about the menu, Marnie murmured agreement, and reviewed her To Do list in her head. She had three appointments with new clients early in the morning tomorrow, one afternoon bachelor meet and greet to host, then her company's Saturday night speed date event—

"Did you hear what I said?" her mother cut in.

"Sorry, Ma. The connection faded." Or her brain, but she didn't say that.

The cab driver fiddled again with the GPS, pushing buttons to zoom in or out, Marnie wasn't sure. He seemed flustered and confused. She leaned forward. "Just take a left up here," she said to him. "Onto Boylston. Then a right on Harvard."

The cabbie nodded.

And went straight.

"Hey, you missed the turn." Damn it. Was the man that green? Marnie gave up the argument and sat back against the seat. After the long day she'd had, the delay was more welcome than annoying. Especially to her feet, which were already complaining about the upcoming three-flight walk upstairs to her condo. She loved the brick building she lived in, with its tree-lined street located within walking distance of the quirky neighborhood of Coolidge Corner. But there were days when living on the third floor—despite the nice view of the park across the street—was exhausting after a long day. Right this second, she'd do about anything for an elevator and a massage chair.

"I said you should wear a dress to brunch on Sunday," her mother said, "because I'm inviting Stella Hargrove's grandson. He's single and—"

"Wouldn't it be nicer just to visit with you and my sisters, Ma? That way, we can all catch up, which we never seem to get enough time to do. A guy would end up being a fifth wheel." Marnie pressed a finger to her temple, but it did little to ward off the impending headache. A headache her sister Erica would say she brought on herself because she never confronted her mother and instead placated and deferred. Instead of saying *Ma, don't fix me up,* she'd fallen back on making nice instead. Marnie was the middle sister, the peacemaker, even if sometimes that peace came with the price of a lot of aspirin. "Besides, if I want a date, I have a whole file of handsome men to go through."

"Yet you haven't done that at all. You keep working and working and…oh, I just worry about you, honey."

Ever since their father had died, Helen had made her three children her top—and only—priority. No matter how many times Marnie and her sisters had encouraged their mother to take a class, pick up a hobby, go on a trip, she demurred, and refocused the conversation on her girls. What her mother needed was an outside life. Something else to focus on. Something like a…

Man.

Marnie smacked herself in the head. For goodness sake, she was a professional matchmaker. Why had she never thought to fix up her mother? Marnie had made great matches for both of her sisters. Oldest sister Kat got married to her match two years ago, and Erica was in a steady relationship with a man Marnie had introduced her to last month. Despite that, Marnie had never thought about doing the same for her widowed mother. First thing tomorrow morning, she would cull her files and find a selection of distinguished, older men. Who appreciated women with a penchant for meddling.

"I'll be there for brunch on Sunday, Ma, I promise," Marnie said, noting the cabbie again messing with the GPS. "Maybe next time we can invite Stella's grandson. Okay?"

Her mother sighed. "Okay. But if you want me to give him your number or give you his…"

"I know who to call." Marnie started to say something else when the cabbie swore, stomped on his brakes—

And rear-ended the car in front of him. Marnie jerked forward, the seatbelt cutting across her sternum but saving her from plowing into the plexiglass partition. She let out an oomph, winced at the sharp pain that erupted in her chest, while the cabbie let out a stream of curses.

"What was that sound?" Helen asked. "It sounded like a boom. Did something fall? Did you hit something?"

"It's, uh, nothing. I gotta go, Ma," Marnie said, and after a breath, then another, the pain in her chest eased. "See you tomorrow." She hung up the phone, then unbuckled, and climbed out of the yellow cab. The hood had crumpled, and steam poured from the engine in angry gusts. The cabbie clambered out of the taxi. He let out another long stream of curses, a few in a language other than English, then started pacing back and forth between the driver's side door and the impact site, holding his head and muttering.

The accordioned trunk of a silver sports car was latched onto the taxi's hood. A tall, dark, handsome, and angry man stood beside the idling luxury car. He shouted at the cab driver, who threw up his hands and feigned non-understanding, as if he'd suddenly lost all knowledge of the English language.

Marnie grabbed her purse from the car, and walked

over to the man. One of those attractive, business types, she thought, noting his dark pinstriped suit, loosened tie, white button-down with the top button undone. A five o'clock shadow dusted his strong jaw, and gave his dark hair and blue eyes a sexy air. The matchmaker in her recognized the kind of good-looking man always in demand with her clients. But the woman in her—

Well, she noticed him on an entirely different level, one that sent a shimmer of heat down her veins and sped up her pulse. Something she hadn't felt in so long, she'd begun to wonder if she'd ever meet another man who interested her.

Either way, Mr. Suit and Tie looked like a lawyer or something. The last thing she needed was a rich, uptight man with control issues. She'd met enough of them that she could pick his type out of the thousands of people in the stands at Fenway on opening day.

"Is everyone okay?" she asked.

The cab driver nodded. Mr. Suit and Tie shot him a scowl, then turned to Marnie. His features softened. "Yeah. I'm fine," he said. "You?"

"I'm okay. Just a little shaken up."

"Good." He held her gaze for a moment longer, then turned on the cabbie. "Didn't you see that red light? Where'd you get your license? A vending machine?"

The cabbie just shook his head, as if he didn't understand a word.

Mr. Suit and Tie let out a curse and shook his head, then pivoted back to Marnie. "What were you thinking, riding around this city with a maniacal cab driver?"

"It's not like I get a resume and insurance record handed to me before I get in a taxi," she said. "Now, I understand you're frustrated, but—"

"I'm *beyond* frustrated. This has been a hell of a day.

With one hell of a bad ending." He shot the cab driver another glare, but the man had already skulked back to his car and climbed behind the wheel. "Wait! What are you doing?"

"I'm not doing any—" Then she heard the sound of metal groaning, and tires squealing, and realized Mr. Suit and Tie wasn't talking to her—but to the cab driver who had just hit and run. The yellow car disappeared around the corner in a noisy, clanking cloud of smoke.

In the distance, she heard the rising sound of sirens, which meant one of the people living in the apartments lining the street must have already called 9-1-1. Not soon enough.

Mr. Suit and Tie cursed under his breath. "Great. That's all I needed today."

"I'm sorry about that." Marnie stepped to the corner and put up her hand for a passing cab. "Well, good luck. Hope you get it straightened out and your night gets better."

"Hey! You can't leave. You're my witness."

"Listen, I'm exhausted and I just want to get home." She raised her arm higher, waving her hand, hoping to see at least one available cab. Nothing. Her feet screamed in protest. Soon as she got home, she was burning these shoes. "I'll give you my number. Call me for my statement." She fished in her purse for a business card, and held it out.

He ignored the card. "I need you to stay."

"And I need to get home." She waved harder, but the lone cab that passed her didn't stop. "This is Boston. Why aren't there any cabs?"

"Celtics game is just getting over," the man said. "They're probably all over at the Garden."

"Great." She lowered her arm, then thought of the

ten-block hike home. Not fun in high heels. Even less fun after an eighteen-hour day, the last four spent dancing and socializing. She should have drunk an entire pot of coffee.

"I'll make you a deal," the man said. "I'll give you a lift if you can wait until I've finished making the accident report. Then you can give your statement and kill two birds with one stone."

She hesitated. "I don't know. I'm really tired."

"Stay for just a bit more. After tonight, you'll never have to see me again." He grinned.

He had a nice smile. An echoing smile curved across her face. She glanced down the street in the direction of her condo and thought of the soft bed waiting for her there. She weighed that against walking home. Option two made her feet hurt ten times more. *Stupid shoes.*

She glanced back at the misshapen silver car. "You're sure you can drive me home? In that?"

"It runs. It's just got a little junk in the trunk." He grinned. "Sorry. Bad joke."

A laugh escaped her and eased some of the tension in her shoulders, the pain in her feet. "Even a bad joke sounds good right now." No cabs appeared, and that settled the decision for her. "Okay, I'll wait."

Not that it was going to be a hardship to wait with a view like that. This guy could have been a cover model. Whew. Hot, hot, hot. She should get his contact information. She had at least a dozen clients who would be—

You're always working.

Marnie could hear her mother's voice in her head. *Take some time off. Have some fun. Date a guy for yourself. Don't be so serious and buttoned up all the time.*

What no one seemed to understand was this buttoned-up approach had fueled Marnie's success.

She'd seen how a laissez-faire approach to business could destroy a company and refused to repeat those mistakes herself. A distraction like Mr. Suit and Tie would only derail her, something she couldn't afford.

The man opened the passenger's side door. "Have a seat. You look like you've had a trying day. And I know how that feels."

She sank into the leather seat, kicked off her shoes and let the platform heels tumble to the sidewalk. The man came to stand beside her, leaning against the rear passenger door. He had the look of a man comfortable in his own skin, at ease with the world. Confident, sexy, but not overly so. A hot combination, especially with the suit and tie. Her stance toward him softened.

"You're right. I have had a long, trying day myself." She put out her hand. "Let's try this again. I'm Marnie Franklin."

"Jack Knight."

The name rang a bell, but the connection flitted away before she could grasp it because when he took her hand in his, a delicious spark ran through her, down her arm. If she hadn't been seated, she might have jumped back in surprise. In her business, she shook hands with dozens of men in the course of a week. None had ever sent that little…zing through her. Maybe exhaustion had lowered her defenses. Or maybe the accident had shaken her up more than she thought. She released his hand, and brushed the hair out of her eyes, if only to keep from touching him again.

The police arrived, two officers who looked like they'd rather be going for a root canal than taking another accident report in the dent and ding city of Boston. For the next ten minutes Marnie and Jack answered questions. After the police were gone, Jack turned to her. "Thanks for staying. You made a stressful day much better."

"Glad to help."

Jack bent down and picked up the black heels she'd kicked onto the sidewalk when she'd sat in his car. He handed them to Marnie, the twin heels dangling from his index finger by their strappy backs. In his strong, capable hands, the fancy shoes looked even more delicate. "Your shoes, Cinderella." He gave her a wink, and that zing rushed through her a second time.

"I'm far from Cinderella." She bent and slipped on the damnable slingbacks. Pretty, but painful. "More like the not-so-evil stepmother, trying to fix up all the stepsisters with princes."

His smile had a dash of sexy, a glimmer of a tease. "Every woman deserves to be Cinderella at least once in her life."

"Maybe so, *if* she believes in fairy tales and magic mice."

She worked in the business of helping people fall in love, and had given up on the fairy tale herself a long time ago. Over the years, she'd become, if anything, more cautious, less willing to dip a toe in the romance pool. When she'd started matchmaking she'd been starry eyed, hopeful. But now...

Now she had a lot of years of reality beneath her and the stars had faded from her vision. She knew her business had suffered as a consequence. Somehow she needed to restore her belief in the very thing she touted to her clients—the existence of true love.

Jack shut her door and came around to the driver's side. The car started with a soft purr. "Where to?"

She gave him her address, and he put the car in gear. She settled into the luxury seat. The dark leather hugged her body, warm and easy. Damn. She needed to step outside the basic car model box because sitting in this sedan made it pretty easy to fall for the whole Cinderella fantasy. It wasn't a white horse, but it was a giant step closer to a royal ride. Having a good looking prince beside her helped feed that fantasy, too.

"I'm sorry for being grumpy earlier. That accident was the icing on a tough day. Thanks again for staying and talking to the cops for me," he said. "I can't believe you remembered all those details about the driver."

She shrugged. "My father used to make me do that. Whenever we went someplace, he made sure I noticed the waiter's name or the cab driver's ID. He'd have me recite the address or license plate or some other detail. He said you never knew when doing that would come in handy, and he was right." She could almost hear her father's voice in her ear. *Watch the details, Daisy-doo, because you never know when they'll matter.* He'd rarely called her Marnie, almost always Daisy-doo, because of her love for the flowers. Kat had been Kitty, Erica had been Chatterbug. Marnie missed hearing her father's wisdom, the way he lovingly teased his daughters. "Besides, the cab driver had his hands on the GPS more than the steering wheel, and that made me doubly nervous. If I could have, I would have jumped in the driver's seat and taken the wheel myself."

He chuckled. "Nice to meet a fellow control freak."

"Me? I'm not a control freak." She wrinkled her nose. "Okay, maybe I am. A little. But in my house, things were a little…crazy when I was a kid and someone had to take the reins."

"Let me guess. You're the oldest? An only?"

"The middle kid, but only younger than the oldest by nine months."

"Oh, so not just the driver, but the peacemaker, too?" He tossed her a grin.

He'd nailed her, in a few words. "Do you read personality trait books in your spare time or something?"

"Nah. I'm just in a business where it's essential to be able to read people, quickly, and well."

"Me, too. Though sometimes you don't like what you read."

"True." Jack glanced over at her, his blue eyes holding her features for a long moment before he returned his attention to the road. "So, Cinderella, what has made you so jaded?"

The conversational detour jolted her. She shifted in her seat. "Not jaded...realistic."

"Well, that makes two of us. I find, in my line of work, that realism is a must."

The amber glow of the street lights and the soft white light coming from the dash outlined his lean, defined profile with a soft edge. Despite the easy tone of his words, something in them hinted at a past that hadn't been easy. Maybe a bad breakup, or a bitter divorce? Either way, despite the zing, she wasn't interested in cleaning up someone else's baggage. *Stick to impersonal topics, Marnie.*

His cell phone started to ring, and the touchscreen in the center of his dash lit up with the word Dad. "Do you mind if I answer this?" Jack asked. "If I don't, he'll just keep calling."

She chuckled and waved toward the screen. "Go right ahead. I totally understand."

Jack leaned forward, pressed a button on the screen, then sat back again. "Hey, Dad, what's up? And before you say a word, you're on speaker, so don't blurt out any family secrets or embarrassing stories."

"You got someone in the car with you?" said a deep, amused voice on the other end. "Someone pretty, I hope."

Jack glanced at Marnie. A slow smile stole across his face and a quiver ran through her. "Yes, someone very pretty. So be on your best behavior."

His father chuckled. "That's no fun. The only thing that gets me out of bed in the morning is the potential for bad behavior."

Beside her, Jack rolled his eyes and grinned. *Parents,* he mouthed.

Seemed she wasn't the only one with a troublesome parent. Jack handled his father with a nice degree of love and humor. That tender touch raised her esteem for him, and had her looking past the suit and tie. Intriguing man. Almost…intoxicating.

She didn't have time, or room, in her life for being intrigued by a man, though, especially since her business took nearly every spare moment. Even one as handsome as him.

She could almost hear her mother screaming in disagreement, but Marnie knew her business and herself. If she got involved with someone right now, it would be a distraction. Maybe down the road, when her business and life were more settled…

Someday when?

She'd been saying "someday" for years. And had to find the right moment—or the right man—to make her open her heart to love.

"I called because I was wondering when you'd be home," Jack's father was saying. "You work more hours than the President, for God's sake."

Marnie bit back a laugh. It could have been her conversation with her mother a little while ago. She half expected his father to schedule a blind date brunch, too.

"I'm on my way." Jack flicked a glance at the dashboard clock. "Give me twenty minutes. Did you eat?"

"Yeah. Sandwiches. *Again*. Lord knows you don't have anything in that refrigerator of yours besides beer and moldy takeout."

"Because I'm never there to eat."

"Exactly." Jack's father cleared his throat. "I have an idea. Maybe…you should bring your pretty companion home for a—"

"Hey, no embarrassing statements, remember?"

His father chuckled. "Okay, okay. Drive safe."

Jack told his father he'd be home soon, then said goodbye and disconnected the call. "Sorry about that," Jack said to Marnie. "My dad is…needy sometimes. Even though it's been a few years since he got divorced, it's like he's been lost."

"My mother is the same way. She calls me every five minutes to make sure I'm eating my vegetables, wearing sunscreen and not working too much."

He chuckled. "Sounds like we have the same parent. Ever since my dad sold his house, he's been living with me, while he tries to figure out if he wants to stay in Boston or high-tail it for sunny Florida. He thinks that means he should comment on everything I do and every piece of furniture in my apartment."

"And what is or isn't in your fridge." Marnie's mom stopped by Marnie's condo almost every Sunday after church, but less to visit than to do a responsible child check. *You need more vegetables,* her mother would say. Or *you should cook for yourself more often.* And the best, *if you had a man in your life, you wouldn't have to do that.* Marnie loved her mother, but had realized a long time ago that a mother's love could be… invasive. "I get the whole you should make more time for homecooked meals and a personal life lecture on a weekly basis. I think my mother forgets how many hours I work. The last thing I want to do when I get home is whip up a platter of lasagna."

"I think they go to school for that," Jack said. "How to Bug Your Adult Kids 101."

She laughed. It did sound like they had the same parent. "Maybe you should get your dad involved in something else, something that keeps him too busy to focus on you. There are all kinds of singles events for people his age. Some of them are dates in disguise, get-togethers centered around hobbies, like cooking or pets," Marnie said, unable to stop work talk from invading every second of her day. My lord, she was a compulsive matchmaker. And one who needed to take her own advice. First thing tomorrow, she was going to look into dates for Ma and someday soon, she'd nicely tell her mother to butt out.

Yeah, right. Marnie had yet to do that to anyone, especially her mother. But she could tell others what to do. *That* she excelled at, according to her sisters.

Jack nodded. "I tried that before, years ago, but it didn't go so well. But you're right—maybe if I try again, now that some time has passed since all that upheaval, my dad will be more open to doing some activities, especially ones that get him dating again."

"And if he meets someone else—"

"He won't have time to worry about my fridge or my hours." Jack laughed. "Ah, such a devious plan we've concocted."

"As long as it works." She grinned.

Jack turned onto Marnie's street. A flicker of disappointment ran through her as the ride came to an end. "It's the fourth one on the right," she said. "With the flowers out front."

Invite him in? Or call it a night?

He slowed the car, then stopped at her building's entrance. "Nice looking place. I love these brick buildings from the early 1900s. It's always nice to see the architecture get preserved when the building gets repurposed. Not every owner appreciates history like that."

"Me, too. Coming home is like stepping into history." She smiled, then put out her hand. Impersonal, business-like. "Well, thank you for the ride."

That zing ran through her again when his large hand enfolded hers. For a second, she had the crazy thought of yanking on his hand, pulling him across the car, and kissing him. His broad chest against hers, his lips dancing around her mouth, his hands—

Wow. She needed to sleep more or get extra potassium or something.

"It was the least I could do after you stayed," Jack was saying. He released her hand. Darn. "Especially after you had a long day yourself."

Focus on the words he's speaking, not the fantasy. She jerked her gaze away from his mouth. "It was no trouble."

He grinned. "You said that already."

"Oh, well, I'm just really…tired."

"Yeah, me, too. I had a long day, made longer by someone who dropped the ball on some important paperwork. I got everything back on track, but…what a day." He ran a hand through his hair, displacing the dark locks. "Anyway, I'm sorry again about losing my temper back there."

"I would have done the same thing if my trunk looked like an origami project," she said.

He glanced in the rearview mirror and shrugged off the damaged rear. "It gives my insurance agent something to do."

She laughed. "True. Anyway, thanks again. Have a good night."

"You, too." He reached for her before she got out of the car, a light, quick touch on her arm. But still enough to send heat searing along her skin. "Would you like to go get a cup of coffee or a drink? We could sit around and complain about our jobs, our meddling parents, bad cab drivers and whatever else we can think of?"

A part of her wanted to say yes, but the realistic part piped up, reminding her of the time and her To Do list, and her no-men-for-the-foreseeable-future resolve. Besides, there was something about that zing, something that told her if she caved, she'd be lost, swept in a tsunami. The mere thought terrified her. "I can't. It's late. And I have an early day tomorrow."

"On Saturday?"

She raised one shoulder, let it drop. "My job is a 24/7 kind of thing."

He chuckled. "Mine, too. And even though every year I vow to work less and play more…"

"You don't."

He nodded.

"Me, too." Because work was easier than confronting the reasons why she worked too much. Because work was easier than taking a chance on love. Work she could control, depend upon. Love, not so much. But she didn't say any of that. She released the door handle, and shifted to face him.

Despite the fear, she didn't want to leave. Right

now, with Jack looking at her like that, his eyes lit by the street light above and his strong jaw cast in a dark shadow, her resistance was at an all-time low. Desire pulsed in her veins. She wished she *had* dragged him across the car and kissed him silly when she'd had the chance. So she delayed leaving a bit longer.

"What do you do for work that keeps you busy late into the day and also on weekends?" She put a finger to her lip and gave him a flirty smile. "Let me guess. Lawyer?"

"Hell, no." He glanced down. "Oh, I get it. Pinstripe suit, power tie. Screams waiting to sue to you?"

"Well, if the Brooks Brothers fits…"

His smile widened, ending with a dimple. *Oh, God.* Dimples. She'd always been a sucker for them.

"I'm…an investor," Jack said. "Of sorts."

"Of sorts?"

"I buy and sell businesses. I find ones that need a cash infusion, and if I think they're viable, I invest. If I think they're not, I buy them and either sell them again or break up the pieces and sell it off."

A shiver ran down her back. The leather seemed to chafe now, not comfort. "You're…a corporate raider?"

"I'm a little nicer than that. And I tend to work with small to medium-sized businesses, not giant Goliaths."

The connection fused in her mind. His job. His name.

Jack Knight. Owner of Knight Enterprises. A "business investor"—a euphemism for his true identity. Jack Knight was a vulture. Feeding off the carcasses of desperate business owners.

It had to have been the exhaustion of the day that had kept her from putting the pieces together until now. How could she have misread all the clues?

And to think she'd wanted to kiss him five minutes

ago. She bristled. "The size doesn't matter to the company that gets sold off, or taken over, or destroyed in the process of that kind of 'help.'"

"I must have given you the wrong impression. There's more to it—"

"No, there really isn't. You destroy people's companies, and their lives." The words sprang to life in her throat, fueled by exhaustion, shock, and surprised even Marnie with their vehemence. She never did this, never showed outrage, never yelled. Jack Knight had brought out this other side of her, with a roar. "Do you even think about what happens to those people after you swoop in and tear their company to shreds? They spent their lives building those companies, and in an instant, you take it all away. And for what? A bottom line? A few more dollars in your pocket? Another sports car for the collection?" She let out a gust, then grabbed the door handle. It stuck, then yielded, and fresh night air washed over her. She'd gotten distracted, by a dimple and a zing. *Idiot.* "Goodnight."

"Wait. What did—"

She shut the door, cutting off his words. She'd confronted him, told him off, and told herself it felt good to finally say what she should say, exactly when she was supposed to say it. Jack idled in the space for a moment, then finally, he drove away, swallowed by the night.

Disappointment hit her first. If only she'd kissed him. If only she'd let herself get talked into that cup of coffee.

If only he'd been someone other than Jack Knight.

Then righteous indignation rose in her chest. He was the one at fault, not her. He was the one who had ruined her father's company, not her. If she'd told him what she really wanted to say to him, if she'd really let the confrontation loose, she'd have resorted to some very unlady-like behavior, and she refused to give him that satisfaction. Jack Knight didn't deserve it, not after what he had done to her father.

So she had said goodnight, got out of Cinderella's carriage, and went back to the real world, where princes didn't come along very often, and there were no mice to do the work for her.

CHAPTER TWO

"ARE YOU GOING to admit I was right?" Marnie whispered to her mother. They were standing to the side of the private dining room of an upscale Boston restaurant on a sunny Saturday afternoon. Soft jazz music filled the air, accented by the rise and fall of a dozen human voices.

A blush filled Helen's cheeks, making her look ten years younger. She had her chestnut hair up tonight, which elongated her neck and offset her deep green eyes. The dark blue dress she'd worn skimmed her calves, and defined the hourglass shape she'd maintained all her life, even after giving birth to three children. Coupled with the light in her eyes and the smile on her face, Helen looked prettier than ever, and far younger than her fifty-eight years.

"Yes, you were right, daughter dear," Helen whispered back. "How'd I get such a smart child?"

"You gave me great genes." Marnie glanced over the room. Cozy and intimate, the private dining space offered a prime location, great parking and an outstanding menu, making it perfect for Matchmaking by Marnie meet and greets. In her experience, full and happy stomachs equaled happy people who then struck up conversations.

Today, she'd invited ten bachelors to meet her mother, and set up a buffet of finger foods on the far right side of the room. While they noshed on chicken satay and mini eggrolls, Helen circulated. Three days ago, when Marnie and Erica had proposed the idea of a mixer to Helen, she'd refused, insisting she didn't need to be fixed up, and didn't want to be, but after a while, she'd relented and agreed to "put in an appearance."

That appearance had lasted more than an hour now. Once the first man talked to Helen, and two more joined the conversation, Marnie had watched her mother transform into a giggling schoolgirl, flattered by all the sudden attention. Marnie made sure each bachelor got equal time, then stepped back and allowed the pieces to fall where they may. She'd paved the way, then let Mother Nature finish giving directions.

"So," Marnie said, leaning in closer so they wouldn't be overheard, "is there one man in particular who you like the most?"

Pink bloomed in Helen's cheeks. "Do you see the one standing by the bar?"

"The tall man with the gray hair?" Marnie and Erica had interviewed so many eligible gentlemen in the fifty- to sixty-plus age range that some of them had become a bit of a blur. She didn't remember the details of this man, only that he had impressed her during the group interviews.

"His name's Dan. He's retired from his landscaping business, hates to golf, but loves to watch old movies." Her mother grinned, and in that smile, Marnie could see the energy of a new relationship already blossoming. "And, you'll never guess what his favorite movie is."

Marnie put a finger to her lip. "Hmm…*Casablanca?*"

Helen nodded. "Just like me. We like the same kind

of wine, the same kind of music, and both of us love to travel."

"Sounds like a match made in heaven." Marnie grinned. "Or a match made by a daughter who knows her mother very well."

Helen chuckled. "Well, I wouldn't say it's a perfect match…yet, but it's got potential. Big potential. Now, if only we could find someone for you." Helen brushed a lock of hair off Marnie's forehead. "You deserve to be happy, sweetheart."

"I am happy." And she was, Marnie told herself. She had a business she loved, a purpose to her life, and a family that might annoy her sometimes, but had always been her personal rock. She gave her mother a quick hug, then headed for the front of the room, waiting until everyone's attention swiveled toward her before speaking. She noticed Dan's gaze remained on her mother, while Helen snuck quick glances back in his direction, like two teenagers at a football game.

"I wanted to thank you all for coming today, and if you weren't lucky enough to be chosen by our amazing and beautiful bachelorette," Marnie gestured toward her mother, who waved off the compliment, "don't worry. My goal at Matchmaking by Marnie is to give everyone a happy ending. So work with me, and I promise, I'll help you find your perfect match."

The bachelors thanked her, and began to file out of the room. Dan lingered, chatting with Marnie's mother. She laughed and flirted, seeming like an entirely different person, the person she used to be years and years ago. Marnie sent up a silent prayer of gratitude. Her mother had been lonely for a long time, and it was nice to see her happy again.

The waitstaff began taking away the dishes and

cleaning the tables. Marnie gathered her purse and jacket, then touched her mother on the arm. "I'm going to get going, Ma. Call me later, okay?"

Her mother promised, then returned her attention to Dan. The two of them were still chatting when Marnie headed out of the restaurant. She stood by the valet counter, waiting for the valet to return with her car, when a black sports car pulled up to the station. The passenger's side window slid down. "You're like a bad penny, turning up everywhere I go."

The voice took a second to register in her mind. It had been a couple weeks since she'd last heard that deep baritone, and in the busy-ness of working twenty-hour days, she'd nearly forgotten the encounter.

Almost.

Late at night, when she was alone and the day had gone quiet, her mind would wander and she'd wonder what might have happened if he'd been someone other than Jack Knight and she'd agreed to that cup of coffee. Then she would jerk herself back to reality.

Jack Knight was the worst kind of corporate vermin— and the last kind of man she should be thinking about late at night, or any time. Of all the people in the city of Boston, how did she end up running into him twice?

She bent down and peered inside the car. Jack grinned back at her. He had a hell of a smile, she'd give him that. The kind of smile that charmed and tempted, all at once. Yeah, like a snake. "Speaking of bad pennies," she said, "what are you doing here?"

"Picking up my father." His head disappeared from view, and a moment later, he had stepped out of the car and crossed to her. He had on khakis and a pale blue button-down shirt, the wrinkled bottom slightly untucked, the top two buttons undone, as if he was just knocking off after putting in a full day of work, even on a Saturday. He looked sexy, approachable. If she ignored his name and his job, that was.

She didn't want to like him, didn't want to find his smile alluring or his eyes intriguing. He was a Knight, and she needed to remember that. She was about to say goodbye and end the conversation before it really had a chance to start, when the restaurant door opened and her mother and Dan stepped onto the sidewalk.

"Marnie, you're still here?" Helen said.

"Jack, you're here early," Dan said.

The pieces clicked together in Marnie's mind. The timing of Jack's arrival. *Picking up my father,* he'd said.

She glanced from one man to the other, and prayed she was wrong. "Dan's your father?" she said to Jack, then spun back to Dan. "But...but your last name is Simpson."

Dan grinned. "Guilty as charged. I'm this troublemaker's stepfather." He draped a loving arm around Jack and gave him a quick hug.

"You know Dan's son?" Helen asked Marnie. "You never told me that."

"I didn't know until just now. And, Ma, I think you should know that Jack..." Marnie started to tell her mother the rest, the truth about who Jack was, but she watched the light in her mother's eyes dim a bit, and she couldn't do it. The urge to keep the peace, to keep everyone happy, overpowered the words and she let them die in her throat.

Dan Simpson. Father of Jack Knight, the man whose company had ruined her family's life.

Dan Simpson. The man her mother was falling for.

Dan Simpson. Another Mr. Wrong in a family teeming with them.

"You should know that, uh, Jack and I met the other night," Marnie said finally. "We sort of…ran into each other."

"Oh, my. What a small world," Helen said, beaming again.

"Getting smaller every day." Jack grinned at Marnie, but the smile didn't sway her. "How do you know my father?"

She gave a helpless shrug. "It seems I just fixed him up with my mother."

"You've got one talented matchmaker standing here," Dan said, giving Helen's hand a squeeze. "You should see if she can fix you up, too, Jack."

Fix him up? She'd rather die first.

"You're a *matchmaker?*" Jack raised a brow in amusement.

"Guilty as charged," she said, echoing Dan's words.

Her brain swam with the incongruity of the situation. How could she have created such a disaster? Usually her instincts were right on, but this time, they had failed her. And she'd created a mess of epic proportion. One that was slipping out of her control more every second.

Beside her, Dan and Helen were chatting, making plans for dinner or lunch or something. They were off to the side, caught in their own world of just the two of them. All of Marnie's senses were attuned to Jack— the enemy of her family and son of the man who had finally put a smile on her mother's face. How was she supposed to tell Ma the truth, and in the process, break a heart that had just begun to mend?

Jack leaned in then, close, his breath a heated whisper against her ear. "I'm surprised you didn't try to fix me up the night we met."

"I wouldn't do that to one of my clients," she whispered back.

Confusion filled his blue eyes, a confusion she had no intent of erasing, not here, not now.

"I'm not sure what I did to make you despise me," he said, "but I assure you, I'm not nearly as bad as you think."

"No, you're not," she said just as the valet arrived with her car. She opened the door, and held Jack's gaze over the roof. "You're worse."

Then she got in her car and pulled away.

A matchmaker.

Of all the jobs Jack would have thought the fiery redhead Marnie Franklin held, matchmaker sat at the very bottom of the list. Yet, the title seemed to suit her, to match her strong personality, her crimson hair, her quick tongue.

His stepfather had raved about Marnie's skills the entire ride from the restaurant to the repair shop to pick up the car the taxi driver had rear-ended, return the rental, then head home. The event had agreed with Dan, giving his hearty features a new energy, and his voice renewed enthusiasm, as if he'd reverse-aged in one afternoon. At six-foot two, with a full head of gray hair, Dan cut an imposing figure offset by a ready smile and pale green eyes. Eyes that now lit with joy every time he talked about Helen.

"I never would have expected to fall for the matchmaker's mother," Dan said. "But I tell ya, Jack, I really like Helen."

"I'm glad," Jack said. And he was. His stepfather had been alone for a long, long time, and deserved happiness. Just with someone other than Marnie Franklin's maternal relatives. The woman had something against him, that was clear.

"Her daughter's quite pretty, too, you know," Dan said.

"Really? I hadn't noticed."

Dan laughed. "You lie about as well as I cook. I saw you checking her out."

"That was a reflex."

"Sure it was." Dan shifted in his seat to study his son. "You know, you should use some of the arguments you used on me."

Jack concentrated on the road. Boston traffic in the middle of the day required all his attention. Yeah, that was why he didn't look Dan in the eye. Because of the cars on the road. "What are you talking about?"

"The list of reasons why I should go to that event—and I'm glad I did, by the way—is the same list I should give you about why you should ask Marnie out."

"I did. She turned me down."

"And?"

"And what? End of story." He didn't want to get into the reasons why he had no intentions of dating anyone right now. He, of all people, should steer far and wide from anything resembling a relationship.

He could bring a business back to life, turn around a lackluster bottom line, but when it came to personal relationships, he was—

Well, Tanya had called him unavailable. Uninvolved. Cold, even. More addicted to his smartphone than her.

A year after the end of their relationship, he'd had to admit she had a point. When he woke up in the morning, his first thought was the latest business venture, not the woman in his life.

Then why had he asked Marnie to coffee?

Because for the first time in a long time, he was intrigued. She'd been on his mind ever since the night they'd met. Confounding, intriguing Marnie Franklin had been a constant thought in the back of his head. After seeing her today, those thoughts had moved front and center. But he didn't tell Dan any of this, because he knew it would give his stepfather more ammunition for his "get back to dating" argument.

Right now, Jack was concentrating on work, and on making amends. Jack Knight, Sr. had ruined a lot of lives, and Jack had spent the last two years trying to undo the damage his father had done, while still keeping the business going and keeping the people who worked for him employed. As soon as he'd moved into his father's office, he'd vowed he would do things differently, approach the company in a new way. He'd gone through all the old files, and had tried to apply that philosophy, one deal at a time.

Tanya might not have thought he had heart when it came to personal relationships, but Jack was determined to prove the opposite in his business relationships. That uninvolved, cold man he'd been was slowly being erased as he gave back more than Knight had taken.

More than he himself had taken.

To try his best to be everything except his father's son.

That, Jack knew, was why he kept putting in all those hours. He'd been part of his father's selfish, greedy machinations, and it was all Jack could do now to restore what had been destroyed, partly by his own hand.

Doing so felt good, damned good, but he knew the time he invested in that goal was costing him a life, a family, kids. Maybe if he could do enough to make amends to all those his father had wronged, when he went to sleep at night, then maybe the past would stop haunting him.

And then he could look to the future again.

Maybe.

It hadn't thus far, and there were days when he wondered if he was doing the right thing. Or just trying to fill an endless well of guilt.

"What do you want to do for dinner?" Jack said, changing the subject.

"You're on your own tonight, kid. I have plans with Helen." Dan grinned, and for a second, Jack envied his stepfather that beaming smile, that anticipation for the night ahead. "I'm taking her to Top of the Hub."

Jack arched a brow at the mention of the famous moving restaurant at the top of the Prudential building. "Impressive. On a first date?"

"Gotta wow her right off," Dan said.

"I must have missed the memo."

Dan chuckled. "You're just a little jaded right now."

"Not jaded. More…realistic about my strengths. I'm good at business, not good at relationships. End of story."

"Hey, you're preaching to the choir here," Dan said. "I'm the king of bad at relationships, or at least I used to be. You live and you learn, and hopefully stop making the mistakes that screwed up your last relationship."

Which was the one skill Jack had yet to master. When it came to businesses and bottom lines, he could shift gears and learn from the past. But with other people… not so much. Maybe it was because he had gone too many years trying to prove himself to a father who didn't love him or appreciate him. Jack had kept striving for a connection that never existed. That made him either a glutton for punishment or a fool. "Or just avoid relationships all together."

Dan chuckled. "What are you going to do? Become a monk?"

"I don't know. Think they're taking applications?" Jack grinned. Nah, he wouldn't become a monk, but he wasn't at a point in his life where he wanted or needed a committed relationship.

He was trying to buckle down and do the right thing where Knight Enterprises was concerned. Juggling yet another commitment seemed like an impossible task. Deep down inside, he worried more about getting too close to a woman. He'd screwed things up with Tanya, and had plenty of relationship detritus in his past to prove his lack of commitment skills. He had been his father's son in business—and a part of Jack wondered if he'd be his son in a marriage, too. The easiest course— keep his head down and his focus on work. Rather than try to fix the one part of his life that had been impossible to repair.

"When do I have time to date?" Jack said. "I barely have enough spare time to order a pizza."

Except he had found plenty of time to think and wonder about Marnie. His wandering mind had set him a good day behind on his To Do list. He really needed to focus, not daydream. By definition, the sassy matchmaker believed in destiny and true love and all of that. Jack, well, Jack hadn't been good at either of those.

"Aw, you meet Miss Right and you'll change your tune," Dan said. "Like me. Helen has me rethinking this whole love in the later years concept."

"All that from one meeting?"

"I told you, she's a special lady. When you know, you know."

Jack would argue with that point. He'd never had that all-encompassing, couldn't-talk-about-anything-else feeling for a woman before.

Well, that was, until he met Marnie. She'd stuck in his mind like bubble gum, sweet, delicious, addictive. Maybe Dan had a point. But in the end, Jack still sucked at relationships and pursuing Marnie Franklin could only end with a broken heart. But that didn't stop him from wanting her or wondering about her. And why her attitude toward him had done a sudden 180.

Had his reputation preceded him? Had he hurt her somehow, too, in the years he'd worked with his father? Jack decided to do a little research in the morning and see if there was a connection. A memory nagged in the back of his head, but didn't take hold.

Jack pulled in front of the renovated brownstone where he lived, a building much like himself—filled with unique character, a speckled history, but still a little rough around the edges.

While his stepfather headed off—whistling—to the shower, Jack grabbed a bag of chips, taking them out to the balcony. He scrolled through his phone, past the endless stream of emails and voice mails. Work called to him, a non-stop siren of demands. On any other day, he'd welcome the distraction and challenges. But not today. Today, he just wanted to sit back, enjoy the sunshine and think about the choices he'd made.

Maybe his stepfather had a point. Maybe it was time to date again, make a serious commitment to something other than a cell phone plan and a profit and loss statement. He'd been working for two years to make up for the past, and still it hadn't fulfilled him like he thought it would. Nor had it eased the guilt that haunted his nights. It was as if he was missing something, some key that would bring it all together. Or maybe Dan was right and Jack needed to open his heart, too. A monumental task, and one he had never tackled successfully before.

He took a chip, the fragile snack crumbling in his hand, and thought maybe he was a fool for believing in things that could crumble at any moment.

CHAPTER THREE

As soon as her mother left on her date with Dan that night, the condo echoed. Empty, quiet. Helen had been at Marnie's house for the better part of the afternoon, indulging in a lot of mother-daughter chatting and taking a whirl through Marnie's closet to borrow a fun, flirty dress. Helen's contagious verve had Marnie in stitches, laughing until her sides hurt. But once Ma was gone, the mood deflated and reality intruded.

Marnie tried working, gave up, and gathered her planner and laptop into a big tote and headed out the door. Five minutes later, she was sweating on a treadmill at the gym near her house. It had been weeks since she'd had time for a good workout and as the beats drummed in her head, and the cardio revved up her heart, the stresses of the day began to melt away.

Someone got on the treadmill beside her, but Marnie didn't notice for a few seconds. As she passed the three-mile mark, she pressed the speed button, slowing her pace to a fast walk. Her breath heaved in and out of her chest, but in a good way, giving her that satisfaction of a hard job done well.

"You're making me feel like a couch potato."

She swiveled her head to the right, and saw Jack Knight, doing an easy jog on the other treadmill. Her hand reached up, unconsciously brushing away the sweat on her brow and giving her bangs a quick swipe. Damn. She should have put on some makeup or lip gloss or something. Then she cursed herself for caring how she looked. She wasn't interested in Jack Knight or what he thought about her, all sweaty and messy. Not one bit.

Then why did her gaze linger on his long, defined legs, his broad chest? Why did she notice the way the simple gray T and dark navy shorts he wore gave him a casual, sexy edge? Why did her heart skip a beat when he smiled at her? And why did her hormones keep ignoring the direct orders from her brain?

"I'm impressed." He glanced at the digital display on her treadmill. "Great pace, nice distance."

"Thanks." She took her pace down another notch, and pressed the cool down button. "Are you a member at this gym? I've never seen you here before."

"That's because most of the time, I'm here in the middle of the night, after I finally leave the office for the day. At that time, I have the whole place pretty much to myself."

She gave him a quizzical look. "I thought the gym closes at ten."

"It does. I have…special privileges." He broke into a light jog, arms moving, legs flexing. His effortless run caused a modest uptick in his breathing, leaving Marnie the one now impressed. She'd have been huffing and puffing by now.

"Let me guess," she said. "A cute girl at the front desk gave you a key?"

"Nope. My key comes from one of the owners."

"You?"

"I don't own it," he said. "I have a…vested interest in this gym. One of my high school friends bought it, and when he was struggling, he needed an investor, so I stepped in."

"You did?" She tried to keep the surprise from her voice, but didn't quite make it. "That's really…nice."

Not the kind of thing she expected from Jack Knight, evil corporate raider. He'd saved the gym owned by his friend, but not her father's business. Did he only help friends? And let a stranger's businesses fall to pieces? Or was there a nice guy buried deep inside him?

Or were there a few things she hadn't accepted about her father's company and his role in its demise?

A part of Marnie had always avoided looking too close at the details, because keeping them at bay let her keep her focus on Knight as the evil conglomerate at fault. But deep down inside Marnie knew her affable, distracted, creative father wasn't the best businessman in the world. Helen refused to talk about it, refused to open those "dark doors" as she called them, to the past. And right now, right here, Marnie didn't want to open them either.

Jack leaned over, the scent of soap and man filling the space between them and sending that zing through Marnie all over again. "See? I told you, I'm not as bad as you think I am."

Her face heated. She reached for the hand towel on the treadmill and swiped at her cheeks, then took a deep gulp of water from her water bottle. "I never said you were a horrible person."

Out loud.

"You didn't have to. It was in the way you drove away from the restaurant earlier and in your stinging rejection of my invitation to coffee." He bumped up the speed on his treadmill and increased his jog pace, his arms moving in concert with his legs. "And it was just coffee, Marnie, not a lifetime commitment."

He was right. A cup of coffee with a handsome man wasn't a crime.

Except this handsome man was Jack Knight, who had destroyed her father's company in one of his "investments." She doubted he even realized what he had done to her family, and how that loss had hurt all of them in more than just Tom Franklin's bank account.

She opened her mouth to tell him what she really thought of him, then stopped herself. That urge to keep the peace resurged, coupled with a burst of protectiveness. If Marnie lashed out at Jack, the conversation would get back to Dan and her mother. She had yet to tell her mother who Dan really was, unable to bring herself to wipe that smile off Helen's face, to hurt her mother or disappoint her. Somehow, she had to tell her the truth, though, and do it soon.

Wouldn't it be smart to go into that conversation armed with information? And the best way to gather information without the other party suspecting? Dine with the enemy.

Maybe her father hadn't been businessman of the year, but she knew as well as she knew her own name that Knight Enterprises had been part of the company's downfall, too. If she could figure out how and why, then she could go to her mother and warn her away from Dan. Maybe then both Franklin women would have closure…and peace.

"You know, you're right. It's not a lifetime commitment," she said before she could think twice. "I'll take you up on your coffee offer."

He arched a brow in surprise, and turned toward her, but didn't slow his pace. "Where and when?"

"As soon as you finish your run. If that works for you."

Jack glanced at the time remaining on the treadmill's display and nodded. "Sounds good. How about if I meet you up front in twenty minutes?"

Enough time for her to hit the locker room and get cleaned up. Not that she cared what she looked like with Jack Knight, of course. It was merely because she was going out in public.

As she stepped into the shower and washed up, she second guessed her decision. Getting close to Jack Knight could be dangerous on a dozen different levels. A matchmaker knew better than to put Romeo and Juliet together—and especially not enemies like her and Jack. She had no business seeing him, dating him, or even thinking about either.

She still remembered her father's heartbreak, how he had become a shell of the man he used to be, sitting at home, purposeless, waiting for a miracle that never came. His life's work, gone in an instant. And all because of Jack Knight.

The last of the lather went down the shower drain. She'd have coffee with Jack, and in the process, maybe find a way to exact a little revenge for how he had let her father fail, rather than help the struggling businessman succeed.

What was that they said about revenge? That it was a dish best served cold? Well, this one was going to be rich, dark and steaming hot.

Seventeen minutes later, Jack stood in the lobby of the health club, showered, changed, and his heart beating a mile a minute. He told himself it was from the hard, short run on the treadmill, but he knew better. There was something about Marnie Franklin that intrigued him in ways he hadn't been intrigued in a hell of a long time.

Her smile, for one. It lit her green eyes, danced in her features, seemed to brighten the room.

Her sass, for another. Marnie was a woman who could clearly give as good as she got, and that was something he didn't often find.

Her love/hate for him, for a third. He knew attraction, and could swear she'd been attracted to him when they first met. Then somewhere along the way, she'd started to dislike him. Yet at the same time, she seemed to war with those two emotions.

He had done some preliminary research before he hit the gym, but his files were filled with Franklins, a common enough last name. Then it hit him.

Tom Franklin.

A printer, with a small shop in Boston. Nice guy, but such a muddled, messy businessman that Jack had at first balked when his father asked him to take on Top Notch Printing as a client. He hadn't realized at the time what his father's real plan was—

Well, maybe he had, and hadn't wanted to accept the truth. Buy up the company for pennies on the dollar, to pave the way for a big-dollar competitor moving into town, another branch of the Knight investment tree. Within weeks, Tom Franklin had been out of business.

Oh, damn. If Marnie was that Franklin, Jack had a hell of a lot to make up for. And no idea how to do it. Jack's memory told him that none of Tom's daughters had been named Marnie, though, so he couldn't be sure. Maybe it was all some kind of weird coincidence.

Just then Marnie came down the hall, wearing a navy and white striped skirt that swooshed around her knees, and a bright yellow blouse that offset the deep red of her hair. She had on flats, which was a change from the heels he'd seen her in before, but on Marnie, they looked sweet, cute. Her skin still had that dewy just showered look, and like the other two times he'd seen her, she'd put her hair back in a clip that left a few stray tendrils curling along her neck. The whole effect was... devastating. His fingers itched to see what it would take to get her to let her hair down, literally and figuratively. To see Marnie Franklin unfettered, wild, sexy.

"Where are we going?" she asked. "There's that chain coffee shop—"

He shook his head. "I'm not exactly a decaf venti kind of guy. When I want coffee, I want just that. So, the question is—" at this he took a step closer to her, telling himself it was just to catch a whiff of that intoxicating perfume she wore, a combination of flowers and dark nights "—do you trust me?"

Her eyes widened and she inhaled a quick breath. Then a grin quirked up on one side of her face, and she raised her chin a notch. Sassy. "No, I don't. But I'll take my chances anyway."

"Pretty risky."

"I'm not worried. I carry pepper spray."

A laugh burst out of him, then he turned and opened the health club door for her. As she ducked past him, he leaned in again and caught another whiff of that amazing perfume. Damn sexy, and addictive. "You surprise me, Marnie Franklin. Not too many people do that."

"I'll keep that in mind." She tossed the last over her shoulder, before walking into the waning sunshine.

He fell into step beside her, the two of them shifting into small talk about the weather and the treadmills at the gym as they walked down the busy main street for a couple of blocks before turning right on a small side street. Dusk had settled on the city. Coupled with the dark overlay of leafy trees it made for a cozy, peaceful stroll. For Jack, the walk was as familiar as the back of his hand.

He knew he should find a way to bring the conversation around to whether her father was the Tom Franklin he'd known, but Jack couldn't do it. He liked Marnie, liked her a lot. If she had a chance to get to know this Jack, the one who had walked away from his father's legacy and now tried to do things differently, then maybe he could explain what had happened before.

"Where are we going?" Marnie asked.

"It's a surprise. You'll see."

"Okay, but I don't have a ton of time—"

He put a hand on her arm, a quick, light touch, but it seemed to sear his skin, and he saw her do another quick inhale and a part of him—the part that had been closed off for so long—came to life. He wanted to let her in, if only for today, to have a taste of that sweet lightness, even though he feared a woman like her wasn't meant for a man like him.

"It's beautiful out. We both work hard. I think we can afford a few extra minutes to enjoy the end of the day."

She gave him a wary glance. "Okay. But just a few."

The side street led straight into a neighborhood, as if stepping into another world after leaving the hectic-ness of the city. Quiet descended over the area, while the constant hum of rush hour traffic behind them got farther away with each step. Elegant brick homes nearly as old as Boston itself decorated either side of the street, fronted by planters filled with bright, happy flowers. Concrete sidewalks lined either side of the street, accented with grassy strips and the minutiae of life in a neighborhood—kids' bikes, lawn tools, newspapers. Neighbors greeted Jack as he walked by, and passing cars slowed to give him a wave.

In the distance, the gold-tipped spire of a church peeked above the leafy green trees, like a crown on top of a perfect cake. His heart swelled the farther he walked. No matter how many times he came back here, he always felt the same—at home.

"How come everyone knows you here?" Marnie said.

"I grew up in this neighborhood, staying in the same house all my life, even after my mom married Dan," he said. "Even though my dad passed away and my mom moved to Florida a couple years ago, this place is still home."

"It's a pretty neighborhood. Lots of great architecture." She raised a hand to touch the black curved iron and aluminum pole of the street light. It was a replica, and a pretty darn close historical copy of the original lights that had been lit by torches a century ago. "I love these lights, too. The old-fashioned ones are my favorite."

"Much nicer than the sodium vapor and high mast ones they use on the main roads. And in keeping with the tradition that's so important to this neighborhood."

"Oh, and look, daisies." She pointed to a house fronted by the bright white flowers. "I loved those when I was a kid, so much that my dad called me Daisy-doo. Silly, but you know, when it's your dad, it's kinda special."

"I bet." His father had never been the kind for anything as superfluous as a nickname. Dan had been the one to tease, make jokes, envelop Jack with warmth and hugs. But the man whose DNA Jack shared, hadn't done so much as offer a hug.

He shrugged off the memories and pointed to the spire. "Back when this neighborhood was built, it was centered around the church. It's still pretty central to the houses here."

They rounded another corner, and as they did, the road opened up, showcasing a simple white building. The small, unpretentious church sat in the middle of the neighborhood, with the rest of the streets jutting off like spokes. Street lights blinked to life, and danced golden light over the sidewalk. "This is my favorite time of day to be here," Jack said. "It looks so beautiful and peaceful. So pristine and perfect, like a new beginning could be had for the asking."

He hadn't realized he'd said that out loud until Marnie turned to him and smiled. "That sounds so... awesome."

"Thanks. But I can't take all the credit." He gestured toward the building.

Marnie stopped walking and stared up at the church. "Wow. It *is* beautiful. Understated. Maybe because it's so...ordinary. There are so many buildings in this city that try to compete for architectural design of the year, and this one is more...wholesome, if that makes sense."

"It does. I guess that's why I like coming here."

"You go to this church?"

He nodded. "I've gone almost every Sunday since the day I was born."

She arched a brow. "Really? You?"

He leaned in again, close enough to see the flecks of gold in her eyes, the soft chestnut wave brushing against her cheek. And close enough to once again, be mesmerized by her perfume. "I told you, I'm not as bad as you think."

She raised her gaze to his, and that smile returned. "You don't know what I think about you, Mr. Knight."

He reached up and trailed a finger down her cheek, whisking away that errant hair before lowering his hand. She inhaled, exhaled, watching him. No, he didn't know what she thought about him. But damn, he wanted to know.

Was it just because she was trying so hard not to like him? Or because he was tired of being seen as the evil corporate raider, painted with the same brush as his father?

Jack just wanted time before he probed deeper, to find out where Marnie's animosity lay. Give her a chance to get to know this Jack Knight, the one who no longer did his father's bidding. Then, when the time was right, he'd broach the subject of the past. Because right now he wanted her. Damn, did he want her.

"Considering how much we have in common, Marnie," he said, "I think you should call me by my first name. Don't you?"

"And what do we have in common?"

"Besides an appreciation for good architecture, and a competitive streak on the treadmill, there's the fact that our parents are dating."

She laughed. "In my world, that's not something in common. Heck, that wouldn't even be enough to invite you to a mixer, *Mr. Knight*."

Damn. Every time he thought they were growing closer, that she was giving him a chance, she retreated, threw up a wall. They started walking again, circling past the church, then turning down another tree-lined street. They walked at an easy pace, no hurry to their step. How long had it been since he'd done that? Taken a walk, with no real hurry to his journey? Even though he had a thousand things to do, at least a dozen phone calls to return and countless emails waiting for his attention, he kept walking. Something about today, or about Marnie, made him want to linger rather than rush back to the office. Right now, he couldn't tell if that was a good or bad thing.

"So how does it work?" he asked.

They passed under a leafy maple tree, the branches hanging so low, they whispered across their heads. "What? Matchmaking?" she said.

He nodded. "Do you use some kind of algorithm or something? A computer program?"

"No." She laughed. "Most of it's instinct. We do log pertinent client and potential match information into the computer, just so it's easier to develop a list of bachelors or bachelorettes for a mixer, but when it comes to picking the best possible matches, it's all in here." She pressed a hand to her chest.

He jerked his gaze up and away from the enticing swell of her breast. He was having a conversation here, not indulging in a fantasy. Except every time he looked at her, his thoughts derailed. Especially when she smiled like she did, or laughed that lyrical laugh of hers. "Sounds sort of like buying a business. Instinctually, I know which ones will be the best choice, and which aren't going to make it, no matter how much of a cash infusion I give it."

Her expression hardened. "Yeah, I bet it's exactly like that. All guts. No logic." She cast her glance to the right and left, away from him. The warm and bubbly moments between them evaporated, and a wall of ice dropped into her voice. "So, where's this coffee shop?"

Her reaction sealed his suspicions. She'd been

burned, either by Knight or someone like him. But most likely his company. Guilt churned in his stomach.

"One more block," he said, trying to redirect the conversation. "Close enough to walk there after church, which is part of what makes the location so ideal."

The wall remained, however. Silence descended on them, an uncomfortable, tense hole in the conversation. They reached the corner where the coffee shop sat, a bright burst amidst the brick and white of the neighborhood.

The door to the Java Depot was propped open, and the rich scent of brewed coffee wafted outside, luring customers in with its siren call of caffeine. Several couples sat at umbrella-covered wrought iron tables, while a trio of kids played on the small playground set up beside the shop's deck. The non-lucrative use of a good chunk of the cafe's land had been a risky move, but one that had paid off, given the number of kids and families that visited this space on a regular basis. The sound system played contemporary jazz and alternative music, lots of it by local artists who often performed on the outdoor patio.

"Cute place," Marnie said. "I never even knew it existed."

"One of those great hidden secrets in Boston." He grinned. "Though the new owner is determined to get the word out via advertising and social media."

Marnie looked around, her intelligent gaze assessing the location and décor. "I like how it's so community oriented, with the local art displays, and the playground for kids. It's almost like being at home."

The words warmed him. He so rarely saw the reaction to his work, the money he invested, the counsel he gave. Too often, he'd seen the effects of the businessman he used to be—the shuttered shops, the For Sale signs, the people filing unemployment. But the Java Depot was a success story, one of many, he hoped. Appreciation and seeing others' success was a far greater reward than any increase in his own bottom line.

"That was the idea. A neighborhood coffee shop should feel like an ingrained part of the neighborhood and reflect the owner's personality. This one does both." He waved her ahead of him, then stepped inside and paused while his eyes adjusted to the dim interior.

"Jack!" Dorothy, a platinum blond buxom woman in her fifties who had been behind the counter of the Java Depot for nearly two years, sent him a wave. She gave him a broad, friendly smile, as if she was greeting a long lost family member. Considering how long he'd known Dot, she practically was family. "I brewed some of your favorite blend today. Let me get you a cup."

"Thanks, Dot. And I'll need a…" He glanced at Marnie.

"Whatever you're having. But with the girly touch of some cream and sugar."

"A second one. Regular, please."

"You got it," Dot said. A few seconds later, she passed two steaming mugs of coffee across the counter. "Got fresh baked peanut butter cookies, too." Before he could respond, she laid two cookies on a plate and slid those over, too, giving Jack a wink.

"You are bad for my diet, Dot." He grinned.

"You work it off in smiles, you charmer, you." She chuckled, then turned to Marnie. "Half my waitstaff trips over themselves to serve him. There's going to be a lot of envious eyes on you, my girl, because you've snagged Mr. Eligible here."

"Oh, I'm not his girlfriend," Marnie said. Fast. So fast, a man could take it personally.

"Well, you're missing out on a hell of a catch," Dot said, then gave Jack a wink. "Why this man is the whole reason I'm in business. Without Jack, there wouldn't be a Java Depot here. He helped me out, encouraged me, gave me great advice, and a big old nudge when I needed one most. Always has, and I suspect even if I tell him not to, he always will." Dot's light blue eyes softened when she looked over at Jack. "It's good to have you in my corner, Jack."

He shifted his weight, uncomfortable under Dot's grateful words. It was what he worked for, but there were days when praise for doing the right thing felt like wearing the wrong shoes. Maybe someday he'd get used to it.

"I needed a place to get my coffee," he said. "And my mom is addicted to your cookies, so if you went out of business and stopped shipping them down to her in Florida, she'd go into serious withdrawal, and I'd have hell to pay."

"Yeah, that's why you helped me out," Dot said with a little snort of disbelief. "Purely selfish reasons."

Jack grinned and put up his hands. "That's me."

Dot shook her head, then gestured toward Marnie. "He's a keeper, I'm telling you. Though you might have to beat off half the women in Boston to get him. And you—" she wagged a finger at Jack "—you need to use some of that legendary Knight charm, and win her over." Dot chuckled, then headed to the other end of the counter to help another customer.

"Legendary charm?" Marnie asked. She reached past him to pick up her mug of coffee, and give him a teasing grin. "Legendary like the Loch Ness Monster and Bigfoot?"

"Exactly." He chuckled, then picked up the second mug and the cookies and followed her to an outdoor table where Christmas lights lit the undersides of the umbrellas over the tables. A soft breeze rippled the bright blue umbrella, and toyed with the ends of Marnie's hair. His fingers ached to do the same.

He'd thought he didn't want to date anyone. That he didn't have room in his life for a relationship. A week ago, he would have sworn up and down that he had no interest in dating anyone on a long-term basis. That he, of all people, shouldn't try to create ties.

Then he met Marnie.

Maybe it was the way she ran hot, then cold. Maybe it was the way she kept him at a distance, like a book he couldn't read in the library. Or maybe it was that none of his "legendary charm" worked on her. Was it about the challenge of wanting what he couldn't have? Or something more?

Either way, he reminded himself, he was his father's son. The offspring of a womanizer who destroyed companies, ruined lives, and broke hearts. Jack had been like that, too, for too long. He'd managed to change his approach to business, but when it came down to making a commitment, would he run like his father had or stick around? Would he shut out the people he cared for, turn his back on them?

Marnie picked up one of the cookies, and took a bite. A smattering of crumbs lingered on her lips, and it took everything in his power not to kiss her. Then the family beside them got up and left, leaving him and Marnie alone on the patio. She reached for her coffee, and before he could think twice, he leaned forward, closing the distance between them to mere inches. Desire thundered in his veins, pounded in his brain. All he wanted right now was her, that sweet goodness, her tempting smile. To hell with later; Jack wanted now. "You have a crumb right—"

And he kissed her. To hell with staying away, to hell with making smart decisions, to hell with everything but this moment.

A gentle kiss, more of a whisper against her lips. She froze for a second, then shifted closer to him, one hand reaching to cup his cheek, her fingers dancing against his skin. She deepened the kiss, her delicate tongue slipping in to tango with his. Holy cow. A hot, insistent need ignited in his veins, and it took near every ounce of his strength to pull back instead of taking her on the table in front of the whole damned neighborhood.

"Uh, I think I got it," he said. Truth was, right now he couldn't think or see straight enough to tell if she was covered in crumbs.

Her fingers went to her mouth, lingered a moment, then she lowered her hand. Her cheeks flushed a deep pink and she let out a soft curse. "That…that wasn't a good idea. At all. I have to go." She got to her feet, leaving the half-eaten cookie on the plate. "Thanks for the coffee."

"Wait, Marnie—"

"Jack, stay out of my life. You've done enough damage already."

Then she turned and left. Jack leaned back in his chair and watched her go, bemused and befuddled. A woman who kissed him back yet claimed not to be interested in him. She was a puzzle, that was for sure. What had she meant by "you've done enough damage already"?

A sinking feeling told him she'd meant more than that kiss. His past had reared its ugly head again. Somewhere, Marnie was connected to the mistakes he'd made years before. He vowed to dig deeper into the files in his office, and find the connection.

Would it always be this way? Would he find his regrets confronting him every time he tried to do the right thing?

Jack watched Marnie hail a cab, get inside the yellow taxi and disappear into the congested streets. Somehow, he needed to find a way to do what he had done before. Mitigate the damage. And find a solution that left everyone happy.

CHAPTER FOUR

JACK LOGGED A hard six miles on the treadmill, but it wasn't enough. He could have run a marathon and it wouldn't have been enough to quiet the demons in his head. He'd tried, Lord knew he'd tried, over the years.

By the time he climbed off the machine, he was drenched in sweat, but his mind still raced with thoughts of Marnie Franklin. Hell, half the reason he'd come to the gym today was because he'd hoped to bump into her.

After their walk to the coffee shop, he'd gone to the office and pulled out Top Notch Printing's file, from the piles stacked on the credenza behind his desk. So many people's lives ruined, so many businesses shuttered, their contents sold like trinkets at a garage sale.

He'd dug through Tom's file, looking for the notes he'd made all those years ago.

Owner: Tom Franklin, married to wife Helen. Three daughters. Calls them Daisy, Kitty and Chatterbug.

Nicknames. That's why Jack hadn't made the connection when he'd met Marnie. He'd never known Tom's daughters' real names, never spent enough time with the man to get that personal.

Jack dropped onto a bench outside the gym and put his head in his hands. He could still see Tom's face. Bright, hopeful, trusting. Believing every word Jack and his father said.

Jack had tried to undo the damage, but by then it had been too late. Too damned late.

He sighed and got to his feet. Instead of taking the left toward the office, he took a right and went back home.

"I thought you just left. What are you doing home so soon?" his stepfather asked when Jack stepped into the apartment.

"I'm off to a slow start today." Because his mind was far from work. Had been ever since Marnie's cab had dented his sports car. That alone was a sign he was in too deep. Then why kiss her? Why go to the gym on the off chance she'd be there, too? Why couldn't he just forget her? Was it all about trying to make up for the past? Or more?

"Maybe I need some protein or something. You want to go grab some breakfast before I head into the office? Unless you already ate."

"Even if I did, I'll eat again." Dan chuckled, and grabbed a light jacket off the back of the kitchen chair. "That's the beauty of retirement. No schedule. Lunch can come five minutes after breakfast."

They headed out into the bright sunshine and around the corner to Hector's cozy little deli. Its glass windows looked out onto two streets, while inside, business bustled along, in keeping with the city's busy pace. Hector greeted them as they walked in with a boisterous hello and a hearty wave. A gregarious guy given to playing mariachi music just because, Hector was a colorful and exuberant addition to the area. His incredible sandwiches drew people far and wide for their unique taste combinations and home-baked breads.

Dan and Jack ordered, then snagged a couple of bar stools at the window counter, and unwrapped their sandwiches. "So, what do you think of Helen?" Dan asked.

Dan and Helen had been on several dates over the last week. Dan had even invited her to dinner at Jack's apartment—and wisely ordered takeout instead of trying to cook. They'd gone to a Red Sox game, played Bingo at a local church and taken several long walks through the neighborhood. After every date, Dan's smile grew broader, his step lighter, like a man falling in love.

"She seems really nice," Jack said. "And she definitely likes you."

A big, goofy grin spread over Dan's face. "I sure like her, too. More and more every day." Dan toyed with the paper wrapper before him. "You're okay with me dating? I mean, it's got to be kind of weird."

"You and my mom divorced years ago, Dad." Even though Dan was his stepfather, he'd been in Jack's life for so long, calling him Dad seemed natural. Jack's real father had left him the business, and not much else, letting his work keep him from seeing his son, and leaving the raising of Jack up to Dan and Helen. Probably for the best, because Dan had been a hell of a stepfather. Jack, Senior had been about as warm and fuzzy as a porcupine.

Still, there'd always been that part of Jack that had craved a relationship with his biological father. Maybe because then he could have the answers he wanted about why Jack, Sr. had walked away from his family. Why he had chosen work over his son. In the end, Jack had realized his father lacked the capacity to love others first.

And that he had been damned lucky to have Dan, who had shown him the way a good father acted.

"I want you to be happy, too," Jack said to Dan, and meant the words.

"Me, too. And hopefully, I do it right this time."

"About doing things right…" Jack sighed. "There's something you should know. Helen is the widow of one of the business owners that Knight put out of business."

"She mentioned something about her husband's company going under after some investors stepped in. I wondered about the connection."

Jack toyed with the napkin. "I was the one that talked Tom into signing with Knight. At the time I was working for my dad and—"

Dan put a hand on his shoulder. "You don't need to explain. We all make mistakes, Jack. We all screw up. The point is you learned and you changed. You're not that man anymore."

Jack nodded, as if he agreed. But he wondered how much distance he had placed between himself and the father he'd idolized. He'd tried so hard to be like him, to get past the wall between them. Had it been at the expense of his heart?

"Why did you and my mom get divorced?" It was a question Jack had never asked. Maybe because he'd been too busy working when the announcement came. Maybe because it was easier to bury himself in work than to call his mom or Dan and ask what had happened. Yet another item to add to his "not good at" list. Family relationships.

Tanya was right. He was cold and uninvolved. He'd cut off the relationships part of his life for far too long. He needed to find more ways to connect, to care. Because if he didn't, he could see the writing on the wall—Jack, Jr., was going to morph into Jack, Sr.

He'd come so close to doing exactly that. Then one day he'd looked in the mirror before the biggest deal of Knight's history, and realized he had become his father, from the mannerisms to the crimson power tie. Jack had walked out of the bathroom, quit his job and walked away.

Dan sighed. "As easy as it would be for me to blame Sarah, truth is, I was a terrible husband."

"You were a great stepdad, though." There'd been after-school softball games in the yard, impromptu weekend camping trips and annual father-son vacations. Dan had gone to every track meet, every Boy Scout canoe trip, every award ceremony.

"Thanks, Jack. You weren't so bad as a stepson yourself." Dan grinned. "But your mother and I, we just didn't have what it took. When we got married, it was a fast decision. Too fast, some would say. We married a week after we met. Crazy, but gosh, I just didn't think it through. I just said I do. By the time I realized we were like oil and water together, it was too late. I'd already started considering you my son, and I couldn't bear leaving. We tried to stick it out after you grew up, but by that time, we'd become two different people, living separate lives. If I had plugged in more, or tried harder, maybe we wouldn't have ended up that way." He sighed. "It was like our marriage died a long, slow death. We were always friends—and we still are—but that wasn't enough to make it work."

Jack had noticed years ago that his mother and Dan rarely hugged or kissed or went out alone. There'd been no drama, no fights, just a quiet existence. Jack couldn't think of anything more agonizing and painful than that.

If he ever settled down, he wanted a woman who challenged him, who made his life an adventure.

A woman like Marnie?

Want if he ended up repeating his father's mistakes? Leaving his wife for one woman after another, ignoring his child, in favor of his company? There was no guarantee Jack would end up doing that, or end up a good man like Dan, but Jack's cautious and logical side threw up a red caution flag all the same.

"I'm glad your mother is happy now with that new guy she's dating," Dan said, bringing Jack back to their conversation. "What's his name? Ray? Seems like he's perfect for her."

Jack had only met Ray once, but he'd have to agree. His mother's new boyfriend was an outgoing, friendly guy who enjoyed the same things as she did—traveling, bike riding, and charitable work. "She needed someone busier than her," Jack said with a chuckle.

Jack's exuberant, spontaneous stepfather had driven his mom crazy sometimes. She was a stick-to-the-schedule, organized woman who never got used to Dan's unconventional approaches. Jack liked to think he'd taken on the best of both their traits. Some of the impulsivity of his stepfather, and some of the dependable keel of his mother. Ray's personality was much closer to Sarah's, which had made them a good fit.

"This time, I'm going to work damned hard to make sure me and the woman I marry are on the same path," Dan said. "And that I let her know all the time how much I appreciate her. Life's too damned short to spend it alone, you know?"

Jack nodded. He'd been feeling the same way himself lately. Was it just because he'd met Marnie? Because he was tired of being alone? Or because he'd glimpsed his future and didn't like the picture it presented? Work-aholic, glued to his desk. A repeat of his namesake's choices. Not the future Jack wanted. "You deserve happiness, Dad. You really do."

"Thanks, Jack. That means a lot." Dan took a bite of his sandwich, swallowed, then looked at Jack and a teasing smile lit his face. "How are things going with the daughter?"

"You mean Marnie?" Jack said the word like he didn't know who Dan meant. Like he hadn't been thinking about Marnie almost non-stop for days.

"She's smart and beautiful, and a hell of a catch, according to her mother. And yes, we have been talking about you two and conspiring behind your backs. We both think you'd be a fool to let her get away."

Get away? He couldn't seem to get her to stay. "She's made it very clear that she's not interested in me."

Well, not exactly crystal clear. There was the matter of that kiss. Mixed messages, times ten.

"I think Marnie's figured out my connection to her father's business. It's no wonder she hates me. Seriously, I hate myself for some of the decisions I made back then."

Dan waved that off. "So? You make better decisions now. That's what counts. We're all allowed a little stupidity."

Jack grinned. "Either way, I won't blame Marnie if she wants to tie me to a stake and light a fire at my feet."

"Since when have you let a little roadblock like that hold you back?" Dan chuckled. "Listen, I saw the truth all over her face outside the restaurant the other day. She *likes* you."

Jack snorted.

Dan leaned an arm over his chair. "You know, there is a way to make her prove it."

"What? A little Sodium Pentothal?"

Dan chuckled then leaned in and lowered his voice. "Have her take you on as a client. When she tries to fix you up, she'll see that the best possible match is…"

"Her." Jack let that thought turn around in his head for a while. "It could work. But, I don't know, Dad. I haven't exactly done a good job of balancing work and a life thus far. There's only twenty-four hours in a day and it seems like twenty-three of them are dedicated to the business."

Well, maybe less than that, if he counted the hours spent walking around Boston with Marnie, then at the gym trying to stop thinking about Marnie, and this morning, avoiding the office because all he could do was think about Marnie.

Distracted had become his middle name. Not a good thing right now. He had three pending deals this month, a few other recently acquired companies that still needed his guiding hand, and a To Do list a mile long. And yet, here he was, sitting with Dan and talking about Marnie. He made no move to leave.

Nor did he answer the nagging doubts in his head. The ones that said all he was doing was making excuses. Because that was easier than getting involved—and being the kind of human iceberg that had ruined relationships before.

"Chicken," Dan teased.

"I'm not chicken. I'm busy. There's a difference."

"Bawk, bawk," Dan said, flapping his arms in emphasis. "You are, too. It's time you had a life, Jack, instead of just watching from the sidelines."

He bristled. He'd had the same thoughts, but wouldn't admit it. "I do have a life. I go out, I go to the gym—"

"You *exist*. That's different." Dan clapped a hand on his shoulder, and his light blue eyes met Jack's square-on. "You deserve to be happy. Your father...well, I don't like to speak ill of the dead, but your father wasn't exactly citizen of the year. But that doesn't mean you'll turn out like him. Don't let one bad apple spoil the rest of the batch."

Jack chuckled. "How many trite phrases do you have in you?"

"As many as it takes to get you over to Marnie's office, and back out into the dating world. Who knows, maybe she'll find your perfect match for you."

"I thought the goal was for her to realize she was the right one for me."

"I'm thinking it might need to work both ways," Dan said. "Now get out of here and go over there before you *chicken* out."

"Very funny," Jack said. He got to his feet and tossed his trash in the bin, then said goodbye to his stepfather and left the deli. He stood on the corner for a long moment. To the north lay the office and a thousand responsibilities. To the east, Marnie and a thousand risks.

"What has you all distracted today?" Erica, Marnie's little sister, said. She was sitting at the desk across from Marnie, while the two of them worked on a menu for the annual client thank-you party. Erica had inherited their father's dark brown locks, but the same green eyes as the other Franklin girls. Two years younger than Marnie, she was the bubbly one in the family, filled with more energy than anyone Marnie had ever met.

"Me? I'm not distracted."

Erica laughed. "Uh-huh. Then why did you write the same thing three times on this list? Do we really need that many napkins?" She pointed to a paper sitting between them. "And you've been staring off into space for the last ten minutes. Heck, most of the day I've had to repeat myself every time I've talked to you. This is totally not like you, oh, organized one."

"Sorry. It's just been a busy day." A lie. She had been distracted by thoughts of Jack Knight. What was it about that man? He was the enemy. A man she had done a good job of despising for years.

When she went for coffee with him yesterday, it had been to gather information and come up with a plan for a little revenge. Instead, he'd turned the tables with that kiss.

And what a kiss it had been. As far as kisses went, that one ranked high on Marnie's Top Ten list. She'd gone home after the coffee, and spent half the day doing what she was doing now—daydreaming and wondering how she could be so attracted to a man yet despise him at the same time. Maybe it was some kind of reverse psychology at work.

Or maybe it was that Jack Knight could kiss like no man she'd ever met, and just the mere thought of him sent a delicious rush through her.

God, she was a mess. She needed to get back on track, not keep letting Jack derail her. If there was one thing Marnie excelled at, it was holding on to the reins. She had her business and her apartment organized to the nth degree, her planner filled with neat little squares. She made quarterly goal lists, daily agendas, and didn't go off on crazy heat-filled dates with Mr. Wrong.

Most of the time, anyway.

Then why had she kissed Jack back? Why had she

let him get close? All the more reason to get a grip and get back to work.

The door opened and a burst of yellow rushed into the room. "Oh. My. God. You guys are the *best!*" a female voice screeched.

"Oh, no," Erica whispered and rolled her eyes. Marnie sucked in a fortifying breath.

Every time she arrived, Roberta Stewart's giant personality exploded. A tall, gangly woman, Roberta's decibel-stretching voice entered a room long before she did. Marnie had known her since the first day she opened her doors, one of her first clients—and one of her least successful. Roberta was likeable, smart, and funny, but few people dated her long enough to realize that, because her first impression was so loud and busy. No matter how many times Marnie tried to counsel Roberta to tone it down just a bit, she didn't listen. And the men ran—until they were out of earshot.

Today, Roberta had on a sunny yellow dress that swirled like a bell around her hips, and a wide-brimmed matching hat trimmed with silk orchids. She let out a dramatic sigh, then plopped onto the sofa in the waiting area, her dress spreading across the brown leather like melting butter. "I just came from my *third* engagement party of the year! You guys did it *again!*" Roberta shook her head. "Amy and Bob looked *so happy!*"

"I'm glad," Marnie said, thinking of the cycling enthusiast couple she had put together a few months ago. "They're a great match."

"And now it's my turn!" Roberta jumped to her feet and clasped her hands together. "So, who do you have for me this week? Tell me, who's my new Mr. Right?"

"Things didn't work out with Alan?" Marnie had

really hoped the bookish accountant would be a great counterbalance to Roberta's exuberance.

"Alan, shmalan." Roberta waved a hand in dismissal. "I need a man with verve! Life! Energy! Strength! Somebody's got to keep up with all this!" She swiveled her hips. "And poor Alan was ready to pass out before we even reached the second nightclub. Give me a man who takes his *vitamins!*"

"Maybe you should try a quiet dinner for your first date," Erica said. "Rather than all-night salsa dancing."

"But these shoes and this body were made for *dancing,*" Roberta said. "I need a man who can keep up with me. Call me as soon as you have another one. Oh, and please make sure he's had a stress test before the date. I was a little worried poor Alan's heart was going to go *kaput!*" She gave them a wave, then headed back out the door.

"Ah, Roberta. Always a memorable visit," Erica said once the door shut. "Who are you going to match her with now?"

"I have no idea. I like Roberta, but she needs a very special man." One that had yet to come along, though not for a lack of trying on Marnie's part. Maybe such a bachelor didn't exist in Boston. Or the greater New England area. Or maybe even on planet Earth.

No, there was someone perfect for Roberta. Marnie just hadn't found him yet. He needed to be a unique man, strong yet confident enough to be with a woman like her.

"Speaking of men," Erica said, "I have a date. Mind if I knock off early?"

"Nope. There are no appointments the rest of the day. I'm just going to finish up this menu, and then head home myself."

"Be sure you do," Erica said softly, laying a hand on her sister's shoulder. "Take a little time to let go and just be, sis. Okay?"

"I do."

Erica laughed. "No, you don't. But maybe if I tell you to do it often enough, you finally will."

CHAPTER FIVE

AFTER ERICA LEFT, Marnie sat in her office, the music cranked up on the mini sound system beside her desk, and hammered out the rest of the details for the next few Matchmaking by Marnie events. She spun around in her chair, facing the window that looked out over Brookline, tapping her feet against the sill in time to a catchy pop tune. She'd kicked off her shoes, and let her hair out of the clip that held it in its usual bun. She grabbed a half-eaten bag of chips and started snacking while she watched the traffic go by, singing along between bites, and enjoying her moment of solitude.

"So this is how a matchmaker works her magic."

Marnie gasped, dropped her feet to the floor and spun around, a chip halfway to her mouth, while several more tumbled onto her lap. She wanted to crawl under her desk and hide, or at least shrivel into a bowl. She told herself she didn't care that her hair was a mess, she was covered in potato chip crumbs, and she'd been caught singing off-key to a teenybopper hit.

"Jack...uh, I mean, Mr. Knight," she said, then covered her mouth and paused to swallow. Did she really think calling him by his last name would erase that kiss, the way he made her feel with a simple smile? That it would put up a wall he couldn't pass? She forced authority into her tone. "What are you doing here?"

Even in a dark gray suit, with his pale blue tie loosened at the neck, he looked sexy, approachable. Hard to resist. "I'm looking for a matchmaker," he said. "And you come highly recommended by a close family member. Apparently my stepfather has fallen head over heels for your mother."

"I've heard all about it, too." There was no denying the happiness in Helen's voice. Marnie had talked to her mother earlier today and heard nothing but joy. Hearing that Helen's feelings were reciprocated—

Well, that was what Marnie worked for. The cherry on top of all the work she put in, building that matchmaker sundae. Except her mother was falling for a man with ties to someone who could hurt their family all over again.

"I don't think you need my help," she said. "What was it Dot said? You've got legendary charm? I'm sure you could find plenty of women on your own."

"Whether I do or not, that hasn't brought me Miss Right yet. I think I need a professional." He came closer, then around her desk, to sit on the edge. He leaned forward, and captured a chip just as it began to tumble off her chest. Her face heated. "Someone who knows what they're doing."

She pushed the chair back, and turned to dump the rest of the chips into the trash. That was the last time she was going to eat a messy snack at her desk. "Well, I'm sorry, but I'm not taking new clients right now." A lie. She rarely turned down new clients. In her business, people came and went as their lives changed, which kept her busy year-round and left room for more. "You'll have to find another matchmaker, or maybe try one of those online dating services. Sorry I couldn't help you."

There. That had been definitive, strong. Leaving no room for negotiation—or anything else. But Jack didn't leave. Instead, he leaned in closer, his gaze assessing and probing.

"Okay, tell me." The sun shone through the window and danced gold lights on his hair, his face. "What did I do to you that makes you hate me? Yet, kiss me five minutes later?"

"For your information, that kiss was an accident. I was reacting on instinct."

Why didn't she just tell him the truth? Why did she keep hesitating, letting this flirtatious game continue?

Because a part of her wondered about the man who had helped the local coffee shop and the neighborhood gym and still knew his old neighbors. A part of her wanted to know who the real Jack Knight was.

And if there was a possibility that for all these years, she might have been wrong about him.

"An instinct?" he said, his voice low, dark. "No more?"

"Yes. No more." The lie escaped her in a rush.

"So if I leaned in now—" and he did just that, coming within a whisper of her lips, then brushing his against hers slow, easy, a feather-light kiss that made her want more, before he drew back "—you wouldn't react the same way?"

"Of course not." She stood her ground, but the temptation to curve into him pounded in her veins. To finish what they'd started back in the parking lot, to let that heady, heated rush run through her again, obliterating thought, reason.

Damn it. She didn't do this. She didn't lose control

of her emotions, get swept away by a nice smile and a shimmer of sexual energy. Stupid decisions were made that way, and Marnie refused to do that.

She clenched her fists, released them, and forced her breathing to stay normal, not to betray an ounce of the riot inside her. To not let him know how much she wanted a real, soul-sucking, hot-as-heck kiss right now. Her gaze locked on his, then dropped to his mouth. *Oh, my.*

"Well, I'm glad to know you can resist that 'legendary charm,'" Jack said, then rose and went around her desk to sit in one of the visitor's chairs.

Disappointment whooshed through her. She let out a little laugh to cover the emotion, then sat back in her chair, because her legs had gone to jelly and her heart wouldn't slow. She had two choices right now. Keep denying she was attracted to him, or fix him up and get him out of her life for good. What did she care if he dated half the female population of Boston?

For a woman who craved calm and order more than chips, erasing Jack Knight from her life was the easiest and best option. No one got hurt. A win-win.

"I might be able to help you find someone," she said, clasping her hands on the desk, tight. Treat him like any other client. Act like he's simply another bachelor. "Let's start with why you think this is the right time in your life to find the perfect match?"

He leaned back, propping one leg atop the other. "I think it's time I settled down and pursued the American dream."

"Really? Right now. That's actually what you think." It wasn't a question. Jack coming to her, now, after she'd refused to get close to him, couldn't be a coincidence. It had to be some kind of game. What did he really want?

"It's true. I woke up, realized all my friends are married, have kids, houses in the suburbs. I'm the lone holdout. I guess I haven't met the right woman yet." He grinned.

She let out a gust. "Why are you really here? Because if it's to get me to go out with you, that's not going to work."

"Oh, I know. I got that message. Loud and clear."

She thought she detected a measure of hurt in his voice. Impossible. Jack Knight was a shark, and sharks didn't get hurt feelings. "Well, good."

"My stepfather was very pleased with how compatible he is with Helen, and I thought you could do the same for me."

If Marnie had anything to say about it, her mother would find someone else and stay far, far away from any relative of Jack Knight's. She had yet to find a way to make him pay for the hurt he'd brought to her family.

Confronting him and demanding answers would only backfire when Helen found out. In Marnie's perfect world, Jack Knight was destroyed and her mother never got hurt.

Marnie hadn't been able to keep her mother from being hurt after the death of Tom, but maybe she could make sure this debacle with Jack didn't impact Helen. All she had to do was find a way to keep Jack far from Helen—and that meant making sure Jack got the message that Marnie wanted him gone. She glanced over at the pile on her desk and realized there might be a way to hurt Jack and get rid of him for good—a much better and smarter way than having coffee with him and taking long walks through Boston neighborhoods. Clearly, that kind of thing distracted her too much. Brought her too close to the shark's teeth. But this way…

"Sure, I'll help you," she said, pulling out a sheet of paper from the file drawer on her desk. "Let's start with the basics. Name, address, occupation."

He rattled off his address. "I believe you know the rest. Especially my name."

Her cheeks heated again when she thought of how she had whispered his first name back at the coffee shop, of the way that same syllable had echoed in her dreams, her thoughts. Oh, yeah, she knew his name. Too well. "Uh, date of birth?"

He gave her that, too, then grinned. "I'm a Taurus, or at least I think I am. And I like long walks on the beach and moonlit dances."

She snorted. "Whatever."

"Would you rather I said monster truck rallies and mud wrestling championships?"

She laughed. "Now *that* I would believe."

"Ah, then you don't know me very well." He leaned forward, propping his elbows on his knees. "I love the beach. I couldn't move away from the ocean if I tried. There's nothing like waking up on a warm Sunday morning, and having the ocean breeze coming in through your window."

"I like that, too," she said, then drew herself up. What was this, connect with Jack time? *Focus, Marnie, focus.* "Favorite music? Movies?"

"I like jazz. The kind of music that makes you think of smoky bars and good whiskey. Where you want to sit in a corner booth with a beautiful woman and listen to the band."

A beautiful woman like her? Marnie glanced down at the sheet, saw she had written the question, then scribbled it out. That made her twice as determined to get

Jack out of her life. Marnie Franklin didn't do scatter-brained or dreamy or infatuated. Damn. "Uh, movies?"

"I don't get to see many movies, and as much as I'd like to say something smart like *Requiem for a Dream*, I have to cave to a cliché. If you check my DVR, there's a lot of action movies on there." He shrugged. "What can I say? In a pinch, I opt for *The Terminator*."

"I'll be baaack, huh?" she said, doing a pretty bad imitation of Arnold.

He chuckled. "Exactly. What about you? What's your favorite movie?"

"I cave to the cliché, too. Any kind of romantic comedy. Especially *You've Got Mail*."

"Isn't that the one where the woman fell in love with her enemy?" Jack's blue eyes met hers, a tease winking in their ocean depths.

Did he know? Did he suspect her hidden agenda? Then he smiled and she relaxed. No. He didn't know who she really was or what she was planning for his "match." He'd been joking, not probing to see if this particular Romeo and Juliet had a shot.

She didn't care if they both liked the ocean, jazz music, and fun movies. If they'd both suffered a loss of a parent, and were still searching for something that would never be. He had ruined her life, her family. More than that, he was the kind of man who encouraged her to let loose, to become some giggly schoolgirl. She'd seen enough women make the mistake of leaping into a relationship without thinking, and refused to do the same. This wasn't a Nora Ephron movie—it was reality.

She glanced down at the paperwork. *Treat him like any other client,* she repeated. Again. "Uh, what about things to do? In your free time?"

"Running at the gym. Seeing outdoor concerts. Walking the streets of Boston."

She sighed, then put down the pen. "This isn't going to work if you keep flirting with me."

"I'm not flirting with you, Marnie. If I was flirting with you, you'd know it."

"That—" she waved a finger between them "—was definitely flirting."

"No. *This* is flirting." He got up again and approached her desk, then placed his hands on the oak surface and leaned over until their faces were inches apart. She caught the dark undertow of his cologne, the steady heat from his body. His blue eyes teemed with secrets. A lock of dark hair swooped across his brow. The crazy urge to brush it back rose in her chest.

"You are a beautiful, intoxicating, infuriating woman," he whispered, his voice a low, sensual growl, "and I can't stop thinking about you. And I love the way you look today. All…unfettered. Untamed."

Heat washed over her body, unfurled a deep, dark flame in her womb. She opened her mouth to speak, and for a moment, could only breathe and stare into those storm-tossed eyes of his. "Okay." Her words shook and she drew in a breath to steady herself. "Yes, that…that was flirting."

He smiled, held her gaze a moment longer, then retreated to the chair. "Glad we got that settled."

Settled? If anything, things between them had become more unsettled. A place Marnie never liked to be. Her concentration had flown south for the winter, and every thought in her head revolved around finding the nearest bedroom and taking her sweet time to "flirt" with Jack Knight.

Jack Knight. The enemy. In more ways than one.

She cleared her throat and retrieved her pen. In a normal client meeting, she'd let the questions flow in a natural rhythm. Her initial meetings were usually more like a chat with a new neighbor than a formal interview, but with Jack, she couldn't seem to form a coherent thought. "I, well, I think that's all I need for now. I'll be in touch in a couple days with some potential matches."

"That was easy. You sure you don't need anything else?"

You, a bedroom, more of those kisses. "Nope, I'm good," she said, too fast.

"Okay." He started to rise, and she put out a hand but didn't touch him.

She refused to let a silly thing like attraction get in the way of her goals. She needed information, and she needed Jack out of her life. Today. She could accomplish both right now.

Here was her opportunity to finally do what she'd been trying to do for weeks—find out about his business and how he operated. Maybe then she'd have the answers she needed, the ones that would close the hole in her heart and answer the what-ifs. She'd finally be able to accept the loss of her father, and move forward.

"Jack, wait a second. You know, lots of the women you'll be paired with work in complimentary fields. It might be good to get to know more about your job."

He sat back down. "Makes sense. I've told you a little about what I do. What else do you need to know?"

She had to word this carefully, or he'd realize she was looking for more than just matchmaking info. "Well, let's start with something general. Pretend we're chatting for the first time."

"Over coffee?" He grinned.

She hardened her features. The last thing she needed

to do was think about that walk to the coffee shop. Or the cookie crumb driven kiss. *Keep this professional.* "Or over a desk in an office."

He nodded agreement. "Okay, shoot."

"Tell me more about how you decide which companies to invest in and which ones you walk away from."

He cleared his throat and when he spoke again, the flirt had left his voice and he was all business. "A lot of that is a matter of numbers. I look at their market share, profit and loss, balance sheets, and weigh that against future potential and opportunities. If the dollars aren't there, it doesn't make financial sense for me to invest. But, sometimes I do anyway." He shrugged. "Because of the Caterpillar Factor."

"The Caterpillar Factor?" She stopped writing. "I've never heard of that before."

"It's something I made up. When you buy a business, there's a lot of data to wade through. But in the end, I let my instincts make the final decision. That's the Caterpillar Factor." He leaned forward in the chair, his eyes bright with enthusiasm. "You know how you can look at a caterpillar and get grossed out by it? I mean, most of them are fat and have a bunch of legs, and aren't exactly something you want crawling on you."

"That's true." She gave an involuntary shudder.

"But those same caterpillars have the *potential* to be something really incredible. When you look at them, you don't know what it will be—you're judging it entirely on its current form. But underneath, buried deep inside that caterpillar, is something that, given enough time and nurturing, will be amazing and beautiful."

"A butterfly," she said, her voice quiet.

"Exactly." He grinned. "Not every business is a butterfly waiting to be unveiled, but some are. And I know that by investing in and coaching them, I can help them become something amazing." He gave a little nod, and a flush crept into his cheeks. "I know, it sounds kind of corny."

She never would have thought she'd see Jack Knight embarrassed or shy or vulnerable. But here he was, admitting that he believed in potential, that he sometimes went with his gut, against conventional wisdom. Wasn't that how she approached her matchmaking? No computer algorithms, no formulas, just instinct?

Why did this one man—the wrong man—discombobulate her so? She'd never met anyone who could do that with nothing more than a smile, a whisper of her name.

Damn it all. She related to him, understood him, and that added another complicated layer to what she'd thought would be a simple matter of revenge. The closer they got to each other, the more she allowed him to burrow his way into her heart, the harder it became to implement her plan.

She glanced down at the paper before her. The words swam in her vision. Why hadn't Jack seen a butterfly in Top Notch Printing, her father's business? Why hadn't he helped her father more? Wasn't Tom Franklin's life and livelihood worth some time and nurturing, too?

"And what about the ones that won't be butterflies? What do you do with those businesses?"

He sighed. "Sometimes, the business is too far gone, or the owner just isn't equipped with the right skill set to help it reach the next level. We could throw millions at the company and it wouldn't be enough. In those cases, we sell off the parts, recoup our investment, and hopefully send the owner off with cash in his pocket."

"Hopefully?" The word squeaked past the tension in her jaw.

"You're a businesswoman, Marnie. I'm sure you understand that there are a million factors that can affect the decision to keep or sell a company. Some owners are great at running a business, some…aren't."

She thought of her affable, fun-loving father. He'd never been much for keeping track of paperwork or receipts. Never one to demand a late payment or argue with a customer. But that meant Tom had needed more help, not less. Why hadn't Jack seen that?

"Sometimes, despite all the due diligence in the world," Jack said, "we make mistakes, and sometimes life throws us a curveball that we didn't expect. A supplier goes under or a major customer takes their sales elsewhere. Sometimes, the companies recoup, sometimes…"

"They die," she finished. She had to swallow hard and remind herself to keep breathing.

He nodded. "Yeah, they do."

"You seem awful cavalier about this." As if there weren't people hurt in the process. As if the only thing that died was a bottom line. She clenched her hands together under her desk, feigning a calm she didn't feel.

"It's a reality. Fifty percent of businesses fail, for a million reasons. You can pump all the cash you want into them, and some just aren't destined to survive. If I got emotional about each one, I'd get distracted and lose sight of the big picture. So I don't make my decisions based on emotion. I think it helps that I don't exactly love my job, but I…respect it. Maybe someday down the road, I'll get a chance to do something else."

"And what is the big picture? Profits?"

"Well, everyone likes to make money. But for me,

it's the businesses I see succeed. Like Dot's coffee shop or my friend Toby's gym. I see the placed filled with happy customers, and that tells me I did the right thing. It's not about profits, it's about quality of life. For the owners, and their clients."

"And the businesses that don't make it?" she said. "What are they to you?"

"The cost of doing business. It sounds harsh, but in the end, when there's nothing more that can be done, a failure is reduced to dollars and cents."

Under the desk, her hands curled into fists. She worked a smile to her face, even though it hurt. The smile, and the truth. "Well, I guess that's all I need."

Please leave, please get out of here before my heart breaks right in front of you.

The chips from earlier churned in her gut. She wished her day was over, because right now, all she wanted to do was go home, draw the shades, and stay in bed.

Not only had Jack just confirmed that her father's business had been a negative number in the general ledger, but his asking her to find him a match confirmed she was a negative in his personal ledger, too. This was what she'd wanted—the truth and to be rid of Jack. But still, the success had a bitter taste.

"Thanks again for taking the time to see me today, Marnie." Jack got to his feet. "I look forward to hearing from you, and seeing who you match me up with." He looked like he wanted to say something more, but all he said was goodbye before heading for the door. One hand on the knob, he turned back. "You know, you should let your hair down more often. And I mean that, literally and figuratively. It suits you. Very nicely."

The door shut behind him with a soft click. Marnie

sat in her chair, watching the space for a long time. She shook off the maudlin thoughts and turned to her contacts database. Jack Knight had asked her for a match, and she intended to give him one—

A match that would challenge him and keep him far from Marnie.

Then maybe he'd stop flirting with her, and tipping her carefully constructed life upside-down. Because there was one thing she knew for sure. Jack Knight was bad for business—the business of Marnie's heart.

CHAPTER SIX

JACK KNIGHT WAS rarely wrong. He had learned over the
years to read people's body language, the subtle clues
they sent out that created a roadmap to their thoughts
and actions. He'd used that skill a thousand times in ne-
gotiations, and in strategic meetings. But when it came
to Marnie Franklin, his instincts had failed him, big
time. He'd completely underestimated how angry she
was—

And how far he was from proving himself as a different man than his father.

He strode into her office a week after their last meeting, waving off the assistant's offer to help him, heading straight for Marnie's desk. "What kind of match
was that?"

"What are you talking about?"

"That date you set me up on. What were you thinking?"

She leaned an elbow on her chair, relaxed, uncon-
cerned. Her eyes widened as he approached, then a
flicker of a smile appeared on her face and disappeared
just as fast. A smile like she knew what she had done.
"I'm sorry you're unhappy with the Matchmaking by
Marnie match, but we truly thought—"

"*Unhappy?* I wouldn't say that. The woman was nice

and very energetic, but not my type, at all." His gaze narrowed. "Did you do that on purpose?"

"I have no idea what you're talking about," Marnie said. With a straight face.

"Marnie, I have to go to that meeting with the caterer," her assistant said. "But if you want, I'll stay awhile longer."

"I'll be fine. Go ahead to the appointment, Erica." Marnie waved her off.

Erica, Marnie's sister. His gaze skipped to her, and he saw the same leery look in her eyes as in Marnie's. Oh, yeah, they knew who he was here—or who they thought he was. Damn. How was he going to prove the opposite?

Once the door shut behind Erica, Jack winnowed the space between himself and Marnie's desk. She looked beautiful today, her hair up in its perpetual clip, her button down white shirt pressed and neat, accented by a simple gold chain and form fitting black skirt.

"I'm sure Miss Stewart will be a great match for someone, but that someone isn't me."

"You just have to give her a chance," Marnie said. "Roberta...takes some time to get to know."

"Oh, I think she's a great person. We went out dancing, and even though I run four days a week, she outdanced me ten to one. And she's funny and enthusiastic, but not my type. What did you think we'd have in common?"

Marnie shrugged. Played innocent. "Sometimes opposites attract."

"And sometimes matchmakers don't play fair. I came to you as a legitimate client—"

"No, you didn't." She got to her feet, and her features shifted from detachment to fire. He could see it in the way her eyes flashed, her lips narrowed. "You might have said you wanted a match, but it didn't take a rocket scientist to figure out your true motive. You came here, hoping I'd think you were my perfect match."

"You have made it abundantly clear that you are not interested in me. That's why I think you should put your money where your mouth is."

"What is that supposed to mean?"

"You go out with me on a real date."

"Why would I do that?"

"Because despite your strong efforts in the opposite direction—" and thinking of the mismatch she'd sent him, he wondered if it wasn't just revenge but that deep down inside, Marnie didn't want to see him connect with another woman "—I think we'd be a great match."

She scoffed. "That's my job, not yours."

"And yet you have not found the perfect man for you." He leaned on her desk and met her green eyes. "Why is that?"

"I...I work a lot. I haven't had time to date."

"Is that all? Time? Because it's the end of the day. We could make time right now."

"Go out with you? Now?"

He grinned. "Why wait?"

"I am not interested in dating you. Ever."

"What was that walk to coffee? To me, it was a trial date."

She snorted. "There's no such thing."

He leaned in closer, until her eyes widened and that intoxicating perfume she wore teased at his senses. "We don't have to follow the rules, Marnie. We can make them up as we go along."

Her mouth opened, closed. She inhaled, and for a second, he thought she'd agree. A smile started to curve up his face, when he noticed the fire return to her green eyes. "I only have one rule. To stay far away from you." She got out of her seat, standing tall in her heels and matching him in height. "Don't think another Franklin will fall for your line of bull again, Jack. You don't get to ruin any more lives in this family. We're done believing in your lies and your charming little pep talks. So stay far away from this family."

And there it was. The past he couldn't run from, sweep under a rug, or ignore. Guilt rocketed through him. If Marnie knew how much of a hand Jack had had in her father's business closing, she'd never forgive him. He wanted her to see him as the man he was today, not the man he used to be, but getting from A to B meant confronting A and dealing with it, once and for all. "Yes, we did work with your father and his shop. And I swear, I had no idea you were his daughter until you told me your nickname. He always called you Daisy when he talked about you."

Hurt flickered in her eyes. "That business would still be operating today under Tom Franklin," Marnie said, the words biting, cold. "If someone didn't destroy it."

"Marnie, there's more to it than that. I—"

"I have no interest in anything you have to say to me, or any claims you intend to make about your 'business practices,'" Marnie said. "My sisters and I watched our father fall apart after you stepped in and 'helped' him. You. Ruined. Him. And helped him…" she bit her lip, and tears welled in her eyes "…die too soon."

"Marnie, I didn't do that." But he had, hadn't he? He'd talked Tom into signing on the dotted line, knowing full well what the true intent of Knight would be. And when Tom needed a friend, Jack was gone. *You're a cold, uninvolved man, Jack.* "I mean, yes, I did invest in your father's business, and yes, I did counsel him, but—"

"Get out of my office," Marnie said, waving toward the door, her face tight with rage. "And don't ever come back. I don't want to hear any more of your lies and I sure as hell don't want to date you."

He opened his mouth, but she pointed at the door again. "For someone who's perfected the art of matching people, you of all people should understand that some matches go well and some don't. It takes two to make it work. And sometimes only one to destroy it."

"Yeah, you."

He took her anger, and let it wash over him. He understood now why she had bristled every time he talked about his job. Why she had been so warm at first, then so cold. And why she had set him up on a date that was bound not to work out. "Sometimes," he said quietly, "our best intentions can go down paths we never saw. I'm sorry, Marnie, about your father and his business. If I could change any of it, I would."

Then he left, and for the first time since he'd taken over Knight Enterprises, he wished for a do-over. Another chance to go back and do a better job.

Her mother had canceled Tuesday night dinner at her house, Thursday night's card game, and Saturday's brunch. And now, the morning after the confrontation with Jack in Marnie's office, Helen was trying to get out of her regular Wednesday lunch with Marnie. "Ma, I haven't seen you in two weeks," Marnie said.

"I'm sorry, honey. We've just been so busy, going to the ball games and Bingo and…"

While her mother talked, Marnie debated the best way to tell her mother the truth. She'd spent a sleep-

less night debating the pros and cons of telling Helen
the truth about Jack, but in the end, there was only one
option.

Put it out there, and let the consequences fall as they
may.

Her family had never been one to tackle the hard topics. They'd put a sunny face on everything, and done
a good job avoiding. This, though, they couldn't avoid
any longer—because Helen was falling hard for Dan.

Marnie hated being in this position. Standing in the
middle of two evils, both of which would hurt the ones
she loved. She'd thought that standing up to Jack and
telling him how she felt would make her feel better. But
instead of relieving the anger and betrayal in her gut,
the confrontation had left her restless, replaying every
word a hundred times in her head.

No. She'd done the right thing. Now she needed to
do the right thing again—

And break her mother's heart.

"Dan and I have just been having so much fun,"
Helen said. "Oh, did I tell you, he's taking me to Maine
for the weekend on Friday? He found this lovely little
cottage in Kennebunkport. If we get lucky, maybe we'll
even see the former president on the beach."

That meant they were getting serious. Damn. Marnie had hoped the relationship between Dan and her
mother would fizzle, saving Marnie from having to tell
her mother the truth about who Dan was.

She'd avoided the truth forever, but where had that
gotten her? Nowhere good. And it had given her mother
and Dan time to get closer, which only added more com-
plications. Marnie took a deep breath. "Are you free for
lunch today, Ma? I'll stop on the way to get us some
Thai food, if you want."

"That sounds wonderful."

Marnie said goodbye, then powered through the rest of her morning appointments, keeping her head on her job instead of what was to come. Lord, how she dreaded this. Her mother had sounded so happy, with that little laugh in her voice that they had all missed over the last few years. And now Marnie was about to erase it all.

But as she got closer to Ma's house, and the scent of the Thai food overpowered the interior of the car, Marnie wanted to turn around. To delay again. It wasn't just about breaking her mother's heart anymore, but about facing the truth herself. All along, she kept hoping to be wrong about Jack. To find out that the guy with the amazing smile and earth-shattering kisses wasn't the evil vulture she'd painted him to be.

But he was, and the sooner she got that cemented in her mind, the better.

Even if the man had asked her out. Why would he do that? Was he truly interested? Or was she just another conquest?

Helen greeted her daughter with a big hug, and a thousand-miles-an-hour of chatter about Dan. "He's just the sweetest guy, Marnie. I can't believe no one has scooped him up. He holds the door for me, brings me flowers, even sings to me." She smiled, one of those soft, quiet smiles. "I really like him."

Guilt washed over Marnie. "Ma, we need to talk. Come on, let's go in the kitchen."

A few minutes later, both women had steaming plates of pad thai in front of them, but no one was eating. "Okay, shoot. What did you want to tell me?" Helen asked.

"Dan isn't…who you think he is," Marnie said, the words hurting her throat. "I should have caught this when I interviewed him, but to be honest, I never ask about kids or stepkids and—"

"What do you mean? I've met Dan's stepson. Remember? After the mixer. He seemed very nice—"

"He's Jack Knight."

Helen froze. "Jack Knight? That's impossible. Dan's last name is Simpson."

"He's his stepfather. Jack is the owner of Knight Enterprises. The same Knight Enterprises that destroyed Dad's business. If you keep dating Dan, you'll be seeing Jack, and the reminder of everything that happened to Dad. I'm so sorry to have to tell you this."

Silence filled the kitchen, and the food grew cold on their plates. Helen got to her feet, waving off her daughter. Ma crossed to the sink, placed her hands on either side of the porcelain basin and stood there a long time, her gaze going to the garden outside the window. The rain pelted soft knocks on the glass, then slid down in little shimmering rivers.

"Ma?" Marnie said. She walked over to her mother, and placed a hand on Helen's shoulder. "Ma, I'm so sorry. If I had known, I never would have fixed him up with you."

"Dan is the best thing to come along in my life in a really long time," Helen said, her voice thick with emotion that made Marnie's guilt factor rocket upward. "Besides you girls, of course." She closed her hand around Marnie's, and gave her daughter a smile. "I'm glad I met him."

"He is a great guy, I agree, and if he wasn't related to Jack—"

"It doesn't matter. Dan and I are happy. I don't care who his stepson is." Helen turned around and placed her back against the sink. Her features had shifted from heartbreak to determination. "We might work out, we might not, but we're going to give it a shot. Life's too short, honey, and I don't want to spend any more of my time alone."

This was a new Helen, Marnie realized. A woman who hadn't been defeated by the loss of her husband, and the prospect of starting her life over again, but rather energized by it. She also showed an amazing strength that had probably always been there, waiting for the right moment to appear. Dating Dan had only emphasized those qualities, not detracted.

Her mother was happy. Taking chances. Making changes. Jumping into the unknown. All things that Marnie had held back from doing, sticking to her organized planner and her rigid schedule.

Still, the urge to protect her mother, to head off any further hurt, rose in Marnie. If Dan and Helen stayed together, it would be nothing but a constant reminder, a cut against an old scab, again and again.

"I just don't want you to be hurt again," Marnie said.

"If there's one thing I've finally learned and accepted, it's that life comes with hurt. But if you're willing to risk that, you can find such amazing happiness, too."

On the wall, one of those kitschy cat shaped wall clocks clicked its tail back and forth with the passing seconds. Helen gestured toward the black plastic body, a stark contrast to the pin-neat, granite and white kitchen. "Do you remember when your father got me that?"

Marnie smiled. "It was a joke Christmas gift. We never thought you'd hang it up."

"It made me laugh. It makes me laugh every time I see it on the wall. That's why I hung it up, and why I kept it there, to remember to have fun sometimes."

"But isn't that the problem?" Marnie said, the words tumbling out of her mouth before she could stop them. "We're always having fun, never talking about the hard stuff. You can't just keep ignoring the facts, Ma."

Helen's soft hands cupped her daughter's face. "Oh, Marnie, Marnie. My serious one. Always trying so hard to keep the rest of us in line."

"I just like things to…stay ordered."

"And our lives when you were younger were far from ordered, weren't they? But we had fun, oh, how we had fun. Your father never had a serious day in his life, bless his heart." Helen released Marnie and the two women retook their seats at the table. "Let's talk about Knight and your father. And what really happened."

All these years, they'd avoided the subject. Whenever it came up, her mother would say she couldn't bear to hear it, and they'd switch to something inane or trivial. But this new Helen, the one who had been tempered by life on her own, had a determination in her eyes and voice that surprised Marnie.

"What do you know about what happened to Dad's company?" Ma said.

"Knight Enterprises invested in the company at first, made big promises about helping him get it profitable again, then deserted him and let him fail. When the business went south, Dad sold the rest of it to them for a fraction of what it was worth." Marnie bit back a curse. "And after that, Dad just…gave up."

"Part of that's true." Helen laid her hands on top of each other on the table. She smiled. "You and I are so much alike, Marnie. We both try to keep the peace, keep everyone happy. Sometimes, you need to rock the boat and tell the truth."

Marnie knew what was coming before her mother

spoke. She'd probably always known, but like her mother, found it easier to pin her anger on Jack, rather than accept the facts.

"That business was on its last legs before your father went to Knight for help. Tom had lost his passion for it years earlier, and in the last couple of years before he sold, he'd spent too many days going fishing on the boat instead of working. A business is like a garden. You have to keep tending it, or it'll die on the vine. And your father stopped tending it." She shrugged. "I knew, but I figured we were okay. And I couldn't blame him. He'd worked so many hours when he first started out and he hated being the boss. The one to hire, fire, and demand. Plus, he missed you girls' soccer games and softball matches, and weekend family trips. I think he just wanted a break, to live his life before he got too old to do so and…"

Her voice trailed off and she bit her lip. "He just wanted time. With his family. With the people most important to him. There was a lot involved in that decision, Marnie. A lot you didn't know. Your father kept things to himself, hated to worry us. All he kept saying was that we'd be fine."

"Keeping the sunshine on his face," Marnie said, repeating her father's oft-used phrase.

"That was his philosophy, right or wrong. And so I couldn't blame him for wanting time to enjoy his days. He said he had put money aside for retirement, and that we would be all right once he got some investors on board. The company would turn around, freeing him up. We'd have time together, we'd travel, we'd treat you girls to all those extras we hadn't been able to afford before. I trusted him. I'd been married to the man nearly all my life, why wouldn't I?"

Marnie's jaw dropped as she put the pieces together. The financial struggle her mother had had over the last few years, her decision to go back to work. "There was no retirement?"

Helen shook her head, sad and slow. "Your father had spent it all, investing it in some fishing charter thing his cousin Rick talked him into, and kept telling him it would pay off. Just be patient, wait, and your dad did. Too long."

Her father, a trusting, optimistic man, who had trusted a family member when he should have had his guard up. In the end, it didn't surprise Marnie as much as reveal a different side of her father.

"Rick's business went belly up before it started, and the money was gone," Ma said. "Our entire future, gone in an instant. All our equity. All we had left was the house and the company, which by then wasn't worth much at all."

"So he sold a majority interest in the business to get the money back," Marnie finished.

Helen nodded. "Your father partnered with Knight on the agreement that they would be there to provide counsel to help him get the printing company back on track. They talked about bringing in an expert to help the operation get leaner, more efficient, hire some sales people to generate more income. Tom thought maybe he could bring about a financial miracle before I realized what happened to the retirement money. But then Knight didn't help. As soon as the paperwork was signed, the help and advice stopped. And the company, like you said, faltered. When Knight came back and offered to buy the remaining assets, your father jumped at the offer, even though it meant taking a loss. By then, he knew there was no way to rebound, and I don't think he had the heart or desire to put in the hours that might take. He wanted to be here, not behind that desk. Still, your father felt so guilty, and I think that's what broke his heart in the end. I had no idea. If I had…" She shook her head, regrets clouding her eyes. "He didn't tell me any of this until shortly before he died. I wish he'd told me sooner. Oh, how I wish he had. Communication was never the strong suit in this family, and we had…so many other worries at the time. If he'd said something—"

"We would have stepped in and helped," Marnie said. "I would have gone to work for him or loaned him some money or…" She paused as the realization dawned in her mind. Her father, sacrificing for his family right to the end. "That's why he didn't tell us. He didn't want us to do any of that."

Helen's soft palm cupped her daughter's cheek. "He was so proud of you. You and your sisters. You found jobs that you love, that speak to your heart, and he would never have asked you to give that up."

"But, Ma, we could have helped him. Done something."

"And it would have made him miserable. He wanted you girls to be happy in your own lives, not make up for his mistakes. Not to worry about him all the time."

"He wasn't perfect," Marnie said, "but he sure was a great dad."

"Before he died, he made me promise not to let hurt or anger fill my heart. That's why he got me that clock the last Christmas before he died. So I'd remember to be happy, to tick along. To not let what happened ruin our future." Her mother got to her feet, took the clock off the wall and pressed it into Marnie's hands. "Take this, hang it on your wall, and remember to be happy, Marnie. To be silly. And most of all, to forgive."

The two of them hugged, two women who had lost a man they loved, and who shared common regrets. Outside, the rain washed over the house, washed it clean, and inside the kitchen, the first steps of healing truly began.

CHAPTER SEVEN

"TELL ME AGAIN why I'm here, besides serving as a fifth wheel," Jack said. They were standing in the lobby of a seafood restaurant located on the wharf. In the distance, he could hear the clanging of the buoys. The scent of the ocean, salty, tangy, carried on the air, a perfect complement to the restaurant's menu.

Dan chuckled. "I thought it'd be nice for you to get to know Helen a little better. And it'll do you good to eat a meal that doesn't come out of a takeout box."

Jack grinned. "You have a point there."

"Parents are always right. Just remember that." Dan arched a brow, a smirk on his face. The door to the restaurant opened, and Helen strode in, shaking off the rain on her coat and her umbrella. Her gaze met Dan's and a smile sparked on her face.

A wave of jealousy washed over Jack. Not that he begrudged Dan a moment of happiness, but seeing Helen's happiness, and the echoing emotion in his stepfather, was a stark reminder to Jack of his solitary life.

"Did you tell him?" Helen asked.

"Nope." Dan grinned again.

That didn't sound good. Jack sent Dan an inquisitive look. "Tell me what?"

Then the door to the restaurant opened again and

Marnie walked in. At first, she was too busy brushing off the rain to notice Jack. She shrugged out of her raincoat, handing it the coat check. Then she turned, and his groin tightened, his pulse skipped a beat and everything within him sprang to attention. Wow.

Marnie had on a clingy dark green dress that accented the blond in her hair, made her eyes seem bigger, more luminous. The dress skimmed her body, showed off her arms, her incredible legs, and dropped in an enticing V in the front.

She smiled when she saw Dan and her mother. Then her gaze swiveled to Jack and the smile disappeared. "Why are you here?"

"I was invited," he said.

"So was I." She tipped her head toward her mother. "Ma?"

Helen took Dan's arm and beamed at both Jack and Marnie. "Our table's ready. Let's go have dinner."

"Ma—"

"Come on, Marnie, Jack." Then Helen turned on her heel and headed into the dining room with Dan, leaving Jack and Marnie two choices—follow or walk out the door. Marnie looked ready to do the latter.

Jack tossed Marnie a grin. "It is their treat, and we do need to eat. Should we call a truce, for the sake of our parents?"

She hesitated, biting her lower lip, then nodded. "If they stay together we'll inevitably see each other once in a while. So we should at least get along tonight. For their sake."

"*If* they stay together? I thought you were the best matchmaker around," he teased. "Hmmm…maybe you were wrong about who you matched me with, too."

"You were a special case."

He laughed. "Now that I agree with."

She rolled her eyes, but a slight smile played on her lips. It was enough. It gave Jack hope that maybe, just maybe, all was not lost between them. She strode into the dining room, with him bringing up the rear.

They sat across from Dan and Helen, who had taken seats together on one side of the table. Another element of Dan and Helen's strategic plan, one Jack had to admit he admired. The waiter took their drink orders, left them with menus, then headed off to the bar.

"I'm glad you both decided to join us for dinner," Helen said.

Dan draped an arm over the back of Helen's chair and she shifted a bit closer to him. "We figured it would take a miracle for you two to see you're as matched as two peas in a pod—"

"Dad—"

Dan put up a hand. "Hear me out, Jack. Marnie's mother and I are pretty damned happy. And we want to see both of you just as happy as we are. Now, maybe you two won't work out. But you'll never know unless you give it a chance."

"You had to get your matchmaking abilities somewhere," Helen said to Marnie. "Dare I suggest your mother's side of the family?"

"They're pretty obvious," Marnie said to Jack.

He nodded, a smirk on his face. "Maybe they've got something here."

Dan and Helen watched the exchange with amusement. "Like I said, you should always listen to your parents," Dan said. "We've got age and experience on our side."

"Definitely the latter," Helen said with a flirtatious tone in her voice. She flushed, then laughed, and gave

Dan a quick kiss on his cheek. He cupped her face, and kissed her again.

A craving for that—that happiness, that ease with another person, that loving attention—rose in Marnie fast and fierce. Her mother had taken this leap, taken the biggest risk of all and fallen for someone else. Could Marnie do the same?

If she didn't, she knew she'd never have what her mother had right now. And oh, how Marnie wanted it. More than she ever had before.

She slid a glance in Jack's direction. Every woman with a pulse had noticed him tonight. He had on a dark blue pinstripe suit, a pale blue shirt the color of the sky on a cold morning, and a green and silver striped tie that coordinated with her dress, as if they'd planned it that way. His dark hair seemed to beg for her to run her fingers through it, while the sharp lines of his jaw urged her to kiss him.

If he was any other man, and she was any other woman, she would want him. She would probably date him. Fall for him. But even the thought of that caused the familiar panic to rise inside her chest.

Falling for Jack would be like jumping off a cliff. It was the kind of heady rush that Marnie avoided at all costs. Not to mention, his mere presence was a constant reminder of what had happened to her father's business. She couldn't do that to herself, but most especially, to her mother or sisters.

"It's very sweet of you both to think we should date," Marnie said, "but this matchmaker doesn't see the logic in that. Jack and I are too…different."

Helen propped her chin on her hands. "Really? Different? How?"

Marnie shifted in her seat. "He's a businessman—"

"As are you."

"Well, I'm in a creative industry. He's…corporate."

"That just means you'll compliment each other's skills," Helen said.

Dan nodded. "Yup. Like ranch dressing and celery sticks."

Jack turned in his chair and put one arm on the back. "There are the things we have in common, too. Like music. Hobbies."

"Not movies," she pointed out, then felt silly for even mentioning it. Really? Her strongest argument was that Jack liked *The Terminator* and she liked tissue-ready chick flicks?

Jack nodded and feigned deep thought. "There is that. Well, that settles it, then."

She breathed a sigh of relief. Good. He wasn't going along with this charade any more than she was. "Great."

"We just won't watch movies," he said, then leaned toward her. His dark, woodsy cologne teased at her senses, urged her to come closer, to nuzzle his neck, taste his lips. "We'll find other ways to entertain ourselves."

Desire roared through Marnie's veins, an instant, insane tsunami of want, as if Jack had reached over, and flicked a switch to On. Across from them, Dan laughed, and Helen gave them a knowing smile.

"I, uh, forgot. I have a meeting with a client." Marnie grabbed her purse and jerked to her feet. The only thing she could do to avoid this disaster was to leave. "I'm so sorry. Maybe we could do this another time."

Helen apologized to the men, then headed out after her daughter.

After the women had left, Dan turned to his stepson

and sighed. "Sorry, son. We thought that would work out better than it did."

"It's okay. She can't forgive me for what Knight did to her father's company. I understand that." Heck, he heard it every day, as he worked to make amends, to try to undo the damage that had been done both by his father and himself.

But there were days when the task felt like pushing back a wall of water. He'd think he was making progress, then unearth another stack of files or get another phone call from a lawyer and realize how far he had yet to go. In between, he was still running Knight Enterprises, and still working on investment deals and helping the businesses he funded. A Herculean task, even with a staff working along with him.

"She'll come around," Dan said. "Look at the people you have helped. You've gotten, what, twenty companies back up and running? Invested in another dozen business owners whose companies had been dissolved? You've got a gift there, son, and you're using it to do good. I'm proud of you."

The tender words warmed Jack. For so long, he had wanted to hear them from his biological father, but never had, even when he'd modeled Jack, Senior's ruthless behavior. Now, in doing the opposite of his biological dad, he had earned respect and pride from the man who had truly been his father, with or without a DNA connection. And that, in the end, meant far more to Jack. His biological father might never have appreciated or understood or supported him, but this man did all three, and that was the mark of a true parent. "Thanks, Dad. That means a lot."

Jack's gaze went to the restaurant exit. A part of him

hoped like hell that Marnie had changed her mind, but no, Helen was making her way back to the table. Alone.

"And don't you worry about Marnie," Dan said as if he'd read his stepson's mind. "You'll figure out the best way to win her heart because that's your specialty. Solving the big problems and creating a happy ending for everyone."

Jack thought of the piles of folders on his credenza. The companies he had yet to find a way to restore or repair. He had a way to go, a hell of a long way to go, in creating those happy endings. And judging by the way Marnie had looked at him tonight, he had a way to go in the romantic happy ending department, too. It was time to admit defeat and quit chasing something that didn't want to be caught.

"If there's one thing I've learned in business, it's when to walk away from the deal," Jack said, getting to his feet, and nodding a goodbye to his stepfather and Helen. "And when it's time to move on to another candidate."

Every time Marnie managed to put him from her mind, Jack Knight popped back into her world, a few days after the dinner with her mother and Dan. Marnie had just locked the door on the office and turned toward home, exhausted and beyond ready for a vacation, or at the very least a weekend away from the calls and emails and meetings, when a familiar silver car pulled into the lot and Jack hopped out of the driver's seat. The trunk had been restored to new condition, all evidence of the wreck erased by some talented body shop.

As for Jack, despite everything, a little thrill ran through her at the sight of him, tall and lean, in a pair of well-worn jeans, a cotton button-down and a dark brown sports jacket. He looked…comfortable. Sexy. Like a man she could lean into and the world would drop away.

"Leaving so soon?" Jack asked.

"It's nearly noon," she said. "On a Sunday. Most people left the office two days ago."

"Just us workaholics still in the city, huh?" He reached into his jacket and withdrew a bright pink flyer. "And people planning on going to the Esplanade this afternoon to soak up some sun and hear the MAJE Jazz Showcase."

"What's that?"

"Top scoring high school bands from around the area get to perform at the Hatch Shell every year. And this year, my cousin is playing in one of the bands that won gold at the state competition, which automatically puts the band into the showcase." He took a couple steps closer to her. "How about it? Would you like to go and support the local arts?"

"Me? Why?"

"Because I think you would enjoy it. We both like jazz, and it's a gorgeous day, one we should take advantage of and spend a few hours enjoying. And—" he took a couple steps closer to her "—because I am officially asking you on a real date."

"Jack—"

"You know, after that dinner at the restaurant, I told myself to walk away. To quit pursuing someone who didn't want to be pursued. And I did. But you know what the problem with my theory is?"

She shook her head.

"I couldn't get you out of my mind. Maybe this is crazy. Maybe this is a really bad idea." He took another step closer, and his cologne teased her nostrils, and her pulse began to race. "But I want to see you again, Marnie."

That sent a zing through her heart, and a smile to her lips. "You are a stubborn man, Jack Knight." No one had ever pursued her this hard before, and if she was honest with herself, it was nice. Very nice.

A part of her wanted to run, to retreat to her familiar comfort of organization and schedules. But the other part of her, the part that had seen hundreds of happy couples walk down the aisle, wanted to take a chance. To trust in the very process she had built her business upon.

Still, she hesitated. This was Jack Knight, she reminded herself. Going out with him would only complicate an already complicated situation. Could hurt those she loved. "I should get home. It's my only day off—"

"And yet you were working."

"Well, my only *half* day off. I have laundry and other things to do."

"Wouldn't you rather grab a picnic lunch, spread a blanket on the grass at the Esplanade, and listen to some really amazing jazz?" he said, his voice like a siren calling to the part of her that craved a break, and the need for more in her life than her work. "Enjoy the beautiful spring day, maybe have a glass of wine, and just…be?"

God, yes, she wanted that. She relaxed far too little, worked far too much. Work kept her from thinking, though, and also prevented her from dwelling on her regrets. Oh, how tempting—and wrong—Jack's offer sounded.

Yet at the same time, he was a man who personified the very thing she avoided—taking risks. Trusting in others. Letting down your guard.

"That walk we took the other day did me some good,

too, and I'm not just talking about in a cardiovascular way," he said. "Sometimes, I need to be forced out the door or I work too many hours. This weekend, the geeks are doing some maintenance on the server. That means I can't work, not while the computers are down. And my cousin is really counting on me to be there. I couldn't bear to let him down." Jack grinned.

Why did he have to keep being so nice? So...normal?

She kept waiting to see the side of him that had swooped down and shredded her father's company, and she hadn't. Now here he was, admitting he was a workaholic like her, striking yet another sympathetic chord in her heart. One who, like her, also spent far too little time in the sun and with close family. She liked him, damn it, and really didn't want to.

She shook her head even as her resistance eroded a little more. "You don't need my company to do that."

"Ah, but a day like today is so much better when it's enjoyed with someone else, don't you agree?" He reached back and opened the rear passenger door of his car. "I already have a picnic and a blanket ready to go."

"So sure I was going to say yes?"

"Quite the opposite. I wanted to sweeten the pot because I knew you'd say no."

He could have read her mind. Five minutes ago, she'd written "take some time off" on a Post-It note and tacked it onto her desk, a reminder to stop working seven days, to have some time to regroup, recharge. Except for her thrice-weekly runs at the gym, there'd been far too much work and far too little relaxation in her days. In her business, a tired matchmaker wasn't as inspired when it came to putting matches together, hence the reminder for time off.

But a picnic with Jack? How could that be a good

choice? He was the kind of man who tempted her to take the very risks she'd avoided all her life. The kind of man who came with heartbreak written all over his face.

The kind of man she tried so very hard to resist. And failed.

She peered past him, and into the car. A bright green reusable shopping bag sat on top of a folded red plaid blanket. The shopping bag bulged, and the amber neck of a bottle of white wine stuck out of the top, alongside a spray of daisies.

Daisies.

Not roses. Not carnations. Not orchids. Daisies, their bright white faces so friendly and inviting.

Jack caught where her gaze had gone, and he reached inside, tugged out the flowers, and presented them to her. "I thought an unconventional woman deserved an unconventional flower."

She took them, and despite everything, her defensive walls against Jack melted a little more. "Did my mother tell you these were my favorites?"

"Nope. You did. When you told me about your nickname."

He'd remembered that tidbit. It touched her more than she wanted to admit. She fingered one of the blooms, and a smile curved across her face. "Every time I see daisies, they bring back great memories."

"Tell me," Jack said, his voice quiet and soft.

She inhaled the light scent of the delicate flowers. "When I was a little girl, there was a field near my house where daisies grew wild. Every spring, I couldn't wait for them to bloom. Once they did, I'd go and gather as many as I could carry and bring them to my mother. She'd arrange them in this big green vase of my grandmother's, set it in the center of the dining room table, and every night over dinner, we'd give one of the daisies a name. She said they have so much personality, they deserve to have their own names."

Jack leaned forward, and ran a finger along the delicate petals of one of the flowers. "And what's this one's name?"

She shook her head. "Jack, I'm too old for that."

"We both are. But it's fun to be young once in a while, don't you think? Believe me, I wish I'd taken more time to be a kid when I had the chance."

She heard something in his voice, something sad, regretful. She wondered again about the Jack Knight she thought she knew—who had ruined her father's company—and the Jack Knight she had met—a man with a definite soft spot. Which was the real Jack? Curiosity nudged her closer to him. "Why didn't you have more kid time?"

"Long, involved, unhappy story. I'll tell it to you if I'm ever on Oprah." He shook off the moment of somberness, then plucked one of the daisies from their paper wrapper. "I'm calling this one Fred."

She shook her head, stepping away. "Jack—"

He plucked a second flower from the arrangement and held it out to her. "Let go of all those rules and regulations you live by, Marnie."

"How do you know I do that?"

"Because we're two peas in a pod, as my stepfather would say. I have kept such a tight leash on everything in my life, trying to make up for the past, trying not to be the man my father was. And where has it gotten me? Working too many hours, eating most of my meals on the run, and living the same lonely work-centered life he lived."

"I'm not…" She shook her head, unable to complete the sentence.

Jack touched her cheek, his blue eyes soft, understanding. "I see a woman who works too much and plays too little. As if she's afraid to go after the very thing she helps her clients find."

It was as if he'd pulled open a curtain in Marnie's brain. How many times had she thought the same thing? Heard those same words from her sisters, her mom? She glanced at the daisies and saw her younger self in those happy white circles. When had she gotten away from that carefree person? When had she become this woman too scared to take a chance on love?

She reached out and took the flower, caught in the game, in Jack's infectious smile, in the echoing need to forget her adult problems for just a little while. "That makes this one Ethel."

"Sounds perfect, Marnie." He closed his hand over hers, capturing the flowers and making her heart stutter at the same time. "Let's put the rest in water, and take Fred and Ethel to the concert. They'll be our table decoration, even if our table is a blanket on the ground."

It was a beautiful day, warm, sunny, the kind of day that begged to be enjoyed. She thought of the things she had planned to do at home—laundry, vacuuming, dusting. Catching up with her life, essentially, after a long week of work. Not an ounce of that appealed to her right now, but the thought of spending time outside, with Fred and Ethel and Jack, did.

He's the enemy. The one who destroyed your father. Every time you see him, it will remind you of that history.

But was that really what had her hesitating? Or was

it what Jack had said, that she was afraid to go after the very things she helped her clients find?

"Come on, Marnie. Enjoy the day. Consider this your civic duty, supporting local high schools," he said, "albeit, civic duty accompanied by a glass of chardonnay."

"Oh, that sounds really good," she said, because it did, and because her resistance had been depleted when he'd named the daisy. She bit her lip, then shoved the doubts to the back of her mind. She wanted this afternoon, this moment. She pressed the Ethel daisy into his hand. "Hold these and I'll be back in two minutes. I have a vase in my office."

She ran back into the building, and up the stairs. In a few minutes, she had the daisies in some water, and had placed the vase by her desk, so she'd see them first thing every day. She was about to leave, then put a hand to her hair, and ducked into the restroom instead. She washed up, then placed her hands on either side of the sink and stared up at her reflection. Excitement and anticipation showed in her eyes, pinked in her cheeks.

Excitement and anticipation because she was going out with Jack Knight.

"What the hell are you doing?" she said to her image. "You can't get involved with him. He's all wrong for you, remember?"

Her image didn't reply. Nor did her brain rush forward with any reasons why Jack was wrong, exactly. For some reason, she couldn't come up with a single objection.

Even as she told herself she didn't care what Jack Knight thought about her appearance, she gave her hair a quick brush, then refastened the barrette holding the chestnut waves off her face. A quick swipe of blush, a little lipstick, then a quick exchange of heels for a pair of flats she kept under her desk. She grabbed a cardigan from the hook by the door, then, at the last second, she unclipped the barrette and dropped it on the counter. Her hair tumbled to her shoulders.

Unfettered, untamed.

His words came back to her, tempting, sexy, urging her to take a chance, to give him a chance. To just…be.

She stopped when she saw him standing by the silver car, holding Fred and Ethel. The last of her reservations melted away.

One day, one concert, wouldn't change anything. She'd have a good time, and be home before dark. Right?

CHAPTER EIGHT

WRONG.

The thick plaid blanket had seemed big when Marnie and Jack spread it on the grassy field that lay in front of the famous Hatch Shell. Hundreds of other families were camped out around them, armed with video cameras to capture their child's performance. The first band sat on the stage under the giant white dome, tuning their instruments while the A/V staff ran back and forth, doing last minute prep.

Marnie took a seat beside Jack and arranged her skirt over her knees and legs. She'd kicked off her shoes, left her cell phone in the car. Sitting in the sun, barefoot, with nowhere to go but right here, right now, had a decadent quality. For a while, the nagging thought that she should be doing something tensed in her shoulders. But as the sun washed its gentle warmth over her, Marnie began to relax, one degree at a time.

Well, relax as much as she could sitting next to Jack. He was so close that she caught the spicy dark notes of his cologne with every inhale. Her hand splayed on the blanket, inches from his. He had strong hands, the kind that looked like they could take care of her in one instant, and send her soaring to new heights in the bedroom in the next.

"Hungry?" Jack asked.

"Oh, yeah," she said, then colored when she realized that her hunger was for him, not food. Damn. What was with this man? Why did he draw her in so easily? She had already made that mistake with someone else. She straightened, putting a few centimeters of distance between them. "Uh, did you say you brought sandwiches?"

"Yep. Ham and cheese good with you?"

"Yes, thank you." She took one of the paper wrapped sandwiches from him and opened it. A thick pile of honey ham, topped with a generous portion of provolone cheese, as well as deep green Boston lettuce and juicy red tomato slices peeked out from between two rustic slices of sourdough bread. She took a bite, and goodness invaded her palate. "Oh, my. This is amazing. What's on this?"

"Hector's own jalapeno/cilantro mayonnaise. He owns the deli, and there are some meals that I think could get him nominated for sainthood."

Marnie took another bite. "Oh, this, definitely."

Jack chuckled, then uncorked the wine and poured it into two plastic cups, handing her one of them. "Plastic isn't exactly high brow, but I'm not exactly a fancy glass kind of guy."

"Really? You strike me as, well, as the opposite. Or at least, you have the other times I've run into you."

"It's those damned suits. They make me look all boring and dull."

She laughed. "Those are *not* the adjectives I'd use to describe you."

"Oh, really?" He arched a brow. "And how would you describe me?"

She thought a minute. "Mysterious. Guarded. An

enigma." That much was true. Every time she thought she had Jack figured out, he threw her a curveball.

"Ah, the elusive guy in the shadows who never opens his heart, is that it?" He raised his cup toward hers. "To guarded hearts."

"You talking about me?"

He laughed. "You, Marnie, have the most guarded heart I've ever seen."

"Touché." She gave him a nod of concession, then a smile. "To guarded hearts. And mysterious enigmas." They touched cups, then drank. Two kindred souls, in relationships at least.

"I don't think I ever thanked you for introducing my stepfather to your mom."

"I should be thanking you for encouraging him to go to the mixer. He really seems perfect for her." Marnie didn't think she'd ever seen her mother this happy, yet at the same time, the caution flags stayed in her head. Dan came with Jack—and could her mother handle that? "He's a nice guy."

Jack nodded. "He was a heck of a stepdad, too. He married my mom when I was eight, and was one of those hands-on dads. The kind that plays catch in the yard and teaches you how to build a fire with a flint and some kindling. But the years before Dan came along were…rough."

"I'm sorry." And she was. No child should have a difficult childhood. Hers hadn't been perfect, but it hadn't been rough, either.

Jack shrugged like it was no big deal, but she got the sense it did bother him. "My father was never there. Not then, not later."

"Did he work a lot?"

Jack snorted. "My father made work a world-class

sport. Heck, I saw the Tooth Fairy more than my own dad. And when he was home, his attention span lasted about five minutes before he was off on another call or writing another memo. Eventually, my mother had enough of being, essentially, a single mom, and divorced him."

"Yet you followed your father into the family business, from the day you graduated Suffolk." When he arched a brow in question, she gave Jack a little smile. "I Googled you."

"So you *are* interested in me?"

"Cautious. You never know who you're riding home with."

Jack laughed and tipped his cup of wine toward her. "True."

She picked off another tiny bite of ham. "So if you and your father had such a bad relationship, why did you go to work for him?"

Jack leaned an arm over his knee. His gaze went to somewhere in the distance, far from the performance at the Hatch Shell, far from her. "Even though I loved Dan, I never got past that need for a father's love and attention. Pretty pathetic, huh?"

"No, not at all." Another thread of connection knitted between them. Her father had worked countless hours as he built his business. She could relate to that craving for a relationship, a connection. She too had missed out on the camping trips and ball games with her father.

Her sympathy for Jack doubled. In his eyes, she could still see that hurting, hopeful boy, and it broke her heart.

Across from them, a mother and father took turns playing peek-a-boo with a baby in a stroller. The baby's laugh carried on the air, infectious, bubbly. That was what a family looked like, she thought, the kind of family Jack should have had his entire childhood, and it added a sad punctuation to their conversation.

Jack sighed. "Anyway, I guess I hoped that if I worked for him, we'd finally have that relationship I had missed out on."

She had wondered the same thing. If she had worked for her father, would she have had a closer relationship with him? Been able to help his business? Help him? "And did you get that relationship?"

"Oh, I saw him at work. When I was getting called into his office for another 'stupid' mistake. We didn't have long, father-son talks or take lunch together or even work on projects together. Everything I learned came from the other guys who worked for my father. Many of those men still work for me today, and they're almost like a second family."

"Why didn't you leave the company?" she asked.

"I did. Took a job at another business brokerage firm, and barely had time to put my pens in the drawer of my desk before I got a call telling me my father had had a heart attack. Two days later, I was in charge. After he died, I stepped into his shoes. Well, his office." A wry, sad grin crossed his face. "I made my own shoes."

She picked at an errant thread on the blanket, hating that they had this in common, too. Of all the people in Boston, why did she have to relate so closely to Jack, and his loss?

Jack's blue eyes met hers and his features softened. "I'm sorry, Marnie. I know your father died too, a few years ago. He was a heck of a nice guy, and I'm sure that loss was hard on you."

She heard true sympathy in Jack's voice and it made tears spring to her eyes. He covered her hand with his.

An easy, comfortable touch. One that eased the loss in her heart, yet at the same time it drove that pain home.

Damn him. Damn Jack for making her care. Damn Jack for caring about her. And damn Jack for being the reason behind all of this.

But he said he had quit, walked away. Then returned to do things his own way. Did that mean he had changed? That other businesses weren't being hurt like her father's? That her biggest argument against him was fizzling?

"I guess we never outgrow the need for a parent, huh?" he said.

She heard the echoes of her own loss in his voice, and it muddled the issues. She wanted to hate him—

And instead commiserated with Jack, this complex, layered man who had gone through so many of the same hurts as she had.

"Jack! Jack!" A blonde waved at them from a few feet away. A dark-haired man stood beside her, loaded down with a diaper bag, two lawn chairs and a small cooler.

Jack grinned, then got to his feet and put a hand out to Marnie. "Come on, let me introduce you to my cousin Ashley. She's the mom of the talented musician we're here to see."

"Oh, I don't think I should..." she said.

"I promise, they won't bite," he said, then took her hand and hauled her to her feet. So fast, she collided with his chest. He grinned and held her gaze for one long, hot moment. "Though I can't promise I won't."

A delicious thrill raced through her veins. Marnie released Jack's hand and bent down to straighten her skirt, and break that hypnotic connection. "Uh, maybe we should hurry because the concert's about to start." Anything to get some distance, some breathing room.

But then Jack took her hand again to help her as they picked their way among the lawn chairs and blankets and people on the lawn. He shifted his touch to the small of Marnie's back when they reached his cousin. "Hey, Ashley," he said. "This Marnie. Marnie, this is my cousin Ashley and her husband Joe."

"Nice to meet you," Ashley said, shaking hands with Marnie. Her husband echoed the sentiment, then nodded toward a little girl running across the back lawn.

"I'll be back. Have to go catch a runaway toddler." Joe lowered the things in his arms to the ground, then headed off at a light jog. Ashley unfolded the lawn chairs and placed them on either side of the cooler and diaper bag.

"I hear you have a talented son," Marnie said.

"Jack likes to brag about him, but yeah." Ashley's face lit with a mother's pride. "We think he's pretty amazing. And thank you, Jack, for making the time to be here."

"You know I'd never miss something like this."

"He'll be thrilled you came." Ashley gave Jack's hand a squeeze. "You're a great godfather." Then she turned to Marnie and grinned. "If the way he treats his godchildren is any indication, this one's going to be a great dad. Just in case you were wondering."

Marnie's face heated. "Oh, he and I, we're not… together."

"Pity," Ashley said. "Because I'd love to spoil Jack's kids rotten. Maybe even buy them a drum set for Christmas, like he did for our kids."

Jack chuckled. "Hey, that drum set led to him being on that stage."

"True. But next time, I'm letting my kids sleep over

at your house when they need to practice." Ashley laughed.

The warmth and love between the cousins mirrored the camaraderie Marnie had with her own family, and again showed another dimension to Jack Knight. A man who loved and was loved, not the man she'd vilified for years. Her resistance lowered even more.

The three of them talked for a little while longer, then Jack took Marnie's hand. "They're about to start," he said. "We better get back to our spot."

Joe returned with a tow-headed toddler in his arms. "She says she wants Uncle Jack."

The girl scrambled out of her father's arms and up into Jack's. "Uncle Jack, are you comin' to our house later? Mamma made cake."

"Cake, huh?" Jack beeped the girl's nose. "Is it as sweet as you?"

She nodded. "Uh-huh. It's chocolate. With bubber dream."

"Buttercream," Ashley corrected, moving to take her daughter and hand her a juice box. "Bad for the hips and the heart, but oh, so good."

Jack chuckled. "Sure. I'll stop by tonight. And I might just have a surprise if you're good."

The little girl straightened and nodded, as solemn as a judge. "Imma good girl."

"Of course you are," he said quietly. Then he ruffled her hair. "Okay, good girl, watch your brother. I'll see you later."

Marnie and Jack walked back over to their blanket, and took their seats again. "Your family was really nice," she said. And they were. She had liked them, a lot.

"Thanks. I never had any brothers or sisters, so my

cousins are like my siblings. Most of them still live in
the area, and I see them pretty often. If I ever have a
kid, I'm calling Ashley and Joe for advice." He sent a
fond look in their direction.

"She's adorable."

"She's four. Smart as a whip, and a bottle full of sass,
according to her mother, but yes, adorable."

Jack's face showed the soft spot in his heart for his
cousin's children. For his family. It drew her in, even as
she tried to keep distance between them. Marnie kept
her hands away from his under the guise of eating, but
really, it was because it had become far too easy and
natural to connect with Jack. To let down that wall, to
let herself…be.

To fall for him.

"How's your sandwich?" Jack asked.

She jerked her attention back to him. "Oh, uh, perfect." And it was. Low-key, easy, simple. Marnie found
herself giving in to the relaxing day, the bucolic setting,
the contentment of good food. Just the two of them—
okay and three hundred other adults and kids—enjoying
a lunch outdoors. The first band began to play, and both
Jack and Marnie sat back and listened, while they ate
their sandwiches and sipped the wine. As the first song
edged into the second, then the third, she started to truly
enjoy herself. Maybe it was the sunshine. The food in
her belly. The wine. But by the time the second band
came on the stage, Marnie was leaning on her elbows,
with Jack so close, she could feel his shoulder brush
hers every once in a while. She didn't move away. She
wasn't sure she could if she wanted to.

"This is my cousin's school coming on stage now,"
he said, turning to speak to her.

She pivoted at the same time, which brought their

mouths within kissing distance. Heat ignited in the space between them, and her gaze dropped to his mouth. Anticipation pooled in her gut.

The band launched into an up-tempo jazz selection. Marnie jerked back, clasped her hands in her lap and concentrated on the music. Not on almost kissing Jack.

The quartet played plucky notes accented by a soft touch on the drums, and occasional taps of the high hat. It was a simple group, with drums, a bass, a sax, and a piano. The players would look up from time to time, grin at one another, and then play through a complex section of the music. The last few notes tapered off and applause began to swell.

"They were terrific," Marnie said over the sound of their clapping hands. "Which one is your cousin?"

"The pianist." Pride beamed in Jack's features. "He's a great kid. Really talented. He's applied at Berklee, and he has a great chance of getting in."

"I can see why." She sat back as the band exited the stage, and made room for the next one. "I wish I had even an ounce of their musical ability. I couldn't carry a tune if you taped one to my mouth."

He chuckled. "Oh, I don't know about that. You have such a pretty voice, I bet you can sing."

She put up her hands to ward off the possibility, but the compliment warmed her. "My sister Kat, who became a graphic designer, got all the creative genes in the family."

"I think matchmaking is pretty creative, don't you?"

"True." She leaned her head on her shoulder and studied him. "What about you? Any creativity in those genes?"

He grinned. "Depends on what kind of creativity you're looking for."

Her face heated—God, what was it with this man, turning her face red all the time—as she realized the double entendre. "I meant the ones in your DNA, not the bedroom kind."

"I know." He leaned over and ran a finger over her cheek. Her pulse skittered. "I just like to see you blush."

Oh, my. This man hit all the right buttons, and as much as part of her cursed him for doing it, another part liked it. Very much. She'd dated men, but none had knocked her so off-kilter, leaving her breathless, distracted, *wanting*.

When he looked at her, she felt beautiful. When he smiled like that, she felt sexy. And when his voice lowered like that, it set off a chain reaction of desire deep, deep inside her body.

She jerked around to a sitting position, drawing her knees up to her chest. "Oh, look, the next band is on stage."

Was she that desperate for a man in her life that she'd fall for the one man who had helped ruin her father?

Or that scared of falling for someone who turned her world so inside-out? Being with Jack was like racing down a track on the back of a runaway car. And that was the one thing that made Marnie want to bolt.

A few minutes later, the concert was over, and the attendees began gathering up blankets and lawn chairs, and start trekking back across the grassy lawn to their cars. The skies had begun to darken, and in the distance, Marnie heard the low rumble of thunder. "We better hurry," she said, "before we get caught in the storm."

But even as she bundled up the blanket and helped gather the remnants of their lunch, Marnie had a feeling she'd already gotten caught by a storm. One made by Jack Knight.

* * *

They didn't move fast enough.

A second later, the thick gray clouds broke open with an angry burst of wind and water, dropping rain in fast sheets over the Esplanade and the hundreds of people scrambling for their cars. Jack grabbed Marnie's hand. "Come on, let's go!"

They charged across the grass, weaving through the other people, as the rain fell. Finally, they reached the car, and collapsed against it in a tangle of arms, legs and picnic supplies. "Wait!" she said. "I dropped the blanket."

"Don't worry about it. I'll get another." He fumbled in his pocket for the keys, then unlocked Marnie's door. A second later, they were both safe inside the dry car. He took the picnic supplies from her and tossed everything onto the back seat. The leather seats would probably end up ruined, but right now, Jack didn't care.

Even with the rain, the day had been one of the best he could remember having. All his life, he'd sucked at personal relationships, putting the people in his life on the sidelines while he concentrated on work. He'd worried that he'd be his father's son with women, too, that he would leave a trail of broken hearts to match the trail of broken companies.

No more.

For the first time in forever, Jack wanted to try harder, to be better, for himself and with others. He didn't want to just give back to companies, or connect with business owners, or repay those his father had hurt, he wanted to do the same turnaround with himself. He used to think that if he could just make amends for his father's choices, he would be complete. But now he wanted more.

He wanted everything his father had never appreciated. The white picket fence, the two kids, the dog in the yard. The woman who greeted him with a smile at the end of the day.

Marnie had brought that out in him. She was a challenge, a puzzle, one he wanted to solve. He had a feeling this complex, beautiful woman would keep him on his toes for a really, really long time. And oh, how he craved that.

Craved *her*.

Marnie shook her head, then swiped off the worst of the rain. Even soaking wet, she looked amazing. Water had darkened her lashes, plastered her hair to her head, and soaked the pale yellow shirt she wore, until it outlined every delicious inch of her torso. She leaned down and plucked at her skirt. "God, I'm soaked. Maybe we should hit a Laundromat and throw ourselves into a dryer." She glanced up, and caught him looking at her. "What?"

Desire pulsed in his veins, pounded in his heart. Coupled with the darkened interior of the car, the intimacy of the black leather seats, and the rain drumming a steady beat on the roof, it seemed as if they were the only two people in the world.

"You're soaking wet," he said.

She laughed. "I know. I said that."

"And still one of the most beautiful women I have ever seen in my life." That caused another blush to fill her cheeks. Damn, he liked that about her. A touch of vulnerable, mixed in with the strong. He reached out, brushed a lock of hair off her cheek. It left a little glistening trail of water, and before he could think better of it, he leaned across the console and kissed that line kissed all the way down her cheek, until he moved a few millimeters to the left and caught her lips with his.

"We…shouldn't do this," Marnie whispered against his mouth.

"Okay," he said, then kissed her again. She tasted of wine and vanilla and all he wanted right now was more, more, and even more of her. He slid one hand up, along the smooth side of her blouse, then around the curve of her breast. The thin, wet fabric offered almost no barrier against the lace edges of her bra, the stiff peak of her nipple.

When his fingers danced over it, Marnie gasped and arched forward. *"Jack."*

He'd heard his name a million times in his life. Never had that single syllable sounded so sweet. He opened his mouth against hers, and with a groan, deepened the kiss, shifting to capture more of her breast, more of her, more of everything.

Her hands came up around his back, clutching at him, nearly dragging him over the console. Her kiss turned wild, ferocious, and that sent him into a dizzying tailspin of want, need. The rain pounded harder, thunder booming above them, lightning crackling in the sky, as the storm between them became a wild ride of hands and tongues.

His fingers went to the buttons on her blouse, then stilled when he heard a horn honk, the rev of an engine. Damn. They were still in the parking lot, surrounded by other people. "We should take this somewhere more private," he said. His breath heaved in and out of his chest.

She drew back, her lips red and swollen, her breath also coming in little fast gasps. Her green eyes met his, held, then her breathing slowed. She shook her head. "How do you do that?"

"Do what?"

"Get me to forget all the very good reasons I have for not letting you get close. We can't do this, Jack. Not now, not ever. It's...wrong."

"It sure felt right. And explosive. And crazy, and a hundred other things."

She sighed. "That's the problem."

The rain began to slow, one of those fast-moving storms that passed almost as fast as it started. The parking lot cleared out, families going home to dinners in the oven, homework at the kitchen table. He put his hand on the ignition but didn't turn the key. "Then why did you kiss me?"

She bit her lip. "Because, for a little while, I forgot. And just...was."

"Forgot what?"

But Marnie just shook her head and asked him to drive her home. He started the car, pulled out of the lot, and headed southwest. But as he watched the Hatch Shell get smaller and smaller in his rearview mirror, Jack had a feeling he'd lost more than just a blanket today.

CHAPTER NINE

JACK HAD RUINED HER.

Ever since the walk to the neighborhood coffee shop and the jazz concert on the lawn, she'd found her office too confining. She'd spent more time outside in the last few days than she had all year, and as the morning wore on and the sun made its journey across the sky, Marnie got more and more antsy. She paced. She hummed. She fiddled. In short, she didn't do a damned thing productive.

Erica got to her feet, and grabbed Marnie's car keys. "Okay, that's it. I'm tired of you bouncing in place. Let's get out of here and go grab something to eat. Preferably something chocolate and really, really bad for us."

"But I've got all this work—"

"To do tomorrow. It can wait, especially considering you haven't done much of it so far today." Erica arched a brow, then grinned.

"Why are you smiling about that?" Marnie ran a hand through her hair and let out a sigh. "All it does is put me further behind. I have this long list of clients waiting for me to find them a match. All these events to organize and—"

"Step out of your comfort zone, Marn, and blow off work today. There are days when you are wound tighter than a ball of yarn, which is pretty much par for the course with you, oh, control freak sister. But these last couple weeks…" Erica shrugged.

"What?"

"These last couple weeks, you've been smiling and laughing, and…" Erica put a hand on her sister's and met Marnie's gaze. "Well, it's been nice."

Marnie refused to give Jack Knight any credit for the change in her attitude. If anything, he'd made things worse, not better. Except…

The walk through the quaint neighborhood and the jazz concert at the Hatch Shell had been fun. Even running in the rain had left her breathless, laughing. It had all been a huge step out of her comfort zone and oddly, she'd enjoyed it. What had he said to her the other day?

You should let your hair down more often.

Right or wrong, Jack Knight had gotten her to do exactly that in the last couple weeks. She'd slept better at night, worked better during the day, and the tension had eased in her shoulders. Maybe Jack had a point. She hated that he did, but he did.

"So…who is he?" Erica asked.

"Who's who?"

"The man who has you all atwitter. You're like a girl in junior high." Erica pointed at her sister. "There, that. You're blushing. You *never* blush."

Marnie sighed. "He's Jack Knight. The owner of Knight Enterprises."

A light dawned in Erica's eyes and she let out a little gasp. "Jack *Knight?* Of Knight Enterprises infamy? The same one that invested in Dad's business years ago?"

Marnie nodded, then explained how she'd met Jack, and what had transpired in the weeks since, leaving off the bit about kissing him.

"Okay, but that still doesn't explain why you blush every time you talk about him," Erica said.

Marnie sighed. "He kissed me."

"He...*what?* He *kissed* you? Really? Oh, my God," she said, her voice reaching Roberta-worthy decibels. "Did you kiss him back?"

"Yes, but only because he took me by surprise. And it won't happen again, I can tell you that. I reacted out of...instinct."

Yeah, right. She'd kissed him because of a reflex, not desire. *Liar.*

Erica typed something into the laptop computer beside her, waited a second, then turned the screen toward Marnie. "Oh, I'm sure it was instinct to kiss *that* hunk of yummy. Any woman with a pulse's instinct."

Marnie looked at Jack's image, one of those professional photos done for the corporate website. He had a serious, no-nonsense look on his face, along with a navy power suit and a dark crimson tie. The Jack Knight in the photo was powerful, commanding. None of the teasing looks or charming grins he'd given her. And yet, her body reacted the same, with that instant zing of desire. Curse the man for being so damned good looking. "Okay, so he's cute."

"So, what are you going to do about him? Now that you're done kissing him?"

"I don't know. I want to hate him, and I do, I really do, but..."

"A part of you is starting to like him?"

Marnie shook her head. "No, not at all."

Erica just laughed. "You do realize that when you shook your head, you then gave a slight nod? If this were an interrogation, it would totally negate your strong protests to the contrary."

"The trouble is, he seems nice. Not at all the evil corporate raider I pictured." Marnie thought of the gym he'd invested in, the coffee shop owner who loved him and raved about him, the family he adored. Twice, Jack had told her he wasn't as bad as she thought he was, yet he represented everything that had hurt her mother, her family. She shook her head. "Either way, he's all wrong for me."

"Then you better stop kissing him," Erica said with a grin. "Or next you'll end up in bed with the enemy."

Later that morning, Marnie and Erica closed up the office and headed across town to the Second Chance shelter and work counseling center. The two of them had been volunteering there for years, a good cause that helped struggling people find work.

Even though her workload had quadrupled because of the distracting thoughts about Jack, Marnie welcomed the break from the office. She'd get away from her sister's prying eyes, the ringing of the telephone, and the daisies that still sat on her desk. All reminders of Jack, and how close she kept coming to falling for Mr. Wrong.

She wanted a steady, dependable man. One who wanted a quiet, predictable life. None of this heady, crazy, spontaneity that came with Jack. He was a risk, a giant one. Hadn't she already seen how bad a risk like that could ruin someone? She had no desire to do the same.

A silver sports car glided to a stop in the lane beside her, and she flicked a quick glance at the driver. Darn it. Every silver car she saw reminded her of Jack Knight. Heck, even though she knew better, he'd been on her mind the better part of the day and nearly all night. Her hormones hadn't gotten the memo from her brain that he was No Good for Her. Maybe she just needed more time.

And less silver sports cars on the Boston roads. Because despite her better judgment, she couldn't stop from looking in the driver's side window, a part of her hoping to see a dark-haired, blue-eyed man.

Erica had dropped the subject of Jack, thank goodness, and talked on the drive about her plans for the weekend. They drove across town, then parked outside a converted two-family home that had been turned into a combination shelter and education center for people down on their luck. Second Chance had been started a few years ago by a group of local businesspeople who wanted to give back to the community, and had been successful with a large percentage of the people it served. Marnie had supported the organization from day one with monetary donations, a couple of career workshops, and clothing donations. She'd used her network to help several of the residents find jobs, and sent numerous leads to the director. It was a good cause, and one she wished every business in Boston would get behind.

She and Erica grabbed two big bags of clothes Marnie had to donate, and headed inside. Linda, the director, came out of her office to help. Linda was a tall, thin, energetic woman who always had a ready smile for everyone she met. Her ash blond hair was pulled back in a ponytail, which gave her blue floral dress and practical white sneakers a fun touch. "Oh, bless you, Marnie. The ladies here will be so glad to see all this."

"No problem. It's the least I can do. Where do you want everything?"

Linda directed her to a room down the hall that had

been converted into a giant closet. "Marnie, if you could just set the items up on the hangers, then they'll be ready for after our event. Oh, and Erica, since you're here, too, can I borrow you to help with lunch service for a little bit? We're short-handed today. We had more people than I expected show up to hear our speaker today."

"Sure. I'd be glad to." Erica headed into the kitchen, while Marnie hung up the clothes and set up the shoes she'd brought. It was good, easy, mindless work that kept her from dwelling on impossible situations.

Ten minutes later, Marnie had finished. The antsy feeling had yet to go away, so she started straightening and pacing again. From down the hall, she heard a strong round of applause and the murmur of voices.

The speaker Linda had mentioned. Whoever it was, he or she was enjoying an enthusiastic response from the attendees. Linda often brought in motivational speakers, who left their listeners with a renewed enthusiasm. Might be worth popping in for a minute and listening, Marnie decided. It was better than rehanging shirts and straightening skirts, or wearing a path from the hall to the window.

She crossed into a large room that used to be a dining room, but had been opened up and turned into a mini auditorium, now utilized for speakers, AA meetings, and other events. Rows and rows of folding chairs filled the space, and not a one was vacant. At the podium stood a tall, thin man Marnie recognized as Harvey, a frequent visitor to Second Chance. He had started out homeless, addicted to drugs, and had turned his life around in recent years, becoming a volunteer and counselor at the very place that helped him. She liked

Harvey, especially his positive attitude and his belief in perseverance.

"I can't thank this man enough for what he did," Harvey was saying. "He gave me a job when no one else would, he told me he believed in me when no one else did, and he became a friend when no one else was around. I'm proud as heck to introduce my mentor and good friend, Jack Knight, to all of you."

Marnie bit back a gasp. Jack? Here? Being touted as the best thing to come along since sliced bread? By Harvey of all people?

She ducked to the right to hide behind a thick green potted plant, just as Jack strode into the room, wearing jeans and a pale green button-down shirt that made his eyes seem even bluer. Her body reacted with a rush of heat, and her mind replayed that kiss in the car. God, she wanted him, even now, even when she shouldn't.

He stepped up to the podium, thanking Harvey for his warm introduction. The crowd greeted Jack with renewed enthusiasm, and several shouted his name and a welcome back. After the applause died down, Jack began to speak.

She expected one of those speeches about corporate responsibility. Or putting your best foot forward in a job interview. But instead, Jack delivered a commentary that had the audience riveted, and Marnie rooted to the spot.

"You will always have people who will tell you that your dreams aren't worth having," Jack said. "People who think their way is the only way, and that anyone who takes another path is wrong. They'll try to cut you down, or talk you out of your plans. Work to convince you that they have the right answers, or maybe even tell you to pull the plug and give up. Move on. Do something else. It can take a great deal of courage to forge forward, to keep believing in yourself. But I'm here to tell you that it's worth it in the end."

Applause, a few whoops of support.

Jack nodded, then went on. He didn't read from cue cards, or anything prepared, but rather, seemed to speak from his heart. His gaze connected with every person in the audience, and they connected right back with him. "You've heard the old adage that you have to fight for what you believe in, and that is true. But they don't tell you that the first fight you have to have is for yourself. Start by fighting for you, and fighting those doubts that keep you stuck in the wrong place, because *you* matter." At this, he pointed at the crowd, then at Harvey, then at himself. "And once you know that, the rest of the battle gets easier."

More applause, more whoops. Marnie felt a hand on her shoulder and turned to find Erica beside her.

"Oh, my God, is that Jack Knight?" Erica asked.

Marnie nodded. "I had no idea he was going to be here today."

"Wow, he's even cuter in person than he is in his picture," Erica whispered. "And without the suit and tie, he's downright sexy."

"He is," Marnie admitted. "And the people here love him. His speech is great."

"Seems to me that's a good enough reason to take a chance on him." Erica shrugged. "We could have him all wrong."

"Or he could be the greatest BS artist to come along in years."

"True. But he did bring you daisies. Doesn't that mean he deserves a second look? Or at least a chance to explain why he did what he did with Dad's business?" Erica cast another glance at Jack. "Until you do, I don't think you can truly know whether to hate him or love him."

"Love him?" Marnie scoffed. "I can barely stand him."

Erica laughed. "Oh, yeah, I can see that in the way you stare at him."

"I fixed him up with other women, Erica. I'm not interested in Jack Knight."

Except she had gone out on two, no, three dates with him, if she counted the dinner with their parents. And she'd been thinking about him non-stop for days. Kissed him twice. Desired him more than she'd desired anyone else.

"Pity. He seems like a really nice guy." Erica glanced over her shoulder, saw Linda heading for the kitchen and gave her sister a light touch on the shoulder. "I have to get back to lunch service. Just remember what Dad used to say. You can't judge the house until you see the inside. You don't know the whole story of Dad's house, and you don't know the whole story of Jack's. You don't know if Jack tried to help Dad and he refused to listen. Our father was a great visionary but not the best businessman in the world."

"All the more reason why he needed an investor who would help him, not just throw some money at him then step back and watch him drown. Regardless, Jack is a constant reminder to all of us of what happened with Dad. We don't need that in our lives."

"Maybe. But you won't know unless *you ask him about it*." Erica leaned in to whisper in Marnie's ear, with emphasis on the last few words. "Stop being afraid to look inside and find out the truth. You keep this tight little leash on everything, Marnie. Sometimes taking a risk is good for you, and your heart."

Erica left the room. Marnie debated following, but Jack's voice drew her in again. "That's the business I'm really in," he was saying, "one where I support dreams. I am honored to have been rewarded for my work, too."

Financially, the cynic in Marnie thought.

"I'm not talking about money," Jack said as if he'd read her mind. "It's the people. When you put passion and belief into what you do, it translates into the people around you, and you pay it forward with every business decision you make. For me, it's the bookstore owner who has the funds to start a literacy program for adult learners. The daycare owner who can now afford to offer a drop-in service for parents who are looking for jobs. The handyman firm that has expanded into two more cities, and hired great people like Harvey here. These are people who took a risk and it paid off. Their thank-yous are worth more than any number on the bottom line, and at the end of the day, bring you a satisfaction you won't find anywhere else." He stepped out from behind the podium and into the audience, as far as the mike's cord allowed. "So take a chance, go after your dreams, and you'll enjoy a return on that investment that is ten-fold."

The audience erupted into applause. People got to their feet, cheering Jack and his words, reaching for him to tell him how impressed they were, thanking him for his message.

Heck of a speech, Marnie thought. Almost had her convinced he was a nice guy.

The crowd began to disperse, some people heading for the platters of cookies and coffee at the back of the room, while others opted for lunch in the kitchen. Many of the people raved about Jack's speech, clear fans of him now. Maybe her father had been sold on some "support the dream" speech, too, and been too blind to see the reality of the situation.

Except that didn't match the father she'd known. Yes, he'd been terrible at business—more of a creative than an accountant—but he'd been an incredible judge of character. Tom could pick a con artist out of a room of a hundred people, and many of the people he'd had handshake deals with over the years had turned out to be his best friends. He'd known in a minute if someone had a good heart or bad intentions.

If that was so, then why had he signed an agreement with Knight Enterprises? How could he have missed the writing on the wall? Or had Jack tried, and failed, to help Tom's business?

He brought you daisies, Erica had said. *Doesn't that mean he deserves a second look?*

Marnie lingered in the room, watching Jack interact with several of the people at Second Chance. She stayed behind her veil of greenery, her feet rooted to the spot. A woman Marnie knew well, a single mom named Luanne, stepped over to Jack. Within seconds, Luanne was crying, and Marnie's heart went out to her. She knew life had been tough for Luanne lately—not only had she lost her job, but also her home after a bitter divorce. She'd been staying at Second Chance for a few weeks now and had been the one with the idea of a donated career dress day to help the women looking for work.

"You told us to follow our dreams," Luanne said to Jack, "but I lost all mine. I don't know what to do now."

Jack's face was kind, his eyes soft. "What did you do before for work?"

"Data entry at a newspaper, working in the subscription department."

"And did you love that?"

The room had emptied out, with most of the people heading for lunch in the kitchen, a few lingering in the hall. Spring sunshine streamed in through the windows, bright, cheery, hopeful, like it was trying to coax Luanne into believing brighter days were on the horizon.

Luanne shook her head. "I hated that job. I only took it because I wanted to be a writer. Then one year turned into two, turned into ten…" She shrugged.

Jack reached into his breast pocket and pulled out a pen, one of those expensive ones, with a heavy silver barrel. He pressed the ballpoint into the woman's hand. "Take this," he said, "and write with it."

"Write what?"

"About your journey. About your life lessons. About anything you want. Back when I was young and had lots to say, I wrote novels and short stories. I even started out in college pursuing a degree in writing, before I switched to a major in business. A part of me still loves writing, the whole process of collecting my thoughts and forming them into stories." Jack shrugged. "No one will ever read what I write, but that's okay because it's just a hobby for me. You, though, you have a dream and a passion. I could see it in your eyes when I gave you the pen and said 'write.' It was as if that lit a fire deep inside you. So go, and write. The world needs more writers, especially ones with life experiences to share."

Luanne scoffed. "Who wants to hear my sob story?"

Jack held her gaze, and that smile Marnie had memorized curved across his face. "I do. And I bet the publisher at the community magazine wants to hear it, too. Send it my way when you're done, and I'll get it to him."

Tears glimmered in Luanne's eyes. She clutched the pen so tight, her knuckles whitened. "Thank you. Thank you so much."

"Don't thank me. Just take this dream, and spread it to another. Someday, you'll give someone else a pen or a kind word or some advice, and that will start them on their journey." Jack gave Luanne a gentle hug, then said goodbye and crossed to the coffeepot.

Marnie told her feet to move. Told herself to leave the room. But she remained cemented where she was, behind the plant, watching Jack approach.

Jack Knight, the demon who had destroyed her father, helping a woman down on her luck. Jack Knight, the man who kept getting her to step out of her comfort zone and let her hair down. Jack Knight, the man who had ignited something raw, urgent, and terrifying, deep inside her. Telling people to go after their dreams. Was it all a front?

A riot of emotions ran through her in the few seconds it took Jack to go from one end of the room to the other. She kept trying so hard to hate him but the feeling refused to stick.

In the end, indecision won out. Jack's blue eyes lit and his smile broadened when he spied her behind the plant. A sweet, delicious warmth spread through Marnie, and despite her better judgment, she found herself stepping out from behind the plant and giving him a smile of her own.

"Marnie."

When he said her name in that soft, surprised way, she was back in the car, the rain pounding on the roof, kissing Jack and thinking of nothing more than how much she wanted him, how he seemed to know every inch of her body so well. "I, uh, heard you talking and came in to listen. You gave a great speech."

"Thanks. I hope it touched a few people."

"It touched Luanne," she said, nodding in the direction the other woman had gone. Luanne had left the room with a lightness in her steps, a hopeful smile on her face, a changed woman. "That was really nice, what you did for her."

Jack shrugged. "It was a small thing."

"Not to Luanne. She's been through a lot, with her ex, and losing her job. I can tell that really touched her, to have someone believe in her." Marnie had to admit, that for all the bad Jack had done in the past, this moment would make a difference. She could already see a renewed enthusiasm and optimism in Luanne's features as she talked to other people in the room, showing off the pen, and spreading the words of encouragement.

"And yet, you run away every time I get close. You give me a laundry list of reasons why we shouldn't date." He took a step closer. "Why?"

She shook her head. "Jack, there's too much between us to make this work. Please stop trying to pretend there isn't."

He took another step closer, and the fronds of the plant brushed against his shoulder. "I'm not trying to pretend there isn't. But I'm willing to take the risk that we have something amazing here, something that is stronger than the past. The question is why you don't think so, too. Why you won't take a risk."

"I'm not interested in you. Or a relationship." But even as she said the words, Marnie knew, deep down inside, that they were a lie. She wanted all of that, and she wanted him—

But her wants couldn't overpower the tight hold she had on her life. If she let him in, if she took a chance—

No. She didn't do that. She didn't go off on haphazard paths, with no clear sense of direction. And that's what being with Jack was like. Insane and delicious, all at the same time. The whole thing made her want to hyperventilate.

"You make me want to take the day off, head for the Common with a bottle of wine and a picnic lunch," Jack said, his blue eyes capturing hers. "Or get in the car and drive up the coastline until we get to the tip of Maine, the edge of the country. Or just sit in a car while the rain falls and watch the way your eyes light up when I move closer and—"

She jerked away. How did he keep doing that? Every time she turned around, Jack wrapped her in his spell. Was that what he had done with her father, too? Spoken pretty words that masked Jack's true intentions? One Franklin had already fallen for Jack's words, had believed him when he'd offered a risky proposition. She refused to be the second one. "I have to go. I'm supposed to be helping my sister in the kitchen."

Then she spun on her heel and got out of the room, before temptation got the better of her. Although a part of Marnie suspected it already had.

CHAPTER TEN

JACK SAT AT his father's desk, in the office his father had spent most of his life in, and wished he could have a second chance, the very thing he'd promoted in his speech the other day. He'd told others they were possible, and had yet to find one in his own life, no matter how many hours he spent here. There were still things from the past catching up with him, nipping at his heels, and reminding him every day that he was his father's son—

And not at all proud of that fact.

The guilt of what he had done, the companies he had destroyed, the people whose hearts he had broken, gnawed at him still. The work he'd done over the last two years hadn't filled that aching hole in his heart the way he'd thought it would. It was as if he was sitting in the wrong chair, making the wrong choices. Impossible. He knew this was the right thing to do. But as he reached the end of the pile of folders, he had to wonder if that was true.

He'd told the people in that room to take a risk, to go after what they wanted. Had he taken his own advice?

He'd pursued Marnie, yes, but he'd also let her go. If he truly wanted her, what the hell was he doing here?

His assistant dropped off a stack of checks for Jack to sign. He thanked her, then began to scrawl his name across the bottom line. Each one he signed represented a new start for someone, a new chance. And another chance for Jack to make amends.

He paused on the last one. Doug Hendrickson's seed money. Jack held the check for a long time, then reached in his drawer, pulled out one of the dozens of keys stored in a box, and headed out of the office. As he left, he paused by his assistant's desk. "Cancel the rest of my appointments for today. And can you make sure this—" he grabbed a piece of paper and an envelope, then jotted a quick note on the white linen stock "—gets delivered immediately?"

"Sure," she said, then looked up at him. "If you don't mind my saying so, you look a little worried today. Everything okay?"

Jack glanced down at the note, then at the key in his hand. "Not yet. But I hope it will be."

Marnie returned from lunch, expecting the office to be empty. Erica had a doctor's appointment, and Marnie's schedule was clear for the rest of the day. But as she got out of her car, she saw a familiar car parked in Erica's spot, and her mother standing on the stoop. "Ma, what a nice surprise!"

Her mother held up a bag of cookies from a local bakery. "And I brought dessert."

"My favorite. And such a decadent treat after I just had a salad." Marnie unlocked the office door and waved her mother inside. "Let me put on some coffee."

Marnie started the pot brewing, then got them two cups and a plate for the cookies, and set it all up in the reception area. "Thanks for bringing these. This is definitely a chocolate kind of day."

Her mother laughed. "I think that goes for every day."

"True, very true." Marnie grinned, then took a bite of a chocolate peanut butter cup cookie. Heaven melted against her palate. "These are...amazing."

Marnie and her mother ate, drank and chatted for a few minutes, catching up on family gossip. The cookies eased the tension lingering in Marnie's shoulders, a tension brought about by too many late-night thoughts about Jack, and their conversation at Second Chance yesterday.

I'm willing to take the risk that we have something amazing here, something that is stronger than the past. The question is why you don't think so, too. Why you won't take a risk.

Trust and fall. Just the thought caused Marnie's chest to tighten. She reached for another cookie and pushed the thoughts of Jack to the back of her mind. Stubborn, they refused to stay there, and lingered at the edge of her every word.

"Aren't you leaving tonight?" Marnie asked her mother. "For your big weekend in Maine?"

"About that..." Helen toyed with her coffee mug. "I'm not sure I should go."

"What? Why?"

"Because you're not okay with us being together, and the last thing I want to do is make you unhappy. You and your sisters are my world, Marnie." Ma's hand covered hers. Her pale green eyes met Marnie's. "I don't want to see you hurting."

"Ma, you were happy with Dan. He was happy with you. You deserve that."

A small, sad smile crossed Ma's face. "Not at the expense of your happiness."

In that instant, Marnie saw what her actions had cost. Not just herself, but those she loved. Her mother had given up the man she cared about—her second chance at love—to avoid hurting her daughter. Because Marnie had yet to be able to get over the past. She kept wanting to make Jack, and anyone associated with Jack, pay for something that had happened three years ago. Her mother had gotten past it, had moved on and started her life over. Marnie needed to do the same. "Here you are, protecting me, when I was trying to protect you." Marnie shook her head.

"Protect me? From what?"

"From being hurt. I thought if I didn't date Jack and you avoided Dan, that you wouldn't see Jack and think about what happened to Dad. But it's clear Dan makes you happy and that this isn't about the past anymore. It's about your future."

"Oh, honey—"

Marnie gave her mother's hand a squeeze. "You took a risk, and fell in love again—"

"Well, it's probably too soon to say fell in love." But the blush in Ma's cheeks belied that statement.

"And I think that's pretty incredible. Because..." Marnie drew back her hand and dropped her gaze to the cookies. Cookies that hadn't erased the issues, just muted them for a few bites. "Because I've been too terrified to do that myself."

There was the truth. Marnie didn't date because she was terrified of falling in love. It was the one emotion that meant giving up control, letting go. Trusting the other person would catch you.

Ma's face softened. "Marnie, don't let fear keep you from love. Or from Jack."

"I'm not talking about Jack." Or thinking about him.

Or dwelling on him. Except she was, all the time. And wondering if she took a risk on love with him, if she'd find the same happiness her mother had.

I'm willing to take the risk that we have something amazing here, something that is stronger than the past.

She realized she'd become the same thing she saw in her clients all the time, a gun-shy single who wanted love, but did everything she could to avoid a relationship. The matchmaker was terrified of matching herself.

How ironic.

"Jack's a good man, Marnie," Ma said as if reading her daughter's mind, "despite what he did in the past. He's changed, Dan said. Doing business in an entirely new way." Her mother's cell phone lit with an incoming call from Dan. A smile stole across Helen's face. The kind of smile of a woman in love, a woman who had found a man who loved her, too. A gift, Marnie realized, that not everyone found.

"Dan's a good man, too," Marnie said. She picked up the phone and placed it in her mother's palm, closing Ma's fingers over the slim silver body. "Tell him you'll go to Maine with him."

Ma hesitated. "Really?"

Marnie nodded. "He makes you smile, Ma, and that's all that's ever mattered to me."

The smile widened on Ma's face, and her eyes lit with joy. She pressed the button on her phone, and answered the call. Within seconds, Ma was giggling like a schoolgirl, and making plans with Dan. "Okay, sounds good," she said. "I'm looking forward to it, too. See you soon, Dan." Then she said goodbye and tucked the phone back into her purse.

Ma got to her feet and leaned over to give her daughter a warm hug. "You're a good daughter," she whispered, then she drew back and met her daughter's gaze with older, wiser, loving eyes. "Now take your own advice and take a chance on the man who makes you smile, too. A man like Jack, perhaps?"

"I don't know." Marnie hesitated. Jack distracted her, set her off her keel. That couldn't be a good thing, could it?

"If I were you," Ma said, "I'd make a list, just like you make your clients do. Figure out what's most important to you in the man you meet. And then use that instinct of yours to point you in the direction of Mr. Right."

Marnie shook her head. "I don't think it works on me. Too close to the work and all that."

"That's because you haven't tried." Ma wagged a finger at her. "And you never know what awaits around the next bend unless you travel down the road."

CHAPTER ELEVEN

AFTER THE COOKIE and coffee and chat with her mother, Marnie got back to work, instead of acting on her promised resolve to let Jack into her life. Erica returned from her appointment, and paused to hang up her coat, then stow her purse in the closet. When she got to her desk, she glanced across the room at her older sister. "Hey! Are those cookies on your desk?"

Marnie chuckled, and slid the plate in Erica's direction. "Ma stopped by with gifts."

"I thought she'd be halfway to Maine by now."

"She is now. She and I talked about Dan, and I'm cool with them dating. Ma is so happy, and it's nice to see. She deserves it."

Erica nodded. "It sure is. And if her being happy means we get cookies for lunch, then by all means, keep Dan around. Oh, I almost forgot!" Erica jumped up and dashed over to her desk, returning a second later with an envelope. "This came for you today when I was coming in the door. Delivered by messenger, so it must be important." She glanced at her watch. "Okay, I really gotta scoot. I'm supposed to meet with the caterer for our next event. Then I've got a date. You gonna be okay here without my astounding help?"

"Of course." Marnie tapped the envelope on her desk.

Plain, nondescript, nothing more than Marnie's name and address on the front. Probably a thank you from a satisfied client. "Thanks, Erica. Have fun on your date."

Erica's smile winged across her face. "You know me, I always do. And don't forget to have some fun yourself."

Marnie just nodded, then got back to work when Erica left. After a while, she stretched, and noticed the envelope again on the corner of her desk. She undid the flap, then pulled out the card inside.

> *I found something of your dad's at his shop that I think you're going to want to have. Your key should still work.*
> *Jack*

Marnie held on to the card for a long, long time. She turned it over, weighing her options. In the end, curiosity won, driven by the urge to see Jack again. Ever since the conversation with her mother, her thoughts had drifted toward the what-ifs. What if she fell for Jack? What if she kissed him again? What if they took things to the next level? Would she be going around with that same goofy, blissful smile on her face?

The card had been the impetus she needed, like a sign from above that she needed to stop dithering and start acting. Wasn't it about time she found out, instead of sitting on the sidelines, giving everyone else the happy ending she wanted, too? She grabbed her keys and headed across town, her heart in her throat.

In her mind, she kept seeing the four letters of *Jack*. Not *Love, Jack,* or *Thinking of you, Jack* or even *Best Wishes, Jack*. Just *Jack*. She should have been glad he'd left the closing impersonal, business-like. But she wasn't. She wanted more. She wanted him to come right out and say what he was feeling, and then let them take it from there. Even that thought made her heart beat a little faster with anxiety.

God, she really was a mess. But as she got closer to the building, and to seeing Jack, a smile spread across her face and anticipation warmed her veins. She thought of that kiss in the car, the one at the coffee shop, and decided...

Yes, she wanted him. Yes, she'd take this risk. Yes, she would put the past behind her and open her heart.

She wove her way through the city streets until the congestion eased and the roads opened up to an area filled with small office buildings and light industrial complexes. Her father's old building came into view, a squat one-story concrete building with a nondescript storefront and a long, rectangular shape. She sat there for a long moment, staring at the building, memorizing the sign. The Top Notch Printing sign had faded, and the white exterior paint that had once been so pristine had faded to a dingy gray. Weeds had sprung up between the cracks in the parking lot. The tidy building now looked sad, defeated.

It hit her then, hard and fast. She would never again drive up here and see Top Notch Printing on the front façade. Never again see the mailbox her father had painted himself one weekend. Never again walk through the door and hear her father call her name.

In the years since her father passed, no one had rented or bought the building, and it seemed to echo now with emptiness, disuse. Marnie parked, got out of the car, and flipped through the keys on her ring until she got to a brass one. The key had been on her father's ring for decades, and had a worn spot where his thumb had sat, morning after morning, when he opened the building for the day.

She slipped the key into the lock. The lock stuck a bit, then gave way, and the door opened with a creak. Once inside, her hand found the light switch, and the overhead fluorescents sputtered to life, providing a sur-real white glow in the foyer. She stepped past the glass partition that divided the receptionist's desk from the main office. A smile curved across her face. Her father had never had a receptionist, but when the girls came in after school or on the weekends, they'd fought over sitting at that desk and answering the phones, as if it was the best job in the world.

Marnie ran a hand over the old corded desk phone, then let her gaze skip over the desk. Nothing there, or on the counter where her father would leave things for customers to pick up. She took a right, and headed down the hall, toward the big oak door that hadn't been opened in three years.

Her steps stuttered and she looked up at the engraved plaque attached to the oak.

Tom Franklin

That was all, no title, nothing fancy. The guys in the shop had made the sign for him one day, and he'd mounted it with the caveat that they all called him Tom, just like always. He'd been a good boss, almost one of the guys, which had made his employees love him, but had often given them license to slack on produc-tion. Still, every person who had ever worked for her father came to his funeral, a testament to his memory, his lasting relationships with people. Tom had been a good guy, a good boss, and an even better father. Oh, how she missed him.

Marnie reached up, her fingers dancing over the engraved lettering. Then she tugged off the plaque and tucked it in her purse. Doing so left a scar on the door, which Marnie liked. It said Tom had been here, and shouldn't be forgotten.

A long, low creak announced the opening of the front door. Marnie wheeled around, raising her fist with the keys in it. Not much of a defense, but better than nothing. She lowered her fist when she saw a familiar figure enter the building. "Jack. You scared the heck out of me."

"Sorry." He stepped into the foyer, and his features shifted from shadows to light. In the white fluorescents, his eyes seemed even bluer, his hair darker, his jaw line sharper. Her heart started beating double-time. "I wanted to get here before you did, but I was running behind."

She took a step closer to him, letting the smile inside her bubble to the surface. "That's okay. You didn't have to be here. I could have picked this up myself."

He took a step closer, reached up a hand, and cupped her jaw, his gaze soft, tender. "Oh, Marnie, you are so determined to fly solo."

"It's safer that way," she whispered.

"But is it better?"

She shook her head, and tears rushed to her eyes. "No, it's not."

"Then stop doing it," he said. He smiled, then closed the distance between them and kissed her. This kiss was tender, gentle. His hands held her jaw, fingers tangling in her hair. She sighed into the kiss and leaned into Jack.

And it all felt so, so right. So perfect. Falling wasn't so bad, she realized. Not so bad at all.

Finally, Jack drew back, but didn't let her go, not right away. The connection between them tightened, as the threads they had been building began to knit into something real and lasting.

It was as if in that kiss, that moment of surrender, something fundamental had shifted between them. Marnie could feel it charging the air, the space between them. The grin playing on Jack's lips said he felt it, too. From here on out, nothing would be the same. And for the first time in her life, Marnie was ready to get on that roller coaster, but still, fear kept her from saying a word.

"Before we get too distracted, let me show you what I found. I put it on your father's desk." Jack reached past her, which whispered his cologne past her senses, and opened the door to Tom's office, allowing Marnie to enter first.

She took a deep breath, squared her shoulders, then went into the office. The second her feet touched the carpet, she jetted back in time. She hadn't been inside her father's office for years. At least four, maybe more. Once she'd gone off to college, then come home to open her own business, free time had become a rare commodity and her days of playing receptionist with her sisters had ended.

Nothing had changed with the passage of time. The worn black leather chair her father had rescued from a salvage sale still sat behind the simple dark green metal desk he'd painted himself. The bookshelf held a haphazard collection of business books—gifts, mostly—that he'd kept meaning to read and never had. A stack of print samples lay against one wall, and a dish of Tootsie Rolls sat on the corner of the desk, beside a hideous green pottery pen holder that Kat had made for Dad in the third grade. Marnie's throat swelled. "It's been three years and it still seems like I could walk in here and find him at his desk."

Jack put a hand on her shoulder. She leaned into his touch, allowed his stronger, broader shoulders to hold her up. "I'm sorry you lost him," he said. "He was a really nice guy."

"Yeah, he was." She stepped away from Jack's touch, and crossed to a box on the credenza behind the desk. Her name had been written across the top, in the same precise script as the note. Jack's handwriting. She danced a finger across the six letters of her name.

"I came across that when I was cleaning out the office," Jack said. "I thought you'd want to have it. For you and your sisters."

She pried open the cardboard. Instant recognition hit her, along with a teary wave of memories. She reached inside and pulled out the wooden photo frame, still filled with a picture of Dad and his girls, the three of them crowding the space in front of him. Ma had taken the picture, out in front of the building, years and years ago. Kat was about ten, Marnie almost nine and Erica just seven, the three of them wearing goofy smiles and matching pigtails. It wasn't the picture that caught her heart, though, it was the frame.

When her mother had brought home the print from the photo developer, Dad had showed it to Marnie and told her a special picture like this needed a special frame. He'd asked her to help him make one, and she'd leapt at the chance. Her father, who worked too many hours and came home to three girls all anxious for him to hear about school or help with homework or go outside to ride bikes, rarely had time to spend with just one daughter.

"My father and I made this together," she said, the memory slipping from her lips in a soft whisper. "He told the other girls that this was going to be a Dad and Daisy-doo project. Kat and Erica pouted, but Dad stuck to his guns. We went out to the garage, and he and I did everything, from cutting the wood to nailing the pieces together. He taught me how to miter the corners and sand the wood filler until it was smooth. When it was done—" she flipped over the frame and ran her fingers over the letters etched there "—he showed me how to use the woodburner to put our names on it."

And there, as deep and clear as the day she'd done it, were the words *Dad and His Daisy-Doo's Great Project.*

A great project, indeed. The best one, and one of the few things that had been just between her and her dad. Her throat clogged. Her vision blurred. *Oh, Dad.*

"I didn't even know he saved it." But of course he would have. Tom had been a sentimental man, who had held on to nearly every school paper his daughters brought home, framed the weekly drawings, and made a big deal out of every life event. Tears welled in her eyes, clung to her lashes. She clutched the frame to her chest. Solid, warm, it held so many memories. "Thank you."

"You're welcome." He let out a breath, then shifted his weight. His stance changed from commiseration to serious, and she knew this was something she might not want to hear. "I've got some things to tell you, Marnie, about the way I handled your father's business."

"It's okay. It's in the past. He's gone now."

"I know, but...this needs to be said. For both of us." Jack heaved a sigh. His gaze skipped around the room, coming to rest on the visitor's chair, as if he was sitting in it, across from her father again. "When I first met with your father, I came to him under false pretences. I promised him we'd help him. It was the same line we gave all the businesses we worked with. Sometimes, yes, we did help them, but sometimes we just invested and walked away, knowing they'd fail."

"How was that a smart strategy?"

Jack took a seat on the corner of the desk. "There's a lot that goes into a buying decision, you know? Pluses and minuses, current earnings versus future. Your father might not have been great at managing a business, but he was amazing at building customer relationships, and that meant his business had incredible future earning potential. Everybody loved the guy, loved working with him, and he had a great rapport with them. But..."

"But what?"

He heard the caution in Marnie's voice, and knew she was bracing herself for something she didn't want to hear. How he wanted to stop here, to not tell her anything. But the guilt had weighed on him heavy for years, and he couldn't keep seeing Marnie or ask anything more of her if she didn't know who he used to be.

"But there was a bigger company in town who wanted those same customers. They were a current client of my father's, and they had tried to buy your dad's business a few times, but he always refused."

"I vaguely remember something about that. My dad didn't talk about work very often."

"The competitor came to my father and I, asking us to go in, get Tom's business from him and then they could have the customers. There'd be a big bonus for Knight, of course, and a very happy client. At the time I thought it was the right thing to do. I justified it a hun-

dred different ways. Your father was older, ready for retirement. He wasn't much of a businessman. He'd been
talking about getting out of the company, having more
time for himself. So I kept telling myself I was doing
the right thing, that in the end, it was the best choice
for Tom. But..."

Across from him, Marnie had gone cold and still.
"But what?"

"But I liked your father. He was a great guy, like I
said. The kind of guy you'd have a few beers with or
split a pizza with. He was honest and forthright and
nice."

"And trusting."

Jack nodded, hating himself for abusing that trust
years ago. "And trusting."

"So you..." She clutched the frame between her
hands, her knuckles whitening. "You threw him under
the bus, for a bottom line?"

Jack sighed, and ran a hand through his hair. "Yes,
I did all those things. I'm the one that talked to your
father about Knight investing in his company. I'm the
one that promised him we'd be there through thick and
thin. And I'm the one who, in the end, deserted him.
But, Marnie, there's more to it than what you know."

But she had already turned on her heel and headed
out of the office. Before he could follow, she had rushed
out. The door slammed in her wake.

Marnie ran. Her mind tried to process what Jack had
told her, but it wouldn't compute. Jack had fed her father a line of lies. Then let him fail on purpose.

She jerked her keys out of her purse and thumbed the
lock. A bright green pickup truck pulled into the lot.

The color triggered a memory in Marnie, and when the man in the truck got out, she remembered.

Doug Hendrickson, the twenty-something son of Floyd Hendrickson, who owned a rival printing company in Boston. Back in the early days of his business, Marnie's father and Floyd had worked together, helping each other build from the ground up, trading jobs, connections, equipment. Marnie could remember going into her father's shop on the weekends, and sometimes seeing Doug when he came in with his father.

Then Floyd and Tom had a falling out, over what Marnie had no idea, and the two had stopped speaking. They'd become fierce competitors then, each trying to grab their corner of the Boston printing market. She hadn't seen Floyd or his son in years, but she knew Doug's wide, friendly face in a second.

Doug cupped a hand over his brow to block the sun. "Is Jack around? I'm supposed to meet him here, but I'm early."

"You're meeting Jack? Jack Knight?" she said, instead of telling him Jack was right inside.

"Yup. You seen him?" Doug's gaze narrowed and he took a step closer. "Hey, aren't you Tom's daughter? Uh, Kat? Or…"

Marnie worked a smile to her face. "I'm the middle one. Marnie."

"I knew you looked familiar!" He grinned. "What a wicked small world. God, I haven't seen you in years. You're not thinking of reopening your dad's place, are you?"

She shook her head. "No."

The door opened behind her and Jack stepped into the sunshine. Damn. She should have left.

"Hey, Jack!" Doug greeted him with a smile. "Glad to see you. You got my check?"

Marnie jerked her gaze from one man to the other. "Check? What check?"

"Gee, Marnie, I would have thought someone would tell you." Doug put his hands in his back pockets and rocked on his heels. "I'm opening up my own shop. With some funding from my dad and Knight, of course. I met Jack here a few years ago and he set me up with this place and a nudge to go out on my own. This place was perfect because, well, it has all the equipment still. A little dusty, but it works." Then Doug seemed to realize what he'd said and his face sobered. "Sorry, Marnie. I know your dad passed and all, and this is probably hard."

She bit her lip. "Harder than you know. I'm glad you're the one giving this place a second life. I'm sorry if I seem short with you, Doug. It's just been a really tough day."

An ache started deep inside her chest and spread through Marnie, fast, painful, until she wanted to collapse, or run, or both. She had trusted Jack, opened her heart to him, begun to fall for him, and what did it get her? Hurt. Why had she taken that risk?

She spun toward Jack. "You did this?"

"It's complicated, Marnie. Your father—"

The anger and hurt inside her ignited. So many emotions, weeks' worth, really, bubbled to the surface. She'd kept it all tamped down, and now she wanted to explode, regardless of who was there or why. "You don't get to tell me anything more about my father. Or me. Or us. Or anything. Just leave me alone, Jack."

Before he could respond, she climbed into her car, started the engine and spun out of the parking lot. Tears blurred her vision, but she swiped them away and drove hard and fast, away from a huge mistake she'd almost made.

Just when she'd begun to think that Jack Knight was a good man, just when she was about to give him a chance, to trust that the man she'd seen at the gym and the coffee shop and the charity was the real Jack, he did something like this.

Sold the remains of her father's company to his competitor. Just like the vulture she knew he was all along.

CHAPTER TWELVE

HE SHOULD HAVE let her go. She was hurting, and like a wounded animal, Marnie wanted to escape from the person she saw as responsible for her pain. She had left the office, and run for the car, dodging the rain that had started to fall again. Her tires squealed against the pavement, spitting gravel in her wake, and then she was gone.

Jack hesitated for a half a second, shouted a *meet you later* at Doug, then he hopped in his car and wove through the traffic, darting left, right, until he saw her gray sedan ahead. He pulled in behind her, following as she navigated the city, driving against the tide of outbound traffic.

She passed her office, took a left instead of the right that would have brought her to her mother's house, and passed by the exit for her condo. She turned down Charles Street, then entered the Boston Common Parking Garage. Jack found a space a half level above her, then hopped out in time to see Marnie heading up the stairs and out one of the parking kiosks located on the Common. She crossed Charles, then entered the Public Garden. He lingered behind, warring with letting her go and running after her. Hadn't he hurt her enough? Done enough damage?

She headed down the wide sidewalk that led to the pond and the swan boat rides. For a moment, he thought maybe that was her destination—a quiet ride on the tranquil pond while swans and ducks bobbed nearby, begging for crumbs. But her steps slowed, then stopped. She took a seat on a bench. When he saw the hunch in her shoulders, the decision was made for him. He couldn't let her hurt for one more second. Because—

Because he was falling in love with Marnie Franklin. Hell, he'd been falling for her ever since they'd met. It had been those shoes, those impractical, uncomfortable shoes that she'd kicked onto the pavement. A barefoot Cinderella who had enticed him with her fiery hair and her feisty attitude.

She might never forgive him, and might hate him for the rest of her life, but that didn't mean he wasn't going to try to rectify the mess he had made years ago. And maybe, just maybe, he'd find some peace finally. He might not be able to fix this enough to allow him and Marnie to be together, but maybe he could make it better for her.

He sat down on the space beside her on the bench. Her eyes widened with surprise. "Let me guess," he said, gesturing to the statue across from them, "favorite book as a child?"

Instead of answering, she wheeled on him. "Why are you here, Jack?"

"Because I'm trying to explain to you what happened."

"You can't. It's too late." Her eyes misted and she turned away, facing the bronze statues across the walkway. A mother duck, followed by several baby ducks, waddled from the nest to the pond. The statues were a Boston Public Garden landmark, based on the famous

Robert McCloskey book about a family of ducks who had battled city traffic and rushing bicycles to settle in this very park.

"That's the statues based on *Make Way for Ducklings,* right?" he said, because he didn't know what else to say. Far easier to focus on some metal ducks than on climbing the wall between himself and Marnie. "That book's a classic."

"My father gave me the book for Christmas when I was a little girl." She turned to him, the anger still in her green eyes, the hurt rising in the bloom of her cheeks. "Do you want to know why?"

"Yes, I do." He wanted to know everything about Marnie, to memorize every detail of this intriguing woman who named flowers and blushed at the drop of a hat.

She bit her lip, then exhaled, but the tears still shone in her eyes. "Because he said no matter how far any of us girls got from him, he'd always be there to make sure we got home okay. He said he'd be there." She stopped, drawing in a breath, then letting it out again with a powerful sigh. "And he's not there. Not now, not ever again. Because of you and your investment. You ruined our lives, Jack, and because of that, he just gave up and…died."

Jack let out a long breath and rested his arms on his knees. "I know I did. And I'm sorry."

She sat beside him, still as the statues. "I don't understand, Jack. You helped Dot and your friend with the gym, and Luanne and Harvey. Why not my father? Why wasn't he worth you doing the same as you did for them?"

Jack's gaze rested on the bronze ducklings, forever frozen in their quest to tag along after their parents.

"When I went to work for my father, all I wanted was a relationship with him. I thought if I became more like him, then he'd, I don't know, start to respect me. Give me an attaboy at least. So I learned his techniques, and I mastered them, and I went in there with his slash and burn and fire sale approach, and did the old man proud." He let out a curse. "I destroyed companies, sold them off like stolen car parts, and waited for my father to say I'd done a good job. He never did. He found fault where there was none, complained about my soft heart when I didn't pull the funding plug fast enough…" Jack threw up his hands. "There was no winning with that man. He was committed to the bottom line and nothing else."

"And my father's business was part of that bottom line? Because it meant more to your father gone than working?"

"Yes." Saying it to Marnie's face hurt Jack far more than speaking to any of the other business owners in that pile of folders on his desk. He wished he could undo the past, flip a switch, and change everything. "Every time I did what my father asked me to do, I died a little inside. I was so caught up in the thrill of it all, the hunt, the chase, the capture, that I couldn't see the impact on the people, or on me."

Marnie just listened.

"When I met your father, and convinced him to sign with us," Jack said, "I liked him. A lot. And for the first time, I felt like the lowest level of scum there was because I knew I was lying and I knew what was going to happen to his business. I realized what I'd been doing and how it had turned me into someone I didn't even like, someone who lied to get what he wanted, who toed the company line no matter what it cost other people. After that, I quit working for my father. I walked away.

It took me a couple weeks to find another job, and in that time, my dad went to your father and told him there was no hope. Nothing to salvage. He convinced your father to sign over the rest of the company to Knight."

"For pennies on the dollar."

Jack nodded. "By the time my father died and I was in that president's chair, it was too late. Your father had left, and didn't want to come back to the business." He still remembered that morning meeting with Tom Franklin. Regrets had haunted Jack for years. He'd been too late, then and now. Too damned late.

"Wait. You offered my father his company back?"

"His was one of the first I tried to fix. It was the one I wanted most to save, but your dad was done, and I think, glad to be out of the chief's role. He said he loved the industry, but hated the stress of being an owner. He seemed…relieved when I talked to him. I kept trying. I called him every week. But he kept saying no. Said he wanted to be retired and enjoy what time he had left. So I stopped."

"What do you mean, what time he had left?"

"He didn't tell you?"

"Tell me what?"

Oh, hell. Jack hesitated. He looked into Marnie's wide green eyes, and wondered if deep inside her, she already knew what he was going to say. "Your father had a heart condition. He'd known about it for years and I think that's what really drove him to get investors, to try to take some of the stress off his shoulders. After I lost my dad from the same thing, I tried to encourage Tom to get to the doctor, listen to the medical advice, but he was…" Jack's voice trailed off.

"A proud and stubborn man." She let out a gust and jerked to her feet. For a moment, she fumed, then she nodded. "My mother had hinted at this. That my father wanted time, and that she wanted him to have it, too. They knew. But they kept it from us."

"He didn't want you to worry, I'm sure. That's why he kept this all secret."

"Secrets are how people get hurt!" The words exploded out of her and she turned away. "If that's love, I don't want it." She waved a hand, as if brushing away a wasp. "Leave it for everyone else."

He stepped to the side, until she looked up at him again. In her face, he saw the scared woman buried deep inside her. So afraid to trust. That had been him, too, for much too long. No more. If he kept letting fear rule his heart, he was going to miss out on someone incredible. Marnie.

"Marnie, your father *did* love you girls and your mother," Jack said. "He talked about you all like his family was the best in the world. He was trying to protect you all, right or wrong."

After a long moment, realization and acceptance dawned in Marnie's eyes. "Because then we'd want to help. We'd want to talk about it. And if there's one thing my family excelled at, it was not talking about anything." She cursed and shook her head, then wrapped her arms around herself, even though the day was warm. "My whole life was like that. Things happening beyond my control. My father would keep his business worries to himself, play the jokester, the happy guy, my mother would act like everything was perfect, and I'd feel like I was missing something. Something necessary and important."

Jack rose and took her hand in his. "Oh, Marnie, I'm sure they didn't do it to hurt you."

"But it did all the same. And so I grew up, and I decided I'd control everything I could. And do the same for them. Protect my mother from…you. From love, from happiness."

"From me?"

"I was afraid that if she saw you, she'd remember what had happened to my father and be hurt all over again. But really, I was just looking for a reason to stay away from this…risk between us." She bit her lip, and finally admitted the truth to herself. Her father had lost his business and her world had been thrust into chaos. Then he died, and the chaos got worse. Both things happened outside her realm of control, and had only made her dig her heels in further. "I have my lists and my organizational things and it all gives me comfort. I went into a business where I can control people's happy endings. And you know what?" She lifted her gaze to his, and felt tears fill her eyes. "Control hasn't made me any happier. It's made me scared and reluctant. And left me alone. The only match I can't make is the one for myself, because falling in love means letting go. Taking a chance. Trusting another person. And maybe getting hurt in the process."

Jack danced his fingers along her cheek. "And would that be so bad?"

She nodded, scared even now. A part of her wanted to hold on to the comfort of that fear, but she had done that for far too long and ended up running from Jack, running from the truth, and most of all, running from the very thing she wanted.

Love.

Her gaze went to the statues again and she realized her father may not have told her everything, but in his own way, he'd always been trying to prepare his daughters for the end. "Whenever he read *Make Way*

for Ducklings to me, my father used to add an epilogue.
He would tell me that there would be a day when Mr.
and Mrs. Mallard could no longer lead the way for the
ducklings to go to the little island, and that the ducklings shouldn't worry. When that day came, that was
when the ducklings knew it was time for them to spread
their wings and find their own ponds. He said the Mal-
lards knew their ducklings would be fine because they
were smart and strong and would always have the love
of their parents at their backs." The tears slid down her
cheeks now, dropping onto her hands and glistening in
the fading light. What she wouldn't give to hear him tell
that story one more time. "He wanted me and my sisters to find our own ponds and not to worry about him."

"Because you are smart and strong and would always have his love."

She nodded, mute, and the tears fell, and Jack pulled
her into his chest, holding her tight and strong. She
cried for a long time, while pigeons cooed at their feet
and the sun began to set over Boston. She cried and his
heart broke for her, and he wished that of all the things
he had fixed, that he could fix this one most of all.
She cried and Jack envied her father, and hoped Tom
Franklin knew how lucky he had been to have people
love him like this.

Finally, Marnie drew back and swiped at her eyes.
"I'm sorry."

He whisked away one more tear with his thumb, then
cupped her jaw. "Don't be. I'm sorry I didn't stand up
to my father sooner. I'm sorry I wasn't here when your
father needed me most. I'm sorry I didn't tell you all
of this sooner. I'm sorry for a thousand things, and a
thousand more. I've been trying to make it up to the
people my father's company destroyed ever since that

day, because that's the only thing that's going to let me sleep at night. I can't change the past, but hopefully I can make the future better."

"And the Hendricksons? Are they part of that?"

Jack shook his head. "That was all your father's idea. He said he wanted to see the next generation carry the company forward. He told me to contact Doug and tell him that after he got out of college, he could buy the building and its contents for a fair price."

"You held on to that property all this time? Because my father asked you to?"

Jack nodded. "It was the least I could do." He brushed back the lock of hair that had fallen across her brow. "I'm sorry, Marnie."

It was as if he couldn't say the words enough. She was the face of his and his father's selfish decisions, the mirror Jack looked into every day. But telling her and getting the truth on the table, as painful as it had been, had eased the guilt in his chest. For the first time since he'd taken a seat behind his father's desk, he felt as if he'd made a difference. Like he could stop beating himself up for the past.

"I'm glad you're helping Doug. I truly am. I couldn't think of a single soul that would take better care of my father's dream." She gave him a grateful smile. "My mother told me once that my father said he thought you were a good man when he met you."

"Really?" Jack thought of who he had been, and couldn't imagine why Tom would say such a thing.

"One of my father's skills, and I think it's something I inherited and use in my matchmaking, is seeing the best in people. He knew who you were inside, and that's what he saw. That's all he saw. That's why he trusted you."

Jack shook his head. "He must have had a crystal ball into the future because I sure wasn't a good man back then."

"But now, you are."

"Now I'm just trying to make up for the past. Going into the same office, day after day, and trying to undo the damage." He shrugged. "I'm not sure that makes me good or bad, more…doing my job."

She thought about that for a second as a trio of bicyclers sped past them, and a family paused to admire the bronze ducklings. The end of the day brought more people to the park, their voices rising and falling like music.

"You know, you and I are a lot alike," Marnie said. "We both keep taking comfort in the things we know, the things we can rein in, rather than risk it all for the unknown. It's like what you said in your speech about taking chances. It's so much easier, isn't it, not to confront, not to upset? It's just another way to control the situation. When really—" at this, she let out a little laugh "—the one you're really not confronting is yourself. Your own fears and insecurities and worries."

How right she was. He'd gone along with his father's plans for years, because he didn't want to look in the mirror at what he'd been doing. And now, he'd avoided relationships under the guise of not wanting to repeat his family history, rather than looking at the inner demons that kept him from making a commitment. He took her hand, letting his thumb rub across the back of her fingers. Her hand felt good in his, right. "All we can do, as my stepfather says, is to live and learn, and do things different going forward."

She nodded. "That's good advice, Jack. You should take it."

"I'm trying." He grinned.

"I mean it. You should go after the things you're afraid of."

"I'm trying to go after you." He moved closer, reaching for her, but she stepped out of his grasp. "But you keep running away from me."

He reached up and cupped her jaw. He could look at her face every day for the rest of his life. Hear her say his name every morning and night, forever. After his engagement ended, he'd been afraid to risk his heart, and it almost cost him this woman. His stepfather had been right. He had been scared, terrified really, of opening his heart to Marnie because it meant taking a risk that he could turn out like his father. He was done with that. Done with worrying. The best thing to do—

Take the leap anyway.

Jack let his thumb trail along her bottom lip. "All that fire and sass, in one woman. No wonder I can't stop thinking about you."

She shook her head. "Don't, Jack. Don't do this."

She was going to bolt, and he didn't know how to stop that. Despite her words, the woman who brought people together for a living still lived in fear of her own happy ending, held that fear like a security blanket. He and Marnie were so alike, he thought, burned by their pasts and using their jobs to cover for their emotions.

"Don't what, fall in love with you? Too late, Marnie."

She swallowed hard and her eyes widened. "But we've only known each other a few weeks and we barely dated or anything."

"When you know, you know. Doesn't that happen to your clients all the time?"

"Yes, but this is different."

"How?"

"It just is."

He wanted to shake her, to tell her to take down that stubborn wall, and open her heart. But he knew she would do that only when she was ready. Pushing her would only push her away, the last thing he wanted.

His gaze dropped to her lips, trembling with the fear still in her heart, then raised his gaze to her eyes, wide, cautious. "Why are you so terrified of the very thing you tell everyone else in the world to go after?"

"I…I'm not." The lie flushed her cheeks.

"Do you know why my engagement ended?" Jack said. "Tanya left me because she said I was cold. Uninvolved. More interested in work than in our relationship. I lost her, and it was all my fault. I've kept my heart closed off ever since, and worked myself half to death, because I thought that was easier. After all, I learned that art from the master." He let out a gust and a low curse. "The irony of the whole thing is that the one man I never wanted to emulate—my father—was the man I had started to become. I won't make that mistake again, nor am I going to spend one more day alone just because I'm afraid of his legacy. I'm done running from relationships. The question is—" he took her hand again "—are you?"

"You think I'm running? Look in the mirror, Jack. You're afraid, too."

"I'm not afraid of anything, Marnie."

"Really? You told Luanne that you originally went to college to be a writer, then changed your major to business. Why? Because you wanted to make your father happy, not you. You told me yourself that you don't love your job, and you had thought about doing something else, but put it off. My question for you is why are you still working in your father's business if your first love was in writing?"

He scoffed. "Any business person will tell you that a job like that, where the sales and return on investment are almost completely out of your hands, is crazy. I've read the statistics. I know how many writers are making poverty level wages, and how many—"

"Are talking themselves out of it because they're afraid. Stop investing in other people, Jack, and invest in yourself. Then maybe…" Her green eyes met his, soft, vulnerable. "Maybe we can be."

Now she did leave, and this time, he didn't follow her. He sat back down on the bench and watched the bronze ducks marching on a perpetual journey to lands unknown. And wondered how a smart man could be so very, very stupid.

Marnie stood at her thirty-first wedding of the year and tried like heck to look happy. Instead, she suspected she had a face fit for a funeral. She shifted on her heels, slipped a glance at her watch, and bit back a groan. She'd only been here for five minutes. She couldn't make a decent exit until at least thirty minutes had passed.

This was what she worked so hard for, this was the icing on the matchmaking cake, and all the other times, she loved the moment when she saw a couple she had brought together pledge to be together forever. But not this time.

Not since Jack.

She hadn't taken any of his calls. Had refused the flowers he'd sent over. He'd even sent over a first edition of *Make Way for Ducklings,* with a little note inside that said:

The only way to get to the right pond is to take the risk and cross the street. Love, Jack.

That one word had scared her spitless, and she'd tucked the book on a shelf. Erica had just shook her head and not said anything. Marnie buried herself with work, staying late and getting to the office early, making matches until her head hurt.

Late at night, Marnie faced the truth. She was doing it again. Running from her own fears. Rather than confronting them. Was she always going to be like this? Afraid to take the very risks she encouraged her clients to take?

Her sisters and her mother had taken a leap of faith when it came to love. All three were happy as could be, and yet Marnie held back. Why?

She stood to the side of the room, watching couples kiss and dance, while the bride and groom waltzed to their favorite song. Marnie stood alone, flying solo, like she did at most of these events. And feeling miserable.

She had thought, when she walked out of the park, that she was doing the right thing. But really, she had been retreating again. All the emotions of the last few days had overwhelmed her, and brought her deepest fears roaring to the surface. So much for that resolve to go ahead and fall for Jack.

Okay, she had done that. She had fallen for him when he named the daisy Fred. But acting on those feelings—

That terrified her.

Jack had told her that people live and learn and then try to do things different going forward. Thus far, all she'd done was stick to her comfort zone. Which sure as heck wasn't keeping her warm at night.

Wedding guests tapped their forks against their wine glasses, the musical sound signaling to the bride and groom to kiss. Marnie watched Janet and Mark Shalvis giggle, then join hands and kiss each other, happiness exuding from them like perfume.

She thought of the cookie crumbs. The daisies. The picnic. The rain storm. Then she glanced in the mirror on the wall, and saw a woman who made her living creating happy endings, and had to make one of her own.

What was she waiting for? Was she going to be at her thirty-second wedding, still alone, still wishing she'd gone after what she wanted?

The only way to get to the right pond is to take the risk and cross the street.

Even if she didn't know what waited for her on the other side of the street. Or if he still wanted her. But if she didn't do it now, she'd always regret not acting, and Marnie Franklin was tired, dog tired, of living with regrets. If there was one thing her father's death should have taught her, it was that life was short. Her mother had moved on and found happiness in her golden years. What was Marnie waiting for?

Marnie drew in a deep breath, then strode across the room, over to the newly married couple. "Congratulations, you guys. I hate to leave, but I really have to go."

Janet pouted. "Can't you stay a little while longer? I really wanted to introduce you to my mom. And I have three single cousins who could use your help. They're like an advertisement for a lonely hearts club."

How tempting it would be to retreat to that default position of work, instead of risk. For a second Marnie considered it. After all, what difference would a day make?

No. She'd wasted enough days already. She shook her head, and gave Janet a smile. "Have them call me tomorrow. Right now, I have to go. I have a very important match to go make. This one needs…my personal touch."

Janet took her arm and gave it a gentle squeeze. "Good. Because no one knows what's right for another's heart like you do, Marnie."

Even her own, she thought, as she waved goodbye and hurried out the door of the ballroom. The need to be out of here, to be across town, filled her, and she couldn't move fast enough. Her heels slowed her steps, and she kicked them off, gathering them up by the straps and running barefoot across the tiled lobby. Once outside the hotel, she raised her arm to call a cab, when that familiar silver sports car glided into the spot beside her. Dare she hope?

The window on the passenger's side rolled down. "I really need to take you shoe shopping."

The deep voice thrilled her, lifted her heart. He was here. Had he read her mind? Or did he have business inside the hotel? She bent down and saw Jack's familiar grin in the driver's side. "What are you doing here?"

"Rescuing Cinderella before the clock strikes midnight." He leaned over and opened the door. "Do you need a ride to the ball?"

"Actually, I'm leaving the ball," she said, then got inside the car and shut the door. "I was going to go look for the prince. But it appears he already found me. How on earth did you do that in a city this size?"

"Bloodhounds." He grinned. "No, I'm kidding. You wouldn't talk to me. I got desperate. So I bribed your sister to tell me where you were."

"You bribed Erica?"

"It's amazing what kind of information a chocolate cupcake can buy." Jack chuckled, then put the car in gear and pulled away from the curb. A light rain started up, casting the city in shades of gray, and reminding Marnie of that afternoon at the jazz festival. "If you hadn't come out of that wedding, I would have ended up making quite a scene."

"Oh, really? And what would you have done?"

Jack turned into an empty parking lot, stopped the car and turned to Marnie. The rain fell faster now, pattering against the glass, the roof. "I had it all planned out. I was going to march in there, daisies blazing—" he reached into the back seat and pulled out a huge spray of white daisies "—and tell the entire world that I loved you."

Joy bubbled in her heart. Once, those words would have filled her with fear, but no more. She'd almost lost him, and that realization had woken her up to the fact that she took this chance now, or lost it forever. She thumbed in the direction they'd just come. "You know, we can always go back."

"Maybe later," he said, then put the daisies on the dash and pulled her to him. "After I'm done kissing you."

She put up a hand to stop him. "Wait. I need to tell you something first."

He drew back, hurt shimmering in his eyes. "Okay. Shoot."

"I told you that you weren't facing your fears, when really, I should have said that to myself. It's just that finding out all that stuff about my father, just kicked me in the gut, and so I retreated to my default position." She let out a gust. "I buried my head in the sand, which is exactly what I blamed my parents for doing for years. Ironic, isn't it? That I did the very thing I hated?"

"Sometimes we repeat what we know, even if we don't realize it at the time."

"I put off confronting you and told myself it was because I didn't want to hurt my mother. But really, I was afraid of looking at *me*. At how I was starting to feel for you, and how much that scared me. I let what happened with my father be the reason to avoid a relationship with you because I was damned afraid of letting go."

"And now?"

"Now, I…" She paused, and the smile inside her heart made its way to her face. "Now I just ditched my clients because I wanted to run across town and tell you how I felt."

When he returned the smile, that zing ran through her, faster and more powerful than ever before. If she'd been a matchmaker with a client, she would have told the client to listen to that zing. To follow its lead. Because it always led to the heart's true desire. She raised her lips to Jack's. "I'm falling for you, Jack. You came into my life with a bang, and scared the hell out of me because you kept trying to get me to let my hair down, to be spontaneous and fun and *unfettered*." She laughed again at the word he'd used to describe her.

He brushed her bangs away from her eyes with two gentle fingers. "You are damned sexy that way, you know."

"Oh, really?" She grinned, then released her curls from the clip that held them in place. Her crimson hair cascaded onto her shoulders.

Jack let out a groan and pulled her closer. "We have got to get out of this car and behind a closed door, because I am not making the same mistake I did in the parking lot." His blue eyes darkened with desire and he leaned toward her.

"Wait. There's one other thing." She bit her lip and

feigned a serious look. "Before you and I go any further, I wanted to set you up on one more match."

He groaned. "Marnie, I don't want to—"

"She's a redhead. Who loves daisies and has this silly habit of naming the flowers she receives. She loves jazz music and peanut butter cookies, and doesn't mind running through the rain, even if she often wears completely impractical shoes." Jack grinned and leaned in closer, but Marnie put up a finger and pressed it to his lips. "I have to warn you. She's complicated and scared as hell of having her heart broken. But that hasn't stopped this reluctant Cinderella from falling in love with a prince in a silver sports car."

"She sounds like the perfect match for me." The words danced across her fingers, followed by a quick, light kiss. His blue eyes lit with a teasing light. "Though she may want to think twice about getting tangled up with that prince. He's a business owner who's writing a book in his spare time. A guy who has made a few bad choices, but is doing his damnedest to make up for them. And before you get too sold on him, you should know he hates romantic comedies but loves action movies."

She shook her head. "Oh, that could be a deal breaker."

He chuckled, then drew Marnie into his arms. "Maybe we'll just watch the news instead."

"Or," she said, and a delicious smile curved up her face, "we could stay in bed and not watch anything."

"Now *that* sounds like a plan." Jack kissed her then, a deep, sweet, tender kiss that soared in Marnie's veins and filled her heart to the brim. She'd taken the risk, and found exactly what she was looking for on the other side—

Her own happy ending. And as she kissed Jack, the

rain fell and the city rushed by in its busy way. But inside the car, the world had slowed to just the two of them, and the match made in heaven.

Three months later, Marnie and Jack stood at the thirty-second wedding of the year, and by far, the biggest success story for Matchmaking by Marnie. From the minute she walked down the aisle, between Dan and Helen, Jack hadn't been able to take his eyes off Marnie. She had to be the most beautiful bride he'd ever seen. She had her hair down, that riot of red curls a stark, sexy contrast to the simple satin sheath dress she wore.

"I love you, Mrs. Knight," he whispered in her ear. They were sitting at the banquet table, with her sisters on either side, while several dozen of their friends enjoyed the food and music. It had been a simple wedding, held outside on the grassy lawn of a country club, with white table and chair sets and a small portable dance floor. Beside them was a small pond, with a pair of ducks making lazy circles through the water. Nothing too fancy, nothing too elaborate. But a day he knew he'd never forget. The summer sun shone over them, like it was smiling down on their happiness. The weatherman had predicted a storm, but so far, everything had been perfect.

"I love you, too, Mr. Knight." She grinned up at him, and Jack thought there was no sight more beautiful in the world than his wife's smile. *His wife*.

He didn't know if he'd ever get used to how amazing that sounded. He hoped not. He owed that cab driver a thank-you for being a distracted driver that night.

"I hope you're ready to dance tonight," Marnie said.

"Always, if it's with you. Though it depends on what you're wearing for shoes, Cinderella."

She chuckled, then lifted the hem of her dress to reveal very sensible and very comfortable decorated tennis shoes. They'd been studded with rhinestones and featured lacy bows. He laughed. Leave it to Marnie to surprise him, even today.

"I didn't want anything to spoil our wedding," she said.

"Nothing would spoil today, not even a freak winter storm," he said, then kissed her. She curved into his arms, a perfect fit. She had been, from the first moment he met her.

"Oh! My! God! You guys are the cutest couple ever! I can't believe you invited me to your wedding!" The high, loud voice of Roberta carried across the lawn, rising several decibels above the music and the murmurs of the guests. Jack and Marnie laughed, then turned toward her. She sent them a wave, then got back to shimmying her bright pink clad self with Hector on the dance floor. The couple had been together for several months now, and had even talked about marriage. A miracle, in Marnie's eyes.

"I think she's finally found her match," Marnie whispered to Jack. "I owe you big time for introducing them. I was worried I'd never find a match for Roberta."

"Oh, and I intend to collect on that debt. For the rest of our lives." He leaned in and kissed his wife, while guests clinked their glasses and cheered them on.

The DJ shifted the music from a fast song to a slow, romantic song. Couples began to head for the dance floor, including her sisters and their dates. Jack put out his hand for Marnie.

There was a rumble, and an instant later, the skies opened up, dropping a fast, furious, soaking summer storm. Guests began to run toward the building, shriek-

ing in the rain, and hurrying to keep from getting wet.
The dance floor emptied out, the DJ pulled the plug and
dashed inside, yelling that his equipment would be ruined. Even Roberta and Hector made a fast break for
the cover of the country club. But Marnie stayed where
she was with Jack.

"Don't you want to get inside?" he said.

She shook her head, even as little rivers of water ran
down her cheeks and arms. Her dress was already plastered to her body, but she didn't seem to care. "They
say that a little rain is lucky on your wedding day. And
I want to make sure we have all the luck we need."

"Oh, Marnie, we already do," Jack said softly and
drew her to him. "We have each other."

They kissed again, while the ducks quacked and
the rain fell and the world around them dropped away.
They kissed until the storm abated and the sun came
out again, as if giving their marriage its own blessing.
They kissed, and for the first time in their lives, Jack
and Marnie put their faith in happily ever after.

* * * * *

The boy who ruined my life.

Macintyre W. Hudson. A voice whispered from her past. *Everybody just calls me Mac.*

Just like that seven years slipped away and she could see him, Mac Hudson, the most handsome boy ever born, with those dark, laughing eyes, that crooked smile, that silky chocolate hair, too long, falling down over his brow.

Just like that a shiver ran up and down her spine, and Lucy remembered exactly why that boy had ruined her life.

Only he wasn't a boy any longer, but a man.

And she was a woman.

"Macintyre Hudson did not ruin your life," Lucy told herself sternly. "At best he stole a few moments of it."

But what moments those had been, a voice inside her insisted.

SECOND CHANCE WITH THE REBEL

BY
CARA COLTER

First published in Great Britain 2013
by Mills & Boon, an imprint of Harlequin (UK) Limited,
Eton House, 18-24 Paradise Road, Richmond, Surrey TW9 1SR

© Cara Colter 2013

ISBN: 978 0 263 90115 3
ebook ISBN: 978 1 472 00488 8

23-0613

Harlequin (UK) policy is to use papers that are natural, renewable and
recyclable products and made from wood grown in sustainable forests. The
logging and manufacturing processes conform to the legal environmental
regulations of the country of origin.

Printed and bound in Spain
by Blackprint CPI, Barcelona

Cara Colter lives in British Columbia with her partner, Rob, and eleven horses. She has three grown children and a grandson. She is a recent recipient of an *RT Book Reviews* Career Achievement Award in the 'Love and Laughter' category. Cara loves to hear from readers, and you can contact her or learn more about her through her website: www.cara-colter.com

CHAPTER ONE

"HUDSON GROUP, HOW may I direct your call?"

"Macintyre Hudson, please."

Could silence be disapproving? Lucy Lindstrom asked herself. As in, you didn't just cold-call a multi-million-dollar company and ask to speak to their CEO?

"Mr. Hudson is not available right now. I'd be happy to take a message."

Lucy recognized the voice on the other end of the phone. It was that same uppity-accented receptionist who had taken her name and number thirteen times this week.

Mac was not going to talk to her unless he wanted to. And clearly, he did not want to. She had to fight with herself to stay on the line. It would have been so much easier just to hang up the phone. She reminded herself she had no choice. She had to change tack.

"It's an urgent family matter."

"He's not in his office. I'll have to see if he's in the building. And I'll have to tell him who is calling."

Lucy was certain she heard faint suspicion there, as if her voice was beginning to be recognized also, and was on the blocked-caller list.

"You could tell him it's Harriet Freda calling." She picked a fleck of lavender paint off her thumbnail.

"I'll take your number and have him call you back when I locate him."

"It's okay. I'll hold," Lucy said with as much firmness as she could muster.

As she waited, she looked down at the paper in her purple-paint-stained hand. It showed a neat list of names, all of them crossed off save for one.

The remaining name stood out as if it was written in neon tubing.

The boy who ruined my life.

Macintyre W. Hudson. A voice whispered from her past, *Everybody just calls me Mac.*

Just like that, seven years slipped away, and she could see him, Mac Hudson, the most handsome boy ever born, with those dark, laughing eyes, that crooked smile, the silky chocolate hair, too long, falling down over his brow.

Just like that, the shiver ran up and down her spine, and Lucy remembered exactly why that boy had ruined her life.

Only, now he wasn't a boy any longer, but a man.

And she was a woman.

"Macintyre Hudson did not ruin your life," Lucy told herself sternly. "At best he stole a few moments of it."

But what moments those were, a voice inside her insisted.

"Rubbish," Lucy said firmly, but her confidence, not in great supply these days anyway, dwindled. It felt as if she had failed at everything she'd set her hand to, and failed spectacularly.

She had never gone to university as her parents had hoped, but had become a clerk in a bookstore in the neighboring city of Glen Oak, instead.

She had worked up to running her own store, Books and Beans, with her fiancé, but she had eagerly divested herself of the coffee shop and storefront part of the business after their humiliatingly public breakup.

Now, licking her wounds, she was back in her hometown of Lindstrom Beach in her old family home on the shores of Sunshine Lake.

The deeding of the house was charity, plain and simple. Her widowed mother had given it to Lucy before remarrying and moving to California. She said it had been in the Lindstrom family for generations and it needed to stay there.

And even though that was logical, and the timing couldn't have been more perfect, Lucy had the ugly feeling that what her mother really thought was that Lucy wouldn't make it without her help.

"But I have a dream," she reminded herself firmly, shoring herself up with that before Mac came on the line.

Despite her failures, over the past year Lucy had developed a sense of purpose. And more important, she felt *needed* for the first time in a long time.

It bothered Lucy that she had to remind herself of that as she drummed her fingers and listened to the music on the other end of the phone.

The song, she realized when she caught herself humming along, was one about a rebel and had always been the song she had associated with Mac. It was about a boy who was willing to risk all but his heart.

That was Macintyre Hudson to a *T*, so who could imagine the former Lindstrom Beach renegade and unapologetic bad boy at the helm of a multimillion-dollar company that produced the amazingly popular Wild Side outdoor products?

Unexpectedly, the music stopped.

"Mama?"

Mac's voice was urgent and worried. It had deepened, Lucy was sure, since the days of their youth, but it had that same gravelly, sensuous edge to it that had always sent tingles up and down her spine.

Now, when she most needed to be confident, was not the time to think of the picture of him on his website, the one that had dashed her hopes that maybe he had gotten heavy or lost all his hair in the years that had passed.

But think of it she did. No boring head-and-shoulders shot in a nice Brooks Brothers suit for the CEO of Hudson Group.

No, the caption stated the founder of the Wild Side line was demonstrating the company's new kayak, Wild Ride. He was on a raging wedge of white water that funneled between rocks. Through flecks of foam, frozen by the camera, Macintyre Hudson had been captured in all his considerable masculine glory.

He'd been wearing a life jacket, a Wild Side product that showed off the amazing broadness of his shoulders, the powerful muscle of sun-bronzed arms gleaming with water. More handsome than ever, obviously in his element, he'd had a look in his devil-dark eyes, a cast to his mouth and a set to his jaw that was one of fierce concentration and formidable determination.

Maybe he didn't have any hair. He'd been wearing a helmet in the photo.

"Mama?" he said again. "What's wrong? Why didn't you call on my private line?"

Lucy had steeled herself for this. Rehearsed it. In her mind she had controlled every facet of this conversation.

But she had not planned for the image that materialized out of her memory file, that superimposed itself above the image of him in the kayak.

A younger Mac Hudson pausing as he lifted himself out of the lake onto the dock, his body sun-browned and perfect, water sluicing off the rippling smooth lines of his muscles, looking up at her, with laughter tilting the edges of his ultra-sexy eyes.

Do you love me, Lucy Lin?

Never *I love you* from him.

The memory hardened her resolve not to be in any way vulnerable to him. He was an extraordinarily handsome man, and he used his good looks in dastardly ways, as very handsome men were well-known to do.

On the other hand, her fiancé, James Kennedy, had been homely and bookish and had still behaved in a completely dastardly manner.

All of which explained why romance played no part in her brand-new dreams for herself.

Fortified with that, Lucy ordered herself not to stammer. "No, I'm sorry, it isn't Mama Freda."

There was a long silence. In the background she could hear a lot of noise as if a raucous party was going on.

When Mac spoke, she took it as a positive sign. At least he hadn't hung up.

"Well, well," he said. "Little Lucy Lindstrom. I hope this is good. I'm standing here soaking wet."

"At work?" she said, surprised into curiosity.

"I was in the hot tub with my assistant, Celeste." His tone was dry. "What can I do for you?"

Don't pursue it, she begged herself, but she couldn't help it.

"You don't have a hot tub at work!"

"You're right, I don't. And no Celeste, either. What we have is a test tank for kayaks where we can simulate a white-water chute."

Lucy had peeked at their website on and off over the years.

The business had started appropriately enough, with Mac's line of outdoor gear. He was behind the name brand that outdoor enthusiasts coveted: Wild Side. First it had been his canoes. It had expanded quickly into kayaks and then accessories, and now, famously, into clothing.

All the reckless abandon of his youth channeled into huge success, and he was still having fun. Who tested kayaks at work?

But Mac had always been about having fun. Some things just didn't change.

Though he didn't sound very good-humored right now. "I'm wet, and the kayak didn't test out very well, so this had better be good."

"This is important," she said.

"What I was doing was important, too." He sighed, the sigh edged with irritation. "Some things just don't change, do they? The pampered doctor's daughter, the

head of student council, the captain of the cheerlead-
ing squad, used to having her own way."

That girl, dressed in her designer jeans, with hun-
dred-dollar highlights glowing in her hair, looked at her
from her past, a little sadly.

Mac's assessment was so unfair! For the past few
years she had been anything but pampered. And now
she was trying to turn the Books part of Books and
Beans into an internet business while renting canoes
off her dock.

She was painting her own house and living on maca-
roni and cheese. She hadn't bought a new outfit for over
a year, socking away every extra nickel in the hope that
she could make her dream a reality.

And that didn't even cover all the things she was
running next door to Mama Freda's to do!

She would have protested except for the inescap-
able if annoying truth: she *had* told a small lie to get
her own way.

"It was imperative that I speak to you," she said
firmly.

"Hmmm. Imperative. That has a rather regal sound
to it. A princess giving a royal command."

He was insisting on remembering who she had been
before he'd ruined her life: a confident, popular honor
student who had never known trouble and never done a
single thing wrong. Or daring. Or adventurous.

The young Lucy Lindstrom's idea of a good time,
pre-Mac, had been getting the perfect gown for prom,
and spending lazy summer afternoons on the deck with
her friends, painting each other's toenails pink. Her idea

of a great evening had been sitting around a roaring bonfire, especially if a sing-along started.

Pre-Mac, the most exciting thing that had ever happened to her was getting the acceptance letter from the university of her choice.

"Pampered, yes," Mac went on. "Deceitful, no. You are the last person I would have ever thought would lower yourself to deceit."

But that's where he was dead wrong. He had brought out the deceitful side in her before.

The day she had said goodbye to him.

Hurt and angry that he had not asked her to go with him, to hide her sense of inconsolable loss, she had tossed her head and said, "I could never fall for a boy like you."

When the truth was she already had. She had been so crazy in love with Mac that it had felt as though the fire that burned within her would melt her and everything around her until there was nothing left of her world but a small, dark smudge.

"I needed to talk to you," she said, stripping any memory of that summer and those long, heated days from her voice.

"Yes. You said. Imperative."

Apparently he had honed sarcasm to an art.

"I'm sorry I insinuated I was Mama Freda."

"Insinuated," he said silkily. "So much more palatable than lying."

"I had to get by the guard dog who answers your phone!"

"No, you didn't. I got your messages."

"Except the one about needing to speak to you personally?"

"Nothing to talk about." His voice was chilly. "I've got all the information you gave. A Mother's Day Gala in celebration of Mama Freda's lifetime of good work. A combination of her eightieth birthday and Mother's Day. Fund-raiser for all her good causes. She knows about the gala and the fund-raiser but has no idea it's honoring her. Under no circumstances is she to find out."

Lucy wondered if she should be pleased that he had obviously paid very close attention to the content of those messages.

Actually, the fund-raiser was for Lucy's good cause, but Mama Freda was at the very heart of her dream.

At the worst point of her life, she had gone to Mama Freda, and those strong arms had folded around her.

"When your pain feels too great to bear, *liebling,* then you must stop thinking of yourself and think of another."

Mama had carried the dream with Lucy, encouraging her, keeping the fire going when it had flickered to a tiny ember and nearly gone out.

Now, wasn't it the loveliest of ironies that Mama was one of the ones who would benefit from her own advice?

"Second Sunday of May," he said, his tone bored, dismissive, "black-tie dinner at the Lindstrom Beach Yacht Club."

She heard disdain in his voice and guessed the reason. "Oh, so that's the sticking point. I've already had a hundred people confirm, and I'm expecting a few more to trickle in over the next week. It's the only place big enough to handle that kind of a crowd."

"I remember when I wasn't good enough to get a job busing tables there."

"Get real. You never applied for a job busing tables at the yacht club."

Even in his youth, Mac, in his secondhand jeans, one of a string of foster children who had found refuge at Mama's, had carried himself like a king, bristling with pride and an ingrained sense of himself. He took offense at the slightest provocation.

And then hid it behind that charming smile.

"After graduation you had a job with the town, digging ditches for the new sewer system."

"Not the most noble work, but honest," he said. "And real."

So, who are you to be telling me to get real? He didn't say it, but he could have.

Noble or not, she could remember the ridged edges of the sleek muscles, how she had loved to touch him, feel his wiry strength underneath her fingertips.

He mistook her silence for judgment. "It runs in my family. My dad was a ditchdigger, too. They had a nickname for him. Digger Dan."

She felt the shock of that. She had known Mac since he had come to live in the house next door. He was fourteen, a year older than she was. When their paths crossed, he had tormented and teased her, interpreting the fact she was always tongue-tied in his presence as an example of her family's snobbery, rather than seeing it for what it was.

Intrigue. Awe. Temptation. She had never met anyone like Mac. Not before or since. Ruggedly independent. Bold. Unfettered by convention. Fearless. She remembered seeing him glide by her house, only four-teen, solo in a canoe heavily laden with camping gear.

She would see his campfire burning bright against the night on the other side of the lake. It was called the wild side of the lake because it was undeveloped crown land, thickly forested.

Sometimes Mac would spend the whole weekend over there. Alone.

She couldn't even imagine that. Being alone over there with the bears.

The week she had won the spelling bee he had been kicked out of school for swearing.

She got a little Ford compact for her sixteenth birth-day, while he bought an old convertible and stripped the engine in the driveway, then stood down her father when he complained. While she was painting her toe-nails, he was painstakingly building his own cedar-strip canoe in Mama's yard.

But never once, even in that summer when she had loved him, right after her own graduation from high school, had Mac revealed a single detail about his life before he had arrived in foster care in Lindstrom Beach.

Was it the fact that he had so obviously risen above those roots that made him reveal that his father had been nicknamed Digger Dan? Or had he changed?

She squashed that thing inside her that felt ridicu-lously and horribly like hope by saying, proudly, "I don't really care if you come to the gala or not."

She told herself she was becoming hardened to re-jection. All the people who really mattered to Mama—except him—had said they would come. But her own mother had said she would be in Africa on safari at that time and many people from Lucy's "old" life, her high-school days, had not answered yet. Those who had, had answered no.

There was silence from Mac, and Lucy allowed herself pleasure that she had caught him off guard.

"And I am sorry about messing up *your* Mother's Day."

"What do you mean, *my* Mother's Day?" His voice was guarded.

That had always been the problem with Mac. The insurmountable flaw. He wouldn't let anyone touch the part of him that *felt*.

"I chose Mother's Day because it was symbolic. Even though Mama Freda has never been a biological mother, she has been a mother to so many. She epitomizes what motherhood is."

That was not the full truth. The full truth was that Lucy found Mother's Day to be unbearably painful. And she was following Mama Freda's own recipe for dealing with pain.

"I don't care what day you chose!"

"Yes, you do."

"It's all coming back now," he said sardonically. "Having a conversation with you is like crossing a minefield."

"You feel as if Mother's Day belongs to you and Mama Freda. And I've stolen it."

"That's an interesting theory," he said, a chill in his voice warning her to stop, but she wasn't going to. Lucy was getting to him and part of her liked it, because it had always been hard to get to Mac Hudson. It might seem as if you were, but then that devil-may-care grin materialized, saying *Gotcha, because I don't really care.*

"Every Mother's Day," she reminded him quietly, "you outdo yourself. A stretch limo picks her up. She flies somewhere to meet you. Last year Engelbert Humperdinck in concert in New York. She wore the corsage until it turned brown. She talked about it for days after. Where you took her. What you ate. Don't tell me it's not your day. And that you're not annoyed that I chose it."

"Whatever."

"Oh! I recognize that tone of voice! Even after all this time! Mr. Don't-Even-Think-You-Know-Me."

"You don't. I'll put a check in the mail for whatever cause she has taken up. I think you'll find it very generous."

"I'm sure Mama will be pleased by the check. She probably will hardly even notice your absence, since all the others are coming. Every single one. Mama Freda has fostered twenty-three kids over the years. Ross Chillington is clearing his filming schedule. Michael Boylston works in Thailand and he's coming. Reed Patterson is leaving football training camp in Florida to be here."

"All those wayward boys saved by Mama Freda." His voice was silky and unimpressed.

"She's made a difference in the world!"

"Lucy—"

She hated it that her name on his lips made her feel more frazzled, hated it that she could remember leaning toward him, quivering with wanting.

"I'm not interested in being part of Lindstrom Beach's version of a TV reality show. What are you planning after your black-tie dinner? No, wait. Let me guess. Each of Mama's foster children will stand up and give a testimonial about being redeemed by her love."

Ouch. That was a little too close to what she did have planned. Did he have to make it sound cheap and smarmy instead of uplifting and inspirational?

"Mac—"

"Nobody calls me Mac anymore," he said, a little harshly.

"What do they call you?" She couldn't imagine him being called anything else.

"Mr. Hudson," he said coolly.

She doubted that very much since, she could still hear a raucous partylike atmosphere unfolding behind him.

It occurred to her she would like to hang up on him. And she was going to, very shortly.

"Okay, then, Mr. Hudson," she snapped, "I've already told you I don't care if you don't come. I know it's way too much to ask of you to take a break from your important and busy schedule to honor the woman who took you in and pulled you back from the brink of disaster. Way too much."

Silence.

"Still, I know how deeply you care about her. I know it's you who has been paying some of her bills."

He sucked in his breath, annoyed that she knew that.

She pushed on. "Aside from your Mother's Day tradition, I know you took her to Paris for her seventy-fifth birthday."

"Lucy, I'm dripping water on the floor and shivering, so if you could hurry this along."

She really had thought she could get through her life

without seeing him again. It had been a blessing that he came back to Lindstrom Beach rarely, and when he had, she had been away.

Because how could she look at him without remembering? But then hadn't she discovered you could remember, regardless?

Once, a long, long time ago, she had tried, with a desperation so keen she could almost taste its bitterness on her tongue, to pry his secrets from him. Lying on the sand in the dark, the lake's night-blackened waters lapping quietly, the embers of their fire burning down, she had asked him to tell her how he had ended up in foster care at Mama Freda's.

"I killed a man," he whispered, and then into her shocked silence, he had laughed that laugh that was so charming and distracting and sensual, that laugh that hid everything he really was, and added, "With my bare hands."

And then he had tried to divert her with his kisses that burned hotter than the fire.

But he had been unable to give her the gift she needed most: his trust in her.

And that was the real reason she had told him she could never love a boy like him. Because, even in her youth, she had recognized that he held back something essential of himself from her, when she had held back nothing.

If he had chosen to think she was a snob looking down her nose at the likes of him, after all the time they had spent together that summer, then that was his problem.

Still, just thinking of those forbidden kisses of so

many years ago sent an unwanted shiver down her spine. The truth was nobody wanted Mac to come back here less than she did.

"I didn't phone about Mama's party. I guess I thought I would tell you this when you came. But since you're not going to—"

"Tell me what?"

She had to keep on track, or she would be swamped by these memories.

"Mac—" she remembered, too late, he didn't want to be called that and plunged on "—something's wrong."

"What do you mean?"

"You knew Mama Freda lost her driver's license, didn't you?"

"No."

"She had a little accident in the winter. Nothing serious. She slid through a stop sign and took out Mary-Beth McQueen's fence and rose bed."

"Ha. I doubt if that was an accident. She aimed."

For a moment, something was shared between them. The rivalry between Mama and Mary-Beth when it came to roses was legendary. But the moment was a flicker, nothing more.

All business again, he said, "But you said it wasn't serious?"

"Nonetheless, she had to see a doctor and be retested. They revoked her license."

"I'll set her up an account at Ferdinand's Taxi."

"I don't mind driving her. I like it actually. My concern was that before the retesting I don't think she'd been to a doctor in twenty years."

"Thirty," he said. "She had her 'elixir.'"

Lucy was sure she heard him shudder. It was funny to think of him being petrified of a little homemade potion. The Mac of her memory had been devil-may-care and terrifyingly fearless. From the picture on his website, that much had not changed.

"I guess the elixir isn't working for her anymore," Lucy said carefully. "I drive her now. She's had three doctors' appointments in the last month."

"What's wrong?"

"According to her, nothing."

Silence. She understood the silence. He was wondering why Mama Freda hadn't told him about the driver's license, the doctor's appointments. He was guessing, correctly, that she would not want him to worry.

"It probably *is* nothing," he said, but his voice was uneasy.

"I told myself that, too. I don't want to believe she's eighty, either."

"There's something you aren't telling me."

Scary, that after all these years, and over the phone, he could do that. Read her. So, why hadn't he seen through her the only time it really mattered?

I could never fall for a boy like you.

Lucy hesitated, looked out the open doors to gather her composure. "I saw a funeral-planning kit on her kitchen table. When she noticed it was out, she shoved it in a drawer. I think she was hoping I hadn't seen it."

What she didn't tell him was that before Mama had shoved the kit away she had been looking out her window, her expression uncharacteristically pensive.

"Will my boy ever come home?" she had whispered.

All those children, and only one was truly her boy.

Lucy listened as Mac drew in a startled breath, and then he swore. Was it a terrible thing to love it when someone swore? But it made him the *old* Mac. And it meant she had penetrated his guard.

"That's part of what motivated me to plan the celebration to honor her. I want her to know—" She choked. "I want her to know how much she has meant to people before it's too late. I don't want to wait for a funeral to bring to light all the good things she's done and been."

The silence was long. And then he sighed.

"I'll be there as soon as I can."

"No! Wait—

But Mac was gone, leaving the deep buzz of the dial tone in Lucy's ear.

CHAPTER TWO

"Well, that went well," Lucy muttered as she set down the phone.

Still, there was no denying a certain relief. She had been carrying the burden of worrying about Mama Freda's health alone, and now she shared it.

But with Mac? He'd always represented the loss of control, a visit to the wild side, and now it seemed nothing had changed.

If he had just come to the gala, Lucy could have maintained her sense of control. She had been watching Mama Freda like a hawk since the day she'd heard, *Will my boy ever come home?*

Aside from a nap in the afternoon, Mama seemed as energetic and alert as always. If Mama had received bad news on the health front, Lucy's observations of her had convinced her that the prognosis was an illness of the slow-moving variety.

Not the variety that required Mac to drop everything and come now!

The Mother's Day celebration was still two weeks away. Two weeks would have given Lucy time.

"Time to what?" she asked herself sternly.

Brace herself. Prepare. Be ready for him. But she already knew the uncomfortable truth about Macintyre Hudson. There was no preparing for him. There was no getting ready. He was a force unto himself, and that force was like a tornado hitting.

Lucy looked around her world. A year back home, and she had a sense of things finally falling into place. She was taking the initial steps toward her dream.

On the dining-room table that she had not eaten at since her return, there were donated items that she was collecting for the silent auction at the Mother's Day Gala.

There were the mountains of paperwork it had taken to register as a charity. Also, there was a photocopy of the application she had just submitted for rezoning, so that she could have Caleb's House here, and share this beautiful, ridiculously large house on the lake with young women who needed its sanctuary.

One of her three cats snoozed in a beam of sunlight that painted the wooden floor in front of the old river-rock fireplace golden. A vase of tulips brought in from the yard, their heavy heads drooping gracefully on their slender stems, brightened the barn-plank coffee table. A book was open on its spine on the arm of her favorite chair.

There was not a hint of catastrophe in this well-ordered scene, but it hadn't just happened. You had to work on this kind of a life.

In fact, it seemed the scene reflected that she had finally gotten through picking up the pieces from the last time.

And somehow, *last time* did not mean her ended engagement to James Kennedy.

No, when she thought of her world being blown apart, oddly it was not the front-page picture of her fiancé, James, running down the street in Glen Oak without a stitch on that was forefront in her mind. No, forefront was a boy leaving, seven years ago.

The next morning, out on her deck, nestled into a cushioned lounge chair, Lucy looked out over the lake and took a sip of her coffee. Despite the fact the sun was still burning off the early-morning chill, she was cozy in her pajamas under a wool plaid blanket.

The scent of her coffee mingled with the lovely, sugary smell of birch wood burning. The smoke curled out of Mama Freda's chimney and hung in a wispy swirl in the air above the water in front of Mama's cabin.

Birdsong mixed with the far-off drone of a plane.

What exactly did *I'll be there as soon as I can* mean?

"Relax," she ordered herself.

In a world like his, he wouldn't be able just to drop everything and come. It would be days before she had to face Macintyre Hudson. Maybe even a week. His website said his company had done 34 million dollars in business last year.

You didn't just walk away from that and hope it would run itself.

So she could focus on her life. She turned her attention from the lake, and looked at the swatch of sample paint she had put up on the side of the house.

She loved the pale lavender for the main color. She thought the subtle shade was playful and inviting, a color that she hoped would welcome and soothe the young girls and women who would someday come here when she had succeeded in transforming all this into Caleb's House.

Today she was going to commit to the color and order the paint. Well, maybe later today. She was aware of a little tingle of fear when she thought of actually buying the paint. It was a big house. It was natural to want not to make a mistake.

My mother would hate the color.

So maybe instead of buying paint today, she would fill a few book orders, and work on funding proposals for Caleb's House in anticipation of the rezoning. Several items had arrived for the silent auction that she could unpack. She would not give the arrival of Mac one more thought. Not one.

The drone of the plane pushed back into her awareness, too loud to ignore. She looked up and could see it, red and white, almost directly overhead, so close she could read the call numbers under the wings. It was obviously coming in for a landing on the lake.

Lucy watched it set down smoothly, turning the water, where it shot out from the pontoons, to silvery sprays of mercury. The sound of the engine cut from a roar to a purr as the plane glided over the glassy mirror-calm surface of the water.

Sunshine Lake, located in the rugged interior of British Columbia, had always been a haunt of the rich, and sometimes the famous. Lucy's father had taken delight in the fact that once, when he was a teenager, the queen had stayed here on one of her visits to Canada. For a while the premier of the province had had a summer house down the lake. Pierre LaPontz, the famous goalie for the Montreal Canadiens, had summered here with friends. Seeing the plane was not unusual.

It became unusual when it wheeled around and taxied back, directly toward her.

Even though she could not see the pilot for the glare of the morning sun on the windshield of the plane, Lucy knew, suddenly and without a shade of a doubt, that it was him.

Macintyre Hudson had landed. He had arrived in her world.

The conclusion was part logic and part instinct. And with it came another conclusion. That nothing, from here on in, would go as she expected it. The days when choosing a paint color was the scariest thing in her world were over.

Lucy had thought he might show up in a rare sports car. Or maybe on an expensive motorcycle. She had even considered the possibility that he might show up, chauffeured, in the white limo that had picked up Mama Freda last Mother's Day.

Take that, Dr. Lindstrom.

She watched the plane slide along the lake to the old dock in front of Mama Freda's. The engines cut and the plane drifted.

And then, for the first time in seven years, she saw him.

Macintyre Hudson slid out the door onto the pontoon, expertly threw a rope over one of the big anchor posts on the dock and pulled the plane in.

The fact he could pilot a plane made it more than evident he had come into himself. He was wearing mirrored aviator sunglasses, a leather jacket and knife-creased khakis. But it was the way he carried himself, a certain sureness of movement on the bobbing water, that radiated confidence and strength.

Something in her chest felt tight. Her heart was beating too fast.

"Not bald," she murmured as the sun caught on the luscious dark chocolate of his hair. It was a guilty pleasure, watching him from a distance, with him unaware of being watched. He had a powerful efficiency of motion as he dealt with mooring the plane.

He was broader than he had been, despite all the digging of ditches. All the slenderness of his youth was gone, replaced with a kind of mouthwatering solidness, the build of a mature man at the peak of his power.

He looked up suddenly and cast a look around, frowning slightly as if he was aware he was being watched.

Crack.

The sound was so loud in the still crispness of the morning that Lucy started, slopped coffee on her pajamas. Thunder?

No. In horror Lucy watched as the ancient post of Mama Freda's dock, as thick as a telephone pole, snapped cleanly, as if it was a toothpick. As she looked on helplessly, Mac saw it coming and moved quickly.

He managed to save his head, but the falling post caught him across his shoulder and hurled him into the water. The post fell in after him.

A deathly silence settled over the lake.

Lucy was already up out of her chair when Mac's head reemerged from the water. His startled, furious curse shattered the quiet that had reasserted itself on the peaceful lakeside morning.

Lucy found his shout reassuring. At least he hadn't been knocked out by the post, or been overcome by the freezing temperatures of the water.

Blanket clutched to her, Lucy ran on bare feet across the lawns, then through the ancient ponderosa pines that surrounded Mama's house. She picked her way swiftly across the rotted decking of the dock.

Mac was hefting himself onto the pontoon of the plane. It was not drifting, thankfully, but bobbing co-operatively just a few feet from the dock.

"Mac!" Lucy dropped the blanket. "Throw me the rope!"

He scrambled to standing, found the rope and turned to look at her. Even though he had to be absolutely freezing, there was a long pause as they stood looking at one another.

The sunglasses were gone. Those dark, melted-chocolate eyes showed no surprise, just lingered on her, faintly appraising, as if he was taking inventory.

His gaze stayed on her long enough for her to think, *He hates my hair.* And *Oh, for God's sake, am I in my Winnie-the-Pooh pajamas?*

"Throw the damn rope!" she ordered him.

Then the thick coil of rope was flying toward her. The throw was going to be slightly short. But if she leaned just a bit, and reached with all her might, she knew she could—

"No!" he cried. "Leave it."

But it was too late. Lucy had leaned out too far. She tried to correct, taking a hasty step backward, but her momentum was already too far forward. Her arms windmilled crazily in an attempt to keep her balance.

She felt her feet leave the dock, the rush of air on her skin, and then she plunged into the lake. And sank, the weight of the soaked flannel pajamas pulling her down. Nothing could have prepared her for the cold as the gray water closed over her head. It seized her; her whole body went taut with shock. The sensation was of burning, not freezing. Her limbs were paralyzed instantly.

In what seemed to be slow motion, her body finally bobbed back to the surface. She was in shock, too numb even to cry out. Somehow she floundered, her limbs heavy and nearly useless, to the dock. It was too early in the year for a ladder to be out, but since Mama no longer fostered kids she didn't put out a ladder—or maintain the dock—anyway.

Lucy managed to get her hands on the dock's planks, and tried to pull herself up. But there was a terrifying lack of strength in her arms. Her limbs felt as if they were made of Jell-O, all a-jiggle and not quite set.

"Hang on!"

Even her lips were numb. The effort it took to speak was tremendous.

"No! Don't." She forced the words out. They sounded weak. Her mind, in slow motion, rationalized there was no point in them both being in the water. His limbs would react to the cold water just as hers were doing. And he was farther out. In seconds, Mac would be help-less, floundering out beyond the dock.

She heard a mighty splash as Mac jumped back into the water. She tried to hang on, but she couldn't feel her fingers. She slipped back in, felt the water ooze over her head.

Lucy had been around water her entire life. She had a Bronze Cross. She could have been a lifeguard at the Main Street Beach if her father had not thought it was a demeaning job. She had never been afraid of water.

Now, as she slipped below the surface, she didn't feel terrified, but oddly resigned. They were both going to die, a tragically romantic ending to their story—after all these years of separation, dying trying to save one another.

And then hands, strong, sure, were around her waist, lifting her. Her head broke water and she sputtered. She was unceremoniously shoved out of the water onto the rough boards of the dock.

Lucy dangled there, her elbows underneath her chest, her legs hanging, without the strength even to lift her head. His hand went to her bottom, and he gave her one more shove—really about as unromantic as it could get—and she lay on the dock, gasping, sobbing, coughing.

Mac's still in the water.

She squirmed around to look, but he didn't need her. His hands found the dock and he pulled himself to safety.

They lay side by side, gasping. Slowly she became aware that his nose was inches from her nose.

She could see drops of water beaded on the sooty clumps of his sinfully thick lashes. His eyes were glorious: a brown so dark it melted into black. The line of his nose was perfect, and faint stubble, twinkling with water droplets, highlighted the sweep of his cheekbones, the jut of his jaw.

Her eyes moved to the sensuous curve of his lips, and she felt sleepy and drugged, the desire to touch them with her own pushing past her every defense.

"Why, little Lucy Lindstrom," he growled. "We have to stop meeting like this."

All those years ago it had been her capsized canoe that had brought them—just about the most unlikely of loves, the good girl and the bad boy—together.

A week after graduation, having won all kinds of awards and been voted Most Likely to Succeed by her class, she realized the excitement was suddenly over. All her plans were made; it was her last summer of "freedom," as everybody kept kiddingly saying.

Lucy had taken the canoe out alone, something she never did. But the truth was, in that gap of activity something yawned within her, empty. She had a sense of her own life getting away from her, as if she was falling in with other people's plans for her without really ever asking herself what *she* wanted.

A storm had blown up, and she had not seen the log hiding under the surface of the water until it was too late.

Mac had been over on the wild side, camping, and he had seen her get into trouble. He'd already been in his canoe fighting the rough water to get to her before she hit the log.

He had picked her out of the water, somehow not capsizing his own canoe in the process, and taken her to his campsite to a fire, to wait until the lake calmed down to return her to her world.

But somehow she had never quite returned to her world. Lucy had been ripe for what he offered, an escape from a life that had all been laid out for her in a predictable pattern that there, on the side of the lake with her rescuer, had seemed like a form of death.

In all her life, it seemed everyone—her parents, her friends—only saw in her what they wanted her to be. And that was something that filled a need in them.

And then Mac had come along. And effortlessly he had seen through all that to what was real. Or so it had seemed.

And the truth was, soaking wet, gasping for air on a rotting dock, lying beside Mac, Lucy felt now exactly as she had felt then.

As if her whole world shivered to life.

As if black and white became color.

It had to be near-death experiences that did that: sharpened awareness to a razor's edge. Because she was so aware of Mac. She could feel the warmth of the breath coming from his mouth in puffs. There was an aura of power around him that was palpable, and in her weakened state, reassuring.

With a groan, he put his hands on either side of his chest and lifted himself to kneeling, and then quickly to standing.

He held out his hand to her, and she reached for it and he pulled her, his strength as easy as it was electrifying, to her feet.

Mac scooped the blanket from the dock where she had dropped it, shook it out, looped it around her shoulders and then his own, and then his arms went around her waist and he pulled her against the freezing length of him.

"Don't take this personally," he said. "It's a matter of survival, plain and simple."

"Thank you for clarifying," she said, with all the dignity her chattering teeth would allow. "You needn't have worried. I had no intention of ravishing you. You are about as sexy as a frozen salmon at the moment."

"Still getting in the last shot, aren't you?"

"When I can."

Cruelly, at that moment she realized a sliver of warmth radiated from him, and she pulled herself even closer to the rock-hard length of his body.

Their bodies, glued together by freezing, wet clothing, shook beneath the blanket. She pressed her cheek hard against his chest, and he loosed a hand and touched her soaking hair.

"You hate it," she said, her voice quaking.

"It wasn't my best entrance," he agreed.

"I meant my hair."

"I know you did," he said softly. "Hello, Lucy."

"Hello, Macintyre."

Standing here against Mac, so close she could feel the pebbles of cold rising on his chilled skin, she could also feel his innate strength. Warmth was returning to his body and seeping into hers.

The physical sensation of closeness, of sharing spreading heat, was making her vulnerable to other feelings, the very ones she had hoped to steel herself against.

It was not just weak. The weakness could be assigned

to the numbing cold that had seeped into every part of her. Even her tongue felt heavy and numb.

It was not just that she never wanted to move again. That could be assigned to the fact that her limbs felt slow and clumsy and paralyzed.

No, it was something worse than being weak.

Something worse than being paralyzed.

In Macintyre Hudson's arms, soaked, her Winnie-the-Pooh pajamas providing as much protection against him as a wet paper towel, Lucy Lindstrom felt the worst weakness of all, the longing she had kept hidden from herself.

Not to be so alone.

Her trembling deepened, and a soblike sound escaped her.

"Are you okay?" he asked.

"Not really," she said as she admitted the full truth to herself. It was not the cold making her weak. It was him.

Lucy felt a terrible wave of self-loathing. Was life just one endless loop, playing the same things over and over again?

She was cursed at love. She needed to accept that about herself, and devote her considerable energy and talent to causes that would help others, and, as a bonus, couldn't hurt her.

She pulled away from him, though it took all her strength, physical and mental. The blanket held her fast, so that mere inches separated them, but at least their bodies were no longer glued together.

History, she told herself sternly, was *not* repeating itself.

It was good he was here. She could face him, puncture any remaining illusions and get on with her wonderful life of doing good for others.

"Are you hurt?" he asked, putting her away from him, scanning her face.

She already missed the small warmth that had begun to radiate from him. Again, she had to pit what remained of her physical and mental strength to resist the desire to collapse against him.

"I'm fine," she said tersely.

"You don't look fine."

"Well, I'm not hurt. Mortified."

His expression was one of pure exasperation. "Who nearly drowns and is mortified by it?"

Whew. There was no sense him knowing she was mortified because of her reaction to him. By her sudden onslaught of uncertainty.

They had both been in perilous danger, and she was worried about the impression her hair made? Worried that she looked like a drowned rat? Worried about what pajamas she had on?

It was starting all over again!

This crippling need. He had seen her once, when it seemed no one else could. Hadn't she longed for that ever since?

Had she pursued getting that message to him so incessantly because of Mama Freda? Or had it been for herself? To feel the way she had felt when his arms closed around her?

Trembling, trying to fight the part of her that wanted nothing more than to scoot back into his warmth, she reminded herself that feeling this way had nearly destroyed her. It had had far-reaching repercussions that had torn her family and her life asunder.

"This is all your fault," she said. Thankfully, he took her literally.

"I'm not responsible for your bad catch."

"It was a terrible throw!"

"Yes, it was. All the more reason you shouldn't have reached for the rope. I could have thrown it again."

"You shouldn't have jumped back in the water after me. You could have been overcome by the cold. I'm surprised you weren't. And then we both would have been in big trouble."

"You have up to ten minutes in water that cold before you succumb. Plus, I don't seem to feel cold water like other people. I white-water kayak. I think it has desensitized me. But under no circumstances would I have stood on the pontoon of my plane and watched anyone drown."

Gee. He wasn't sensitive, and his rescue of her wasn't even personal. He would have done it for anyone.

"I wasn't going to drown," Lucy lied haughtily, since only moments ago she had been resigned to that very thing. He'd just said she had ten whole minutes. "I've lived on this lake my entire life."

"Oh!" He smacked himself on the forehead with his fist. "How could I forget that? Not only have you lived on the lake your entire life, but so did three generations of your family before you. Lindstroms don't drown. They die like they lived. Nice respectable deaths in the same beds that they were born in, in the same town they never took more than two steps away from."

"I lived in Glen Oak for six years," she said.

"Oh, Glen Oak. An hour away. Some consider Lindstrom Beach to be Glen Oak's summer suburb."

Lucy was aware of being furious with herself for the utter weakness of reacting to him. It felt much safer to transfer that fury to him.

He had walked away. Not just from this town. He had walked away from having to give anything of himself. How could he never have considered all the possibilities? They had played with fire all that summer.

She had gotten burned. And he had walked away.

And he had never even said he loved her. Not even once.

CHAPTER THREE

"YOU KNOW WHAT, Macintyre Hudson? You were a jerk back then, and you're still a jerk."

"May I remind you that you begged me to come back here?"

"I did not beg. I appealed to your conscience. And I personally did not care if you came back."

"You were a snotty, stuck-up brat and you still are. Here's a novel concept," Mac said, his voice threaded with annoyance, "why don't you try thanking me for my heroic rescue? For the second time in your life, by the way."

Because of what happened the first time, you idiot.

"If I needed a hero," she said with soft fury, "you are the last person I would pick."

That hit home. He actually flinched. And she was happy he flinched. *Snotty, stuck-up brat?*

Then a cool veil dropped over the angry sparks flickering in his eyes, and his mouth turned upward, that mocking smile that was his trademark, that said *You can't hurt me—don't even try.* He folded his arms over the deep strength of his broad chest, and not because he was cold, either.

"You know what? If I was looking for a damsel in

distress, you wouldn't exactly be my first pick, either. You're still every bit the snooty doctor's daughter."

She felt all of it then. The abandonment. The fear she had shouldered alone in the months after he left. Her parents, who had always doted on her, looking at her with hurt and embarrassment, as if she could not have let them down more completely. The friends she had known since kindergarten not phoning anymore, looking the other way when they saw her.

She felt all of it.

And it felt as if every single bit of it was his fault.

"Just to set the record straight, maybe it's you who should be thanking me," she told him. "I came down here to rescue you. You were the one in the water."

"I didn't need your help...."

So, absolutely nothing had changed. She was, in his eyes, still the town rich girl, the doctor's snooty daughter, out of touch with what he considered to be real.

And he was still the one who didn't *need*.

"Or your botched rescue attempt."

The fury in her felt white-hot, as if it could obliterate what remained of the chill on her. Lucy wished she had felt *that* when she had seen him get knocked off the dock by the post. She wished, instead of running to him, worried about him, she had marched into her house and firmly shut the door on him.

She hadn't done that. But maybe it was never too late to correct a mistake. She could do the right thing this time.

She stepped in close, shivered dramatically, letting him believe she was weak and not strong, that she needed his body heat back. Mac was wary, but not wary enough. He let her slip back in, close to him.

Lucy put both her hands on his chest, blinked up at him with her very best will-you-be-my-hero? look and then shoved him as hard as she could.

With a startled yelp, which Lucy found extremely satisfying, Macintyre Hudson lost his footing and stumbled off the dock, back into the water. She turned and walked away, annoyed that she was reassured by his vigorous cursing that he was just fine.

She glanced back. More than fine! Instead of getting out of the water, Mac shrugged out of his leather jacket and threw it onto the dock. Then, making the most of his ten minutes, he swam back to his plane.

Within moments he had the entire situation under control, which no doubt pleased him no end. He fastened the plane to the dock's other pillar, which held, then reached inside and tossed a single overnight bag onto the dock.

She certainly didn't want him to catch her watching. Why was she watching? It was just more evidence of the weakness he made her feel. What she needed to be doing was to be heading for a hot shower at top speed.

Lucy had crossed back into her yard when she heard Mama's shout.

"Ach! What is going on?"

She turned to see Mama Freda trundling toward her dock, hand over her brow, trying to see into the sun. Then Mama stopped, and a light came on in that ancient, wise face that seemed to steal the chill right out of Lucy.

"Schatz?"

Mac was standing on the dock, and had removed his soaking shirt and was wringing it out. That was an unfortunate sight for a girl trying to steel herself against him. His body was absolutely perfect, sleek and strong, water sluicing down the deepness of his chest to the defined ripples of his abs.

He dropped the soaked shirt beside his jacket and sprinted over the dock and across the lawn. He stopped at Mama Freda and grinned down at her, and this time his grin was so genuine it could have lit up the whole lake. Mama reached up and touched his cheek.

Then he picked up the rather large bulk of Mama Freda as if she were featherlight, and swung her around until she was squealing like a young girl.

"You're getting me all wet," she protested loudly, smacking the broadness of his shoulders with delight. "*Ach.* Put me down, galoot-head."

Finally he did, and she patted her hair into place, regarding him with such affection that Lucy felt something burn behind her eyes.

"Why are you all wet? You'll catch your death!"

"Your dock broke when I tried to tie to it."

"You should have told me you were coming," Mama said reproachfully.

"I wanted to surprise you."

"Surprise, schmize."

Lucy smiled, despite herself. One of Mama's goals in life seemed to be to create a rhyme, beginning with *sch,* for every word in the English language.

"You see what happens? You end up in the lake. If you'd just told me, I would have warned you to tie up to Lucy's dock."

"I don't think Lucy wants me tying up at her dock."

Only Lucy would pick up his dry double meaning on that. She could actually feel a bit of a blush moving heat into her frozen cheeks.

"Don't be silly. Lucy wouldn't mind."

He could have thrown her under the bus, because Mama would not have approved of anyone being pushed into the water at this time of year, no matter how pressing the circumstances.

But he didn't. Her gratitude that he hadn't thrown her under the bus was short-lived as Mac left the topic of Lucy Lindstrom behind with annoying ease.

"Mama, I'm freezing. I hope you have *apfelstrudel* fresh from the oven."

"You have to tell me you're coming to get strudel fresh from the oven. That's not what you need, anyway. Mama knows what you need."

Lucy could hear the smile in his voice, and was aware again of Mama working her magic, both of them smiling just moments after all that fury.

"What do I need, Mama?"

"You need elixir."

He pretended terror, then dashed back to the dock and picked up his soaked clothing and the bag, tossed it over his naked shoulder. He returned and wrapped his arm around Mama's waist and let her lead him to the house.

Lucy turned back to her own house, her eyes still smarting from what had passed between those two. The love and devotion shimmered around them as bright as the strengthening morning sun.

That was why she had gone to such lengths to get

Macintyre Hudson to come back here. And if another motive had lain hidden beneath that one, it had been exposed to her in those moments when his arms had wrapped around her and his heat had seeped into her.

Now that it was exposed, she could put it in a place where she could guard against it as if her life depended on it.

Which, Lucy told herself through the chattering of her teeth, it did.

Out of the corner of his eye, Mac saw Lucy pause and watch his reunion with Mama.

"Is that Lucy?" Mama said, catching the direction of his gaze.

"Yeah, as annoying as ever."

"She's a good girl," Mama said stubbornly.

"Everything she ever aspired to be, then."

Only, she wasn't a girl anymore, but a woman. The *good* part he had no doubt about. That was what was expected of the doctor's daughter, after all.

Even given the circumstances he had noted the changes. Her hair was still blond, but it no longer fell, unrestrained by hair clips or elastic bands, to the slight swell of her breast.

Plastered to her head, it hadn't looked like much, but he was willing to bet that when it was dry it was ultra-sophisticated, and would show off the hugeness of those dazzling green eyes, the pixie-perfection of her dainty features. Still, Mac was aware of fighting the part of him that missed how it used to be.

She had lost the faintly scrawny build of a long-distance runner, and filled out, a fact he could not help but notice when she had pressed the lusciousness of her freezing body into his.

She seemed uptight, though, and the level of her anger at him gave him pause.

Unbidden, he wondered if she ever slipped into the lake and skinny-dipped under the full moon. Would she still think it was the most daring thing a person could do, and that she was risking arrest and public humiliation?

What made her laugh now? In high school it seemed as if she had been at the center of every circle, popular and carefree. That laugh, from deep within her, was so joyous and unchained the birds stopped singing to listen.

Mac snorted in annoyance with himself, reminding himself curtly that he had broken that particular spell a long time ago. Though if that was completely true, why the reluctance to return Lucy's calls? Why the aversion to coming back?

If that was completely true, why had he told Lucy Lindstrom, of all people, that his father had been a ditchdigger?

That had been bothering him since the words had come out of his mouth. Maybe that confession had even contributed to the fiasco on the dock.

"What's she doing?" Mama asked, worried. "Is she wet, too? She looks wet."

"We both ended up in the lake."

"But how?"

"A comedy of errors. Don't worry about it, Mama."

But Mama was determined to worry. "She should

have come here. I would look after her. She could catch her death."

Mama Freda, still looking after everyone. Except maybe herself. She was looking toward Lucy's house as if she was thinking of going to get her.

He noticed the grass blended seamlessly together, almost as if the lawns of the two houses were one. That was new. Dr. Lindstrom had gone to great lengths to accentuate the boundaries of his yard, to lower any risk of association with the place next door.

Despite now sharing a lawn with its shabby neighbor, the Lindstrom place still looked like something off a magazine spread.

A bank of French doors had been added to the back of the house. Beyond the redwood of the multilayered deck, a lawn, tender with new grass, ended at a sea of yellow and red tulips. The flowers cascaded down a gentle slope to the fine white sand of the private beach.

On the L-shaped section of the bleached gray wood of the dock a dozen canoes were upside down.

What was with all the canoes? He was pretty sure that Mama had said Lucy was by herself since she had come home a year ago.

A bird called, and Mac could smell the rich scent of sun heating the fallen needles of the ponderosa pine.

As he gazed out over the lake, he was surprised by how much he had missed this place. Not the town, which was exceptionally cliquey; you were either "in" or you were "out" in Lindstrom Beach.

Lucy's family had always been "in." Of course, "in" was determined by the location of your house on the lake, the size of the lot, the house itself, what kind of boat you had and who your connections were. "In" was determined by your occupation, your membership in the church and the yacht club, and by your income, never mentioned outright, always insinuated.

He, on the other hand, had been "out," a kid of questionable background, in foster care, in Mama's house, the only remaining of the original cabins that had been built around the lake in the forties. Her house, little more than a fishing shack, had been the bane of the entire neighborhood.

And so the sharing of the lawn was new and unexpected.

"Do you and Lucy go in together to hire someone to look after the grounds?" he asked.

"No, Lucy does it."

That startled him. Lucy mowed the expansive lawns? He couldn't really imagine her pushing a lawn mower. He remembered her and her friends sitting on the deck in their bikinis while the "help" sweated under the hot sun keeping the grounds of her house immaculate. But he didn't want Lucy to crowd back into his thoughts.

"You look well, Mama," he said, an invitation for her to confide in him. He should have known it wouldn't be that easy.

"I look well. You look terrible." She gave his freezing, naked torso a hard pinch. "No meat on your bones. Eating in restaurants. I can tell by your coloring."

He thought his coloring might be off because he had just had a pretty good dunking in some freezing water, but he knew from long experience that there was no telling Mama.

They approached the back of her house. The porch

door was choked with overgrown lilacs, drooping with heavy buds. Mac pushed aside some branches and opened the screen door. It squeaked outrageously. He could see the floorboards of her screened porch were as rotten as her dock.

He frowned at the attempt at a repair. Had she hired some haphazard handyman?

"Who did this?" he said, toeing the new board.

"Lucy," she said, eyeing the disastrous repair with pride. "Lucy helps me with lots of things around here."

His frown deepened. Somehow that was a Lucy he could never have imagined, nails between teeth, pounding in boards.

Though Mama had said nothing, he had suspected for some time the house was becoming too much for her, and this confirmed it.

"You should come to Toronto with me," he said. It was his opening move. In his bag he had brochures of Toronto's most upscale retirement home.

"Toronto, schmonto. No, you should move back here. That big city is no place for a boy like you."

"I'm not a boy anymore, Mama."

"You will always be my boy."

He regarded her warmly, searching her face for any sign of illness. She was unchanging. She had seemed old when he had first met her, and she really had never seemed to get any older. There was a sameness about her in a changing world that had been a touchstone.

Why hadn't she told him she had lost her license?

She was going to be eighty years old three days before Mother's Day. He held open the inside door for her, and they stepped through into her kitchen.

It, too, was showing signs of benign neglect: paint chipping from the cabinets, a door not closing properly, the old linoleum tiles beginning to curl. There was a towel tied tightly around a faucet, and he went and looked.

An attempted repair of a leak.

"Lucy's work?" he guessed.

"Yes."

Again, the Lucy he didn't know. "You just have to tell me these things," he said. "I would have paid for the plumber."

"You pay for enough already."

He turned to look at Mama, and without warning he was fourteen years old again, standing in this kitchen for the first time.

Harriet Freda's had been his fifth foster home in as many months, and despite the fact this one had a prime lakeshore location, from the outside the house seemed even smaller and dumpier and darker than all the other foster homes had been.

Maybe, he had thought, already cynical, they just sent you to worse and worse places.

The house would have seemed beyond humble in any setting, but surrounded by the magnificent lake houses, it was painfully shacklike and out of place on the shores of Sunshine Lake.

That morning, standing in a kitchen that cheerfully belied the outside of the house, Mac had been fourteen and terrified. That had been his first lesson since the death of his father: never let the terror show.

She had been introduced to him as Mama Freda, and she looked stocky and ancient. Her hair was a bluish-white color and frizzy with a bad perm. She had more wrinkles than a Shar-Pei. Mac thought she was way too old to be looking after other people's kids.

Still, she looked harmless enough, standing at her kitchen table in a frumpy dress that showed off her chunky build, thick arms and legs, ankles swollen above sensible shoes. She had been wearing a much-bleached apron, once white, aged to tea-dipped, and covered with faded blotches of berry and chocolate.

The niceties were over, the social worker was gone and he was standing there with a paper bag containing two T-shirts, one pair of jeans and a change of underwear. Mrs. Freda cast him a look, and there was an unmistakable friendly twinkle in deep-set blue eyes.

Well, there was no sense her thinking they were going to be on friendly terms.

"I killed a man," he said, and then added, "With my bare hands." He thought the *with my bare hands* part was a nice touch. It was actually a line from a song, but it warned people to stay back from him, that he was dangerous and tough.

And if Macintyre Hudson had wanted one thing at age fourteen, it was for people to stay back from him. He had been like a wounded animal, unwilling to trust again.

Mama Freda glanced up from what she was doing, stretching out an enormous piece of dough, thin and elastic, over the edges of her large, round kitchen table. She regarded him, and he noticed the twinkle was gone from her eyes, replaced with an immense sorrow.

"This is a terrible thing," she said, sinking into a chair. "To kill a man. I know. I had to do it once."

He stared at her, his mouth open. And when she beckoned to the chair beside hers, he abandoned his meager bag of belongings and went to it, as if drawn to her side by a magnet.

"It was near the end of the war," she said, looking at her hands. "I was thirteen. A soldier, he was—" she glanced at Mac, trying to decide how much to say "—hurting my sister. He had his back to me. I picked up a cast-iron pan and I crept up behind him and I hit him as hard as I could over his head. There was a terrible noise. Terrible. He fell off my sister. I think he was already dead, but I knew if he ever got up we were all doomed, and so I hit him again and again and again."

Mac had never heard silence like he heard in Mama Freda's kitchen right then. The clock ticking sounded explosive.

"So I know what this thing is," she said finally, "to kill a man. I know how you carry it within you. How you think of his face, and wonder who he was before the great evil overcame him. I wonder what his mother felt when he never came home, and if his sisters grieve him to this day, the way I grieve the brother who went to war and never came home."

Her hand crept out from under her apron and she laid it, palm up, on the table. An invitation. And Mac surprised himself by not being able to refuse that invitation. He put his hand on the table, too. Her hand closed around his, surprisingly strong for such an old lady.

"Look at me," she said.

And he did.

She did not say a word. She didn't have to. He looked

deep into her eyes, and for the first time in a long, long time, he felt he was not alone.

That someone else knew what it was to suffer.

Later they ate the *apfelstrudel* she had finished rolling out on her kitchen table, and it felt as if his taste buds had come awake, as if he could taste for the first time in a long, long time, too, as if he had never tasted food quite so wondrous.

He started, in that moment, with warm strudel melting in his mouth, to do what he had sworn he would never do again. But he was careful never to call it that, and never to utter the words that would solidify it and make it real. For him, the admission of love was the holding of a samurai's sword that you would eventually plunge into your own heart.

But he had never altered the story he had told her that day, not even when she had said to him once, "I know, *schatz,* there is nothing in you that could kill another person. Or anything. Not even a baby robin that fell from its nest. I have watched you carry bugs outside rather than swat them."

But he had never doubted that she really had killed that soldier, and she, too, carried bugs outside rather than swatting them.

Mama, with her enormous capacity to care for all things, had saved him.

And he owed it to her to be there for her if she needed him. It was evident from the state of her house that he hadn't been there in the ways she needed. And that Lucy, the one he had called the spoiled brat, had been. He felt the faintest shiver of something.

Guilt?

"Go shower," Mama said, and he drew himself back to the present with a shake of his head. "Nice and hot."

She was already reaching up high into her cabinet and Mac shuddered when the ancient brown bottle of elixir came down, and he hightailed it for the tiny bathroom at the top of the stairs.

When he came down, in dry clothes, she had a tumbler of the clear liquid poured.

"Drink. It will ward off the cold."

"I'm not cold."

"The cold you will get if you don't drink it!" She had that look on her face, her arms folded over her ample bosom.

There was no sense explaining to Mama you didn't get colds from being cold, that you got them from coming in contact with one of hundreds of viruses, none of which were very likely to be living in the freezing-cold water of Sunshine Lake.

He took the tumbler, plugged his nose and put it back. It burned to his belly and he felt his toes curl.

He set the glass down, and wiped his watering eyes. "For heaven's sakes, its schnapps!"

"Obstler," she said happily. "Not peppermint sugar like they drink here. Ugh. Mine is made with apples. Herbs."

She was right, though—if there was any sneaky virus in him, no matter what the source, it would be gone now.

"Homemade, from my great-grandmother's recipe. Now, take some to Lucy. I have it ready." She passed him an unlabeled brown bottle of her secret elixir.

"I'm not taking it to Lucy." After that encounter on the dock, the less he had to do with Lucy the better.

He'd wanted to believe, after all this time, that Lucy, the girl who had not thought he was good enough, would have no power over him. He had seen the world. He'd succeeded. He'd expected Lucy and this town to be nothing more than a speck of dust from the past.

What he hadn't expected was the rush of feeling when he had seen her. Even dripping wet, near frozen, seeing Lucy on the dock calling to him, he had felt a pull so strong it felt as if his heart was coming from his chest. He'd been vulnerable, caught off guard, but still, there had always been something about her.

She still had that face, impish, unconventionally beautiful, that inspired warmth and trust, that took a man's guard right down, and left him in a place where he could be shoved into a lake by someone who weighed sixty pounds less than he did.

An old hurt surfaced, its edges knife-sharp.

I could never fall for a boy like you.

That was the problem with coming back to a place you had left behind, Mac thought. Old hurts didn't die. They waited. And those words, coming from Lucy, the one he had trusted with his ever-so-bruised heart…

"She needs the elixir! She'll catch her death."

Since he didn't want to tell Mama why he didn't want to see Lucy—because he had fully expected to be indifferent and had been anything but—now might be a good time to explain viruses. But his explanation, he knew, would fall on deaf ears.

"She's a doctor's daughter. I'm sure she knows what she needs."

Mama looked stubborn.

"Mama, it's probably illegal to make this stuff, let alone dispense it."

She regarded him, her eyes narrow, and then without warning, "Are you speaking to your mother yet, *schatz?*"

He glared at her stonily.

"Nearly Mother's Day. Just two weeks away. She must be lonely for you."

The only thing his mother had ever been lonely for was her bank account. But he wasn't being drawn into this argument. And he could clearly see Mama had grabbed on to it now, like a dog worrying meat off a bone.

"How many years?" she asked softly, stubbornly.

He refused to answer out loud, but inside, he did the math.

"It's time," she said.

On this, and only this, he had refused her from the first day he had come here. There would be no reconciliation with his mother.

"Just a card, to start," she said, as if they had not played out this scene a hundred times before. "I think I have the perfect one right here."

It was one of Mama's things. She always had a cupboard devoted to greeting cards. She had one suitable for every occasion.

Except son and mother estranged for fourteen years.

Without a word he picked up the bottle of homemade schnapps and went out the squeaking door. When he glanced back over his shoulder, Mama had her back to him, rummaging through the card cupboard, singing with soft satisfaction.

He noticed how hunched she was.

Frail, somehow, despite her bulk.

He noticed how badly the house needed repair, and felt guilty, again, that he had somehow let it get this bad.

Mac was not unaware that he had been back in Lindstrom Beach all of half an hour and all these uncomfortable feelings were rising to the surface. He didn't like feelings.

Lucy had been here when he had not. Well, he'd take over from her now.

It occurred to him that this trip was probably not going to be the quick turnaround he had hoped for. Still, a few days of intense work, and he'd be out of here, leaving all these uneasy feelings behind him.

"Make sure she drinks some," Mama shouted as the screen creaked behind him. "Make sure. Don't come back here unless she does."

And much as he didn't want Lucy to be right about anything, and much as he didn't like the unexpected feelings, he realized, reluctantly, she had been right to insist he come back here.

Mama needed him.

And yes, the time to honor his foster mother was definitely now. But he would leave the gala to Lucy, and honor his foster mother by making sure her house was livable before he left again.

CHAPTER FOUR

MAC CROSSED THE familiar ground between the two houses. He noted, again, that Lucy's property was everything Mama's was not. Even with the lawns melting together, the properties were very different: Mama's ringed in huge trees—that were probably hard to mow around—the Lindstrom place well-maintained, oozing the perfect taste of old money.

From the tidbits of information dropped by Mama, Mac knew Lucy had taken over the house from her mother a year or so ago. Hadn't there been something about a broken engagement?

How did she find time to do the work that it used to take an entire team of gardeners to do?

Unless she doesn't have a life.

Which, also from tidbits dropped by Mama, Lucy didn't. She ran some kind of online book business. A life, yes, but not the life he had expected the most popular girl in high school would have ended up with.

I don't care, Mac told himself, but if he really didn't, would he even have to say that to himself?

He debated going to the front of the house, keeping everything nice and formal, but in the end, he stayed in the back and went across the deck. He stopped and surveyed the house. The stately white paint was faded and peeling; a large patch of a sample paint color had been put up.

It was a pale shade of lavender. Several boards underneath it had samples of what he assumed would be trim color, ranging from light lilac to deep purple.

The paint color made him think he didn't know Lucy at all.

Which, of course, he didn't. She was no more the same girl she had been when he'd left than he was the same man. He became aware of the sound of water running inside the house, assumed Lucy was showering and was grateful for the reprieve from another encounter with her.

He wasn't a little kid anymore. And neither was Lucy. He respected Mama, but he couldn't take her every wish as a command. *Make sure she drinks it.* Lucy could find the bottle and make up her own mind whether to drink it.

He would take his chances. If he didn't return for a while, Mama might not question how he had completed his assignment. And, hopefully, she would be off the topic of his mother by then, as well.

Mac set Mama's offering at Lucy's back door, and then strolled down to her dock to look over the canoes. They weren't particularly good quality—different ages and makes and colors. Then he saw a sign, fairly new, nailed to a wharf post like the one that had broken at Mama's.

Lucy's Lakeside Rentals. It outlined the rates and rules for renting canoes.

Lucy was renting canoes? He *really* didn't know her anymore. In fact, it almost seemed as if their roles were reversed. He had arrived, he knew every success he had ever hoped for, and she was mowing lawns and scraping together pennies by renting canoes.

He thought he should feel at least a moment's satisfaction over that. A little gloating from the kind of guy Lucy could never fall for might be in order. But instead, Mac felt oddly troubled. And hated it that he felt that way.

He looked at the house. He could still hear water running. He eased a canoe up with his toe. The paddles were stored underneath it.

Then Mac maneuvered the canoe off the dock and into the water, got into it and began to paddle toward the other side of the lake.

Even more than Mama's embrace, the silent canoe skimming across the water filled him with what he dreaded most of all—a sense of having missed this place, a sense that even as he had tried to leave it all behind him, this was home.

An hour later, eyeing Lucy's house for signs of life and relieved to find none, Mac put the canoe back on the dock. He felt like a thief as he crept up to her back door. The elixir was gone. He could report to Mama with a clear conscience. Still, the feeling of being a thief was not relieved by sticking twenty bucks under a rock to cover the rental of the canoe.

"Hey," Lucy cried, "Wait!"

He turned and looked at her, put his hands into his pockets. He looked annoyed and impatient.

"What are you doing?" Lucy called.

"I took one of your canoes out. There's rental money under the rock." This was said sharply, as if it was obvious, and she was keeping him from something important.

"I never said you could rent my canoe."

"I have to pass a character test?"

Below the sarcasm, incredibly, Lucy thought she detected the faintest thread of hurt. After all these years, could it still be between them?

I could never fall for a boy like you.

No, he was successful and worldly, and it was written in every line of his stance that he didn't give a hoot what she thought of him.

"I didn't say that. You can't just take a canoe."

"I didn't just take it. I paid you for it."

"You need to tell me where you're going. What if you didn't come back?"

"I've been paddling these waters since I was fourteen. I've kayaked some of the most dangerous waters in the world. I think I can be trusted with your canoe."

Trust. There it was again. The missing ingredient between them.

"It's not the canoe I'm worried about. I need to give you a life jacket."

"You're worried about me, Lucy Lin?" Now, aggravatingly, he was pulling out the charm to try to disarm her.

"No!"

"So what's the problem?"

"You should have asked."

"Maybe I should have. But we both know I'm not the kind of guy who does things by the book."

Again she thought she heard faint challenge, a hurt behind the mocking tone.

She sighed. "I don't want your money, Mac. If you want to take a canoe, take one. But let someone know where you're going. At least Mama, if you don't want to talk to me."

She was unsettled to realize now she was the one who felt hurt. Not that she had a right to be. Of course he wouldn't want to talk to her. She'd pushed him into the lake. Though she had a feeling his aversion to her went deeper than that recent incident.

"I don't need your charity," he said, "I'd rather pay you."

"Well, I don't need your charity, either."

"You know what? I'll just have my own equipment sent up."

"You do that."

She watched him walk away, his head high, and felt regret. They needed to talk about Mama, if nothing else. But he hadn't returned her calls, and he didn't want to talk to her now, either.

Lucy picked up his twenty-dollar bill, stuck it in an envelope, scrawled his name across it. Not bothering to dress, she crossed the lawns between the two houses in her housecoat, but didn't knock on the door.

She followed his lead. She put the envelope under a rock and walked away. When she got home, she inspected the canoes, saw which one he had been using, and shoved a life jacket underneath it.

* * *

"What's this?" Mama said, handing him the envelope.

Mac looked in it and sighed with irritation. Trust Lucy. She was always going to have the last word.

Except this time she wasn't, damn her. He folded the envelope, tucked it in his pocket and went out the back door. The last person he would ever accept charity from was Lucy. He owed her for the canoe, fair and square, and the days of her—or anyone in this town—feeling superior to him were over.

He lifted his hand to knock on her back door to return the money to her. Raised voices drifted out the open French doors and he moved away from the paint and peered into Lucy's house.

"You're wrecking the neighborhood!" someone said shrilly.

"It's just a sample." That voice was Lucy's, low and conciliatory.

"Purple? You're going to paint your house purple? Are you kidding me? It's an absolute monstrosity. When Billy and I saw it from the boat the other day, I nearly fell overboard."

Lucy had a perfect opportunity to say, *too bad you didn't,* but instead she defended her choice.

"I thought it was funky."

"Funky? On Lakeshore Drive?"

No answer to that.

Mac tried the door, and it was unlocked. He pulled it open and slid in. After a moment, his eyes adjusted to being inside and he saw Lucy at her front door, still wrapped in a housecoat, her hands folded defensively over her chest, looking up at a taller woman, the other woman's slenderness of the painful variety.

Now, there was a face from the past. Claudia Mitchell-Franks. Dressed in a trouser suit he was going to guess was linen, her makeup and hair done as if she was going to a party. Her thin face was pinched with rage.

Lucy was everything Claudia was not. Fresh-scrubbed from the shower, her short hair was towel-ruffled and did not look any more sophisticated than it had fresh out of the drink. She was nearly lost inside a white housecoat, the kind that hung on the back of the bathroom door in really good hotels.

Her feet were bare, and absurdly that struck him as far sexier than her visitor's stiletto sandals.

"And don't even think you're renting canoes this year! Last summer it increased traffic in this area to an unreasonable level, and you don't have any parking. The street above your place was clogged. And I had riffraff paddling by my beach."

"There's no law against renting canoes," Lucy said, but without much force.

This was the same Lucy who had just pushed him into the water? Why wasn't she telling old Claudia to take a hike?

"I had one couple stop and set up a picnic on my front lawn!" Claudia snapped.

"Horrors," Lucy said dryly. He found himself rooting for her. *Come on, Lucy, you can do better than that.*

"I am not spending another summer explaining to people it's a private beach," Claudia said.

Shrilly, too, he was willing to bet.

"It isn't," Lucy said calmly. "You only own to the

high-water mark, which in your case is about three feet from your gazebo. Those people have a perfect right to picnic there if they want to."

Mac felt a little unwilling pride in her. That was information he'd given her all those years ago when he'd thumbed his nose at all those people trying to claim they owned the beaches.

"I hope you don't tell *them* that," Claudia said.

"I have it printed on the brochure I give out at rental time," she said, but then backtracked. "Of course I don't. But can't we share the lake with others?"

The perfectly coiffed Claudia looked as if she was going to have apoplexy at the idea of sharing the lake. Mac was pretty sure Claudia was one of the girls who used to sit on that deck painting her toenails while the "riffraff" slaved in the yard.

"Well, you won't be giving out any brochures this year, no, you won't! You'll need a permit to run your little business. And you're not getting one. And you know what else? You can forget the yacht club for your fund-raiser."

"I've already paid my deposit," Lucy said, clearly rattled.

"I'll see that it's returned to you."

"But I have a hundred confirmed guests coming. The gala is only two weeks away!" There was a pleading note in her voice.

"This is what you'll be up against if you even try rezoning. This is a residential neighborhood. It always has been and it always will be."

"That's what this is really about, isn't it?"

"We finally no longer have to put up with the endless parade of young thugs next door to this house, and you do this?"

He'd heard enough. He stepped across the floor.

"Lucy, everything okay here?"

Lucy turned and looked at him. He could see her eyes were shiny, and he hoped he was the only person in the room who knew that meant she was close to tears.

He thought she might be angry that he had barged into her house, but instead he saw relief on her delicate features as he approached her. Despite the brave front, he could tell that for some reason she felt as if she was in over her head. Maybe because this attack was coming from someone who used to be her friend?

"You remember Claudia," she said.

He would have much rather Lucy told Claudia to get the hell out of her house instead of politely making introductions.

Claudia was staring at him meanly. Oh, boy, did he ever remember that look! The first time he'd taken Lucy out publicly, for an ice cream cone on Main Street, they had run into her, and she'd had that same look on her skinny, malicious face.

"I know you," she said tapping a hard, bloodred-lacquered fingernail against a lip that matched.

He waited for her to recognize him, for the mean look to deepen.

Instead, when recognition dawned in her eyes, her whole countenance changed. She smiled and rushed at him, blinked and put her claw on his arm, dug her talon in, just a little bit.

"Why, Macintyre Hudson." She beamed up at him.

"Aren't you the small-town boy who has done well for himself?"

He told himself he should find this moment exceedingly satisfactory, especially since it had happened in front of Lucy. Instead, he felt a sensation of discomfort—which Lucy quickly dispelled.

Because behind Claudia, Lucy crossed her arms over her chest and frowned. Then she caught his eye and pantomimed gagging.

He didn't want to be charmed by Lucy, but he couldn't help but smile. Claudia actually thought it was for her. He didn't let the impression last. He slid out from under her fingertips.

"I seem to remember being one of the young thugs from next door. *And* the riffraff who had the nerve to paddle by your dock. I might even have had the audacity to eat my lunch on your beach now and again."

She hee-hawed with enthusiasm. "Oh, Mac, such a sense of humor! I've always *adored* you. My kids— I have two boys now—won't wear anything but Wild Side. If it doesn't have that little orangey kayak symbol on it, they won't put it on."

He tried not to show how appalled he was that his brand was the choice of the elite little monkeys who lived around the lake.

"What brings you home?" Claudia purred.

Over Claudia's bony shoulder, he saw Lucy now had her hands around her own neck, the internationally recognized symbol for choking. He tried to control the twitching of his lips.

"Lucy's having a party to honor my mother. I wouldn't have missed it for the world."

Considering that it had given him grave satisfaction to snub Lucy by giving the event a miss, this news came as a shock to him.

"Oh. That. I wasn't expecting *you* would come for *that*. There's been a teensy problem with location. Anyway, it's not as if she's your *real* mother."

Unaware how insensitive that remark was, Claudia forged ahead, her red lips stretched over teeth he found very large.

"I'm afraid the committee has voted to revoke our rental to Lucy. And we don't meet again until next month, and that's too late. But you know, the elementary-school gym is probably available. I'd be happy to check for you."

"No thanks."

"Don't be mad at *me*. It's really Lucy's fault. Norman Avalon is president of the yacht club this year. Do you remember him?"

An unpleasant memory of a boy throwing a partially filled Slurpee cup on him while he was shoveling three tons of mud out of a ditch came to mind.

"They live right over there. If Lucy paints the place purple, his wife, Ellen—you remember Ellen, she used to be a Polson—will have to look at it all day. She's ticked. Royally. And that was before the rezoning application. Macintyre, it is just sooo nice seeing you."

He didn't respond, tried not to look at Lucy, who had her eyes crossed and her tongue hanging out, her hands still around her own throat.

"Congrats on your company's success. I know Billy would love to see you if you have time. We generally have pre-dinner cocktails at the club on Friday."

Behind Claudia, Lucy dropped silently to her knees, and was swaying back and forth, holding her throat.

"The club?" As if there was only one in town, which there was.

"You know, the yacht club."

"Oh, the one Lucy isn't renting anymore. To honor *my* mother."

"Oh." With effort, since her expression lines had been removed with Botox, Claudia formed her face into contrite lines and lowered her voice sympathetically. "If you wanted to drop by on Friday and talk to Billy about it, he might be able to use his influence for *you*."

Lucy keeled over behind her, her mouth moving in soundless gasping, like a beached fish.

"Billy who?"

"Billy. Billy Johnson. Do you remember him?"

"Uh-huh," he said, noncommittal. He seemed to remember smashing his fist into the face of the lovely Billy after he had made a guess about his heritage.

Claudia held up a hand with an enormous set of rings on it. "That's me now, Mrs. Johnson. Don't forget—cocktails. We dress, by the way."

"As opposed to what?"

"Oh, Mac, you card, you. Toodle-loo, folks."

She turned and saw Lucy lying on the ground, feigning death.

She stepped delicately over her inert body, and hissed, "Oh, for God's sake, Lucy, grow up. This man's the head of a multimillion-dollar company."

And she was gone, leaving a cloying cloud of perfume in her wake.

For a moment Lucy actually looked as if she'd allowed Claudia's closing barb to land. Her eyes looked shiny again. But then, to his great relief, she giggled.

"Oh, for God's sake, Lucy," he said sternly, "grow up."

She giggled more loudly. He felt his defenses falling like a fortress made out of children's building blocks. He gave in to the temptation to play a little.

"Hey, I'm the head of a multimillion-dollar company. A little respect."

And then she started to laugh, and he gave in to the temptation a little more, and he did, too. It felt amazingly good to laugh with Lucy.

"You are good," he sputtered at her. "I got it loud and clear. Charades. Three words. *She's killing me.*"

He went over, took her hand and pulled her to her feet. She collapsed against him, laughing, and for the second time that day he felt the sweetness of her curves in his arms.

"Mac," she cooed, between gasps of laughter. "I've always *adored* you."

"The last time you looked at me like that, I got pushed in the lake."

She howled.

"What was that whole horrid episode with Claudia about?" he finally said, putting her away from him, wiping his eyes.

The humor died in her eyes. "Apparently if you even think of painting your house purple, you're off the approved list for renting the yacht club."

He had a sense that wasn't the whole story between the two women, but he played along.

"Boo-hoo," he said, and they were both laughing again.

"I haven't laughed like that for a long time."

She hadn't? Why? Suddenly, protecting himself did not seem quite as important as it had twenty minutes ago when he had come across her lawn to give her her money back.

"It's really no laughing matter," Lucy said, sobering abruptly. "Now I've gone and ticked her off—"

"Royally," he inserted, but she didn't laugh again.

"And I've got a caterer coming from Glen Oak, but they have to have a kitchen that's been food-safe certified. The school won't do."

"Don't worry. We'll fix it."

"We?" she said, raising an eyebrow at him, but if he wasn't mistaken she was trying valiantly not to look relieved.

"I told Claudia I came back for the party."

"But you didn't."

"When I saw Mama's place falling down, I realized I might be here a little longer than I first anticipated."

"Her place *is* in pretty bad repair," Lucy said. "I was shocked by it when I first came home. I've done my best."

"Thanks for that. I appreciate it. But don't quit your day job."

"She would love it if you were here for a while. Being at the gala would be a bonus. For her, I mean."

Mama *would* love it. But staying longer than he'd anticipated was suddenly for something more than getting Mama's house back in order. When he'd seen that barracuda taking a run at Lucy, he'd felt protective.

He didn't want to feel protective of Lucy. He wanted to hand her her money and go. He wanted to savor the fact she was on the outs with her snobbish friends.

But he was astonished to find that not only was he not gloating over Lucy's fall from grace, he felt as if he couldn't be one more bad thing in her day. Mama Freda would be proud: despite his natural inclination to be a cad, he seemed to be leaning toward being a better man.

Lucy seemed to realize she was in her housecoat and inappropriately close to him. She backed off, and looked suddenly uncomfortable.

"Claudia is right. I'm embarrassed. What made me behave like that? You, I suppose. You've always brought out the worst in me."

"Look, let's get some things straight. Claudia is *never* right, and I *never* brought out the worst in you."

"You didn't? Lying to my parents? Sneaking out? You talked me into smoking a cigar once. I drank my first beer with you. I—" Her face clouded, and for a moment he thought she was going to mention the most forbidden thing of all, but she said, "I became the kind of girl no one wanted sitting in the front pew of the church."

"That would say a whole lot more about the church than the kind of girl you were. I remember you laughing. Coming alive like Sleeping Beauty kissed by a prince. Not that I'm claiming to be any kind of prince—"

"That's good."

"I remember you being like a prisoner who had been set free, like someone who had been bound up by all these rules and regulations learning to live by your own guidelines. And learning to be spontaneous. I think it was the very best of you."

"There's a scary thought," she said, running a hand through her short, rumpled hair, not looking at him.

"I think the seeds of the woman who would paint her house purple were planted right then."

"You like the color?" she asked hopefully. "You saw my sample when you came in, didn't you?"

He hated it that she asked, as if she needed someone's approval to do what she wanted. "It only matters if you like the color."

"I wish that were true," she said ruefully.

"I remember when you used to be friends with Mrs. Billy-Goat Johnson," he said.

"I know. But I think the statute of limitations has run out on that one, so I won't accept responsibility for it anymore." She tried to sound careless, but didn't quite pull it off.

Suddenly it didn't seem funny. Lucy had changed. Deeply. And that change had not been accepted by the people around her. He suspected it went a whole lot deeper than her painting her house purple.

Well, so what? People did change. He had changed, too. Though probably not as deeply. He tended to think he was much the same as he had always been, a self-centered adrenaline junkie, driven by some deep need to prove himself that no amount of success ever quite took away. In other words, when Lucy had called him a jerk she hadn't been too far off the mark.

The only difference was that now he was a jerk with money.

She had helped Mama when he had not, and for that, if nothing else, he was indebted to her.

But now Lucy seemed somehow embattled, as if she desperately needed someone on her side.

Not me, he told himself sternly. He wasn't staying here. He owed Lucy nothing. He was getting a few of the more urgent things Mama needed done cleared up. Okay, it wouldn't hurt to stay a few more days for Lucy's party. That would make Mama happy. It wasn't about protecting Lucy from that barracuda. Or maybe it was. A little bit. But tangling his life with hers?

It occurred to him that he may have lied to himself about his reasons for never coming back to Lindstrom Beach. He had told himself it was because it was the town that had scorned him. The traditional place full of Brady Bunch families, where he'd been the kid with no real family and a dark, secret history.

He'd played on that and developed a protective persona: adrenaline junkie, renegade, James Dean of the high-school set. It had brought a surprising fan base from some of the kids, though not their parents.

Not the snooty doctor's daughter, either. Not at first.

But now, standing here looking at Lucy, it occurred to him none of that was the reason he had avoided returning to this place.

Had he always known, at some level, that coming home again would require him to be a better man?

But would that mean looking out for the girl who had rejected him?

"May I use your phone?" he asked. "My cell got wrecked in the lake."

Her expression asked if he had to, she suddenly

seemed eager to divest herself of him. But she looked around and handed him a cordless. Now that he had decided to be a better man, he was going to follow through before he changed his mind.

He could look at it as putting Claudia in her place as much as helping Lucy.

"Casey?" he said to his assistant. "Yeah, away for a few days…My hometown…You didn't know I had a hometown?…Hatched under a rock? Thanks, buddy." He waggled his eyebrows at Lucy, but she was pretending not to listen.

"Look, I need twenty thousand dollars of clothing products, sizes kid to teen, delivered to the food bank, boy's and girl's club and social services office of Lindstrom Beach, British Columbia. Make sure some of it gets to every agency that helps kids within a fifty-mile radius of that town…Yeah, giveaways.

"Of course you've never heard of Lindstrom Beach. When that's done—if you can have the whole area blanketed by tomorrow—take out a couple of ads on the local TV and radio stations thanking the Lindstrom Beach Yacht Club for donating their facilities for the Mother's Day Gala.

"Thanks, buddy. Don't know when I'll be back and don't bother with the cell. I made the mistake of not bringing the Wild Side waterproof case. Oh, throw some of those in with the other donations. I'll pick up another cell phone in the next few days."

Lucy was no longer pretending not to listen. She was staring at him as he found the button and turned off her phone. He handed it back to her. If he was not mistaken, she was struggling not to look impressed.

"Just admit it," he said. "That was great. Two birds with one stone."

"Everybody does not call you Mr. Hudson," she said, pleased. "Two birds?"

"Yeah. Claudia's stuck-up kids just became a whole lot less exclusive, and unless I miss my guess, you are *in* at the yacht club."

"You hate the yacht club," she reminded him.

"I've always had a strange hankering for anything anybody tells me I can't have."

Her arms folded more tightly over her chest and her eyes looked shiny again.

"I didn't mean you," he said softly.

"Let's not kid ourselves. That was part of the attraction. Romeo and Juliet. Bad boy and good girl."

"I don't think that was part of the attraction for me," he said, slowly. "It was more what I said before. It was watching you come into yourself, caterpillar to butterfly."

"Actually," she said, and she shoved her little nose in the air, reminding him of who she had been before he'd taught her you didn't go to hell for saying *damn*, "I don't want to have this discussion. In fact, if you don't mind, I need to get dressed."

"I have to give this to you first. Special delivery," he said, holding out the money to her. "What was that about rezoning?"

She ignored the envelope. "I think it had to do with the canoes. I think you're supposed to rezone to run a business."

But she suddenly wasn't looking at him. He was startled. Because, scanning her face, he was sure she was being deliberately evasive. What did renting canoes have to do with finally getting rid of the young thugs next door? Though it was Claudia they were dealing with. That was a leap in logic she could probably be trusted to make.

"I can put a lawyer on it if you want."

"I don't need you to fix things. I already told you I'm not in the market for a hero."

"Take your money."

"No. Are you in my house without an invitation?" she asked, annoyed.

"Boy, I saved you from drowning *and* from Claudia, and your gratitude, in both instances, seems to be almost criminally short-lived."

"Oh, well," she said.

"Anyone could come in your house without an invitation. You should consider locking the back door at least."

"Don't you dare tell me what to do! This is not the big city. And don't show up here after all these years and think you are going to play big brother. I don't need one."

But it was evident from what he had just seen that she needed something, someone in her court. Still, he was no more eager to play big brother to her than she was to cast him in that role.

But again, if that was what being a better man required of him, he'd suck it up. No looking at her lips, though. Or at the place her housecoat was gapping open slightly, revealing the swell of a deliciously naked breast.

"Lindstrom Beach may not be the big city," he said,

reaching out and gently pulling her housecoat closed. "But it's not the fairy tale you want to believe in, either."

She glanced down, slapped his hand away, and held her housecoat together tightly with her fist. "As a matter of fact, I gave up on fairy tales a long time ago."

"You did?" he said skeptically.

"I did," she said firmly.

He looked at her more closely, and there was that subtle anger in her again suddenly. He missed the girl who had lain on the floor, clutching her throat. He also felt the little ripple of unease intensify—the one that had started when he saw her clumsy repair job in Mama's porch. It was true. There was something very, very different about her.

In high school she had been confident, popular, perky, smart, pretty. She'd been born with a silver spoon in her mouth and had the whole world at her feet. Her crowd, including Claudia, expected it that way.

But Claudia had always had a certain hard smoothness to her, like a rock too polished. In Lucy, he remembered a certain dewy-eyed innocence, a girl who really did believe in Prince Charming, and for some of the happiest moments of his life, had mistakenly believed it was him.

But Lucy Lindstrom no longer had the look of a woman waiting for her prince.

In fact, from behind the barrier of her newly closed housecoat, she looked stubborn and offended. So, she did not want a hero. Or a prince. Good for her. And he was not looking for a damsel in distress. Or a princess.

So they were safe.

Except, he didn't really feel safe. He felt some danger he couldn't identify, so heavy in the air he might be able to taste it, the same way a deer could taste a threat on the wind.

"What happened to your fiancé?" he asked.

"What fiancé?"

"Mama told me you were going to get married."

"I changed my mind."

"She told me that, too."

"But she didn't give you the details?"

"No. Why would she know the details?"

"You're not from around these parts, are you, son?" She did a fairly good impression of a well-known TV doctor.

"I don't know what you mean."

"My engagement breakup was front-page news after my fiancé was chased naked down a quiet residential street in Glen Oak by a gun-wielding man who just happened to be the cuckolded husband of a woman who was my friend and the barista in our bookstore coffee shop."

It seemed Lucy Lindstrom's fall from grace had been complete. Mac ordered himself to feel satisfied. But that wasn't what he felt at all. He couldn't even pretend.

"Aw, Lucy." Her eyes had that shiny look again. He wanted to reach for her and hold her, but he knew if he did she would never forgive him.

"Don't feel sorry for me, please." She held up her hand. "Everything is on film these days. Someone caught the whole thing on their phone camera. It was a local sensation for a few days."

"Aw, Lucy," he said again, his distress for her genuine.

"Aren't you going to ask me if I never guessed something was going on? Everyone else asks that."

"No, I'm going to ask you if you want me to track him down and kill him."

"With your bare hands?" she asked, and though her voice was silky her eyes were shining again.

"Is he the one who made you quit believing in fairy tales?"

"No, Mac," she said quietly. "That happened way before him."

Her eyes lingered for just a moment on his lips, and then she licked hers, and looked away.

Mac turned from the sudden intensity, and made himself focus on the house—anything but her lips and the terrible possibility it was him who had made her stop believing in fairy tales.

"This isn't how I remember it."

Once, he had made the mistake of going to the front door when she was late meeting him at the dock for a canoe trip.

He'd stepped inside and it had reminded him of an old castle: dim and grim, the front room so crowded with priceless antiques that it felt hard to breathe. He found out he'd been invited inside to get a piece of her father's mind, and that's when he'd discovered that Lucy had been seeing him on the sly.

I forbid you to see my daughter.

After all these years Mac wasn't sure, but the word *riffraff* might have come into play. Of course, being *forbidden* to see Lucy had only made him come up with increasingly creative ways to spend time with her.

And it had intensified the pleasure of sneaking into this very room, when her parents were asleep upstairs, and kissing her until they had both been breathless with longing.

That first meeting with her father had been nothing in comparison to the last one.

There's been a rash of break-ins around the lake. My house is about to be broken into. The police are going to find the stolen goods next door, in your bedroom. You'll be arrested and it will be the final straw for that rotten place. I've always wanted to buy it. Someday, Lucy and the man she marries will live there.

Mac had known for a long time that he had to go. That there was no future for him in Lindstrom Beach and never would be.

He'd told her about her father's threat and said he couldn't stand it in this town for one more second. And that's when she had said it.

I could never fall for a boy like you.

Had her father convinced her he was a thief? That he was behind the break-ins that had happened that summer?

Or had she just come to her senses and realized it wasn't going to work? That a guy like him was never going to be able to give a girl like her the things she had become accustomed to?

It seemed to him that there was a lot of space between them that was too treacherous to cross. They'd caused each other pain, he was sure, but he was sure he had caused her more than she had caused him.

Maybe he had been the one who wrecked fairy tales for her.

But he'd already been a world away from fairy tales by the time he met her.

Safer to focus on the here and the now.

"There used to be a wall here," he said. *And a couch here.* He decided that focusing on the here and now meant not mentioning the couch. Not even thinking about it would have been good, too, but it was too late for that.

"My mom actually opened the walls ups after my dad died."

Which meant they were not, technically, even in the same room they had once made out in. The ghosts of their younger selves, breathless with need, were not here.

Mac somehow doubted her mother had achieved the almost tangible quality of sanctuary that the room had. Her mother, as he recalled her, had been much like Claudia. This room would have had the benefit of an interior designer, the magazine-shoot-perfect layout. It would have been designed with an eye for entertaining. And impressing.

But Lucy had created a space that was casual and inviting. It was a place where a person could read a book or stay in their housecoat all day. But there was something about it that he couldn't quite put his finger on.

Mac went through to the dining-room table to set down the envelope of money. There were papers stacked neatly on it. It was not the space of someone who entertained or had large dinner parties. He put his finger on it: her space had a feeling of surprising solitude clinging to it.

Lucy? Who had been at the heart of a crowd, directing all the action, without even knowing she was?

Imposing her standards on others as unconsciously as breathing?

Lucy? Who had been the most popular girl in her graduating class, not standing up for herself with the likes of Claudia Mitchell-Franks?

Lucy? Who had always been "in," now suddenly having to beg for use of the yacht club in the town named for her grandfather?

Lucy? Who had been as conservative as her parents before her, now tentatively painting her house purple and enraging the community by running a commercial venture from her dock?

"What happened to you?" he asked softly.

And he saw more than secrets in her eyes—enormous, green, dazzling. But if he didn't allow himself to be dazzled, he was sure he saw something he really didn't want to see. He saw fear.

CHAPTER FIVE

FOR ONE MOMENT Lucy was almost overcome by a desire to tell him. Everything. That after he had left that summer, her whole world as she had known it had changed irrevocably and forever.

But she was not giving in to impulses—she already regretted the charade behind Claudia's back—and especially not where Mac was concerned.

"Nothing happened to me. I grew up. That's all."

She didn't want him to look too closely at the table. The charitable foundation registration was sitting there. So was the rezoning application that would allow her to turn this house into a group home for unwed mothers.

She was not getting into that. Not with him. Not now and not ever.

Still clutching her housecoat closed, she went over and inserted herself between him and her secrets.

"Is there something on that table you don't want me to see?"

She was close enough that she could smell him, the scent of the pure lake water not quite eradicated by a faint soapy scent.

"No."

"Unlike Claudia," he said, "you are developing a little worry furrow right here."

He touched between her brows.

And she wanted, weakly, to lean into his thumb and share her burdens. She had secrets. She was worrying. It was none of his business. He was a man she had known back when he was a boy. To think she knew anything about him now, on the basis of that, would be pure folly.

Unless she remembered she couldn't trust him.

"Seven years," he said, peering over her shoulder. "What could possibly be on your table after seven years that you wouldn't want me to see?" He waggled his eyebrows at her in that fiendish way that he had. "The possibility of a lingerie catalog is making me look harder."

Enough. She snatched the money from where he had set it on the table, and looked at it with exaggerated interest. "I don't want this."

Mac shrugged. "Donate it to your favorite charity."

"All right," she said stiffly. There was an irony in that that he never had to know about. In fact, he did not need to know one more thing about her. She was all done laughing for the day. It felt like a total weakness that he coaxed that silly part from her. And the story of her broken engagement.

She didn't like how that had changed him, some wariness easing in him as he looked at her.

"Now, I have to go get dressed, so if you'll excuse me…"

"What *is* your favorite charity?"

She shook her head, felt put out that he was trying to make conversation with her instead of obediently heading for the door.

"Why? Do you want the receipt?"

He turned, and relieved, Lucy thought that she had insulted him and he was going. Instead, he went into her living room and sat down in one of her overstuffed chairs. If she was not mistaken, the only reason he was still here was that he was devilishly enjoying her discomfort.

At least he'd moved away from the rezoning documents.

He appeared totally relaxed, deeply enjoying the view out her window.

She cocked her head at him, unforthcoming. Who could outwait whom?

He picked up the book that was open on the arm, but she raced over and snatched it away—not quickly enough.

"Interesting reading material for a girl who has given up on fairy tales. *To Dance with a Prince?*"

She bit back an urge to defend her choice of reading material, but he had already moved on.

"I like what you've done to the place," he said. "Kind of ski-lodge chic instead of Victorian manor house. I doubt that was your mom. I bet the exterior paint color wasn't her choice, either. It's surprisingly Bohemian for this neck of the woods."

"The paint is barely dry and the neighbors have lost no time in letting me know they don't appreciate me indulging my secret wild side."

And then it was there, the danger. It sizzled in the air between them. Her secret wild side was interwoven with their history. Those heated summer nights of discovery, bodies melting together. That hunger they'd had, an almost desperate sense of not being able to get enough of each other.

She found his eyes on her lips and the memory was scalding.

She was shocked by what she wanted. To be wild. To taste him just one more time. To throw caution to the wind.

"I would have pictured you in a very different life, Lucy."

"Really?"

"Traditional. A big house. A busy husband. A vanload of kids, girls who need to get to ballet lessons, boys who need to be persuaded not to keep their frogs in the kitchen sink."

She was silent.

"I thought you would be living a life very similar to that of your parents, that you'd be hanging with all those kids you grew up with. Friday drinks with friends at the yacht club, water-skiing on weekends in the summer, trips to the ski hill in the winter."

She arched an eyebrow at him. "I'm surprised you pictured me at all."

It was his turn to be silent. The view out the window seemed to hold his complete attention. And then he said, quietly, "A man never forgets his first love."

Something trembled inside her. "I didn't know I was your first love."

"How could you not know? Those crazy weeks, Lucy. I'd wake up thinking of you. I'd go to sleep thinking of you. We spent every moment we could together. It felt as if I couldn't breathe unless you were there to give me air."

How well she remembered the intensity of those few weeks.

"You never said you loved me," she whispered.

He looked at her and smiled. She distrusted that smile. It could still turn her insides to jelly. That devil-may-care smile made him the most handsome man alive, but it said that nothing mattered to him. It was the wall he put up.

"I never say I love anyone," he said. "Not even Mama."

"You've never told Mama you love her?"

"I don't think so."

"Well, that just stinks."

"Anyway, those days are a long way behind us, Lucy."

Yes, they were and it would do nothing but harm to dredge them up. Even now, she could feel her heart beating way too quickly at his admission that he had spent night and day doing nothing but thinking of her. At the time, he certainly hadn't let on that's what was going on for him!

"So, what does the grown-up Lucy do for fun?"

The question took her aback. "Fun?" she asked uncomfortably.

"You were the girl at the center of the fun, as hokey and wholesome as I found it at the time. The water fight on the front lawn of the high school. The fund-raising car wash where they shut down Main Street and brought out the fire truck. The three-day bike excursion to Bartlett. The canoe trip across the lake, camping on the Point.

"I remember standing over at Mama's one night

when you had a group of kids here at your fire pit. You know what I couldn't believe? You had them all singing! All these kids who considered themselves cooler than cool, singing *Row Row Row Your Boat*."

"I thought those days were a long way behind us," she muttered. "Besides, you never participated in any of those things!"

"No, I didn't."

"Why?"

"I felt I didn't fit in."

It was an admission of something real about him, and for the second time Lucy was startled. He had never once said anything like that when they were together. He had revealed more about himself in the last ten minutes than he had the whole time they were together.

"That never showed," she said. "You always seemed so supremely confident. Everybody thought you were so cool. Unafraid, somehow. Bold. If you wore a pair of jeans with a rip in the knee, half the school had ripped their jeans by the next week."

"It wasn't that I didn't have the right stuff—the clothes, the great bike, though I didn't—it wasn't that. It was that your crowd was all so damn *normal*. Two parents. Nice houses. A dog. Allowances. Born into expectations of how they would behave and what they would become. I felt excluded from that. Like I could never belong, only be a visitor."

"I hope I never made you feel like that."

"No, Lucy, you never did. In fact, for those few weeks—" He stopped.

"For those few weeks what?" she breathed.

But he rolled his shoulders, like a fighter shrugging off a blow. "Nothing."

And the veil was down over his eyes, and that was what she remembered most about him. Get close, but not too close.

"You kind of bucked all those expectations of you, didn't you, Lucy?"

Oh, yeah. Because she had had one life before Mac and a completely different one after.

"My life may not be what my father and mother expected, but I have a really good life. I love what I do."

"Mama keeps me posted."

She felt mortified, and he saw it and laughed.

"Don't worry, nothing juicy, just tidbits of news. I heard about your online bookstore, and according to Mama, you do very well at it, too."

"Ah, well," Lucy said, wryly self-deprecating, "You know Mama. When she loves you, you can do no wrong."

"When did you two become so close? When I lived here there was always a kind of barrier, imposed by the doctor, between your family and her. You and Mama were polite to each other, and good neighbors, but you weren't mowing her lawn or repairing her house."

Again, Lucy had to fight with a voice inside her that said, *Wouldn't it be nice to tell him?*

But she reminded herself, firmly, that that summer when she had loved him, she had given and given and given until she had not a secret left. And he had not divulged anything about himself. Laughing at her efforts to find out.

I killed a man. With my bare hands.

"I don't remember the exact details," she lied. But oh, she remembered them so clearly. Flying across that lawn in the dark, the emotional pain in her so great, she was unaware she had stepped on a sharp rock and her foot was bleeding.

The door opening and Mama standing there.

Liebling! *What is it?*

"So, to get back to my original question, what do you do for fun?"

"My work's fun," she said firmly.

"I hope you're joking."

She felt mutinous. "What do you do for fun?"

"My work *is* fun. I developed a company that's all about fun. I think the roots of Wild Side started right here."

"So, your work is what you do for fun, too."

"Touché," he said. "But I do love the white-water kayaking. It is so physical and requires such intense concentration. It makes me feel more alive than just about anything I've ever done."

But a sudden memory flashed through his eyes and it was as if she could see it, too: lying in the sand beside him, the moonlight bathing them, never having ever felt quite so alive as that before.

Or since.

"I guess that's what I'm asking, Lucy. What makes you feel like that?"

"Like what?' she stammered.

"The way I feel when I am in a kayak. Alive. Totally engaged. Intensely in the moment. What makes you feel like that?"

If she said nothing, he would think she was a total

loser. And in fact there was something that made her feel exactly like that.

"I have something," she said reluctantly. And she did. "It makes me feel alive, but I'm pretty sure you wouldn't call it fun."

"Try me."

"Not today." To tell him would just make her feel way too vulnerable.

"Drink the schnapps and I'll ask again."

She marched into her kitchen, got down a shot glass, filled it from Mama's bottle and went back out. She slammed the liquid back. She blinked hard.

"Okay," he said. "What do you do for fun, Lucy Lin?"

"You already figured it out," she said, "I work. Now, shoo. Because I have a lot of that to do today."

Shoo. She wished she had worded that differently. He looked way too closely at her. He was too close to striking a nerve.

He turned to go. "I'll be back."

"I was afraid you would say that," she muttered as she watched him go. Even though she ordered herself not to, even though she knew she shouldn't, Lucy went and watched him cross the yards back to Mama's house.

He was whistling and the melody drifted in her open door, mingled with the scent of the trees, and tingled along her spine.

Rebel. It was a warning if she had ever heard one, and yet Lucy was aware that she felt alive in ways she had not for a long, long time.

Mac went back across the lawns, pensive. Something was so different about Lucy. What had changed in her?

He got the sense that maybe she had become an out-cast from the Lindstrom Beach crowd, which was the most surprising thing of all.

As surprising as her mowing lawns and trying to fix floorboards and renting canoes.

Her new aloneness in this community, was it her choice or theirs?

What mattered, really, was that Lucy was shoulder-ing all that responsibility for Mama and he had let her. She seemed alone, and she seemed just a little too grim about life.

Somewhere in her was a woman who wanted to paint her house purple, and probably wasn't going to.

Without an intervention. He was going to be the man Mama expected him to be.

Before he left here, he was going to help Lucy have some fun.

Lucy actually felt light-headed.

It was the schnapps, she told herself, not Mac Hudson crash-landing in her world. She went back upstairs and looked at herself critically in her bedroom's full-length mirror. First soaking wet, now in her housecoat! These were not the impressions she had intended!

She had intended to look sophisticated and coolly professional. Even if she did have a job where she could work in her pajamas if she wanted to.

Lucy found herself dressing for the potential of an-other meeting with him, and then made herself get to work. First, she turned on her computer and reviewed orders that had come in overnight. There were also a dozen more RSVPs for the Mother's Day Gala, three of them from girls she had gone to high school with, saying "will NOT be able to attend."

She felt something sag within her, and told herself it was not disappointment. It was pragmatic: the people refusing to come were the ones who could make the best donations to her cause.

But, of course, her cause was at odds with their vision for life around the lake.

Lucy forced herself to think of something else. She went into a spare room that had become the book room, retrieved the book orders and began to package them.

Later, she would review her rezoning proposal for Caleb's House, the documents lying out on her dining room table where she hadn't wanted Mac to see them.

As the day warmed, Lucy moved out onto her deck to work, as she often did. She told herself it was a beautiful day, but was annoyed at herself for sneaking peeks at Mama's house.

She could hear enormous activity—saws and hammers—but she didn't see Mac.

She wanted to go see what he was doing over there, but pride made her stay at home.

When she had finally succeeded in putting him out of her mind, the radio was on and she heard the ad about the donation of the Wild Side clothing in thanks for the donation of the yacht club for the Mother's Day Gala.

Within an hour she had been phoned by several representatives of the yacht club—notably not Claudia—falling all over themselves to make sure she knew she was most welcome to the space for the Mother's Day Gala, and that the regular charge had been waived.

Now, as evening fell, Lucy was once again cozy

in her pajamas, trying to concentrate on a movie. She found herself resentful that he was next door. She and Mama often watched a movie or a television show together in the evenings.

She hated it that she felt lonely. She hated it that she was suddenly looking at her life differently.

When had she allowed herself to become so boring? Her phone rang.

"Hello, Lucy."

"Mac," she said. "I've been meaning to call and thank you. The yacht club has confirmed."

He snickered. So did she.

"You didn't tell me Mama's car isn't even insured."

"Why would she insure a car she can't drive?"

"I took it to town three times for building materials before she remembered to tell me, ever so casually, that the insurance had lapsed. I could have been arrested!"

From loneliness to this: laughter bubbling up inside her.

"Anyway, Mama would like to see a movie tonight. Can you drive me to town so I can get one for her?"

"You're welcome to borrow my car anytime you need one."

"I'll keep that in mind, thanks, but Mama says I'm not allowed to pick a movie without you there. She says I'll bring home something awful. A man movie, she called it. You know. Lots of action. Blood. Swearing."

"Yuck."

"Just what Mama said. On the other hand, if we send you to get a movie without me, it'll probably be a two-hanky special, heavy on the violin music."

"Why don't you and Mama go get the movie?"

"She's making *apfelstrudel*." He sighed happily. "She says it's at the delicate stage. It'll be ready by the time we bring the movie back. She says you have to come have some."

It was one of Mama's orders. Unlike an invitation, you could not say no. As if anyone could say no to Mama's strudel, anyway. Still, it was not as if Lucy was agreeing to spend time with him. Or plotting to spend time with him. It was just happening.

"She hasn't stopped cooking since you got there, has she?"

"No, because I also made a grocery run before I found out I was driving illegally. She made schnitzel for supper," he said happily. "You know something? Mama's schnitzel would be worth risking arrest for. She's already started a new grocery list. Would you mind if we picked up a few things while we're in for the movie?"

Lucy did mind. She minded terribly that she had been feeling sorry for herself and lonely, and that now she wasn't. That life suddenly seemed to tingle with possibility.

From going for a movie and to the grocery store.

Her life *had* become too boring.

Of course, she wasn't kidding herself. The tingle of possibility had nothing to do with the movie or groceries.

Sternly, Lucy reminded herself she was not a teenager anymore. Back then, being around Mac had seemed like pure magic. But she'd been innocent. As he had pointed out earlier, she had believed in fairy tales. She'd been a hopeless romantic and a dreamer and an optimist.

It would be good to see how Mac fared with her adult self! It would be good to do a few ordinary things with him. Certainly that would knock him down off the pedestal she had put him on when she was nothing more than a kid. It would be good to see how her adult self fared around Mac.

It was like a test of all her new intentions, and Lucy planned on passing it!

"Meet me in the driveway," she said. "In ten minutes."

Did she take extra care in choosing what to wear? Of course she did. It was only human that while she wanted to break her fascination with Mac, it would be entirely satisfying to see his with her increase.

She wanted to be the one in the power position for a change.

If she looked at her life that was the whole problem. She had always given away too much power to others. Fallen all over herself trying to win approval.

If she had a fatal flaw, it was that she had mistaken approval for love.

"You know," Mac said, a few minutes later, "they say that people's choice of cars says a lot about them."

Lucy looked at her car, a six-year-old compact in an almost indistinguishable color of gray.

She frowned. The car was almost a perfect reflection of the life she seemed to be newly reassessing. "It's reliable," she said defensively.

"I can cross driving off the list of things you do for fun."

"What do you drive?"

"What do you think?" he said.

"I'm guessing something sporty that guzzles up more than your fair share of the world's resources!"

"You'd be guessing right, then. I have two vehicles. One a sports car and the other an SUV great for hauling equipment around."

"Both bright red?" she asked, not approvingly.

"Of course. One's a convertible. You'd like it."

"Flashy," she said.

"I don't enjoy being flashy," he said without an ounce of sincerity. "I just want to find my vehicle in the parking lot. It's crowded in the big city."

They got in the car. She did not offer to let him drive. It wasn't that her car would be a disappointment after what he was accustomed to. It was that she was not letting him take charge. It was a small thing, but she hoped that it said something about her, too.

"I'm glad you came with me," he said after her disapproving silence about his flashy car lengthened between them.

Something in her softened. What was the point of being annoyed at him? He wanted to be with her. She ordered her heart to stop. She glanced at him, and he was frowning at the list.

"I didn't want to have to ask a clerk where to find this." He held the list under her nose.

"Hey! I'm trying to drive."

It was a good reminder that the point of being annoyed with him was to protect herself.

"It's after seven. There's no traffic on this road." Still he withdrew the list. "C-u-m-i-n."

"Cumin?"

"I wouldn't have pronounced it like that. What is it, anyway?

"A spice."

He rapped himself on the forehead. "See? I thought it had something to do with feminine hygiene."

"Mac. You're incorrigible! What an awful thing to say!"

"Why are you smiling then?"

"My teeth are gritted. Do not mistake that for a smile! I do not find off-color remarks funny."

"Now you sound like you've been at finishing school with Miss Claudia. Don't take life so seriously, Lucy. It's over in a blink."

That was twice as annoying because she had said almost the very same thing to herself earlier. Lucy simmered in silence.

CHAPTER SIX

"SAME OLD PLACE," Mac said, as they entered the town on Lakeshore Drive, wound around the edge of the lake, through a fringe of stately Victorian houses, and then passed under the wooden arch that pronounced it Main Street.

Lucy's house was two miles—and a world—away from downtown Lindstrom Beach. Main Street had businesses on one side, quaint shops that sold antiques and ice cream and rented bicycles and mopeds. Bright planters, overflowing with petunias, hung from old-fashioned light standards.

On the other side of the street mature cottonwoods formed a boundary to the park. Picnic tables underneath them provided a shaded sitting area in the acres of white-sand beach that went to the water's edge.

"Charming," she insisted.

"Sleepy," he said. "No. Make that exhausted."

The shops would be open evenings in the peak of the summer season, but now they were closed, their bright awnings rolled up, outdoor tables and chairs put away against the buildings. There were two teenagers sitting at one of the picnic tables. She was pretty sure they were both wearing Wild Side shirts.

They left downtown and the main road bisected a residential area. Lucy Lindstrom loved her little town, founded by her grandfather. This part of it had wide tree-shaded boulevards, a mix of year-round houses and enchanting summer cottages.

Under the canopy of huge trees, in the dying light, kids had set up nets and were playing street hockey. They heard the cry of "car!" as the kids raced to get their nets out of the way.

"I bet you don't see that in the big city."

"See?" he said. "You still believe in the fairy tale."

"I don't really think it's so much a fairy tale," she said, a trifle defensively. "This town, my house, the lake, they give me a sense of sanctuary. Of safety. Of the things that don't change."

In a few weeks, as spring melted into summer, the lake would come alive. Main Street Beach, which Lucy could see from her dock, would be spotted with bright umbrellas, generations enjoying it together.

There would be plump babies in sun hats filling buckets with sand, mothers slathering sunscreen on their offspring and passing out sandy potato chips and drinks, grandmothers and grandfathers snoozing in the shade or lazily turning the pages of books.

Along Lakeshore Drive, boards would come off the windows of the summer houses. Power boats, canoes and the occasional plane would be tied up to the docks. The floats would be launched and quickly taken over by rowdy teenagers pushing and shoving and shouting. There would be the smell of barbecues and, later, sparks from bonfires would drift into a star-filled sky.

"I'm unchanging. As incorrigible as ever."

"Can you ever be serious?"

"I don't see the point."

"I love this town," she said, stubbornly staying on the topic of the town, instead of the topic of *him*. "How could anyone not love it?"

Now, added to that abundance of charm that was Lindstrom Beach, Lucy had her dream, and it was woven into the peace and beauty and values of her town. The dream belonged here, even if Claudia Johnson didn't think so!

And so did she. Even if Claudia Johnson disapproved of her.

"How could anyone not like it here?" She could have kicked herself as soon as it slipped out. It sounded suspiciously like she cared that he didn't like it here.

"How much you like Lindstrom Beach depends on your pedigree." Suddenly he sounded very serious, indeed.

She glanced at him. His mouth had a firm line to it, and he took a pair of sunglasses out of his pocket and put them on. She was pretty sure those sunglasses had been in the lake yesterday.

"It does not."

"Spoken by the one with the pedigree. You have no idea what it was like to be a kid from the wrong side of the tracks in Lindstrom Beach."

This time the chill in the voice was hers. "That may be true, but it certainly wasn't for lack of trying."

Suddenly, the pain felt fresh between them, like fragile skin that had been burned only an hour or two before. He had been right. There was no point being so serious.

If she could, she would have left things as they were, lived contentedly in the lie that she was all over that, the summer she had spent loving Mac nothing more than the foolish crush of a woman barely more than a girl. She'd only been seventeen, after all.

He had teased her about it then. The perfect doctor's daughter having her walk on the wild side. When she had first heard the name of his company, she had wondered if he was taunting her for what she had missed. But he had never asked her to go on that journey with him. And besides, that brief walk on the wild side had been a mistake.

The repercussions had torn her oh-so-stable family apart. And then, there was the little place on a knoll behind the house, deeply shaded by hundred-year-old pines, that she went to, that reminded her what a mistake it had been.

Leave it, a voice inside her ordered. But she was not at all sure that she could.

"Macintyre Hudson," Lucy said, her voice deliberately reprimanding, "you lived next door to me, not on the wrong side of the tracks."

But underneath the reprimand, was she still hoping she could draw something out of him? That she could do today what she had not been able to do all those years ago?

Find out who he really was, what was just beneath the surface of the incorrigible facade he put on for the world?

He snorted. "The wrong side of the tracks is not a physical division. Your father hated Mama's old cottage, hardly more than a fishing shack, being right next door to his mansion. He hated it more that she brought children of questionable background there. His failures in life: he failed to have Mama's place shut down, and he failed to bully her in to moving."

Mac didn't know that, in the end, her father had considered *her* one of his failures, too.

"But it looks like Claudia Johnson née Mitchell-Franks has taken over where he left off," he said drily. And then he grinned, as if he didn't care about any of it. "I think we should attend her little shindig on Friday night at the yacht club."

The grin back, she knew her efforts to get below the surface had been thwarted. Again. She should have known better than to try.

"I wouldn't go there on Friday night if my life depended on it," she said.

"Really? Why?"

"First of all, I wasn't invited."

"You need an invitation?"

A little shock rippled through her. All those years ago, was it possible that he had never thought to invite her to go with him when he left Lindstrom Beach? That he had just thought if she wanted to go, she would have taken the initiative?

Lucy did not want to be thinking about ancient history. She was not allowing herself to dwell on what might have been.

But still, she said, "Yes, I need an invitation."

"Your grandfather built the damned place."

"I never renewed my membership when I came back."

"You're going to allow Claudia to snub you? I'd go just to tick her off. It could be fun."

But Lucy felt something dive in the bottom of her stomach at the thought of going somewhere where she wasn't wanted, all that old crowd looking at her as if she was the one who had most surprised them all, and not in a good way.

Fun. His diversionary tactic when anything got too serious, when anything threatened the fortress that was him.

"Well, showing up where I'm not wanted is not exactly my idea of a good time."

"I have a lot to teach you," he said, then, "And here we are at the grocery store. Which is open at—" he glanced at his watch "—half past seven. Good grief." He widened his eyes at her in pretended horror and whispered, "Lucy! Are they open Sunday?"

"Since I've moved back, yes."

"I'll bet there was a petition trying to make it close at five, claiming it would be a detriment to the town to have late-night and Sunday shopping. Ruin the other businesses, shut down the churches, corrupt the children."

She sighed. "Of course there was a petition."

The tense moment between them evaporated as he got out of the car and waited for her. "Come on, Lucy Lin, let's go find the cumin. And just for fun, we have to buy one thing that neither of us has ever heard of before."

"Would you quit saying the word *fun* over and over as if you don't think I know what it is? Besides, this is Lindstrom Beach, I don't think you'll find anything in this whole store that you've never heard of before."

"You're already wrong, because I'd never heard of cumin. Would you like to make a bet?"

Don't let him suck you into his world of irreverence, she ordered herself sternly.

"If I find something neither of us has ever heard of, you have to eat it, whatever it is," he challenged her.

"And if you don't?"

"You can pick something I have to eat."

It was utterly childish, of course. But, reluctantly she thought, it did seem like it might be fun. "Oh, goody. Pickled eggs for you."

"You remember that? That I hate those?"

Unfortunately, she remembered everything.

And suddenly it was there between them again, a history. An afternoon of canoeing, a picnic on an undeveloped beach on the far shore. Her laying out the picnic lunch she had packed with a kind of shy pride: basket, blanket, plates, cold chicken, drinks. And then the jar of eggs. Quail eggs, snitched from her mother's always well-stocked party pantry.

She had made him try one. He had made a big deal out of how awful it was. In fact, he had done a pantomime of gagging that surpassed the one she had done of Claudia yesterday. But, at that moment that he had started gagging on the egg, they had probably been going deeper, talking about something that mattered.

"I'm not worried about having to eat pickled eggs," he said. "I'm far too competitive to worry. I'll find something you've never heard of before. Unlike you, who are somewhat vertically challenged, I am tall enough to see what they tuck away on the top shelves."

As he grabbed a grocery cart, Lucy desperately wanted to snatch the list from him and just do it the way she had always done it. Inserting playfulness into everyday chores seemed like the type of thing that could make one look at one's life afterwards and find it very mundane.

And with Mac? There was going to be an afterward, because he was restless and he would never be content in a place like this.

"Here's something now," he said, at the very first aisle. "Sasquatch Bread. I mean, really?"

"It's from a local bakery. It's Mama's favorite."

"We'll get some, then. How about this?" He picked up a container. *"Chapelure de blé?"*

"What?"

"I knew it. Here less than thirty seconds, and I've already won."

She looked at what he was holding. "You're reading the French side. It's bread crumbs."

"Trust the French to make bread crumbs sound romantic. We'll take some of these, too. You never know when you might need romantic bread crumbs."

She was not sure she wanted to be discussing romance with Mac, not even lightly, but the truth was he was hard to resist. Even complete strangers could see how irresistible he was. She did not miss the sidelong glance of a mother with a baby in her buggy or the cheeky smile of leggy woman in short shorts.

But it seemed as if his world was only about her. He

didn't even seem to notice those other women, his focus so intent she could be giddy with it.

If she didn't know better than to steel herself.

But even with steeling herself against his considerable charm, just like that the most ordinary of things, shopping for groceries, was fun! He scoured the store for oddities, blowing dust from obscure items on the top shelves.

He thought he had her at quinoa, but when she said she made a really good salad with it, that went in the cart, too.

The strangest thing was that she was in a grocery store that she had been in thousands of times. And it felt as if she was discovering a brand-new world.

"Got it," he finally said. He held out a large jar to her. "You have never heard of this!"

"Rolliepops," she read. "Pickled herring wrapped around a savory filling. Ugh!"

"Gotcha!"

He bought the largest size he could find, and they found the rest of the things on the list, plus items he deemed essential for movie night: popcorn, red licorice and chocolate-covered raisins.

"You are really going to enjoy snacking on your Rolliepops during the movie," he told her as they strolled out of the store with their laden cart.

"I'd rather eat the bread crumbs."

"Then you shouldn't have admitted you knew what they were. Retribution for the quail eggs all those years ago," he said happily as he stowed all the things he had bought—most of them not on the list and completely impractical—in the trunk of her car.

The video store was also fun as they wrangled over movies. This was the part of being with him that she had forgotten: it was easy.

It had always astonished both of them what good friends they became and how quickly. They had thought they would be opposites. Instead, they made each other laugh. They thought their worlds would be miles apart, instead they were comfortable in the new world they created.

And now it was as if seven years didn't separate them at all. She felt as if she had seen him just yesterday.

Finally, after much haggling, they settled on a romantic comedy.

By the time they got back, it never even occurred to Lucy not to join him at Mama's house for the movie and fresh strudel. They parked the car back in her driveway and walked over with the groceries.

The strudel was excellent, the movie abysmal, Mama got up halfway through it and went to bed.

Suddenly, they were alone. Too late, Lucy remembered what else had come so easily and naturally to them.

When they were alone, an awareness of each other tingled in the air between them.

Back then, they had explored it. She with guilt, he with hunger, both of them with a sense of incredible discovery. The memory of that made her ache with wanting.

He was so close. She could smell the familiar, intoxicating scent of him. If she reached out, she could touch his arm.

"I have to go," she said, jumping up abruptly.

"Something urgent to do? Feed your fish? Put up a new swatch of color?"

"Something like that," she said.

"Don't forget, you owe me. You still have to eat a Rolliepop."

She grimaced. "I think I'd have nightmares. Herring wrapped around something 'savory'? Not my idea of a bedtime snack, but you know what? A bet is a bet."

"Yes, it is, but even though we had a deal, I'll let you off the hook. For tonight. I'll enjoy having something to hold over you."

He insisted on walking her back across the darkened lawns. A loon called on the lake and they both stopped to listen to its haunting cry.

"I don't like it that Mama was tired tonight," she said as they stood there. "She always insists on watching every movie to the end, even if it's awful. She told me once she always gives it a chance to redeem itself."

"People. Movies. She's all about second chances, our Mama. I'm concerned she's wearing herself out cooking for me. I told her to stop, but she won't."

"What rhymes with stop?" Lucy asked.

"Schnop," he said, and they shared a quiet laugh, but grew serious again as they continued walking across the backyard.

"I'm worried that it's not cooking that's wearing her out."

"Me, too."

It felt entirely too good to have someone to share these worries with.

"Has she said anything? About her health?" Lucy asked.

"No. I've been probing, too, but she says she's fine. While repairing the bathroom, I looked through the medicine cabinet. There was a prescription bottle, but she doesn't have internet, so I couldn't check what it's for."

"I can."

"I know, but it makes me feel guilty. Like I'm spying on her. It's kind of an affront to her dignity. So, I'm just going to hang out and fix the house, and keep my eyes and ears open and see if she tells me."

He stopped on her back porch.

"Good night, Lucy."

"Mac." It seemed to her suddenly she was a long way from her goal of proving to herself that he had no power over her anymore.

In fact, it felt like everything it had always felt like with him: as if the ordinary became extraordinary, as if she'd been sleeping and was coming awake, feeling the utter glory of life shimmering through her very pores.

The moonlight and the call of the loons wrapped her in their spell.

On an impulse she stepped in close to him. She needed to know.

On an impulse she stood up on her tiptoes. She needed to know if that was the same.

She wasn't sure why she had to do this. Maybe because she felt he believed she was way too predictable, from her car to her loyalty to her little town to what he presumed was the lack of fun in her life.

She had kissed other men since then. She had something to compare him to now. She had not back then. She would not be as easy to dazzle as that girl, a virgin whose only experiences with kisses had been spin-the-bottle at parties.

Or maybe she just had something to prove to herself when she took his lips.

That she could have the power. That she didn't need to wait for other people to instigate.

But whatever her intention was, it was lost the second their lips connected. He groaned and pulled her close to him, surrendered to her and claimed her at the very same time.

Oh, no. It was the same.

It was the same way as it had always been. She had never felt it before him, and never after, either. Certainly not with the man she had nearly married.

Oh, God, had she picked James precisely because he didn't make her feel like this? No wonder he had gone elsewhere for his passion!

When Mac's lips met hers, it was as if the world melted, as if the stars began to swirl in that dark sky, faster and faster until they melted right into it and everything became one. The stars, the sky, the loons, the lake, her, Mac.

All one incredible, swirling energy that was life itself.

How was it possible that she had convinced herself she could live without this?

She could feel the danger of being sucked right into the vortex of all that energy. She could feel the danger of wanting to be sucked into it.

Instead, she forced herself to yank away.

"Damn it all to hell," she said.

"Whoa. Not the normal reaction when a woman kisses me."

Was that often? Of course it was! Look at the man!

"You stud muffin, you," she said to hide how rattled she was.

"I have the feeling if we were on the dock, I'd be getting shoved in again. Why are you so angry with me, Lucy Lin?"

"I'm not!" she said.

And she wasn't. That was the whole problem. She wasn't angry with him at all. She loved it that he was making her laugh, and making ordinary things seem fun, and carrying the burden of Mama with her.

She loved the taste of his lips and the way his arms closed around her. It felt like a homecoming for one who had wandered too long in foreign lands.

She loved the way women looked at him in the grocery store, confirming what she always knew: Mac Hudson was about the most handsome man ever born.

And she hated herself for loving all those things.

She was angry with herself because she hadn't proved what she wanted at all. In fact, the exact opposite was true!

She had proved her life was empty and passionless, despite all her good causes!

She went in her house and closed the door, and forced herself not to look back to see him crossing the lawn in the moonlight.

"Stay on your own side of the fence!" she ordered herself grimly.

When Mac got back in, Mama was up, watching the end of the movie.

"I thought you were tired," he said.

"*Ach,* at my age, being tired doesn't mean you get to sleep. I thought the movie might redeem itself."

"Has it?"

"No. Why is this funny, people treating each other so badly?"

"I don't know, Mama." He sat down beside her, and she turned off the movie.

"What's wrong, *schatz?*"

"Mama, have I ever told you that I love you?"

"Of course," she said, with no hesitation. "Just not with words. You take time from your busy work and come to help me. What is that, if not love?"

"Too bad all women aren't as wise as you."

"When you look like me, you develop wisdom."

"I think you're beautiful," he said.

"See? What is that, if not love?"

"I'm worried about you, Mama. Living here by yourself. The house getting to be too much for you. I'm worried you're sick and not telling anyone."

"This is a good thing, my boy. To worry about someone else, hmm? It means you are not thinking of yourself all the time."

It was hard to be offended when it was true. He lived a hedonistic lifestyle. Self-indulgent. His business had allowed him to travel the world. Collect every toy. Seek increasing levels of adventure to fill himself, for a while. His lack of commitment made him responsible to no one but himself.

When he started feeling vaguely empty, he raced to the next rush, hoping it would be the thing that would fill him.

"When you feel pain, you have to do something for another."

"I can build you a new house."

"Would that make *you* feel better?"

"Wouldn't you like it?"

"I consider having more than what I need a form of stealing."

Hmm. Hadn't Lucy said something almost the same? About his vehicles. Taking more than his share of the world's resources?

"Everybody filling up their lives full, full, full with stuff," Mama said. "What is it they don't want to feel?"

"Lonely, I guess," he surprised himself by saying. "Less than."

"Do something for someone else."

"I am. I'm doing something for you."

"You should do something nice for Lucy."

Wasn't that what he'd already decided? But now, that kiss changed everything. He felt as if he was floundering.

"She seems angry at me."

"So, that stops you? You can only offer kindness if there is something in it for you? Why is she angry at you?"

"I don't know. I mean, you know we had a little thing that summer before I left. I knew she couldn't come with me. She loved it here. The little bit of time that she was with me put her at odds with her friends and family. Her dad threatened to have me arrested he was so put out by the whole thing. We were both stupidly young. How could that have worked?"

Mama was silent, and then she said, "You left her to

the only life she'd ever known. Maybe that was love, also, hmm, *schatz?*"

He was suddenly nearly blinded with a memory of how it had felt being with Lucy. Waking up with a smile on his face, needing to be with her. Practically on fire with the sensation of being alive.

He shook it off and sighed. "I'm not sure I'm capable of such nobility," he said. "She wanted more of me than I could give her."

"Ah."

"Maybe," he said hopefully, "it's not me that she's angry with. Her recent fiancé took a pretty good run at her self-esteem by the sounds of it. And something is going on with her old crowd. I hate it that Claudia Stupid-Johnson feels better than her."

"No," Mama said softly. "What you hate is that Lucy lets her."

He felt like he was getting a headache. This was all way too deep and complicated for a guy as dedicated to the rush as he was. But while he was tackling the hard stuff, there was no sense stopping halfway.

"You didn't answer me, Mama. Are you sick?" He hesitated, and said softly, feeling the anguish of it, "Are you going to die?"

"Yes, *schatz,* sooner or later. We are all dying. From the very minute we are born, we are marching toward the other end. Why does everybody act surprised when it comes? Why does everyone waste so much time, as if time is endless, when it is the most finite of all things?"

"I don't know," he said.

"Do something nice for Lucy. It will make you feel better. And send a card to your mother."

Mama patted his cheek, got up and went up the stairs.

Well, since he wasn't sending a card to his mother, that left doing something nice for Lucy. And he knew exactly what that was. She'd somehow lost sight of who she was. She was uncomfortable going to the yacht club! Hell, she should walk in there like the queen that she was!

He thought about her lips on his.

And wondered if Mama had any idea how complicated things could get.

CHAPTER SEVEN

LUCY WAS SITTING on her deck with her laptop. Her mother had sent her an email from Africa with a picture attached. Her mother looked happy. Her hair wasn't done, and she had a sunburn. It was odd, because Lucy didn't really recall her mother not having her hair done. And she was not what she would have ever called a happy person.

Her inbox had more RSVPs, two more from her old high-school crowd, saying no, they would not be able to attend the gala.

It didn't have quite the sting it had had previously. Of course, it was a beautiful mild spring day, the sun on the lake and her skin and in her hair. How could you feel bad on a day like this?

Was there a possibility she was able to dismiss negative things more easily and feel beautiful things more intensely since that kiss?

"Of course I'm not!" It was days ago! She hadn't, thank goodness, seen Mac since.

But think of the devil, and he will appear!

"Hey, Lucy Lin!" Mac was on the other side of her deck, peering through the slats of the deck railing at her. "Are you talking to yourself?"

Which would seem pathetic. Thankfully, she was not in her pajamas. It felt as if she was experiencing his sudden appearance intensely, too.

Her heart began to beat a little faster, her cheeks felt suddenly flushed. She was so aware of how incredibly handsome he was. And sexy. She was a little too aware of how his lips tasted.

He didn't wait for an answer.

"It doesn't look like you've made much progress on that paint."

"I'm not sure about the color anymore," she admitted a bit grumpily.

"Come and see what I found in Mama's shed."

She needed to pretend he wasn't there, go in her house and follow his suggestion of locking her doors.

But, of course, if she reacted like that, he would *know* he was affecting her way too deeply.

She set her laptop aside, got up and reluctantly padded over and looked over the railing, bracing herself. With Mac it could be anything, from a snake to an antique washboard.

He grinned up at her, and she knew that was what she really needed to brace herself against.

That, and the fact Mac was holding the handlebars of a bicycle built for two. It might have been gold once, now it was mostly rust. The leather seats were cracked.

"If you promise to keep your lips off of me, I'll take you for a ride."

"Look, let's get something straight. I didn't kiss you because I find you in any way attractive."

"Hey! That was just plain mean."

"Not that you aren't." Oh! This was going sideways.

"I kissed you as a way of saying thank you for caring so deeply about Mama."

"Well, I'm glad you cleared that up. Let's go for a ride."

She looked at him. She looked at the bike. She had cleared up the lip thing. Well, she hadn't really, but he had accepted her explanation. It was a beautiful day. An unexpected gift was being offered to her.

You are giving in to temptation, she told herself. "No," she told Mac.

"Look, princess, it's a bike ride or the Rolliepop. You owe me."

Her lips twitched. Once, for a few weeks, it had felt as if Macintyre Hudson was her best friend. She could tell him anything, be totally herself around him. In many ways, it felt as if she had found out what that meant—to be totally herself—around him.

She was aware of missing that.

Could they be friends? Without the complication of becoming lovers? What would it hurt to find out?

"You're even dressed for it," he said, sensing her weakening. "Aren't those things called pedal pushers?"

Those *things* were a pair of eighty-dollar trousers she had ordered well before her self-imposed austerity program. "It said capris when I ordered them online."

"Ah, well, you know, one born every minute."

And even though she had practiced saying no to him over and over again in her mind, she might as well not have practiced at all.

Because he was in possession of a bicycle built for two, and she wasn't in the mood to eat a Rolliepop. Plus, she was wearing an eighty-dollar pair of pedal pushers.

It seemed like it would be something of a waste not to try them out!

She came down off her deck, and they pushed the bike, which was amazingly heavy, up her steep driveway to the relative flatness of Lakeshore Drive above it.

"Hop on." He took the front.

She folded her arms over her chest. "Why would you automatically get the front?"

"I assumed it would be harder."

"I think you want control. That's where the brakes are. And the steering."

"Maybe *you* want control!"

"Maybe I do," she admitted.

He sighed as if she was really trying his patience. "If you want the front, you can have it. Look, you even have the bell." He rang a rusty old bell.

He surrendered the front, and she got on the bike. He got on the back. After a few false starts, they were off.

It felt as if she was pulling him. It was really the most awful experience. Because even though his handlebars were stationary and didn't move, he acted as if they did, and every time he wrenched on them the whole bicycle shook precariously.

"Quit trying to steer!"

"I can't help myself."

"Are you pedaling?" she gasped.

"With all my might. Ring the bell and wave, we're going by your neighbor gardening."

She giggled, rang the bell and waved. The bike veered, and he tried to correct it with his handlebars that didn't work. He nearly threw them both off the bicycle. Mrs. Feldman looked up, startled, and then smiled, unaware of the problems they were having, and waved back.

They rode by the houses with name plaques at the tops of the driveways. Her father had disapproved of naming the lake properties, saying he found it corny. But Lucy liked the names, ranging from whimsical: Bide Awhile, Pair-a-Dice, Casa Costallota, to the imposing: The Cliff House, Eagle's Rest, Thunder Mountain Manor. Sometimes you could catch a glimpse of the house from the road, other times lawns, gardens, trees, lake, the odd tennis court or swimming pool.

Had she been asked, Lucy would have said Lakeshore Drive was perfectly flat. Now, it was obvious that from her house toward town, it sloped substantially upward.

She was gasping for air. "Don't run over my tongue."

"Ready to trade places?"

She did, gladly.

Though the back position was slightly more relaxing than the front, the feeling of being out of control was terrible. She had to trust him.

"Hey, you got the easy part," she complained. The road that had been sloping upward crested, and began a gradual incline down.

"Woo-hoo! Look, no hands!"

"Put your hands back down."

"No, you put yours up. Come on, Lucy, fly!"

And so she did, and found herself shrieking with laughter as they catapulted down the hill, arms widespread, chins lifted.

His hands went back to the handlebars and so did hers.

"I think we need to slow down," she said. They were

approaching the bottom of the rise, the road banked sharply to the right.

"You think I'm not trying?"

In horror, she leaned by him to see he was squeezing the handbrakes with all his might. Nothing was happening.

"Try pushing backwards on the pedals."

He did. She did. The bike did not slow. They were coming up to the last curve into Lindstrom Beach.

He put his feet down to slow them. She was afraid he would break his leg. What his feet did was alter the course of the bike. It veered sharply left as the road went right. Her yanking away on her handlebars did nothing for their perilous balance.

They flew off the road and into a patch of thick bracken fern. She flew over her handlebars into him, and together they tumbled through the ferns. She landed on top of him, and the bike landed on top of her.

He reached up, and with one hand tenderly cupped the side of her face.

"Are you okay, Lucy Lin?" he asked with such gentleness it made her ache.

"I am," she heard herself saying. "I am okay. I haven't been for a long, long time, but I am right now."

"That's good. That's perfect. Did I mention where we were going before we were so rudely interrupted?" Mac asked her.

"I didn't think we were going anywhere. For a bike ride."

He reached around and shoved the bike off them. She sat up, then got up. The capris were probably ruined, a dark oily-looking smudge across the front leg, a grass stain on the other side.

"Ah, actually, no. We were going to cocktail hour at the yacht club."

She glanced at him, realized he must be kidding. "You have to *dress*," she reminded him, joking.

He was picking up the bike, inspecting it for damage. "We are dressed."

"That's not what she meant."

"Claudia had her opportunity to clarify and she didn't. So, we're dressed or we're naked. You pick."

She suddenly saw he was serious.

"I'm not going. I've scraped my knee. I think there are leaves in my hair."

He wheeled the bike over, picked the leaves out of her hair, bent down and inspected her knee. Then he kissed it.

"You're going," he said.

"There are smudges on the front of my pants."

"Well, there's one on your derriere, too."

"I am not going to the yacht club all disheveled and smudged, with leaves in my hair! What would they think of me?"

"Why do you care what they think of you?" he asked softly.

"I wish I didn't care, but I do, okay? So far, not one of them is coming to the Mother's Day Gala."

"Why not?"

"No one in this set has ever liked Mama. My father set the tone for that years ago. They're all for doing good on paper, but they don't do it in their backyard."

"That makes me all the more committed to attending their little cocktail hour."

"Not me," she said with a shiver.

"We are going," he said, firmly. "And you're walking into that room like a queen. Do you understand me?"

She looked at him. He wasn't kidding.

"I don't want to go."

"Life's about doing lots of things you don't want to do. You're going."

And suddenly Lucy knew, with him beside her, she could do just what he had said. She could go. And she could hold her head high, too.

Suddenly, she knew he was absolutely right. She *had* to go.

She sighed. "I love it when you're masterful."

"Really? I'll have to try that more often. Back on the bike, wench."

And just like that she was riding toward what she had feared the most for a long, long time. Only, she didn't feel at all afraid.

They rode up on their now quite wobbly bicycle built for two. She would have left it at the back door, but Mac was in the control position, and he rode along the pathway that twisted to the front of the club, where it faced the lake. Some of the cocktail crowd were out on the deck.

There was a notable pause in the conversation as they parked the bike.

Mac threw his arm over her shoulder as they went up the steps, and she glanced at his face.

He had that smile on.

If you didn't know him, you might be charmed by it.

She said quiet hellos to people on the deck, sucked in her breath and, with Mac at her side, entered the yacht club.

"Macintyre Hudson!" Claudia squealed, just in case anyone hadn't recognized him, "I'm so glad you came. Look, folks—" she looped her arm through his "—Mac is back!"

If he cared that he was in shorts when every other man was in a sports jacket and slacks, you couldn't tell.

As always, he carried himself like a king.

And she took her cue from him. Claudia was pointedly ignoring her, so she pointedly ignored Claudia.

"Ellen!" she said, finding a familiar face, "I haven't seen you for ages. What's this I hear that you don't like my paint color on my house?"

"Don't you, Ellen?" Her husband, Norman, turned and looked at her. "I like it."

Claudia's mouth puckered and pointed down. "Let me get you a drink, Mac."

"I'll have lemonade. Lucy?"

"The same."

She grinned at Mac. He had Claudia fetching her a drink!

He winked at her.

And suddenly, in this crowd of people who had once been her friends, she felt lighthearted. Had she bumped her head on the bike?

Because all these people *had* once been her friends. The girls she had known and chummed with since kindergarten. They had stopped calling her. Looked the other way when she came into a room.

And suddenly, she really didn't care. Wasn't that

more about them than her? Why hadn't she picked up the phone? When had she forgotten who she was?

They all seemed so stuffy! The atmosphere in this room seemed subdued and stifling. Mac's question came back to her. *What do you do for fun?*

"Why are we all inside?" Lucy asked. "It's a gorgeous day. And Mac and I brought a bicycle built for two!"

People were looking at her! Good!

"Anyone want to try the bike?" she asked.

Silence. It was obvious no one here was dressed for this. But even so, how could they be so young and still so set in their ways? Where were their kids, for heaven's sake? Didn't they like being with their kids? That made her feel almost sorry for them.

Lucy felt determination bubbling up in her. Not to change who they were. No, not that at all. But not to hide who she was, either. Not anymore.

"There will be a prize," she said, "It's trickier than it looks!"

Still, silence. They were going to reject her. She didn't care! She was stunned by the freedom of not caring!

"The prize is complimentary tickets to the Mother's Day Gala. I have a few left."

Some of them looked uncomfortable then!

"I might throw in a free canoe rental for an afternoon. Much more romantic than those power boats tied up at the dock. That's if I'm still in business."

She was throwing their snubs back in their faces, and loving it.

"Don't pass up on this! Mac is going to serenade

you with that famous song about a bicycle built for two while you ride."

She was aware of Mac giving her a sidelong look, but also of a little smile tickling the edges of his mouth that was quite different from his devil-may-care smile.

"Well, that I can't resist!" And then quiet little Beth Adams, whom she had always liked, stepped forward. "I'll try it." She gave Lucy a quick, hard hug, and said quietly, "It is so good to see you."

It was so sincere that Lucy felt tears sting her eyes.

After that it was as if a dam had burst. People coming and hugging her, shaking Mac's hand, saying how good it was to see them both.

The party moved out onto the lawn as everyone lined up to watch Beth try the bike. Beth hitched up her skirt and kicked off her shoes. Lucy got on the backseat. There was laughter and encouragement as they wobbled down the path.

"Sing," Lucy ordered Mac.

He was a good sport.

"Ring the bell," Lucy called as they turned around at the parking lot and came back, the assembled crowd scattering off the walkway. "Don't get going too fast, the brakes are faulty."

Beth rang the bell, as Mac sang.

The way his eyes rested on her, it almost felt as if he was singing to her. He looked so proud of her!

Then Beth called her sister, Prue, to try it with her. Prue gamely hitched up her dress and tossed her shoes on the grass.

Mac started the song all over. Lucy sang with him.

And then to her amazement, everyone was singing.

Laughter flowed as others tried the bike, first some of the women together, and then couples.

It seemed everyone had to have a turn.

Mac nursed his lemonade, delivered to him and Lucy on the lawn by a very sulky Claudia. He was glad to be out of the clubhouse and back into the sunshine.

The yacht club had surprised him. Once, it had seemed like *the* place that meant you'd arrived, the exclusive enclave of the old and wealthy Lindstrom Beach families. He'd never been invited here when he lived here, nor had he attended the functions that had been open to the public, a kind of reverse snub.

Now, all these years later he'd been to places that were truly exclusive. Many of them.

And in comparison the Lindstrom Beach Yacht Club seemed like a three trying to be a nine. It had a "clubhouse" feel to it, but not in a good way. There was carpet, which was always a bad idea in a place close to water. The paneling was too dark and the paintings too somber.

He smiled as Lucy got everyone moving to the deck and then down on the lawn.

There was quite a gathering of people he'd gone to school with, some of them relatively unchanged, some changed for the worse. Most had arrived in the powerboats that were tied to the dock, and most of the women, at least, were "dressed," their opportunity to haul out the expensive cocktail dresses they normally wouldn't get a chance to wear.

Billy Johnson had aged poorly and had a tortured comb-over hairdo, and a potbelly.

Lucy was as he remembered her, finally. At the heart of it all. Encouraging them to laugh and have fun. Just as in the old days, they thought they were so cool, but they were chirping along to that hokey old song.

In her smudged pants and sleeveless top, with her knee bashed up, he thought she did look like queen.

He loved how she was getting everyone on that bicycle.

He loved how they were all singing that song, Lucy waving her arms around like a bandleader.

He noticed Claudia simmering beside him.

"You and Billy should try it," he said.

"Why would I?" she snapped.

"Come on, Claudia," Billy said. "Everybody but us has tried it. We could win the prize!"

She had been getting drinks when Lucy had announced the prize so Mac had to bite back a shout of laughter.

Annoyed, Claudia nonetheless did not want to seem like the only spoilsport on the lawn.

And Billy still had a bit of the captain of the football team in him. Or a few too many drinks. Because where everyone else had gone up the path and around the parking lot a few times, Billy began to go up the long steep driveway that people used to get their boats into the water.

At the top, he and Claudia disappeared onto Lakeshore Drive.

"Riding to town," someone guessed.

"Had a wreck," someone else said. "Impaired driving!"

"Oh, here they come!"

They had just turned around somewhere on the road. Claudia had obviously missed the part about the brakes, Billy had possibly already had too many drinks to get it.

As they whirred down the hill on the ancient bicycle, the little crowd burst into song.

The bike was wobbling but picking up speed. Billy was yelling, happily, "Faster! Faster!" He put his head down, pedaled with fury.

Claudia, her cocktail dress flying in the wind behind her was shrieking to him to slow down.

The crowd sang boisterously, saluting the couple with their wineglasses.

The bike careened down the hill and past the crowd. It went down the cement ramp that allowed boats to be backed gently into the lake.

Mac wasn't sure that Billy even tried the brake.

In fact, he seemed to be yelling "Ta-da" as they entered the water in a great spray of foam.

Claudia, on the backseat, flew off and into him, just as he and Lucy had done earlier.

It was spectacular! They both plunged into the water with a great splash.

Claudia floundered and squealed until Billy picked her up and hauled her out of the water. People swarmed around them. Claudia's dress looked as if it was made out of soggy toilet paper. Her hair hung in horrible ropes. Her makeup was running.

Her husband whirled her around. "Now, honey, *that* was fun! Hey, Lucy, did we win the prize?"

"Oh, you sure did," Lucy said. She was doubled over with laughter.

"What prize?" Claudia sputtered.

Mac could not take his eyes from Lucy. This is what he remembered. At the very center of it all. Only, there was something about it that was even better.

Because before, there had been no shadows in her.

And now that there were, it was twice as gratifying to see them go away. And now that there were, it was like seeing the sun after weeks of rain.

Beautiful.

The most beautiful thing he had ever seen.

CHAPTER EIGHT

"I'VE GOT TO make some changes to the gala," Lucy panted. She was on the front of the bike, pedaling with all her might. They had left the yacht club and were on the final hill before her house. "I had it all wrong. It was like, when I was planning it, I was trying to win their approval. And none of them were even coming!"

"Well, they're all coming now," he said.

"That remains to be seen. They could all come to their senses before then."

"I think they just did come to their senses."

"I don't want it to be stuffy."

"Like cocktail hour was before you arrived?"

"Exactly. We need something more fun for the gala. I mean, still a dinner, and obviously it's too late to change the black-tie part, but what would you think of a comedian?"

"Lucy, please be quiet and pedal the bike!" She didn't even seem to be tired, bursting with a new energy. Mac wondered what the heck he had unleashed.

Since they knew the bike had no brakes, they walked the final decline in the road. Now that he had seen her light flicker back on, Mac felt honor bound to fan it to life, to keep it going, and it didn't take much.

Over the next few days, he did simple things. He brought a pack of hot dogs and some sticks to her place, and they roasted wieners over an open fire. And then cooked marshmallows, and ate them until their hands and faces were sticky.

He had the bike fixed and they rode it into town for ice cream.

He had one of his double kayaks sent up, and they began to explore the lake in the afternoons.

All this wholesome fun was great, but he wanted to show her more. He wanted to show her a bigger world than Lindstrom Beach. He wanted to show her he was more than the boy he had once been. That he had succeeded in a different place and moved in that place with comfort and confidence.

It occurred to him that his need to show her something more of himself was not strictly within the goal he had set for himself of showing Lucy some fun.

But since he already knew just how he would do it, he refused to ask the question whether he was going deeper than he had ever intended to go.

"Miss Lindstrom?" a deep voice, faintly muffled voice said.

"Yes?" Lucy shook herself awake, played along. She was still in bed. She looked at the clock. It was 6:00 a.m. A girl could live to wake up to the sound of his voice, even when he was trying to disguise it.

"You have won an all-expense-paid trip to Vancouver, B.C. Your flight is departing from the Freda dock in ten minutes."

That sounded so fun. And exciting. Lucy marveled

at this woman she had become. But maybe they'd better set some limits.

"Mac!"

His voice became normal. "How did you guess?"

"You're the only one I know with a plane tied up at Mama's dock. I can't come—for goodness' sake, the gala is days away. This is no time to be taking off."

"Literally, taking off."

"Ha-ha."

"I'm coming over."

Something in her sighed. Mac coming over, them passing back and forth between houses as if it was the most natural thing in the world.

The truth was she couldn't wait to see him. Seeing him for the first time in a day always felt so wonderful. She told herself she had to stop this. She told herself she was playing with fire.

But she had set it off, all those days ago when he had shown up with the bicycle to see if they could be friends.

And it seemed as if they could.

Okay, so she yearned to taste him. To hold him. To kiss him. But no, that had ruined everything last time.

This time she was going to be satisfied with friendship.

She wrapped her housecoat around her and went to the door. Mac looked incredible, of course, in a nice shirt and khakis.

"You spend an awful lot of time in that housecoat, Lucy Lin."

"It's six in the morning."

He grinned wickedly. "So, what do you say? You want to come play?"

"One of us has to be a responsible adult! The gala—"

"Part of the reason for the trip," he said with sincerity.

She folded her hands over her chest, waiting to see how he was going to pull this off.

"Mama found out it's not just about Mother's Day. That it's in her honor. She's quite impressed that something at the yacht club is being held in her honor. She considers it *swanky*."

"But it's supposed to be a surprise!"

"Come on. There are no secrets in Lindstrom Beach."

That, Lucy knew firsthand. "Did you tell her?"

He looked hurt. "No. Agnes Butterfield. It slipped out, apparently. Mama thinks it's a good thing she found out, because, according to her, she has nothing suitable to wear to such a *swanky* venue."

"Could you quit saying *swanky* like that? As if we're a bunch of small town hicks putting on airs?"

"Consider swanky banned from my vocabulary. If you'll come."

Really? A fly-in shopping trip to the big city? How on earth could she refuse that? Apparently he still thought she was resisting, and it was fun to make him try and convince her to do something she'd already decided she wanted to do.

"Mama says a galoot-head like myself cannot be trusted to help her pick a dress."

He was pushing all the right buttons. "Mac, she has more dresses and matching hats than the queen." But she said it weakly.

The carefree look melted from his face. He turned from her and looked over the inky darkness of the lake. His voice was low when he spoke. "She told me nothing she owns fits, that she lost a lot of weight last winter."

Lucy felt that ripple of fear. "I never noticed that," she said, biting a nail.

"I didn't, either. I thought it was because I hadn't seen her for a while. She said it's because she walks more, now that she doesn't have a driver's license."

Lucy closed her eyes, tried to swallow the fear and think rationally. She realized she was really dealing with two kinds of fear.

One, that something was wrong with Mama that had her losing weight and planning her own funeral.

And two, that Mac Hudson was standing on her back deck, and he still made her feel as though she was melting.

There was something quintessentially sexy about a man who could fly an airplane.

As if he knew she had given in, he said, "I told her I'd get her a new dress for her birthday. Lucy, we'll leave in a few minutes, shop, have a nice private birthday lunch with Mama and be home by early evening. It will be fun."

Oh, more fun. Didn't it seem like she was setting herself up for a heartbreak? Because he would leave and all the fun she was becoming so accustomed to would stop.

It was only a heartbreak if there was love involved she told herself. They were just friends. Besides, when was the last time she had just had a lighthearted shopping trip?

Come to think of it, Lucy realized, she was going to need a dress, too.

And come to think of it, she needed a dress that would show Mac she was not quite the stick-in-the-mud, fun-free creature he seemed to believe she was.

And maybe that she had come to believe she was, too!

Besides, wouldn't it be the best of exercises to prove that not only was she capable of embracing a spontaneous day of pure fun, but that she didn't have anything to fear from her reactions to Mac anymore?

She was a grown-up. So was he.

They could be friends. They had been proving that all week, with their strongest bond being their mutual caring for Mama Freda.

Still, this felt different than hanging out over a bonfire, eating marshmallows until they were sticky and sick.

Lucy found herself choosing what to wear very carefully. Finally, she settled on jeans, high heels, a white tailored shirt and a leather jacket. She'd finished with a dusting of makeup, a few curls in her too-short hair, and big gold hoop earrings. The look she was hoping for was casual but stunning.

And from the almost surprised male appreciation in his eyes, she had achieved it.

Mac helped Mama into the plane. Then it was her turn, and his hand closed around hers to hand her up. Given that the plane was bobbing on water, and they were stepping from the dock, this took more physical contact than Lucy had prepared herself for, but at least she didn't end up with his hand on her backside!

Her reaction to it, she told herself, was only evidence that it was time for her to stop being such a hermit.

Mama insisted on sitting in the back.

Apparently she was terrified of flying, a small detail that she was not going to allow to get in the way of a shopping trip and a new dress.

Mac leaned into the back to help her with her seat belt, but she refused the headset Mac passed to her. Instead, out of a gargantuan red handbag, she pulled a bulky eight-track tape player. After checking batteries, she plugged in an eight-track cassette. Then, she fished through the enormous purse, pulled out a book of word searches and a pencil and hunkered down in her seat.

"Mama, there's nothing to be worried about," Mac told her.

"Worried, schmurried," she muttered without looking up from the book.

He shrugged and grinned at Lucy, then helped her buckle in, and adjusted her headset for her. There was something entirely too sexy about Mac at the controls of the plane. He was confident and professional, on a two-way radio filing a flight plan, going through a series of checks.

As the plane taxied along the lake, Lucy looked over her shoulder to see Mama jacking up the volume of her eight track and squinting furiously at her book.

"Is that Engelbert Humperdinck?" Mac asked.

"I'm sure that's what she's listening to." Lucy confirmed.

She thought she heard a sound from Mama, but when she turned around again it was to see Mama glance out the window at the lakeshore rushing by them, go pale and jack up the volume yet again.

The plane wrested itself from gravity, left water and found air. Lucy found herself holding her breath as the plane lifted over the trees at the far end of the lake and then banked sharply.

"Have you ever been in a small plane before?"

"No."

"Nervous?"

Lucy contemplated that. "No," she decided. "It's exhilarating."

Mac flew back over her house and she knew he had done that just for her. Her house from the air was so cute, like a little dollhouse, all the canoes lined up like toys on her dock.

She thought it looked very nice in white.

"Is the lavender going to be a mistake?" she said into the headset. Then, "No! No, it isn't!"

He smiled at her as if she had passed a test—not that devil-may-care smile that held people at a distance. But a real smile, so genuine she could feel tears smart behind her eyes.

She turned and tried to get Mama's attention so she could see her own house from the air, but Mama was muttering along to her music, licking her pencil furiously, and scowling at her word-puzzle book, determined not to look out that window.

"What's Caleb's House?" Mac asked.

She went from feeling safe and happy to feeling as if she was on very treacherous ground. Lucy felt her heart race. "What? Why do you ask?"

"That's the charity Mama told me she wants the

money from the fund-raiser to go to. I'd never heard of it. She said to ask you."

She was aware she could tell him now. That there was something about hearing him say Caleb's name that made her want to be free of carrying it all by herself.

But the time was not right, and it might never be right. He was here only temporarily. Why share the deepest part of her life with him? Why act as though she could trust him with that part of herself?

She had trusted him way too much once before. She had talked and talked until she had no secrets left. Now, she had a secret.

After he had left here, seven years ago, Lucy had found out she was pregnant. Terrified, she had confided in one friend.

Claudia.

Claudia had felt a need to tell her mother and father, who had told Lucy's mother and father, and maybe a few other members of their church, as well.

Lucy's decent, upstanding family had been beyond dismayed.

"How could you do this to us?" her mother had whispered. "I'll never be able to hold up my head again."

Her father's disgust had been visited on her in icy silence. Her plans for college had gone up in smoke. Her friends had abandoned her. She had been terrified and alone, an outcast in her own town.

She had never felt so lonely.

And still, that life that grew within her had not felt like an embarrassment to her. It felt like the love she had known was not completely gone. She whispered to her baby. When she found out it was a boy, she went and bought him the most adorable pair of sneakers, and a little blue onesie.

When it had ended the way it had, in a miscarriage, it was as if everyone wanted to pretend it had never happened.

But by then she had already named him, crooned his name to him to make him feel welcome in a world where he was not really welcome to anybody but her. That was the night she had run to Mama's in her bare feet, needing to be somewhere where it would be okay to feel, to grieve, to acknowledge she could never pretend it hadn't happened.

That was the night she had spoken out loud the name of the little baby who had not survived.

Caleb.

Lucy was careful to strip her voice of all emotion when she answered.

"It's a house for young girls who are pregnant," she said. "It's still very much in the planning stages."

"One thing about Mama," he said wryly. "There's never any shortage of causes in her world."

To him it was just a cause. One of many. She took a deep breath. Was it possible he had changed as much as she had?

"Mac," she said, "tell me about you."

Part of her begged for him to see it for what it was, an invitation to go deeper.

Maybe it was different this time. If it was, would she tell him about Caleb?

"Remember I built that cedar-strip canoe?"

She nodded.

"My first sales were all those kind of canoes. It was

hard to make money at it, because they were so labor-intensive, but I loved doing it. I started getting more orders than I could keep up with, so I went into production. Pretty soon, I was experimenting with kayaks, too. Two things set me apart from others. Custom paint that no one had ever seen before—canoes were always green or red or yellow, some solid, nature-inspired palette, and I started doing crazy patterns on them. It appealed to a certain market."

As much as she genuinely enjoyed hearing about the building of his business, it hardly struck her as intimate.

"The other thing was, when you bought a canoe from me, you became part of a community. I kept in touch with people, put them in touch with other people who had purchased stuff from me. Eventually, it got big enough I had to do a newsletter and a website, a social-media page and all that stuff. I didn't realize I was setting something in place that was going to be marketing gold."

Was there something a little sad about him regarding the building of relationships as marketing gold?

"They didn't just buy a canoe. They belonged to something. They were part of Wild Side. Everybody wants to belong somewhere."

"It's kind of ironic," Lucy said. "Because you seemed like you didn't have that thing about belonging." *Even to me.*

"I guess I never found anything in Lindstrom Beach I wanted to belong to."

She looked swiftly out the window.

"I didn't mean that the way it sounded."

"No, it's okay," she said stiffly. "It was just a little

summer fling. I'm sure you moved on to bigger and better things. I mean, that's obvious."

"It's true I've become a successful businessman. And it's true I seem to have found my niche in life. But I've never been good at the relationship thing, Lucy. I have not improved with time. People want something I can't give them."

Was it a warning or a plea? She turned back and looked at him.

"And what is that?" she asked.

"They want to connect on a deep and meaningful level," he said, and there was that grin, devil-may-care and dashing. "And I just want to have fun."

She was not sucked in by the smile. "That sounds very lonely to me."

He raised an eyebrow. "I'm looking for someone to rescue me," he said, rather seductively, teasing.

Lucy turned back to the window and studied the panoramic views, water, earth and sky. He had always been like this. As soon as it started to go a little too deep, he turned up the wattage of that smile, kidded it away.

"Aren't you going to try and rescue me, Lucy Lin?" he prodded her.

"No," she said, and then looked back at him. "I'm going to get you a cat."

"I killed my last three houseplants."

"Wow. That takes commitment phobia to a new level. You can't even care about a plant?"

"Just saying. The cat probably isn't your best idea ever."

She sighed. "Probably not." Then she realized they

were in an airplane. It wasn't as if he could jump out. She could probe his inner secrets if she wanted to.

"You always seemed kind of set apart from everyone else. It seemed like a choice, almost as if you saw through all those superficial people and scorned them."

"I don't know if *scorn* is the right word," he said. "I've always liked being by myself. I'll still choose a tent in the woods beside a lake with not another soul around over just about anything else."

"It sounds to me like someone hurt you."

His face was suddenly remote.

"It sounds to me as if you don't trust anyone but yourself."

He didn't even glance at her, suddenly intently focused on the operation of the plane, and the instrument panel.

"I'm sure my father didn't help any. I'm sorry about the way Lindstrom Beach treated you. And especially my father. When you told me how he threatened you, said he was going to set you up as a thief, I was stunned. I was more stunned that you let it work. That you let him drive you away. I always figured you for the kind of guy who would stick around and fight for what you wanted."

"And I figured you would say something to your old man in my defense, but you never did, did you?"

All these years that she had nursed her resentment against Mac, and it had never once occurred to her that she had hurt him.

"That summer," he continued quietly, "I'd never felt like that with another person. So close. So connected. Not alone."

Lucy felt as if she couldn't breathe. It was the most Mac had ever said about how he was feeling.

"And the fact it was you, the rich girl, the doctor's daughter, loving *me*. Only, it was like you weren't the rich girl, the doctor's daughter. You stepped away from that role. You were so real, so authentic. And so was I around you. Myself. Whatever that was."

"Why didn't you at least ask me to go with you, Mac?"

"When you didn't take a stand with your dad, I guess I already knew what you would tell me later. That in the end, you would never fall for a boy like me. It would be too big a stretch for you. And unfair even to ask it."

But she was surprised by the pain, ever so briefly naked in his face. He had trusted her, and she had let him down. She could see his trust had been a most precious gift.

Lucy tried to explain. "It was only when it was obvious you were going, and you weren't going to ask me to go, that it was not even an option you had considered, that I said that. *I could never fall for a boy like you.*"

He glanced at her, searching. "It cut me to the quick Lucy. It made me so aware of everything that was different about us when I had been living and br said everything that was the same. I guess before ne and that, I thought we'd keep in touch. That dn't meant write. And maybe come back to visit meant it as in

Now was the time to tell him th it as in he wasn't worthy of her. rable with her. he was too closed, he couldn's if he had already

"Mac, I'm so sorry."

But she suddenly look

revealed more about himself than he wanted to, been as vulnerable as he cared to get. Some things didn't change, and she did not feel she could repair that hurt caused all those years ago by trying to clarify it now.

He must have felt the same way.

"It's all a long time ago," he said with an uncomfortable shrug. "Look where it led me. Hey, and look where we are. We're almost there. Look out your window. We'll be passing right over the Pacific Ocean in two minutes, and then making our approach to the Vancouver Flight Centre at Coal Harbour."

His face was absolutely closed. If she pursued this any farther, she was pretty sure if he had a parachute tucked behind his seat he was going to strap it on and jump.

They still had the trip home! And maybe he needed a rescuer, even as he kidded about it. She didn't know how long he was going to stick around, but she had him for today.

Maybe, just for today, neither of them needed to be lonely.

"It's only been two hours! It takes four or five times long to drive here from Lindstrom Beach!"

now. It's great, isn't it?"

to let she said, and suddenly felt a new willingness for her, embrace whatever surprises the day held had thro race the fact that for some reason fate left her pre back together with the man who had And who those years ago. Who had hurt her. a second chan hurt, too. Were they being given they just take it and embrace it without completely rehashing the past? Lucy found herself hoping.

"Are we landing?" Mama demanded from the back.

"Yes."

She put her puzzle book away and fished through her bag. She drew out her rosary beads.

"Hail Mary…"

Whether it was Mama's prayers or his expertise, or some combination of both they landed without incident and docked at one of the eighteen float-plane spaces at the dock.

A chauffeur-driven limousine was waiting for them, and it whisked them by the Vancouver Convention Centre to the amazing Pacific Centre Mall.

He pressed them into a very posh-looking store. The salesclerks in those kind of stores always recognized power and money, even when it came dressed as casually as Mac was.

"My two favorite ladies need to see your very best in evening wear," he said.

The clerk took it as a mission. Lucy and Mama were whisked back to private dressing rooms. Mac was settled in a leather chair and brought a coffee.

"Would you like something to read? I have a selection of newspapers."

He shook his head, but after Mama and Lucy had modeled the saleslady's first few selections, he wandered off. Lucy assumed he was restless, and didn't blame him.

Lucy had grown up with privilege, but even so, it had been Lindstrom Beach. She had never worn designer labels like these. She and Mama were in awe of how good clothes fitted, the fabric, the drape of them. Of course, even if she weren't on an austerity program, she would never be able to afford dresses like these. Even so, it was so much fun to try them on.

Mac came back, a dress over each arm. "The black for Mama, the red for you."

"Red," she said, and wrinkled her nose. "You know I'm not flashy, so you must be afraid of losing me in the parking lot. Do you have any idea what dresses like these cost?"

"The saleslady asked for my gold card before she'd even take those down for me."

"I shouldn't even try it on," she said, but heard the wistfulness in her own voice.

"You're trying it on."

"What can I say? You know I love it when you're masterful."

And so she did. She wasn't going to buy this dress, and she certainly wasn't going to allow him to buy it for her, but why not just give herself over to the experience?

Mama went first. Lucy and Mac had "oohed" and "aahed" over the selection of designer dresses that had been brought out for Mama so far, but the one he had chosen was the best. Simple, black, silk: it was classic. Lucy and Mac applauded as Mama modeled, as if she had been on the runway all her life. She sauntered down the walkway between the change rooms, hand on her ample hip, turned, winked, flipped the matching scarf over her shoulder.

The salesclerk, Mac and Lucy applauded. Mama beamed. "This is it."

It was Lucy's turn. The clerk came into the fitting

room with her to help slide the yards of red silk over her head.

Even before she looked in the mirror, Lucy could tell by the way she felt that this dress was the kind of dress a woman dreamed of.

The clerk stared at her. "That man has taste," she said.

Lucy turned and looked in the mirror. The dress had slender shoulder straps and a neckline that was a sensual V without being plunging. It had an empire waistline, tight under her breasts, and then it floated in a million pleats to the floor.

She came out of the dressing room.

"Walk like a queen," the clerk said.

That's what Mac had said, too, when he had forced her to go to the yacht club. *Walk like a queen.* In a dress like this it was easy enough to do.

When Mac saw her, his reaction was everything she could ever hope for.

She had never seen him look anything but in control, but suddenly he looked flustered.

"You," he said hoarsely, "are not a queen. Lucy Lin, you are a goddess."

She could not resist walking with swaying hips, spinning in a swirl of rich color, tossing a look over her shoulder. She licked her lips and winked.

She was trying to add a bit of levity, but Mac, for once, did not seem to find it funny.

After she had taken off the dress, Lucy came out of the dressing room, feeling oddly out of sorts. What woman tried on a dress like that and then felt okay when she walked away from it?

She went and waited outside the store while Mac bought Mama the black dress to wear at the gala.

Mama was hugging her package to her and chastising him in a mix of German and English about spending too much money on her. But they could both tell she was utterly thrilled.

They went for a fabulous lunch at a waterfront restaurant, and then, almost as if the whole thing had been a dream, they were back in the plane.

They were home before supper.

He helped her get down from the plane, then they watched Mama waddle happily across the yard with all her bags.

"Thank you for a beautiful day, Mac. It was like something out of a dream. Honestly."

He finished mooring the plane. He turned back to her.

"Okay," he said. "That's it. The whole show. I've shown you everything I do for fun. And you still haven't shown me. You said there was something."

"Oh." She felt doubtful. And then she decided to be brave. What if, by showing him, she eased that loneliness that he wore like a shield? Even for a few more hours?

"Let me make some phone calls. I'll call you in the morning."

"Phone calls to arrange fun," he said. "Skydiving? Horseback riding? I've got it! Bungee jumping!"

"I'm afraid I'm going to be a big disappointment to you, Mac."

Or maybe to herself. Because once again, even though he had given nothing, she had made a decision to be vulnerable. She would show him that thing she did that made her feel so alive.

And he most likely wouldn't understand that there were ways a person could not feel lonely.

And how could that be anything but a good thing if he didn't understand how connected this one thing made her feel? She could have her world back the way it had been before he landed again.

Only, she had a feeling it was not going to be quite that simple.

Mac picked up the phone on the first ring in the morning.

"Are you ready for your big outing, Mr. Hudson?" Lucy asked. "Be ready in ten minutes."

"Should I be dressing for bungee jumping or horse-back riding?"

"Actually, whatever you wear normally will be okay."

That could be anything from a wet suit to a suit suit, so Mac just put on some khakis and a sports shirt with the little kayak emblem on it.

He tried to take a clue from what Lucy was wearing and came to the conclusion it would be nothing too exciting. She might have been dressed for a day clerking at the bookstore. She was not the goddess he had seen in that dress yesterday.

And wasn't that a mercy?

Still, as they got in the car, he was so aware of her. Aware he liked being with her.

"We're going to Glen Oak."

They picked up coffees and conversation flowed freely between them. They talked of Mama and house repairs, the swiftly approaching gala and last-minute details, he made her laugh by doing an impression of Claudia receiving her free tickets to the gala, which he had delivered personally.

Having spent years in Lindstrom Beach, Mac was familiar with Glen Oak. Sixty miles from Lindstrom Beach, Glen Oak was the major city that serviced all the smaller towns around it. All the large chain stores had outlets there, there was an airport, hotels, golf courses and the regional hospital.

"Golfing," he guessed. "I have to warn you, I'm not much of a golfer. Too slow for me."

"That's okay, we're not golfing."

"Not even mini?" he said a little sadly as they passed a miniature golf course. He was aware he would like to go miniature golfing with her.

And horseback riding, for that matter. He wondered what it would take to talk her into bungee jumping.

He frowned as Lucy pulled into the hospital parking lot.

"We're going to a hospital for fun?" Mac asked. "Oh, boy, Lucy, you are in worse shape than I thought."

"I tried to warn you."

Perplexed, he followed her through the main doors. She did not stop at the main desk, but the receptionist gave her a wave, as if she knew her.

What if she was sick? What if that's what she was trying to tell him? Mac felt a wave of fear engulf him, but it passed as she pushed through doors clearly marked Neonatal.

She went to an office and a middle-aged woman

smiled when she saw her and came out from behind her desk and gave her a heartfelt hug.

"My very favorite cuddler!" she said.

Cuddler?

"This is Macintyre Hudson, the man I spoke to you about this morning. Mac, Janice Sandpace."

"Nice to meet you, Mr. Hudson. Come this way."

And then they were in a small anteroom. Through a window he could see what he assumed were incubators with babies in them.

"These babies," Janice explained, "are premature. Or critically ill. Occasionally we get what is known as a crack baby. We instigated a cuddling program several years ago because studies have shown if a baby has physical contact it will develop better, grow better, heal better, and have a shorter hospital stay. It also relieves stress on parents to know that even if they can't be here 24/7, and many can't because they have other children at home or work obligations, their baby is still being loved."

Lucy had already donned a gown with bright ducks all over it, and she turned for Janice to do up the back for her.

"You'll have to gown up, Mr. Macintyre."

He chose a gown from the rack. It had giraffes and lions on it. Lucy was already donning a mask and covering her hair.

Her eyes twinkled at him from above the mask.

He followed suit, as did Janice. She showed him how to give his hands a surgical scrub.

"Today we have multiples," Janice told him from behind her mask. "Twins. Preemies."

She gestured to a rocking chair. Lucy was already settled in one.

Side by side in their rocking chairs.

And then Janice brought Lucy the tiniest little bundle of life he had ever seen. Tightly swaddled in a pink blanket, the baby was placed in Lucy's arms. It stared up at her with curious, unblinking eyes.

"Amber," Janice said, smiling.

In seconds, Lucy was lost in that world. It was just the baby and her. She crooned to it. She whispered in its tiny little ear. She rocked.

This was what she did for fun.

Only, the look on her face said it wasn't just fun.

What Lucy did had gone way beyond fun. Her eyes on that baby had a light in them that was the most joyous thing he had ever seen.

Suddenly fun seemed superficial.

Lucy glanced at him. Even though she had a mask on, he could tell she was smiling. More than smiling— she was radiant.

"This is Sam," Janice said.

He looked up at her. His panic must have been evident.

"Don't worry," she said. "I'll walk you through it. Support his neck. See how Lucy is holding the baby?"

And then Mac found a baby in his arms. It looked up at him, eyes like buttons in the tiniest wrinkled face he had ever seen.

"Talk to him," Janice suggested.

"ET, call home," he said softly. If he was not mistaken, the baby sighed. "I was just kidding. You look more like Yoda. A very handsome Yoda."

He looked over at Lucy, crooning away as if she'd been born to this.

He didn't know what to say.

And then he did.

He sang softly.

It felt as if they had been there for only seconds when Janice came back in and took the now sleeping baby from him. "Thank you," she said.

"No, thank you."

And he meant it.

They were quieter on the way home. When she drove by the mini-golf course, he didn't feel like playing anymore.

Seeing her with that baby, he had known. He had known what he had wanted his whole life and had been so afraid of never being able to have that he had pretended he didn't want it at all.

She drove into her driveway. "I have so much to get done for the gala!"

But he wasn't letting her go that easily. "Is that a charitable organization, the baby thing?" he asked Lucy.

"Yes. It's called Cuddle-Hugs."

"Why aren't we doing Mama's fund-raiser in support of that?"

"Of course they need money to operate, but that's not what Mama chose."

"I'll talk to Corporate this afternoon. I'll have them call Janice. Anything they want. Anything. They'll get it."

"That's not why I took you there, to solicit a donation."

"I know. And we didn't go to Vancouver to buy you a dress, but I bought it for you anyway."

"You bought me that dress?" she gasped.

"So, what do you think now, Lucy Lin? Could you fall for a boy like me now?"

CHAPTER NINE

IT WAS ALL wrong. It was not what he had wanted to say at all.

Mac could have kicked himself. He didn't know where the question had come from. It certainly hadn't been on his agenda to ask something like that. That certainly hadn't been the reason for his donation, the reason for the fly-in shopping trip yesterday. He hadn't done it to impress her.

It was all just a gift to her. He had found his better side after all.

But now somehow he'd gone and spoiled it all by bringing up the past. Over the past few days Mac had convinced himself that they had pretty much put the past behind them.

But really, wasn't it was always there, the past? Wasn't that why he'd made her go to the yacht club and stand up for herself? Wasn't it true that he could not look at her without seeing her younger self, without remembering the joy of her trust in him, the way she had felt in his arms, the way her heated kisses had felt scattering across his face?

She took a startled step back from him. "Oh, Mac,"

she said, "when I said that all those years ago, it was never about what you had or didn't have."

He gave her his most charming smile. "It wasn't? You could have fooled me."

"I guess I did fool you. Because I didn't want you to know how deeply it hurt me that you never, ever told me a single thing about you. Not one single thing about you that mattered. And then when you left, you didn't even ask me to go with you. It seems nothing has changed. Even these gifts, so wonderful and grand, are like a guard you put up. That smile you are smiling right now? That's the biggest defense of all."

"You want to know why I never asked you to go with me, Lucy? It wasn't because I wasn't willing to fight for you. It was because you loved this place more than me. It was because I could see your family being torn up and your friends looking at you sideways as if you'd lost your mind. I gave you your life back. The part I don't get is that you didn't take it back. At all."

"No," she said, quietly, "I didn't."

"Why?"

"This isn't how it works, Mac, with you keeping everything to yourself, while I spill my guts."

"You know what? I've had about as much of Lindstrom Beach as I can handle. I wish I had never come back here."

"I wish you hadn't, either!"

He watched, stunned, as she walked away, went into her house and closed the door behind her.

With a kind of soft finality.

"Mama," he said a few minutes later, "something's

come up. I have to go back to Toronto. I bought that
dress for Lucy. Will you give it to her?"

"Give it to her yourself," Mama said, and went up
the stairs. He heard her bedroom door slam.

Both the women he loved were mad at him.

Wait a minute! He loved Lucy? Then he was getting
out of here just in the nick of time....

Lucy listened to Mac's plane take off.

"I don't care if he's gone," she told her cat. "I don't.
I always knew he wasn't staying."

She had a gala to finish organizing. She had her
dream of Caleb's House to hold tight to.

She burst into tears.

When the phone rang, she rushed to it. Maybe it was
him. Could he phone her from the plane? Was he telling her he was turning around?

"Hello from Africa, Lucy!"

Her mother was brimming with excitement. She'd
seen an elephant that day. She'd seen a lion. Somehow,
Lucy didn't remember her mother like this.

"Anyway," her mother said, "I know you'll be busy
on Mother's Day, so I thought I'd phone today. I didn't
want you having to track me down adding an extra
stress to your day."

That was unusually thoughtful for her mother. It
made Lucy feel brave.

"Mom," she said, "do you mind if I paint the house
purple? I mean, it's not purple, exactly, a kind of lavender."

It was kind of a segue to *Do you mind if I turn our
old family home into a house for unwed mothers?*

"Lucy! I don't care what color you paint the house. It's your house!"

"Mom, did you give me this house because you felt sorry for me? Because you thought I'd never get my life together without help from you?"

"No, Lucy, not at all. I gave you that house because I hated it."

"What?"

"It was the perfect house, I was the perfect doctor's wife and you were the perfect doctor's daughter."

"Until I ruined everything," Lucy said.

"It's only in the last while that I've seen how untrue that is, Lucy. When you got pregnant, it blew a hole in the facade. When you miscarried, I thought we could patch up the hole. That everything would be the same. That you would be the same.

"But you didn't come back. You didn't want what you had always wanted anymore. I think, at first, we were all angry with you for not coming back to your old life. Me, certainly. Your friend Claudia, too.

"Now I can see how we were really all prisoners in that house. Trying to live up to your father's expectations of us. Which was a nearly impossible undertaking. Everything always had to look so good. But keeping it that way took so much energy—without my even knowing it, had sucked the life force out of me.

"That hole you blew in all our lives? I glimpsed freedom out that hole. If your dad hadn't died, I would have left him."

Lucy was stunned.

"Lucy, paint the house purple. Swim naked in the moonlight. Dream big and love hard. I'm glad you didn't marry James. He was like your father—in every way, if you get my drift. He was cold and withholding and a control freak. And he was a philanderer."

"Mom? Mac came back." Somehow this was the talk she had always dreamed of having with her mother.

"And?"

"I love him!" she wailed. "And he left again!"

"Sweetie, I can't be there. If I was I would take you on my lap and hold you and comb your hair with my fingers until you had no tears left. That's what I wish I had done all those years ago. The night the baby died."

A baby. Not a fetus. "Thanks, Mom."

"Life has a way of working out the way it's supposed to, Lucy. I am living proof of that. I love you."

"You, too, Mom. I'll be thinking of you on Mother's Day."

"Now, go eat two dishes of chocolate ice cream. Then go and skinny-dip in the lake!"

Lucy was laughing as she hung up the phone. Her mother was right. Everything would work out the way it was supposed to.

Mac was gone.

But she still had Mama, and the gala, and the babies to cuddle. Sometime, somewhere, she had become a woman who would paint her house purple, and who had a dream that was bigger than she was.

And he was part of that. Loving him was part of that.

He hadn't ruined her life. Her mother had made her so aware of that. He had given her a gift. He had broken her out of the life she might have had. He had made her see things differently and want things she had not wanted before.

That's what love did. It made people better. Even if it hurt, it was worth the pain.

Lucy was going to cry. And eat the ice cream. She'd skip the dip in the lake. She was going to feel every bit of the glorious pain.

Because it meant she had loved. And her mother was right. Love, in the end, could only make you better. Not worse.

Mac was aware he was cutting things very close to the wire. He'd gone back to Toronto. His life had seemed empty and lonely, and no amount of adrenaline had been able to take the edge off his pain.

He loved her. He loved Lucy. He always had.

He had to give that a chance. He had to. And if it required more of him, then he had to dig deep and find that.

He was aware he was cutting things close. He arrived back in Lindstrom Beach the night before the gala.

He had never felt fear the way he felt it when he crossed back over those lawns and knocked on Lucy's door.

"Can I come in?"

When she saw it was him, Lucy looked scared to open that door. And he didn't blame her. But hope won out. She stood back from the door.

"You're in your housecoat," he said.

"It *is* nighttime." She scanned his face. "Come sit down, Mac."

The room was beautiful at night. She had a small fire burning in the hearth, and it cast its golden light across fresh tulips in a vase, a cat curled up on the rug in front of it, a book open on its spine on the arm of the chair. What would it be like to have a life like this?

Not a life of adrenaline rush after adrenaline rush, but one of quiet contentment?

A life of Lucy sharing evenings with him?

He couldn't think about that. Not until she knew the full truth. He sat on the couch, she took the chair across from him, tucked those delectable little toes up under her folded legs.

"Lucy, if you care to listen, I'm going to tell you some things I've never told anyone. Not even Mama."

Why was he doing this?

But he knew why. He could see it all starting again. She loved him. She wanted more from him. She always had.

She was leaning toward him, and he could see the hope shining in her face.

He considered himself the most fearless of men. No raging chute of white water ever put fear into his heart, only anticipation.

But wasn't this what he had always feared? Being vulnerable? Opening up to another? Tackling a foaming torrent of raging water was nothing in comparison to opening your heart. Nothing in comparison to letting someone see all of you.

But once she knew all his secrets would she still love him? Could she? Now seemed like the time to find out.

Mac took a deep breath. It was time. It was time to let it all go. It was time to tell someone. It involved the scariest thing of all. It involved trust. Trusting her.

He hesitated, looking for a place to start. There was only one starting point.

"When I was five, my mom left my dad and me. I remember it clearly. She said, I'm looking for something. I'm looking for something *more*.

"As an adult, I can understand that. We didn't have much. My dad was a laborer on a construction crew in a small town, not so different from Lindstrom Beach. He didn't make a pile of money, and we lived pretty humbly in a tiny house. As I got older I realized it was different from my friends' houses. No dishwasher, no computer, no fancy stereo, no big-screen TV. We heated with a wood heater, the furniture was falling apart and we didn't even have curtains on the windows.

"To tell you the truth, I don't know if he couldn't afford that stuff, or if it just wasn't a priority for him. My dad loved the outdoors. Since I could walk, I was trailing him through the woods. In retrospect, I think he thought of *that* as home. Being outside with his rifle or his fishing rod or a bucket for picking berries. And me.

"Mom left in search of something *more,* and I don't remember being traumatized by it or anything. My dad managed pretty well for a guy on his own. He got me registered for school, he kept me clean, he cooked simple meals. When I was old enough, he taught me how to help out around the place. We were a team.

"My mom called and wrote, and showed up at Christmas. She always had lots of presents and stories about her travels and adventures. She was big on saying 'I love you.' But even that young, I could tell she *hated* how my dad lived, and maybe even hated him for being content with so little.

"When she left, there was always a big screaming match about his lack of ambition and her lack of responsibility. I was overjoyed when she came, and guiltily glad when she left.

"Then she found her something *more*. Literally. She found a very, very rich man. I was eight at the time, and she came and got me and took me to Toronto for a visit with her and the new man. Walden, her husband, had a mansion in an area called the Bridle Path, also called Millionaire's Row. They had a swimming pool. She bought me a bike. There was a computer in every room. And a theater room.

"That first time I went for a visit with them, I couldn't wait to get home. But what I didn't know was that the visit there was the opening shot in a campaign.

"My mom started phoning me all the time. Every night. Why didn't I come live with them? They could give me so much *more*.

"I love you. I love you. I love you.

"What I didn't really get was how she had started undermining my dad, how she was working at convincing me only her kind of love was good. She would ask questions about him and me and how we lived, and then find flaws. She'd say, in this gentle, concerned tone, *'Little boys should not have to cook dinner.'* Or do laundry. Or cut wood. Or she'd say, mildly shocked, *'He did what? Oh, Macintyre, if he really cared about you, you would have gotten that new computer you wanted. Didn't you say he got a new rifle?'*

"In one particularly memorable incident, I told her my dad wouldn't let me play hockey because he couldn't afford it.

"She expressed her normal shock and dismay over his priorities, and then told me she would pay for hockey. I was over the moon, and I ran and told my dad as soon as I hung up the phone.

"I can play hockey this year. My mom's going to pay for it!"

"You know, I'd hardly ever seen my dad really, really mad, but he just lost it. Throwing things around and breaking them. Screaming, 'She's never paid a dentist's bill or for school supplies, but she's going to pay for hockey? She's never coughed up a dime when you need new sneakers or a present to bring to a birthday party, but she's going to pay for hockey? What part of hockey? The fee to join the team? The equipment? The traveling? The time I have to take off work?' And then the steam just went out of him, and he sat down and put his head in his hands and said, 'Forget it. You are not playing hockey.'

"This went on for a couple of years. Her planting the seeds of discontent, literally being the Disneyland Mama while my dad was slugging it out in the trenches.

"When I was twelve, I went and spent the summer with her and Walden. I made some friends in her neighborhood. I had money in my Calvin Klein jeans. I was swimming in my own pool. She bought me a puppy. She didn't have rules like my dad did. It was kind of anything goes. She actually let me have wine with dinner, and the odd beer.

"And when summer was over, she sat down on the side of my bed and wept. She loved me so much, she couldn't bear for me to go back to *that* man. She told me I didn't have to go back. She said I didn't have to think about my dad or his feelings. I should have seen the irony in that—that my dad's feelings counted for nothing, but hers were everything, but I didn't.

"I was twelve, nearly thirteen. At home, my dad made me work. By then, I was in charge of keeping our house supplied with firewood. I did a lot of the cooking. Sometimes he took me to work with him and handed me a shovel. I was allowed to go out with my friends only if I'd met all my obligations at home.

"And here she was offering me a life of frolic. And ease. I saw all the *stuff* I could ever want. I could be one of the rich, privileged kids at school instead of Digger Dan's son.

"I phoned my dad and told him I was staying. I could hear his heart breaking in the silence that followed. But she had convinced me that didn't matter. Only *I* mattered.

"And that's what I acted like for the next few months. Like only I mattered. She encouraged that. When my dad called, sometimes I blew him off. I was supposed to spend Christmas with him, but I didn't want to miss my best friend's New Year's Eve party, so I begged off going to be with him."

Mac took a deep shuddering breath. "Do you remember, a long time ago, I told you I killed a man?"

"With your bare hands," she whispered.

"Not with my bare hands. With my self-centeredness. With my callousness. With my utter insensitivity.

"He died. My dad died on Christmas Day."

"Oh, Mac," she whispered.

"At home, all by himself. He managed to call for help, but by the time they got there he was gone. They said it was a massive heart attack, but I knew it wasn't. I knew I'd killed him."

"Oh, Mac."

"Killed that man who had been nothing but good to me. He might not have been big on words. I don't think I heard him say 'I love you' more than twice in my whole life. But he was the one who had been there when no one else was, who had stepped up to the plate, who had done his best to provide, who had taught me the value of hard work and honesty. I had traded everything he taught me for a superficial world, and I hated myself for it.

"And her. My mother. I hated her. When she told me she didn't see the point in me going to the funeral, that was the last straw. I ran away and went back. To his funeral, to sort through our stuff.

"I never lived with her again. I couldn't. When they tried to make me go back to her, I ran away. That's how I ended up in foster care.

"I haven't spoken to her in fourteen years. I doubt I ever will again. I can see right through her clothes and her makeup, her perfect hair and her perfect house. She plays roles. For a while I was the role and she could play at being the fun-loving, cool mom, because it filled something in her. It relieved her of any guilt she felt about leaving me when I was little.

"But underneath that veneer she was mean-spirited and manipulative, and basically the most selfish and self-centered person ever born. She was using me to meet her needs, and I was done with her.

"I went through a series of foster homes, crazy with grief and guilt. And then I came here. To Mama Freda.

"And Mama saw the broken place in me, and didn't even try to fix it. She just loved me through it.

"I owe Mama my life."

The silence was so long. There, Lucy had it all. She knew the truth about him. He was the man who had killed his own father.

"When you told me, all those years ago, that you had killed a man, I thought you were blowing me off," Lucy whispered.

When had she moved beside him? When had her hand come to rest on his knee?

"I started to tell you. Back then. I saw the look on your face and retreated to the default defense. I always told people that when I was trying to drive them away, protect myself. I added the part about *with my bare hands* because it seemed particularly effective."

"You feel as if you killed your father," she said, looking at him. The firelight reflected off her face. In her eyes he saw the same radiance he had seen when she held the baby.

It hadn't been pity for the baby. And it wasn't pity for him.

It was love. It was the purest love he'd ever seen.

"I did kill my father," he whispered, daring her to love him anyway.

"No," she said, firmly, with almost fierce resolve. "You didn't."

Three words. So simple. *No. You. Didn't.*

Her hand came to his face, and her eyes were so intent on his.

It felt like absolution. It felt as if, by finally naming

it out loud, the monster that had lived in the closet was forced to disappear when exposed to light.

He'd been a teenage boy who did what teenage boys do, so naturally. He had been selfish and thoughtless and greedy. He'd thought only of himself.

It didn't have to be who he was today. It wasn't who he was today.

"You're terrified of love," she said.

"Terrified," he whispered, and knew he had never spoken a truer word.

And she didn't try to fix him. Or convince him. She laid her head on his chest, and wrapped her arms hard around him. He felt her tears warm, soaking through his shirt, onto the skin of his breast.

Her tenderness enveloped him.

And he knew another truth.

That she would see him through it.

Mama's love had carried him so far. Now it was time to go the distance. If he was strong enough to let her. If he was strong enough to say yes to something he had said no to for the past fourteen years.

Love.

He suddenly felt so tired. So very tired. And with her arms wrapped around him, with his head on her breast, he slept, finally, the sleep of a man who did not have to go to his dreams to do battle with his guilt.

When he awoke in the morning, she was gone. The coffee was on, and there was a note.

"Sorry, three zillion things to do. The gala is to-night!"

He went back over to Mama's. Overnight the pop-ulation there had exploded. Her many foster children wandered in and out, many of them with children of their own. There were tents on the lawn and inflatable mattresses on the floor.

"You stayed with Lucy?" Mama asked, in a happy frenzy of cooking.

"Not in the way you think. Mama, come outside with me for a minute." He found a spot under the trees, and took a deep breath. "Lucy asked some of your foster children to speak at the gala tonight. She chose a few. I was one of them and I've said no. But I think, with your permission, I'll change my mind. But only if you'll allow me to share that story you told me all those years ago."

"*Ach.* For what purpose, *schatz?*"

"For the same purpose you told it to me. To let everyone know that in the end, if you hold tight, love wins."

Her eyes searched his. She nodded.

The gala was sold out. He had seen Lucy flitting around in her red dress. He had told her he would speak.

But it seemed to him strange that with the big day here, the day that she had given her heart and soul to, she seemed wan.

"Are you not feeling well?" he asked her.

"Oh," she said. "No. I'm fine. I thought my doing this…" Her voice faltered. "Mother's Day is hard on me."

"Why? Because your own mother is so far away?"

"I'm just being silly," she said. "Sorry. I think I'm a little overwhelmed."

"Everything looks incredible. The silent auction is racking up bids."

She smiled, but it still seemed wan, disconnected.

He had the awful thought it might be because of what he had shared with her last night.

"I think the custom-painted Wild Ride kayak is going to be the high earner of the night."

"It will be. I keep pushing up the bid on it."

He expected her to laugh. She ran a hand through her hair, looked distracted.

"Oh," she said brightening slightly. "He's here."

"Who?"

"I couldn't find a comedian on such short notice. I found something Mama will like even better. An Engelbert impersonator."

He waited for her to smile. But she didn't. She looked as if she was going to cry.

"Later," she said, and walked away.

After dinner, some of Mama's foster children spoke. Ross Chillington talked about his parents being killed in an accident and about coming to Mama's house, how she was the first one who ever applauded his skill in acting.

Michael Boylston told how Mama had given him the courage and confidence to take on the world of international finance and how now he lived a life beyond his wildest dreams in Thailand.

Reed Patterson told of a drug-addicted mother and a life of pain and despair before Mama had made him believe he could take on the world and win.

And then it was his turn. But he didn't talk about himself.

"A long time ago," he said, "in a world most of us in this room had not yet been born into, there was a terrible war." And then he told Mama's story.

When he finished, the room was as silent as it had been that day fourteen years ago when he had first heard this story.

Into the silence he laid his next words with tenderness, with care.

"Mama spent the rest of her life finding that soldier. She found him over and over again. She found him in every lost boy she took into her home. She found him and she saved him. She saved him before the great evil had a chance to overcome him.

"I am one of those boys," he said quietly, proudly. "I am one of the boys who benefited from Mama's absolute belief in redemption, in second chances.

"I am one of those boys who was saved by love. Who was redeemed by it. And as a result, finally, was able to love back.

"Mama." He looked right at her. "I love you."

The words felt so good. She was weeping. As was most of the audience. His eyes sought Lucy. It wasn't hard to find her in her bright red dress. She had her face buried in her hands, crying.

Mac realized right then that he had a new mission in life. He had not killed his father. But it was possible that he had contributed to his death.

He could not change that. But he could try to redeem himself. He could spend the rest of his life on that. Make up for every wrong he had ever done by loving Lucy. And their children. By believing all that love was a light, and when it grew big enough it would envelop the darkness. Obliterate it.

Lucy still didn't look right. She was in her element,

surrounded by people. She had just pulled off something incredible. But she was still crying.

And suddenly she spun around and went into the night.

He waited for her to come back, especially when the Engelbert impersonator geared up and the tables were cleared away for dancing.

Mama stood right in front of the stage. She took off her scarf and threw it at the man's feet.

He picked it up and wiped his sweaty brow, and tossed it back to Mama, who looked as if she was going to die of happiness. Michael Boylston came and asked her to dance. Mac watched and shook his head.

If Mama was unwell, there was no sign of that now. None.

It occurred to Mac that there was something of the miraculous in this evening.

Those foster kids who had grown into adults seemed to be the first to take to the floor, having embraced so much of Mama's enthusiasm and joy for life. They were asking others to dance with them, and, in some instances, were dancing with the people who had once snubbed them as the riffraff from Mama's house.

Claudia was trying to get Ross to sign a movie poster with him on it. Over in the corner, Billy was drinking too much and talking football with Reed Patterson.

Lucy had done what she always did best. She had brought people together.

It hit him out of nowhere.

Things on her dining-room table she didn't want him to see.

Rezoning that had the neighbors in an uproar.

Caleb's House: a home for unwed mothers.

Finding joy in holding little babies.

Mother's Day is hard on me.

It hit him out of nowhere: all her plans had been altered. Claudia feeling superior to her. Her friends not being her friends anymore. No college. Moving away from here. And coming back. Changed.

"Oh my God," he said out loud, and he headed for the door.

There was still, thankfully, a little light in the evening sky. If it had been darker, he might not have been able to see her.

But as it was, her red dress was like a beacon in the thick greenery above her house.

Mac went toward that beacon as if he was a sailor lost at sea. There was a trail, well-traveled along the side of her house, that led him to her.

She was in a small clearing above her house, sitting on a small stone bench. There was a little flower bed cut from the thick growth. In the center of that bed was a stone, hand-painted in the curly cursive handwriting of a girl.

Caleb.

He went and sat beside her on the bench. "There was a baby," he said, and it was a statement not a question. His mouth had the taste of dust in it.

"They said not to name him," she choked. "They said he wasn't even a baby yet. A fetus. They wouldn't let me bury him. He was disposed of as medical waste."

She was sobbing, and he felt a grief as deep as anything he had ever felt.

"He was mine, wasn't he?"

"Yes, Mac, he was yours."

So many questions, and all of them poured out, one on top of the other. "Why didn't you tell me? Were you planning on telling me? Would you have told me if he lived?"

"Mac, I was at the scared-out-of-my-mind stage. I knew Mama would know where you were. I'd decide to tell you. I'd even cross the lawn to Mama's house. And then I'd talk myself out of it. I felt that you would come back—not for love, but because I'd trapped you into it."

"I had a right to know."

"Yes," she said softly, ever so softly, "Yes, you did. And I think, eventually, I would have finished that million-mile journey across her lawn. But then the baby was gone, and the pain was so bad that the last person I was thinking of was you."

Mac was silent. He could feel that pain unfurling in him. *His baby. His and hers.* It made life as he had lived it so far seem unreal. How would he have been different if he had known?

"When were you going to tell me?" he finally asked.

"Soon," she whispered. "I hoped to get through Mother's Day. If you hadn't come back I was going to call you. I knew it was time. To trust you with it."

He looked at her, and knew it was true. And he knew something else. That he had to rise to the fragile trust she was handing him. This had been her secret, her intensely personal grief, but it was no longer. This pain would be an unbreakable bond between them.

Something that they, and they alone, would know the full depth of.

In this instant he sat beside her and felt her grief, and he felt his own. He felt a momentary hurt that he had been excluded from one of the biggest events of his own life.

And yet looking into her eyes, he felt his hurt dissolve and he was taken by the bravery he saw in her. Her hands were clutched around something, and he unfolded them from around it.

It was a small box.

"I bring it with me when I come here."

"May I look?" His voice sounded gruff, hoarse with unshed emotion.

Lucy nodded through her tears, her eyes on his face, begging him.

Inside was a tiny pair of sneakers. A blue onesie with a striped bear embossed on it. And an ultrasound picture.

Begging him to what? To love her anyway, when everyone else had stopped? That was a given.

He touched the little sneakers to his lips. He had not wept since his father died. But he wept now, on Mother's Day, for the baby who would have been his son.

And that's when he saw what she was really begging him for. Someone to share this love with him. The love she had carried alone for too long.

He vowed to himself she would not be alone with it anymore. Not ever.

He saw so clearly what was being given to them both. A chance at redemption. A chance to make good come from bad.

A chance for love to grow from this garden where there had been sorrow.

A long time later they sat in silence, their hands intertwined. The sounds from the party below them grew more boisterous.

The sounds of "I Can't Take My Eyes Off You" floated up through the air.

"You know we would have never made it if I'd asked you to come with me all those years ago."

"I know."

"But I think we could make it now."

She turned to him, her eyes wide with love and hope.

Mac felt now what he could never have felt back then, as a callow youth. The complexity of loving someone.

"I'm asking you to marry me, Lucy Lin, I'm half crazy all for the love of you."

"Yes," she whispered, and then stronger, "Yes."

"You know, Lucy," he said, softly, his voice still gruff with emotion, "it won't all be a bicycle built for two. There are going to be hurts. And misunderstandings. I have places in me that are so tender they will bruise if you try to touch them. It's going to be a lifelong exercise in building trust."

She leaned her head on his shoulder. "I know what I'm getting into."

He watched the moonlight in her eyes and saw that the light coming from them was radiant.

"I do believe you do, Lucy Lin."

Mac took Lucy in his arms, and her soft warmth melted into him and he thanked God for second chances.

EPILOGUE

MACINTYRE HUDSON SIGHED AS a rush of girlish laughter filled the air. Mother's Day was still a whole week away, but Caleb's House, next door to this one, was filled to capacity. There were two trucks with campers on them parked up on the road. No doubt Claudia would be by shortly to complain about that.

There was no official Mother's Day celebration at Caleb's House, but they always came back, those girls, turned into young women, who had stayed there.

They came back whether they had kept their babies or given them up for adoption.

They were drawn back there as if by a spell. Every year, at the same time, they came.

Some came with families—mothers and fathers they had reconciled with, or young husbands who had accepted their history and stepped up to the plate for their future. They came with new young babies and toddlers.

They joined whoever was in residence now, and pretty soon the giggling started and carried across the lawns of that beautiful lavender house to this one.

Mama's house was long since gone. He'd torn it down, and he and Lucy had built a new one. It had what was called a mother-in-law suite, but they moved back and forth between the two living spaces seamlessly. Mama particularly liked their kitchen with all its shiny stainless-steel appliances, even though she didn't make *apfelstrudel* very often anymore.

But it was still *her* house, and ever since the gala, so many of those children Mama had fostered came back on Mother's Day weekend. Came back to the place where they had learned the meaning of home.

Right now, this part of Lakeshore Drive looked like a carnival.

"Did you see this?" Lucy came up behind him.

The funeral-planning kit was out on the table, where they could not miss it.

"Do you know what it's about?" she asked, that cute little worry line puckering her forehead.

"She was staring out the window the other day, lamenting the fact she might not see our children before she dies."

"I guess we should tell her, hmm?" Lucy said.

"No! I don't want her thinking every time she produces that brochure we're going to have a baby for her. Aren't there enough of them next door?"

"Ach," Lucy said, imitating Mama, "a baby is always a blessing."

Those words were a motto, and hung on a smaller sign right below the one that read Caleb's House.

Lucy wrapped her arms around him from behind, nestled into him for a moment and sighed with utter contentment. Then she went to the fridge and took out a jar of Rolliepops.

She popped one in her mouth.

"Those things can't be good for the baby."

"Who are you kidding? You hate kissing me after I've had one. Can't help it. Cravings." She removed a large stainless-steel bowl of potato salad.

"Potluck at Caleb's tonight," Lucy said. "Between Mama's kids and my kids, I think there must be a hundred people out there. Have you seen my mom?"

"She went through here with Donald on her hip a while ago, muttering about diapers." Donald was the baby she had brought back from Africa.

Next year there would be one more added to this amazingly diverse, huge and loving family Mac found himself a part of.

"Are you coming?" Lucy asked. "They'll be starting in a few minutes."

"Give me a minute."

Funny how even after all this time, the sound of his son's name, the son whom had never been born and who he had never known, still squeezed at his heart.

Mac went back to the table. Beside the funeral-planning kit, Mama had set out a card.

He picked it up. On the front it said, "Happy Mother's Day." Inside was completely blank. He set it back down, then went and stood at the window and looked over the familiar sparkling waters of Sunshine Lake.

His own child would be coming into this world soon.

It would require more of him.

Love required more of him. He had thought it would be a lifetime exercise to build trust, but he had never been so wrong.

He trusted Lucy implicitly. He trusted himself to be the man she and Mama believed he was. He trusted in life. Hadn't it become joyous and sweet beyond his wildest dreams?

Mac fished through the junk drawer until he found a pen, and then he went and sat down at the old kitchen table that they could never replace. It was the *apfelstrudel* table. He stared at the card for a long time, and then opened it.

How to start?

And so he started like this.

Dear Mom,

Not too much. A few lines. That she would be a grandmother soon. That she had not met his wife yet. That maybe they could get together the next time he was down east.

He signed it, licked the envelope, addressed it and put a stamp on. Maybe, just maybe, they would have a chance to redeem themselves.

Mama waddled in and went right to the fridge. "Where's the potato salad? My German one. Not like the stuff they call potato salad here."

"Lucy took it already."

"Are you coming, my galoot-head? Listen. They're singing grace."

All those voices raised in a joyous song of thanks. His Lucy would be at the very center of it, where she belonged.

"I'll be along in minute. I'm going to run up to the mailbox first."

Mama's eyes shot to the table, where the card had been.

Mac thought you could live for moments like this: a heart filled with love, the sound of gratitude drifting in the window and a smile like the one Mama gave him.

* * * * *

A sneaky peek at next month…

Cherish™

ROMANCE TO MELT THE HEART EVERY TIME

My wish list for next month's titles…

In stores from 21st June 2013:

☐ Falling for the Rebel Falcon – Lucy Gordon

& The Man Behind the Pinstripes – Melissa McClone

☐ Marriage for Her Baby – Raye Morgan

& The Making of a Princess – Teresa Carpenter

In stores from 5th July 2013:

☐ Marooned with the Maverick – Christine Rimmer

& Made in Texas! – Crystal Green

☐ Wish Upon a Matchmaker – Marie Ferrarella

& The Doctor and the Single Mum – Teresa Southwick

Available at WHSmith, Tesco, Asda, Eason, Amazon and Apple

Just can't wait?

Visit us Online

You can buy our books online a month before they hit the shops! **www.millsandboon.co.uk**

0613/2

Join the Mills & Boon Book Club

Want to read more **Cherish**™ books?
We're offering you **2 more** absolutely **FREE!**

We'll also treat you to these fabulous extras:

- Exclusive offers and much more!

- FREE home delivery

- FREE books and gifts with our special rewards scheme

Get your free books now!

visit www.millsandboon.co.uk/bookclub
or call Customer Relations on 020 8288 2888

The World of Mills & Boon®

There's a Mills & Boon® series that's perfect for you. We publish ten series and, with new titles every month, you never have to wait long for your favourite to come along.

Blaze®

Scorching hot, sexy reads
4 new stories every month

By Request

Relive the romance with the best of the best
9 new stories every month

Cherish™

Romance to melt the heart every time
12 new stories every month

Desire™

Passionate and dramatic love stories
8 new stories every month

Visit us Online

Try something new with our Book Club offer
www.millsandboon.co.uk/freebookoffer

M&B/WORLD2